SHE'S TRYING TO FOLLOW THE RULES

When Elizabeth Hotchkiss stumbles upon a most intriguing book, *How to Marry a Marquis*, in her employer's library, she's convinced someone is playing a cruel joke. With three younger siblings to support, she knows she has to marry for money, but who might have guessed how desperate she's become? A guidebook to seduction might be just the thing she needs—and what harm could there be in taking a little peek?

BUT HE'S MAKING HIS OWN

James Sidwell, the Marquis of Riverdale, has been summoned to rescue his aunt from a blackmailer, a task that requires him to pose as the new estate manager—and he immediately sheds suspicion on his aunt's companion, Elizabeth. Intrigued by the deliciously alluring young woman with the curious little rulebook, he gallantly offers to help her find herself a husband . . . by practicing her wiles on him. But when practice becomes all too perfect, James decides there's only one rule worth following—that Elizabeth marry her marquis.

JULIA QUINN

How to Marry a Marquis

An Avon Romantic Treasure

AVON BOOKS ◆ NEW YORK

Dictionary definition on page 317 reprinted from The Compact Oxford English Dictionary, Second Edition, 1991. Used by permission of Oxford University Press.

This is a work of fiction. Names, characters, places, and incidents either are the product of the author's imagination or are used fictitiously. Any resemblance to actual events, locales, organizations, or persons, living or dead, is entirely coincidental and beyond the intent of either the author or the publisher.

AVON BOOKS, INC.
1350 Avenue of the Americas
New York, New York 10019

Copyright © 1999 by Julie Cotler Pottinger
Inside cover author photo by Paul Pottinger
Published by arrangement with the author
Library of Congress Catalog Card Number: 98-93786
ISBN: 0-380-80081-0
www.avonbooks.com/romance

First Avon Books Printing: April 1999

AVON TRADEMARK REG. U.S. PAT. OFF. AND IN OTHER COUNTRIES, MARCA REGISTRADA, HECHO EN U.S.A.

Printed in the U.S.A.

WCD 10 9 8 7 6 5

In loving memory

Ted Cotler, 1915-1973
Rutherford Swatzburg, 1910-1992
Betty Goldblatt Swatzburg, 1910-1997
Edith Block Cotler, 1917-1998
Ernest Anderson, 1911-1998

I stand upon your shoulders every day of my life.

And for Paul, even though he seems to think
he can get out of just about anything by saying,
"You're very cute, though."

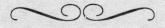

Chapter 1

Surrey, England
August 1815

Four plus six plus eight plus seven plus one plus one
plus one, mark down eight, carry the two . . .

Elizabeth Hotchkiss added up the column of numbers
for the fourth time, came up with the same answer she'd
come up with three times before, and groaned.

When she looked up, three somber faces were staring
at her—the three faces of her younger siblings.

"What is it, Lizzie?" nine-year-old Jane asked.

Elizabeth smiled weakly as she tried to figure out how
she was going to put away enough money to buy fuel to
heat their little cottage that winter. "We, ah . . . we
haven't much in the way of funds, I'm afraid."

Susan, who at fourteen was closest in age to Elizabeth,
frowned. "Are you absolutely certain? We must have
something. When Papa was alive we always—"

Elizabeth silenced her with an urgent stare. There were
a lot of things they'd had when Papa was alive, but he'd
left them nothing aside from a small bank account. No
income, no property. Nothing but memories. And those—
at least the ones Elizabeth carried with her—weren't the
sort that warmed one's heart.

1

"Things are different now," she said firmly, hoping to put an end to the subject. "You can't compare the two."

Jane grinned. "We can use the money Lucas has been stuffing away in his toy soldier box."

Lucas, the only boy in the Hotchkiss clan, yelped. "What were you doing in my things?" He turned to Elizabeth with an expression that might have been termed "glowering" had it not been gracing the face of an eight-year-old. "Is there no privacy in this household?"

"Apparently not," Elizabeth said absently, staring down at the numbers before her. She made a few marks with her pencil as she tried to devise new methods of economy.

"Sisters," Lucas grunted, looking excessively put out. "I am plagued with them."

Susan peered at Elizabeth's ledger. "Can't we shuffle some of the money about? Do something to stretch it a bit further?"

"There's nothing to stretch. Thank goodness the rent on the cottage is paid, or we'd be out on our ears."

"Is it really as bad as that?" Susan whispered.

Elizabeth nodded. "We've enough to last the rest of the month, and then a bit more when I receive my wages from Lady Danbury, but then . . ." Her words trailed off, and she looked away, not wanting Jane and Lucas to see the tears pricking her eyes. She'd been caring for these three for five years, ever since she'd been eighteen. They depended on her for food, shelter, and, most importantly, stability.

Jane nudged Lucas, and then, when he didn't respond, jabbed him in the soft spot between his shoulder and collarbone.

"What?" he snapped. "That hurt."

" 'What' is impolite," Elizabeth said automatically. " 'Pardon' is preferable."

Lucas's little mouth fell open in outrage. "It wasn't *polite* of her to poke me like that. And I'm certainly not going to beg *her* pardon."

Jane rolled her eyes and sighed. "You must remember that he is only eight."

Lucas smirked back. "You're only nine."

"I shall always be older than you."

"Yes, but I shall soon be bigger, and then you'll be sorry."

Elizabeth's lips curved into a bittersweet smile as she watched them bicker. She'd heard the same argument a million times before, but she'd also spied Jane tiptoeing into Lucas's room after dark to give him a goodnight kiss on the forehead.

Theirs might not be a typical family—it was just the four of them, after all, and they'd been orphans for years—but the Hotchkiss clan was special. Elizabeth had managed to keep the family together five years ago when her father had died, and she was damned if she'd let a shortage of funds tear them apart now.

Jane crossed her arms. "You should give Lizzie your money, Lucas. It isn't right to hoard it away."

He nodded solemnly and left the room, his little blond head bowed. Elizabeth glanced back up at Susan and Jane. They were also blond, with the bright blue eyes of their mother. And Elizabeth looked just like the rest of them—a little blond army, they were, with no money for food.

She sighed again and leveled a serious stare at her sisters. "I'm going to have to marry. There is nothing else for it."

"Oh, no, Lizzie!" Jane shrieked, jumping out of her chair and practically clambering across the table to her sister's lap. "Not that! Anything but that!"

Elizabeth looked at Susan with a confused expression,

silently asking her if she knew why Jane was so upset. Susan just shook her head and shrugged.

"It's not that bad," Elizabeth said, stroking Jane's hair. "If I marry, then I shall probably have a baby of my own, and then you get to be an auntie. Won't that be nice?"

"But the only person who's asked you is Squire Nevins, and he's horrid! Just horrid."

Elizabeth smiled unconvincingly. "I'm sure we can find someone besides Squire Nevins. Someone less . . . ah . . . horrid."

"I won't live with him," Jane said with a mutinous cross of her arms. "I won't. I'd rather go to an orphanage. Or one of those horrid workhouses."

Elizabeth didn't blame her. Squire Nevins was old, fat, and mean. And he always stared at Elizabeth in a way that made her break out in a cold sweat. Truth be told, she didn't much like the way he stared at Susan, either. Or Jane, for that matter.

No, she couldn't marry Squire Nevins.

Lucas returned to the kitchen carrying a small metal box. He held it out to Elizabeth. "I've saved one pound, forty," he said. "I was going to use it for—" He swallowed. "Never mind. I want you to have it. For the family."

Elizabeth took the box silently and looked in. Lucas's one pound, forty, was there, almost all in pennies and ha'pennies. "Lucas, honey," she said gently. "This is your savings. It has taken you years to collect all of these coins."

His lower lip quivered, but somehow he managed to expand his little chest until he stood like one of his toy soldiers. "I'm the man of the house now. I have to provide for you."

Elizabeth nodded solemnly and moved his money into

the box where she kept household funds. "Very well. We shall use this for food. Perhaps you can come shopping with me next week, and you may pick out something you like."

"My kitchen garden should begin to produce vegetables soon," Susan said helpfully. "Enough to feed us, and maybe a bit extra we could sell or barter in the village."

Jane started to squirm on Elizabeth's lap. "Please tell me you didn't plant more turnips. I hate turnips."

"We all hate turnips," Susan replied. "But they're so easy to grow."

"Not so easy to eat," Lucas grumbled.

Elizabeth exhaled and closed her eyes. How had they come to this? Theirs was an old, honorable family—little Lucas was even a baronet! And yet they were reduced to growing turnips—which they all detested—in a kitchen garden.

She was failing. She had thought she could raise her brother and sisters. When her father had died, it had been the most impossible time in her life, and all that had kept her going was the thought that she had to protect her siblings, keep them happy and warm. Together.

She'd fought off aunts and uncles and cousins, all of whom offered to take on *one* of the Hotchkiss children, usually little Lucas, who, with his title, could eventually hope to marry a girl with a nice large dowry. But Elizabeth had refused, even when her friends and neighbors had urged her to let him go.

She'd wanted to keep the family together, she had said. Was that so much to ask?

But she was failing. There was no money for music lessons or tutors, or any of the things Elizabeth had taken for granted when she'd been small. The Lord only knew how she was going to manage to send Lucas to Eton.

And he had to go. Every Hotchkiss male for four hundred years had attended Eton. They hadn't all managed to graduate, but they'd all gone.

She was going to have to marry. And her husband was going to have to have a lot of money. It was as simple as that.

"Abraham begat Isaac, and Isaac begat Jacob, and Jacob begat Judas . . ."

Elizabeth quietly cleared her throat and looked up with hopeful eyes. Was Lady Danbury asleep yet? She leaned forward and studied the older lady's face. Hard to tell.

". . . and Judas begat Phares and Zara of Thamar, and Phares begat Esrom . . ."

The old lady's eyes had definitely been closed for some time now, but still, one couldn't be too careful.

". . . and Esrom begat Aram, and . . ."

Was that a snore? Elizabeth's voice dropped to a whisper.

". . . and Aram begat Aminadab, and Aminadab begat Naasson, and . . ."

Elizabeth closed the Bible and began to tiptoe backward out of the drawing room. Normally she didn't mind reading to Lady Danbury; it was actually one of the better parts of her position as companion to the dowager countess. But today she really needed to get back home. She had felt so dreadful leaving while Jane was still in such a tizzy about the prospect of Squire Nevins entering their little family. Elizabeth had assured her she wouldn't marry him if he were the last man on earth, but Jane hadn't been very confident that anyone else would ask, and—

THUMP!

Elizabeth nearly jumped out of her skin. No one knew

how to produce more noise with a cane and a floor than Lady Danbury.

"I am *not* asleep!" Lady D's voice boomed.

Elizabeth turned around and smiled weakly. "So sorry."

Lady Danbury chuckled. "You're not in the least bit sorry. Get back over here."

Elizabeth suppressed a groan and returned to her straight-backed chair. She liked Lady Danbury. She truly did. In fact she longed for the day when she could use age as an excuse and carry on with Lady D's signature brand of outspokenness.

It was just that she really needed to get home, and—

"You're a tricky one, you are," Lady Danbury said.

"I beg your pardon?"

"All those 'begats.' Hand-chosen to put me to sleep."

Elizabeth felt her cheeks grow warm with a guilty blush and tried to phrase her words as a question. "I don't know what you mean?"

"You skipped ahead. We should still be on Moses and the great flood, not that begat part."

"I don't think that was Moses with the great flood, Lady Danbury."

"Nonsense. Of course it was."

Elizabeth decided that Noah would understand her desire to avoid a protracted discussion of biblical references with Lady Danbury and shut her mouth.

"At any rate, it matters not who got caught in the flood. The fact of the matter is that you skipped ahead just to put me to sleep."

"I . . . ah . . ."

"Oh, just admit it, girl." Lady Danbury's lips spread into a knowing smile. "I admire you for it, actually. Same thing I would have done at your age."

Elizabeth rolled her eyes. If this wasn't a case of

"damned if you do and damned if you don't," she didn't know what was. So she just sighed, picked up the Bible, and said, "What portion would you like me to read?"

"None of it. Bloody boring, it is. Haven't we anything more exciting in the library?"

"I'm sure we must. I could check, if you like."

"Yes, do that. But before you go, could you hand me that ledger? Yes, that one on the desk."

Elizabeth rose, walked over to the desk, and picked up the leather-bound ledger. "Here you are," she said, handing it to Lady Danbury.

The countess flipped the ledger open with military precision before looking back up at Elizabeth. "Thank you, my girl. I've a new estate manager arriving today and I want to get all these numbers memorized so I can be sure he isn't robbing me blind in a month's time."

"Lady Danbury," Elizabeth said with the utmost sincerity, "even the devil wouldn't dare to rob you blind."

Lady D thumped her cane by way of applause and laughed. "Well said, my girl. So nice to see a young one with a brain in the head. My own children— Well, bah, I'm not going to get into that now except to tell you that my son once got his head caught between the bars of the fence 'round Windsor Castle."

Elizabeth clapped her hand over her mouth in an effort to stifle a laugh.

"Oh, go ahead and giggle," Lady Danbury sighed. "I've found that the only way to avoid parental frustration is to view him as a source of amusement."

"Well," Elizabeth said carefully, "that does seem a wise course of action. . . ."

"You'd make a fine diplomat, Lizzie Hotchkiss," Lady Danbury chortled. "Where's my baby?"

Elizabeth didn't even bat an eyelash. Lady D's abrupt changes of subject were legendary. "Your *cat,*" she emphasized, "has been sleeping on the ottoman for the last hour," she said, pointing across the room.

Malcolm lifted his furry head, tried to focus his slightly crossed blue eyes, decided it wasn't worth the effort, and settled back down.

"Malcolm," Lady Danbury cooed, "come to Mama."

Malcolm ignored her.

"I have a treat for you."

The cat yawned, recognized Lady D as his primary source of food, and hopped down.

"Lady Danbury," Elizabeth scolded, "you know that cat is too fat."

"Nonsense."

Elizabeth shook her head. Malcolm weighed at least a stone, although a good portion of that was fur. She spent the better part of every evening after she returned home defurring her clothing.

Which was really quite remarkable, since the snobby beast hadn't deigned to let her hold him in five years.

"Good kitty," Lady D said, holding out her arms.

"Stupid cat," Elizabeth muttered as the ecru-colored feline stopped, stared at her, then went on his way.

"You're such a sweet thing." Lady D rubbed her hand against his furry belly. "Such a sweet thing."

The cat stretched out on Lady Danbury's lap, laying on his back with his paws hanging over his head.

"That isn't a cat," Elizabeth said. "It's a poor excuse for a rug."

Lady D raised a brow. "I know you don't mean that, Lizzie Hotchkiss."

"Yes, I do."

"Nonsense. You love Malcolm."

"Like I love Attila the Hun."

"Well, Malcolm loves you."

The cat lifted his head, and Elizabeth would swear he stuck his tongue out at her.

Elizabeth stood, letting out an indignant squeak. "That cat is a menace. I'm going to the library."

"Good idea. Go find me a new book."

Elizabeth headed for the door.

"And nothing with 'begat'!"

Elizabeth laughed in spite of herself and headed across the hall to the library. The clicking sound of her footsteps disappeared as she stepped onto the carpet, and she sighed. Good heavens, there were a lot of books here. Where on earth to start?

She selected a few novels, then pulled down a collection of Shakespeare's comedies. A slim volume of romantic poetry joined the pile, and then, just as she was about to cross the hall back to Lady D's drawing room, another book caught her eye.

It was very small, and bound in quite the brightest red leather Elizabeth had ever seen. But what was most odd about the book was that it was sitting sideways on a shelf in a library that gave new meaning to the word "order." Dust wouldn't dare settle on these shelves, and certainly no book would ever lie sideways.

Elizabeth set down her pile and picked up the little red book. It was upside down, so she had to flip it over to read the title.

How To Marry A Marquis

She dropped the book, half expecting lightning to strike her, right there in the library. Surely this had to be some kind of joke. She'd only decided that afternoon that she had to marry, and well.

"Susan?" she called out. "Lucas? Jane?"

She shook her head. She was being ridiculous. Her

siblings, cheeky as they may be, would not sneak into
Lady Danbury's house and deposit a fake book, and—

Well, actually, she thought, turning the slim red volume over in her hand, when it came right down to it, the
book didn't really look fake. The binding looked sturdy,
and the leather on the cover appeared to be of high quality. She glanced around to make sure that no one was
watching—although she wasn't quite certain why she
should feel so embarrassed—and carefully opened it to
the first page.

The author was a Mrs. Seeton, and the book had been
printed in 1792, the year of Elizabeth's birth. A funny
little coincidence, Elizabeth decided, but she wasn't a su-
perstitious sort of person. And she certainly didn't need
a little book to tell her how to live her life.

Besides, when it came right down to it, what did this
Mrs. Seeton really know? After all, if *she* had married a
marquis, wouldn't she be *Lady* Seeton?

Elizabeth slammed the book shut decisively and returned it to its spot on the shelf, making certain that it
laid sideways, just the way she had found it. She didn't
want anyone to think she'd actually been looking at the
silly thing.

She picked up her stack of books and crossed back to
the drawing room, where Lady Danbury was still sitting
in her chair, stroking her cat and staring out the window
as if she were waiting for someone.

"I found some books," Elizabeth called out. "I don't
think you'll find many 'begats' in these, although perhaps
in the Shakespeare—"

"Not tragedies, I hope."

"No, I thought that in your current frame of mind,
you'd find the comedies more entertaining."

"Good girl," Lady Danbury said approvingly. "Anything else?"

Elizabeth blinked and looked back down at the books in her arms. "A couple of novels, and some poetry."

"Burn the poetry."

"I beg your pardon?"

"Well, don't *burn* it; the books are certainly more valuable than firewood. But I certainly don't want to hear it. My late husband must have bought that. Such a dreamer."

"I see," Elizabeth said, mostly because she thought she was expected to say something.

With a sudden movement, Lady Danbury cleared her throat and waved her hand in the air. "Why don't you go home early today?"

Elizabeth's mouth dropped open. Lady Danbury never dismissed her early.

"I have to deal with that blasted estate manager, and I certainly don't need you here for that. Besides, if he's an eye for pretty young girls, I'll never get him to pay attention to me with you around."

"Lady Danbury, I hardly think—"

"Nonsense. You're quite an attractive thing. Men love blond hair. I should know. Mine used to be as fair as yours."

Elizabeth smiled. "It still is fair."

"It's white, is what it is," Lady Danbury said with a laugh. "You're a sweet thing. You shouldn't be here with me, you should be out finding a husband."

"I . . . ah . . ." What to say to that?

"Very noble of you to devote yourself to your siblings, but you have to live as well."

Elizabeth just stared at her employer, horrified by the tears pooling in her eyes. She'd served Lady Danbury for five years, and never had they spoken of such matters. "I'll—I'll be off, then, since you say I might leave early."

Lady Danbury nodded, looking oddly disappointed. Had she been hoping Elizabeth would pursue the topic further? "Just put that book of poetry back before you go," she instructed. "I'm sure I won't look at it, and I can't trust the servants to keep my books in order."

"I will." Elizabeth set the rest of the books down on an end table, gathered her things, and said her farewells. As she was walking out of the room, Malcolm jumped off of Lady Danbury's lap and followed her.

"See?" Lady D crowed. "I told you he loved you."

Elizabeth eyed the cat suspiciously as she headed out into the hall. "What do you want, Malcolm?"

He flicked his tail, bared his teeth, and hissed.

"Oh!" Elizabeth exclaimed, dropping the poetry book. "You beast. Following me out here just to hiss—"

"Did you throw a book at my cat?" Lady D hollered.

Elizabeth decided to ignore the question, instead jabbing her finger in Malcolm's direction as she snatched up her book. "Go back to Lady Danbury, you awful creature."

Malcolm stuck his tail in the air and stalked away.

Elizabeth let out a long breath and walked into the library. She headed toward the poetry section, scrupulously keeping her back to that little red book. She didn't want to think about it, she didn't want to look at it—

Drat, but that thing was practically giving off heat. Never in her life had Elizabeth been so aware of an inanimate object.

She reshelved the volume of poetry and stomped to the door, starting to get really annoyed with herself. That silly little book shouldn't affect her one way or another. By avoiding it like the plague, she was actually giving it power it didn't deserve, and—

"Oh, for heavens sake!" she finally burst out.

"Did you say something?" Lady Danbury called out from the next room.

"No! I just—uh, I just tripped over the edge of the rug. That's all." Elizabeth muttered another "Good heavens" under her breath and tiptoed back over to the book. It was lying face-down, and much to Elizabeth's surprise, her hand shot out and flipped it over.

HOW TO MARRY A MARQUIS

There it was, same as before. Staring up at her, mocking her, sitting there as if to say she didn't have the gumption to read it.

"It is just a book," she muttered. "Just a stupid, garishly red little book."

And yet . . .

Elizabeth needed money so desperately. Lucas had to be sent to Eton, and Jane had cried for a week when she'd used up the last of her watercolors. And both of them were growing faster than weeds on a summer day. Jane could make do with Susan's old frocks, but Lucas would need clothing befitting his station.

The only road to riches was marriage, and this brazen little book claimed to have all the answers. Elizabeth wasn't so foolish as to believe that she might capture the interest of a marquis, but maybe a little advice could help her snare a nice country gentleman—one with a nice comfortable income. She'd even marry a Cit. Her father would turn over in his grave at the thought of her making an alliance with someone in trade, but a girl had to be practical, and Elizabeth would wager that there were a number of wealthy merchants who'd like to marry the impoverished daughter of a baronet.

Besides, it was her father's fault that she was in this bind, anyway. If he hadn't . . .

Elizabeth gave her head a shake. Now wasn't the time to dwell on the past. She needed to concentrate on her present dilemma.

When it came right down to it, she didn't know much about men. She didn't know what she was supposed to say to them or how she was supposed to act to make them fall in love with her.

She stared at the book. Hard.

She looked around. Was anyone coming?

She took a deep breath, and quick as lightning, the book found its way into her reticule.

Then she ran out of the house.

James Sidwell, Marquis of Riverdale, liked to go unnoticed. He liked nothing better than to blend into a crowd, his identity unknown, and ferret out plots and facts. It was probably why he'd so enjoyed his years of work for the War Office.

And he'd been damned good at it. The same face and body that commanded such attention in London ballrooms disappeared into crowds with startling success. James merely removed the confident gleam from his eyes, stooped his shoulders, and no one ever suspected that he was of noble lineage.

Of course the brown hair and brown eyes helped, too. It was always good to have common coloring. James doubted there were very many successful redheaded operatives.

But one year earlier, his cover had been blown when a Napoleonic spy had revealed his identity to the French. And now the War Office refused to assign him to any mission more exciting than the occasional rounding up of low-stakes smugglers.

James had accepted his boring fate with a heavy sigh and an air of resignation. It was probably time he devoted himself to his estates and title, anyway. He had to marry at some point—distasteful as the prospect might be—and produce an heir to the marquisate. And so he had turned his attention to the London social scene, where a marquis—especially one so young and handsome—never went unnoticed.

James had been alternately disgusted, bored, and amused. Disgusted because the young ladies—and their mamas—viewed him as nothing so much as a large fish to be hooked and reeled in. Bored because after years of political intrigue, the color of ribbons and the cut of a waistcoat just didn't strike him as fascinating topics of conversation. And amused because, to be frank, if he hadn't held on to his sense of humor throughout the ordeal he would have gone mad.

When the note from his aunt had arrived by special messenger, he had nearly whooped with joy. Now, as he approached her house in Surrey, he pulled it out of his pocket and reread it.

Riverdale—

I need your help urgently. Please report to Danbury House with all possible haste. Do not travel in your best finery. I shall tell everyone that you are my new estate manager. Your new name is James Siddons.

Agatha, Lady Danbury

James had no idea what this was all about, but he knew it was just what he needed to alleviate his boredom and allow him to leave London without feeling guilty over shirking his duties. He traveled by hired coach, since an estate manager would not own horses as fine as his, and walked the last mile from the center of town to Danbury House. Everything he needed was packed in one bag.

In the eyes of the world, he became plain Mr. James Siddons, a gentleman, to be sure, but perhaps just a little down on funds. His clothing came from the back of his closet—well-made, but worn at the elbows and two years out of style. A few snips with the kitchen shears effectively marred the expert haircut he'd received just the week before. For all intents and purposes, the Marquis of Riverdale had disappeared, and James could not have been more pleased.

Of course his aunt's scheme did have a major flaw, but that was only to be expected when one let amateurs do the planning. James hadn't visited Danbury House in nearly a decade; his work for the War Office hadn't afforded him much time to visit family, and he certainly hadn't wanted to put his aunt in any kind of danger. But surely there was someone—some aging retainer, the butler, perhaps—who would recognize him. He had, after all, spent most of his childhood here.

But then again, people saw what they expected to see, and when James acted like an estate manager, people generally saw an estate manager.

He was nearly to Danbury House—practically on the front steps, actually—when the front door flew open and a petite blond woman came tearing out, head down, eyes to the ground, and moving just a fraction slower than a filly at full gallop. James didn't even have a chance to call out before she'd run right into him.

Their bodies connected with a dull thump, and the girl let out a feminine squeak of surprise as she bounced off of him and landed inelegantly on the ground. A clip or ribbon or whatever it was females called those things flew from her hair, causing a thick lock of white-gold hair to slip out of her coiffure and settle awkwardly on her shoulder.

"I beg your pardon," James said, holding out his hand to help her up.

"No, no," she replied, brushing off her skirts, "it was my fault entirely. I wasn't looking where I was going."

She didn't bother to take his hand, and James found himself oddly disappointed. She wasn't wearing gloves, and neither was he, and he felt a strange compulsion to feel the touch of her hand in his.

But he could not say such things out loud, and so he instead bent down to help her retrieve her things. Her reticule had flown open when it hit the ground, and her belongings were now strewn around their feet. He handed her her gloves, which caused her to blush.

"It's so hot," she explained, looking at the gloves with resignation.

"Don't don them on my account," he said with an easy smile. "As you can see, I have also chosen to use the fine weather as an excuse to leave mine off."

She stared at his hands for a moment before shaking her head and murmuring, "This is the oddest conversation."

She knelt to gather the rest of her things, and James followed suit. He picked up a handkerchief and was reaching for a book when she suddenly made the strangest noise—nothing so much as a strangled cry—and snatched it out from beneath his fingers.

James found himself really wanting to know what was in that book.

She cleared her throat about six times and said, "You're very kind to help me."

"It was no trouble, I assure you," he murmured, clearly trying to get a look at the book. But she'd already shoved it back into her reticule.

Elizabeth smiled nervously at him, letting her hand slip into her bag, just to reassure herself that the book was really there, hidden safely out of sight. If she was caught reading such a thing, she'd be mortified beyond words. It was a given that all unmarried women were looking for a husband, but only the most pathetic of females would actually be caught reading a *manual* on the subject.

He didn't say anything, just looked her over in an assessing sort of way that made her even more nervous. Finally she blurted out, "Are you the new estate manager?"

"Yes."

"I see." She cleared her throat. "Well, then I suppose I ought to introduce myself, as I'm sure our paths will cross. I am Miss Hotchkiss, Lady Danbury's companion."

"Ah. I am Mr. Siddons, recently of London."

"It was very nice meeting you, Mr. Siddons," she said with a smile that James found oddly engaging. "Terribly sorry about the accident, but I must be off."

She waited for his acknowledging nod, then dashed off down the drive, clutching her bag as if her very life depended on it.

James just stared as she ran off, strangely unable to take his eyes off of her retreating form.

Chapter 2

"James!" Agatha Danbury didn't often squeal, but James was her favorite nephew. Truth be told, she probably liked him better than any of her own children. He, at least, was smart enough not to stick his head between iron fence beams. "How lovely to see you!"

James dutifully bent down and offered his cheek for a kiss. "How lovely to see me?" he queried. "You almost sound surprised by my arrival. Come, now, you know I could no more ignore your summons than one sent by the Prince Regent himself."

"Oh, that."

He narrowed his eyes at her dismissive response. "Agatha, you're not playing games with me, are you?"

Her posture suddenly became ramrod straight in her chair. "You would think that of me?"

"In a heartbeat," he said with an easy smile as he sat down. "I learned all my best tricks from you."

"Yes, well, someone had to take you under her wing," she replied. "Poor child. If I hadn't—"

"Agatha," James said sharply. He had no wish to involve himself in a discussion of his childhood. He owed

21

his aunt everything—his very soul, even. But he didn't want to get into this now.

"As it happens," she said with a disdainful sniff, "I am not playing games. I am being blackmailed."

James leaned forward. Blackmailed? Agatha was a crafty old thing, but proper as anything, and he couldn't imagine her having done anything that might warrant blackmail.

"Can you even fathom it?" she demanded. "That someone would dare to blackmail *me*? Hmmph. Where is my cat?"

"Where is your cat?" he echoed.

"Mallllllllllllllcolmmmmmmmm!"

James blinked and watched as a monstrously obese feline padded into the room. He walked over to James, sniffed, and hopped up onto his lap.

"Isn't he just the friendliest cat?" Agatha asked.

"I hate cats."

"You'll love Malcolm."

He decided that tolerating the cat was easier than arguing with his aunt. "Do you have any idea who your blackmailer might be?"

"None."

"May I ask *why* you are being blackmailed?"

"It is so very embarrassing," she said, her pale blue eyes growing bright with tears.

James grew concerned. Aunt Agatha never cried. There had been few things in his life that were completely and utterly constant, but one of them had been Agatha. She was sharp, she had a biting sense of humor, she loved him beyond measure, and she never cried. Never.

He started to go to her, then held back. She wouldn't want him to comfort her. She would only see it as an acknowledgment of her momentary display of weakness. Besides, the cat showed no inclination to get off his lap.

"Do you have the letter?" he asked gently. "I assume you received a letter."

She nodded, picked up a book that was sitting on the table next to her, and drew from its pages a single sheet of paper. Silently, she held it out to him.

James gently tossed the cat onto the carpet and stood. He took a few steps in his aunt's direction and took the letter. Still standing, he looked down at the paper in his hands and read.

Lady D—

I know your secrets. And I know your daughter's secrets. My silence will cost you.

James looked up. "Is that all?"

Agatha shook her head and held out another sheet of paper. "I received this one as well."

James took it.

Lady D—

Five hundred pounds for my silence. Leave it in a plain sack behind The Bag of Nails Friday at midnight. Tell no one. Do not disappoint me.

"The Bag of Nails?" James asked with an arched eyebrow.

"It's the local public house."

"Did you leave the money?"

She nodded, shamefaced. "But only because I knew you couldn't be here by Friday."

James paused while he decided how best to frame his next statement. "I think," he said gently, "that you had better tell me about this secret."

Agatha shook her head. "It is too embarrassing. I cannot."

"Agatha, you know that I am discreet. And you know I love you like a mother. Whatever you tell me shall never go beyond these walls." When she did nothing other than bite her lip, he asked, "Which daughter shares this secret?"

"Melissa," Agatha whispered. "But she doesn't know."

James closed his eyes and let out a long exhale. He knew what was coming next and decided to save his aunt the embarrassment of having to say it herself. "She's illegitimate, isn't she?"

Agatha nodded. "I had an affair. It lasted only a month. Oh, I was so young and so silly then."

James fought to keep his shock off of his face. His aunt had always been such a stickler for propriety; it was inconceivable that she could have dallied ouside of marriage. But, as she said, she'd been young and perhaps a little foolish, and after all she'd done for him in his life, he didn't feel he had the right to judge her. Agatha had been his savior, and if the need arose, he would lay down his life for her without a second's hesitation.

Agatha smiled sadly. "I didn't know what I was doing."

James weighed his words carefully before asking, "Your fear, then, is that your blackmailer will reveal this to society and shame Melissa?"

"I don't give a fig about society," Agatha said with a huff. "Half the lot of them are bastards themselves. Probably two-thirds of those not firstborn. It's Melissa I fear for. She's safely married to an earl, so the scandal won't touch her, but she was so close to Lord Danbury. He always said she was his special favorite. It would break her heart if she were to learn that he was not her true father.''

James didn't remember Lord Danbury being much closer to Melissa than he was to any of his other children. In fact, he didn't recall Lord Danbury being close to his children, period. He had been a genial man, but distant. Definitely of the ''children belong in the nursery and should be brought down for viewing no more than once a day'' variety. Still, if Agatha felt that Melissa had been Lord Danbury's special favorite, who was he to argue?

''What are we going to do, James?'' Agatha asked. ''You are the only person I trust to help me through this unpleasantness. And with your background—''

''Have you received any more notes?'' James interrupted. His aunt knew that he had once worked for the War Office. There was no harm in that, as he was no longer an active operative, but Agatha was ever curious, and always asking him about his exploits. And there were some things one just didn't want to discuss with one's aunt. Not to mention the fact that James could get himself hanged for divulging some of the information he'd learned over the years.

Agatha shook her head. ''No. No notes.''

''I'll do a bit of preliminary investigating, but I suspect we won't learn anything until you receive another letter.''

''You think there will be another one?''

James nodded grimly. ''Blackmailers don't know how to quit while ahead. It's their fatal flaw. In the meantime, I shall play at being your new estate manager. But I do wonder how you expect me to do this without being recognized.''

''I thought not being recognized was your particular forte.''

''It is,'' he replied easily, ''but unlike France, Spain,

and even the south coast, I grew up here. Or at least I almost did.''

Agatha's eyes suddenly lost their focus. James knew that she was thinking of his childhood, of all the times she'd faced his father in silent, angry showdowns, insisting that James was better off with the Danburys. ''No one will recognize you,'' she finally assured him.

''Cribbins?''

''He passed on last year.''

''Oh. I'm sorry.'' He'd always liked the old butler.

''The new one is adequate, I suppose, although he had the effrontery the other day to ask me to call him Wilson.''

James didn't know why he bothered, but he asked, ''That wouldn't be his name, would it?''

''I suppose,'' she said with a little huff. ''But how am I to remember that?''

''You just did.''

She scowled at him. ''If he's my butler, I'm calling him Cribbins. At my age it's *dangerous* to make any big changes.''

''Agatha,'' James said, with far more patience than he felt, ''may we return to the matter at hand?''

''About your being recognized.''

''Yes.''

''Everyone's gone. You haven't visited me for nearly ten years.''

James ignored her accusing tone. ''I see you all the time in London and you know it.''

''It doesn't count.''

He refused to ask why. He knew she was dying to give him a reason. ''Is there anything in particular I need to know before assuming my role as estate manager?'' he asked.

She shook her head. ''What would you need to know?

I raised you properly. You should know everything there is to know about land management."

That much was true, although James had preferred to let managers watch over his estates since he'd assumed the title. It was easier, since he didn't particularly enjoy spending time at Riverdale Castle. "Very well, then," he said, standing up. "As long as Cribbins the First is no longer with us—God rest his eternally patient soul—"

"What is that supposed to mean?"

His head fell slightly forward and to the side in an extremely sarcastic fashion. "Anyone who butlered for you for forty years deserves to be canonized."

"Impertinent bugger," she muttered.

"Agatha!"

"What's the use of holding my tongue at my age?"

He shook his head. "As I was trying to say earlier, as long as Cribbins is gone, being your estate manager is as good a disguise as any. Besides, I rather fancy spending some time out-of-doors while the weather is fine."

"London was stifling?"

"Very."

"The air or the people?"

James grinned. "Both. Now, then, just tell me where to put my things. Oh, and Aunt Agatha"—he leaned down and kissed her cheek—"it's damned fine to see you."

She smiled. "I love you, too, James."

By the time Elizabeth reached her home, she was out of breath and covered with mud. She'd been so anxious to be away from Danbury House that she'd practically run the first quarter mile. Unfortunately, it had been a particularly wet summer in Surrey, and Elizabeth had never been especially coordinated. And as for that protruding tree root—well, there was really no way to avoid it, and so, with a splat, Elizabeth saw her best dress ruined.

Not that her best dress was in particularly good condition. There certainly wasn't enough money in the Hotchkiss coffers for new clothing unless one had completely outgrown one's old garments. But still, Elizabeth had some pride, and if she couldn't dress her family in the first stare of fashion, at the very least she could make certain they were all neat and clean.

Now there was mud caked onto her velvet sash, and even worse, she'd actually stolen a book from Lady Danbury. And not just any book. She'd stolen what had to be the stupidest, most asinine book in the history of bookbinding. And all because she had to auction herself off to the highest bidder.

She swallowed as tears formed in her eyes. What if there *were* no bidders? Then where would she be?

Elizabeth stamped her feet on the front stoop to shake off the mud, then pushed her way through the front door of her small house. She tried to sneak through the hall and up the stairs to her room without anyone seeing her, but Susan was too fast.

"Good heavens! What happened to you?"

"I slipped," Elizabeth ground out, never taking her eyes off of the stairs.

"Again?"

That was enough to make her twist around and stab her sister with a murderous glare. "What do you mean, again?"

Susan coughed. "Nothing."

Elizabeth swung back around with every intention of marching to and up the stairs, but her hand connected with a side table. "Owwwww!" she howled.

"Ooh," Susan said, wincing in sympathy. "I'll bet that hurts."

Elizabeth just stared at her, eyes narrowing into angry slits.

"Terribly sorry," Susan said quickly, clearly recognizing her sister's bad mood.

"I am going to my room," Elizabeth said, enunciating every word as if careful diction would somehow remove her to her private chamber more quickly. "And then I am going to lie down and take a nap. And if anyone bothers me, I shall not answer to the consequences."

Susan nodded. "Jane and Lucas are out playing in the garden. I shall make certain they are quiet if they return."

"Good, I— Owwwwwwww!"

Susan winced. "What now?"

Elizabeth bent down and picked up a small metal object. One of Lucas's toy soldiers. "Is there any reason," she said, "that this is sitting on the floor where anyone may step upon it?"

"None that I can think of," Susan said with a half-hearted attempt at a smile.

Elizabeth just sighed. "I am not having a good day."

"No, I didn't think you were."

Elizabeth tried to smile, but all she did was stretch her lips. She just couldn't manage to get the corners to turn up.

"Would you like me to bring you a cup of tea?" Susan asked gently.

Elizabeth nodded. "That would be lovely, thank you."

"It's my pleasure. I'll just— What's that in your bag?"

"What?"

"That book."

Elizabeth cursed under her breath and shoved the book down under a handkerchief. "It's nothing."

"Did you borrow a book from Lady Danbury?"

"In a manner of speaking."

"Oh, good. I've read everything we possess. Not that we possess much any longer."

Elizabeth just nodded and tried to dash past her.

"I know it broke your heart to sell off the books," Susan said, "but it did pay for Lucas's Latin lessons."

"I really must go—"

"Can I see the book? I should like to read it."

"You can't," Elizabeth snapped, her voice coming out *much* louder than she'd have liked.

Susan drew back. "I beg your pardon."

"I have to return it tomorrow. That's all. You won't have time to read it."

"Can't I just look at it?"

"No!"

Susan lunged forward. "I want to see it."

"I said no!" Elizabeth hopped to the right, just barely managing to elude her sister's grasp, and then dashed toward the stairs. But just as her foot hit the first step, she felt Susan's hand grabbing the fabric of her skirts.

"I have you!" Susan grunted.

"Let me go!"

"Not until you show me that book."

"Susan, I am your guardian and I order you to—"

"You're my sister, and I want to see what you're hiding."

Reason wasn't going to work, Elizabeth decided, so she grabbed her skirt and yanked hard, which only resulted in her slipping off the step and her bag tumbling to the floor.

"Aha!" Susan yelled triumphantly, snatching up the book.

Elizabeth groaned.

"HOW TO MARRY A MARQUIS?" Susan looked up, her expression somewhat puzzled and wholly amused.

"It's just a silly book." Elizabeth felt her cheeks grow

warm. "I just thought . . . that is, I thought I—"

"A *marquis?*" Susan asked dubiously. "Setting rather lofty goals for ourselves, aren't we?"

"For the love of God," Elizabeth snapped, "I'm not going to marry a marquis. But the book might have some sort of useful advice in it, since I have to marry someone, and nobody is asking."

"Except Squire Nevins," Susan murmured, flipping through the pages.

Elizabeth swallowed down a little dash of bile. The thought of Squire Nevins touching her, kissing her . . . it made her skin turn to ice. But if he was the only way she could save her family . . .

She squeezed her eyes shut. There had to be *some*thing in that book that would teach her how to find a husband. Anything!

"This is really quite interesting," Susan said, plopping down on the carpet next to Elizabeth. "Listen to this: 'Edict Number One—' "

"*Edict?*" Elizabeth echoed. "There are edicts?"

"Apparently so. I say, this business of catching a husband is more complicated than I'd thought."

"Just tell me what the edict is."

Susan blinked and looked back down. " 'Be unique. But not too unique.' "

"What the devil does that mean?" Elizabeth exploded. "If that isn't the most ridiculous thing I've ever heard. I'm putting that book back tomorrow. Who is this Mrs. Seeton, anyway? Not a marchioness, so I don't see why I should listen—"

"No, no," Susan said, waving her arm at her sister without looking at her. "That's just the title of the edict. She goes on to explain."

"I'm not certain I want to hear this," Elizabeth grumbled.

"It's actually quite interesting."

"Give me that." Elizabeth snatched the book back from her sister and read silently:

IT IS IMPERATIVE THAT YOU BE A WOMAN WHO IS WHOLLY UNIQUE. THE MAGIC THAT IS YOU MUST ENTRANCE YOUR LORD UNTIL HE CANNOT SEE THE ROOM BEYOND YOUR FACE.

Elizabeth snorted. " 'The magic that is you'? 'See the room beyond your face'? Where did this woman learn how to write? A perfumery?"

"I think the bit about the room and your face is rather romantic," Susan said with a shrug.

Elizabeth ignored her. "Where is the bit about not being too unique? Ah, here it is."

YOU MUST STRIVE TO CONTAIN YOUR UNIQUENESS SO THAT ONLY HE MAY SEE IT. YOU MUST PROVE TO HIM THAT YOU WILL BE AN ASSET AS HIS WIFE. NO LORD OF THE REALM WISHES TO BE SHACKLED TO EMBARRASSMENT AND SCANDAL.

"Did you get to the part about the shackles yet?" Susan asked.

Elizabeth ignored her and kept on reading.

IN OTHER WORDS, YOU MUST STAND OUT IN A CROWD, BUT ONLY IN HIS CROWD. FOR HE IS THE ONLY ONE WHO MATTERS.

Elizabeth looked up. "There is a problem here."

"There is?"

"Yes." She tapped her finger against her forehead, as was her habit whenever she was thinking hard on a subject. "All of this presupposes that I have set my sights on a single male."

Susan's eyes bugged out. "You certainly cannot set your sights on a married man!"

"I meant one *particular* man," Elizabeth retorted, swatting her sister on the shoulder.

"I see. Well, Mrs. Seeton does have a point. You cannot marry two."

Elizabeth pulled a face. "Of course not. But I should think I must indicate my interest in more than one if I am to secure a proposal. Didn't Mother always say we must not place all of our eggs in one basket?"

"Hmmm," Susan mused, "you have a point. I shall research the matter this evening."

"I beg your pardon?"

But Susan had already sprung to her feet and was dashing up the stairs. "I shall read the book tonight," she called out from the landing, "and I shall report to you in the morning."

"Susan!" Elizabeth used her sternest voice. "Bring that book back to me immediately."

"Have no fear! I shall have worked out our strategy by breakfast!" And the next thing Elizabeth heard was the sound of a key turning in a lock as Susan barricaded herself in the room she shared with Jane.

"Breakfast?" Elizabeth muttered. "Is she planning to skip supper, then?"

Apparently she was. No one saw hide nor hair of Susan, nor even heard the veriest peep from her room. The Hotchkiss clan numbered only three that night at the table, and poor little Jane couldn't even get into her room to go to bed and had to sleep with Elizabeth.

Elizabeth was not amused. Jane was a sweetheart, but she stole all the blankets.

* * *

When Elizabeth went down to breakfast the next morning, Susan was already at the table, little red book in hand. Elizabeth noted grimly that the kitchen showed no signs of use.

"Couldn't you have started breakfast?" she asked grumpily, searching the cupboard for eggs.

"I've been busy," Susan replied. "Very busy."

Elizabeth didn't reply. Blast. Only three eggs. She'd have to go without and hope that Lady Danbury was planning a hearty luncheon that day. She positioned an iron skillet on a tripod over the hearth fire and cracked the three eggs open.

Susan got the hint and started slicing bread for toast. "Some of these rules aren't so terribly difficult," she said as she worked. "I think even you could follow them."

"I am overwhelmed by your confidence in me," Elizabeth said dryly.

"In fact, you should begin practicing now. Isn't Lady Danbury going to host a party later in the summer? There will surely be prospective husbands in attendance."

"*I* won't be in attendance."

"Lady Danbury doesn't plan to invite you?" Susan burst out, clearly outraged. "Well, I never! You may be her companion, but you are also the daughter of a baronet, and thus—"

"Of course she will invite me," Elizabeth replied evenly. "But I shall refuse."

"But why?"

Elizabeth didn't answer for a moment, just stood there watching the egg whites turn opaque. "Susan," she finally said, "look at me."

Susan looked at her. "And?"

Elizabeth grabbed a handful of the faded green fabric of her dress and shook. "How can I go to a fancy house party dressed as I am? I may be desperate, but I have my pride."

"We shall cross the bridge of your clothing when we get to it," Susan decided firmly. "It shouldn't matter, anyway. Not if your future mate cannot see the room beyond your face."

"If I hear that phrase one more time——"

"In the meantime," Susan interrupted, "we must sharpen your skills."

Elizabeth fought the urge to smash the yolks.

"Didn't you say there was a new overseer at Lady Danbury's?"

"I said no such thing!"

"You didn't? Oh. Well, then, it must have been Fanny Brinkley, who must have heard it from her maid, who must have heard from——"

"Get to the point, Susan," Elizabeth ground out.

"Why don't you practice on him? Unless he's horribly repulsive, of course."

"He's not repulsive," Elizabeth mumbled. Her cheeks started to burn, and she kept her face down so that Susan wouldn't see her blush. Lady Danbury's new estate manager was far from repulsive. In fact, he was just about the most handsome man she'd ever seen. And his smile had done the strangest things to her insides.

Too bad he didn't have buckets of money.

"Good!" Susan said with an excited clap of her hands. "All you have to do is make him fall in love with you."

Elizabeth flipped the eggs. "And then what? Susan, he's an estate manager. He isn't going to have enough money to send Lucas to Eton."

"Silly, you aren't going to marry him. Just practice upon him."

"This sounds rather coldhearted," Elizabeth said, frowning.

"Well, you haven't anyone else upon whom to test your skills. Now, listen carefully. I picked out several rules with which to start."

"Rules? I thought they were edicts."

"Edicts, rules, it all amounts to the same thing. Now, then—"

"Jane! Lucas!" Elizabeth called out. "Breakfast is ready."

"As I was saying, I think we should begin with edicts two, three, and five."

"What about four?"

Susan had the grace to blush. "That one, ah, concerns dressing in the first stare of fashion."

Elizabeth just barely resisted the urge to fling a fried egg at her.

"Actually"—Susan frowned—"you might want to begin all the way at number eight."

Elizabeth knew she shouldn't have said a word, but some devil inside forced her to ask, "And what is that?"

Susan read: " 'Your charm must appear effortless.' "

"My charm must appear effortless? What the devil does that me— Ow!"

"I think," Susan said in an annoyingly bland voice, "it might mean that you're not meant to wave your arms about so that your hand smacks the tabletop."

If looks could have killed, Susan would have been bleeding profusely from the forehead.

Susan stuck her nose in the air. "I can only speak the truth," she sniffed.

Elizabeth continued glaring as she sucked on the back of her hand, as if pressing her lips to the spot were actually going to make it stop hurting. "Jane! Lucas!" she called again, this time practically yelling. "Hurry, now! Breakfast will get cold!"

Jane came skipping into the kitchen and sat down. The

Hotchkiss family had long ago dispensed with serving a formal morning meal in the dining room. Breakfast was always served in the kitchen. Besides, in the winter, everyone liked to sit near the stove. And in summer—well, habits were hard to break, Elizabeth supposed.

Elizabeth smiled at her youngest sister. "You look a touch untidy this morning, Jane."

"That's because *some*body locked me out of my room last night," Jane said with a mutinous glare toward Susan. "I haven't even had a chance to brush my hair."

"You could have used Lizzie's brush," Susan replied.

"I like my brush," Jane shot back. "It's silver."

Not real silver, Elizabeth thought wryly, or she would have had to sell it off already.

"It still works just the same," Susan returned.

Elizabeth put a halt to the bickering by yelling, "Lucas!"

"Have we any milk?" Jane asked.

"I'm afraid not, dear," Elizabeth replied, sliding an egg onto a plate. "Just enough for tea."

Susan slapped a piece of bread on Jane's plate and said to Elizabeth, "About Edict Number Two . . ."

"Not *now*," Elizabeth hissed, with a pointed look toward Jane, who, thankfully, was too busy poking her finger into the bread to take notice of her older sisters.

"My toast is raw," Jane said.

Elizabeth didn't even have time to yell at Susan for forgetting to make the toast before Lucas came bounding in.

"Good morning!" he said cheerfully.

"You seem especially chipper," Elizabeth said, tousling his hair before serving him breakfast.

"I'm going fishing today with Tommy Fairmount and his father." Lucas gobbled three-quarters of his egg before adding, "We shall eat well tonight!"

"That's wonderful, dear," Elizabeth said. She glanced at the small clock on the counter, then said, "I must be off. You lot will make certain the kitchen gets cleaned?"

Lucas nodded. "I shall supervise."

"You shall *help*."

"That, too," he grumbled. "May I have another egg?"

Elizabeth's own stomach growled in sympathy. "We haven't any extras," she said.

Jane looked at her suspiciously. "You didn't eat anything, Lizzie."

"I eat breakfast with Lady Danbury," Elizabeth lied.

"Have mine." Jane pushed what was left of her breakfast—two bites of egg and a wad of bread so mangled that Elizabeth would have had to have been far, far hungrier even to sniff at it—across the table.

"You finish it, Janie," Elizabeth said. "I'll eat at Lady Danbury's. I promise."

"I shall have to catch a very big fish," she heard Lucas whisper to Jane.

And that was the final straw. Elizabeth had been resisting this husband hunt; she hated how mercenary she felt for even considering it. But no more. What kind of world was it when eight-year-old boys worried about catching fish, not because of sport, but because they worried about filling their sisters' stomachs?

Elizabeth threw her shoulders back and marched to the door. "Susan," she said sharply, "a word with you?"

Jane and Lucas exchanged glances. "She's going to get it because she forgot to cook the toast," Jane whispered.

"Raw toast," Lucas said grimly, shaking his head. "It goes against the very nature of man."

Elizabeth rolled her eyes as she walked outside. Where did he come up with these things?

When they were safely out of earshot, she turned to

Susan and said, "First of all, I want no mention of this— this *husband hunt* in front of the children."

Susan held up Mrs. Seeton's book. "Then you're going to follow her advice?"

"I don't see how I have any choice," Elizabeth muttered. "Just tell me those rules."

Chapter 3

Elizabeth was muttering to herself as she entered Danbury House that morning. Truth be told, she'd been muttering to herself the entire walk over. She had promised Susan that she would try to practice Mrs. Seeton's edicts on Lady Danbury's new estate manager, but she didn't see how she could do this without immediately breaking Edict Number Two:

> NEVER SEEK OUT A MAN. ALWAYS FORCE HIM TO COME TO YOU.

Elizabeth supposed that was one rule she was going to have to break. She also wondered how to reconcile Edicts Three and Five, which were:

> YOU MUST NEVER BE RUDE. A HIGHBORN GENTLE-MAN NEEDS A LADY WHO IS THE EPITOME OF GRACE, DIGNITY, AND GOOD MANNERS.

And:

> NEVER SPEAK TO A MAN FOR MORE THAN FIVE MINUTES. IF YOU END THE CONVERSATION, HE WILL

41

FANTASIZE OVER WHAT YOU MIGHT HAVE SAID
NEXT.

EXCUSE YOURSELF AND DISAPPEAR TO THE LA-
DIES' RETIRING ROOM IF YOU MUST. HIS FASCINA-
TION WITH YOU WILL GROW IF HE THINKS YOU
HAVE OTHER MATRIMONIAL POSSIBILITIES.

This was where Elizabeth was really confused. It
seemed to her that even if she excused herself, it was
rather rude to leave a conversation after only five
minutes. And according to Mrs. Seeton, a highborn man
needed a lady who was never rude.

And that didn't even begin to include all of the other
rules Susan had yelled at her as she left the house that
morning. Be charming. Be sweet. Let the man talk. Don't
let on if you're smarter than he is.

With all this nonsense to worry about, Elizabeth was
rapidly warming to the idea of remaining Miss Hotchkiss,
aging spinster, indefinitely.

When she entered Danbury House, she proceeded immediately to the drawing room, as was her habit. Sure
enough, Lady Danbury was there, sitting in her favorite
chair, scribbling out some sort of correspondence and
muttering to herself as she did so. Malcolm was lazing
on a wide windowsill. He opened one eye, judged Elizabeth unworthy of his attention, and went back to sleep.

"Good morning, Lady Danbury," Elizabeth said with
a shake of her head. "Would you like me to do that for
you?" Lady Danbury suffered from achy joints, and Elizabeth frequently wrote out her correspondence for her.

But Lady Danbury just shoved the paper into a drawer.
"No, no, not at all. My fingers feel quite the thing this
morning." She flexed her hands and jabbed them in the
air at Elizabeth, like a witch casting some sort of spell.
"See?"

"I'm glad you're feeling so well," Elizabeth replied hesitantly, wondering if she'd just been hexed.

"Yes, yes, a very fine day. Very fine indeed. Provided, of course, you don't go and start reading to me from the Bible again."

"I wouldn't dream of it."

"Actually, there is something you can do for me."

Elizabeth raised her blond brows in question.

"I need to see my new estate manager. He is working in an office adjoining the stables. Could you fetch him for me?"

Elizabeth managed to keep her jaw from falling open at the very last minute. Brilliant! She was going to get to see the new estate manager and she wasn't going to have to break Edict Number Two doing it.

Well, technically she supposed that she still was seeking him out, but it couldn't really count if she'd been ordered to do so by her employer.

"Elizabeth!" Lady Danbury said loudly.

Elizabeth blinked. "Yes?"

"Pay attention when I speak to you. It is quite unlike you to daydream."

Elizabeth couldn't help but grimace at the irony. She hadn't daydreamed in five years. She'd once dreamed of love, and marriage, and of going to the theater, and of traveling to France. But all of that had stopped when her father died and her new responsibilities made it obvious that her secret thoughts were mere pipe dreams, destined never to come true. "I'm terribly sorry, my lady," she said.

Lady Danbury's lips twisted in such a way that Elizabeth knew she wasn't truly annoyed. "Just fetch him," Lady D said.

"At once," Elizabeth said with a nod.

"He has brown hair and brown eyes and is quite tall.

Just so you know of whom I'm speaking.''

"Oh, I met Mr. Siddons yesterday. I bumped into him while I was leaving for home.''

"Did you?'' Lady Danbury looked perplexed. "He didn't mention anything.''

Elizabeth cocked her head in puzzlement. "Was there any reason he should have done? I'm not likely to have any effect upon his employment here.''

"No. No, I suppose not.'' Lady Danbury wrinkled her mouth again, as if she were considering some great, unsolved philosophical problem. "Off with you, then. I shall require your company once I'm through with J—er, Mr. Siddons. Oh, and while I am consulting with him, you may bring me my embroidery.''

Elizabeth fought back a groan. Lady Danbury's idea of embroidering consisted of watching Elizabeth embroider and giving her copious instruction and supervision as she did so. And Elizabeth hated to embroider. She did more than enough sewing at home, what with all the clothing that needed mending.

"The green pillowcase, I think, not the yellow one,'' Lady Danbury added.

Elizabeth nodded distractedly and backed out the door. "Be unique,'' she whispered to herself, "but not too unique.'' She gave her head a shake. The day she figured out what *that* meant would be the day a man walked on the moon.

In other words, never.

By the time she reached the stable area, she had repeated the rules to herself at least ten times each and was so bleary-headed with it all that she would have gladly pushed Mrs. Seeton off of a bridge had the lady in question been in the region.

Of course there were no bridges in the region, either, but Elizabeth preferred to overlook that point.

The estate manager's office was housed in a small building directly to the left of the stables. It was a three-room cottage with a heavy stone chimney and thatched roof. The front door opened to a small sitting room, with a bedroom and office to the back.

The building had a neat and tidy appearance to it, which Elizabeth supposed made sense, since estate managers tended to be concerned with good upkeep of buildings. She stood outside the door for about a minute, taking a few deep breaths and reminding herself that she was a reasonably attractive and personable young woman. There was no reason that this man—whom she really wasn't that interested in, when it came right down to it—should scorn her.

Funny, Elizabeth thought wryly, how she'd never been nervous about meeting new people before. It was all the fault of this blasted husband hunt and that double-blasted book.

"I could strangle Mrs. Seeton," she muttered to herself as she raised her hand to knock. "In fact, I could do so quite cheerfully."

The door wasn't properly latched, and it swung open a few inches as Elizabeth knocked. She called out, "Mr. Siddons? Are you present? Mr. Siddons?"

No answer.

She pushed the door open a few more inches and stuck her head in. "Mr. Siddons?"

Now what was she to do? He clearly was not at home. She sighed, letting her left shoulder lean against the doorframe as her head slid forward into the room. She supposed she was going to have to go hunt him down, and heaven knew where he might be. It was a large estate, and she wasn't particularly excited about the prospect of hiking the length of it looking for the errant Mr. Siddons, even if she needed him desperately to practice Mrs. Seeton's edicts.

While she was standing there procrastinating, she let her eyes skim over the contents of the room. She'd been inside the small cottage before and knew which items belonged to the Lady Danbury. It didn't look as if Mr. Siddons had brought many belongings with him. Just a small bag in the corner, and—

She gasped. A little red book. Sitting right there on the end table. How on earth had Mr. Siddons obtained a copy of HOW TO MARRY A MARQUIS? She couldn't imagine that it was the sort of thing displayed in gentlemen's bookshops. Her mouth hung open in surprise as she strode across the room and snatched up the book.

ESSAYS by Francis Bacon?

Elizabeth shut her eyes and cursed herself. Dear Lord, she was growing obsessed. Thinking she saw that stupid little book around every corner. "Stupid, stupid, stupid," she muttered, swinging around to put the book back down on the table. "Mrs. Seeton does *not* know everything. You have to stop— Ow!"

She howled as her right hand connected with the brass lantern sitting on the table. Still clutching the book in her left hand, she shook her right from the wrist, trying to ward off the stinging pain. "Oh oh oh oh oh!" she grunted. This was worse than a stubbed toe, and the Lord knew she had more than enough experience with those.

She closed her eyes and sighed. "I am the clumsiest girl in all England, the biggest nodcock in all Britain—"

Crunch.

Her head snapped up. What was that? It sounded like a foot scraping against loose pebbles. And there were pebbles right outside the estate manager's cottage.

"Who's there?" she called out, her voice sounding rather strident to her ears.

No answer.

Elizabeth shivered—a bad sign, considering that it had been unseasonably warm all month. She had never been much of a believer in intuition, but something was definitely wrong here.

And she feared that she was the one who would suffer the consequences.

James had spent the morning riding through the estate. He knew it from top to bottom, of course; as a child he'd spent more time here at Danbury House than he had at his own Riverdale Castle. But if he was to keep up his charade as the new estate manager, he needed to inspect the grounds.

It was a hot day, however, and by the time he finished his three-hour ride, his brow was wet with perspiration and his linen shirt was sticking to his skin. A bath would have been perfect, but in his guise as estate manager he didn't have access to the Danbury House servants to fill a tub, and so he was looking forward to a cool washcloth dipped in the basin of water he'd left in his bedroom.

He hadn't expected to find the front door to his cottage wide open.

He adjusted his gait to make his footsteps as quiet as possible and crept up to the door. Peering in, he saw the back of a woman. Aunt Agatha's companion, if her pale blond hair and small frame were any indication.

He had been intrigued with her the day before. He didn't realize just how much until he saw her just now leaning over his copy of Francis Bacon's ESSAYS.

Francis Bacon? For a burglar, the chit had rather highbrow reading tastes.

Watching her was almost hypnotic. Her face was in

profile, and her nose scrunched up in the most amusing manner as she examined the book. Silky tendrils of flaxen hair had escaped her bun and curled along the back of her neck.

Her skin looked warm.

James sucked in his breath, trying to ignore the heat that was curling in his belly.

He leaned in as close to the doorframe as he could without revealing himself. What the devil was the girl saying? He forced himself to concentrate on her voice, which wasn't easy, since his eyes kept swaying to the gentle curve of her breasts, and that spot on the back of her neck where—

He pinched himself. Pain usually acted as decent antidote to one's baser needs.

Miss Hotchkiss was muttering something, and she sounded rather annoyed.

". . . stupid . . ."

He'd agree with that. Sneaking into his rooms during the light of day was not a smart move on her part.

". . . Mrs. Seeton . . ."

Who the hell was that?

"Ow!"

James peered at her more closely. She was shaking her hand and glaring at his lamp. He had to smile. She looked so furious that he wouldn't have been surprised if the lamp had spontaneously burst into flame.

And she was letting out little mewls of pain that did strange things to his stomach.

His first instinct was to rush to help her. He was still a gentleman, after all, beneath any disguise he chose to don. And a gentleman always came to the aid of a woman in pain. But he hesitated. She wasn't in *that* much pain, after all, and what the devil was she doing in his cottage, anyway?

Could she be the blackmailer?

And if so, how could she have known that he was here to investigate? Because if she weren't investigating him, why would she rifle through his belongings? Nice girls— the sort that acted as companions to aging countesses— didn't do that sort of thing.

Of course she might be nothing more than a petty thief, hoping that the new estate manager might be a down-on-his-luck gentleman with a few family heirlooms in his possession. A watch, a piece of jewelry of his mother's— the type of thing a man might be loath to part with, even if his circumstances had forced him to seek employment.

She closed her eyes and sighed, turning around as she did so. "I am the clumsiest girl in all England, the biggest nodcock in all Britain—"

He moved in closer, arching his neck as he tried to catch all of her words.

Crunch.

"Damn," James mouthed, moving quickly so that his back was pressed up against the outside wall of the cottage. It had been years since he'd taken such a careless step.

"Who's there?" she called out.

He couldn't see her any longer; he'd moved too far away from the door for that. But she sounded panicked. As if she were going to run outside at any moment.

He scooted away, quickly positioning himself between the stables and the cottage. When he heard Aunt Agatha's companion leave the building he would stroll out into the open, looking for all the world as if he'd just arrived on the scene.

Sure enough, he heard the front door to his cottage click shut a few seconds later. Footsteps followed, and then James made his move.

"Good day, Miss Hotchkiss," he called out, his long strides taking him right into her path.

"Oh!" she yelped, jumping a foot. "I didn't see you."

He smiled. "I apologize if I gave you a fright."

She shook her head, her cheeks beginning to turn pink.

James pressed a finger against his mouth to hide a triumphant smile. She was guilty of something. A blush like that didn't come about for no reason.

"No, no, it's all right," she stammered. "I—ah—I really must learn to watch where I'm going."

"What brings you out this way?" he asked. "It was my impression that most of your duties required your presence in the house."

"I do. I mean, they do. But actually, I was sent to find you. Lady Danbury would like to speak with you."

James's eyes narrowed. He didn't disbelieve the girl; she was obviously too intelligent to lie about something that could be so easily disproved. But why, then, would she have sneaked into his rooms?

The chit was up to something. And for his aunt's sake, he had to find out what. He'd had to question women before, and he had always been able to get them to tell him what he needed to know. In fact, his superiors at the War Office had often laughed that he had perfected the art of questioning women.

Women, he'd long since realized, were a somewhat different breed from men. They were basically self-absorbed. All one had to do was ask a woman about herself, and she was likely to spill all of her secrets. There were one or two exceptions to this rule, of course, Lady Danbury for instance being one, but—

"Is something amiss?" Miss Hotchkiss asked.

"I beg your pardon?"

"You were so silent," she pointed out, then bit her lip.

"Merely woolgathering," he lied. "I confess I cannot

think of why Lady Danbury should require my presence. I saw her just this morning."

She opened her mouth, but had no answer. "I do not know," she finally said. "I have found it best not to question Lady Danbury's motives. It's far too taxing on the brain to try to understand how her mind works."

James chuckled despite himself. He didn't want to like this girl, but she seemed to approach life with rare grace and humor. And she had certainly figured out the best way to deal with his aunt. Indulge her and do what you liked—it had always worked for him.

He held out his arm, prepared to charm her until she revealed all of her secrets. "Will you accompany me back to the house? Provided, of course, that you have no further business outside?"

"No."

He raised his brows.

"I mean no, I have no further business." She smiled weakly. "And yes, I would be happy to accompany you."

"Excellent," he said smoothly. "I cannot wait to further our acquaintance."

Elizabeth let out a long breath as she slid her arm through his. She had botched her last statement, but other than that, she thought she was holding fast to Mrs. Seeton's rules with admirable diligence. She had even managed to make Mr. Siddons laugh, which had to be in those edicts somewhere. And if it wasn't, it should have been. Surely men appreciated women who knew how to form a witty turn of phrase.

She wrinkled her brow. Perhaps that fell under the bit about being unique. . . .

"You look rather serious," he said.

Elizabeth started. Drat. She had to keep her mind focused on this gentleman. Wasn't there something in the book about giving gentlemen one's full attention? That would have to be during the five minutes *before* one cut off the conversation, of course.

"Almost," he continued, "as if you're concentrating a bit too hard on something."

Elizabeth almost moaned out loud. So much for her charm appearing effortless. She wasn't precisely certain how it applied to the present situation, but she was fairly sure that one was not supposed to actually appear as if one were following a guidebook.

"Of course," Mr. Siddons continued, clearly oblivious to her distress, "I have always found serious women to be most intriguing."

She could do this. She knew she could. She was a Hotchkiss, damn it, and she could do anything she set her mind to. She had to find a husband, but more importantly she first had to *learn* how to find a husband. And as for Mr. Siddons, well, he was right here, and maybe it was a little heartless to use him as some sort of test case, but a woman had to do what a woman had to do. And she was one desperate woman.

She turned, pasting a brilliant smile on her face. She was going to charm this man until—until—well, until he was charmed.

She opened her mouth to slay him with something utterly witty and sophisticated, but before she could form even a sound, he leaned in closer, his eyes warm and dangerous, and said, "I find myself unbearably curious about that smile."

She blinked. If she didn't know better, she'd think that *he* was trying to charm *her*.

No, she thought with a mental shake of her head. That was impossible. He barely knew her, and while she wasn't the ugliest girl in all of Surrey, she was certainly no siren.

"I do apologize, Mr. Siddons," she said prettily. "Like you, I am prone to getting lost in my own thoughts. And I certainly did not mean to be rude."

He shook his head. "You weren't rude."

"But, you see . . ." What was that Susan had read to her from the book? Always invite a man to talk about himself. Men were basically self-absorbed.

"Miss Hotchkiss?"

She cleared her throat and affixed yet another smile on her face. "Right. Well, you see, I was actually wondering about you."

There was a brief pause, and then he said, "Me?"

"Of course. It's not every day we have a new person here at Danbury House. Where are you from?"

"Here and there," he evaded. "Most lately, London."

"How exciting," she replied, trying to keep her voice suitably excited. She hated London. It was dirty and smelly and crowded. "And have you always been an estate manager?"

"Nooo," he said slowly. "There aren't many large country estates in London."

"Oh, yes," she muttered. "Of course."

He cocked his head and gazed down at her warmly. "Have you always lived here?"

Elizabeth nodded. "My entire life. I couldn't imagine living anywhere else. There's really nothing as lovely as the English countryside when the flowers bloom. And one certainly can't—" She cut herself off. She wasn't supposed to be talking about herself.

James's instincts leaped to attention. What had she been about to say?

She fluttered her lashes. "But you don't want to know about me."

"Oh, but I do," he replied, gifting her with his most intensely heated stare. Women loved that stare.

Not this woman, apparently. She jerked her head back and coughed.

"Is something wrong?" he asked.

She shook her head quickly, but she looked as if she had just swallowed a spider. Then—and this made no sense, but he could swear he saw it—she steeled her shoulders as if preparing for some hideous task, and said with impossible sweetness, "I'm certain you have led a much more interesting life than I, Mr. Siddons."

"Oh, but I'm sure that's not true."

Elizabeth cleared her throat, ready to stamp her foot in frustration. This wasn't working at all. Gentlemen were supposed to want to talk about themselves, and all he was doing was asking about her. She had the oddest impression that he was playing some sort of game with her.

"Mr. Siddons," she said, hoping that she had been able to eliminate all traces of frustration from her voice, "I have lived in Surrey since I was born. How could my life possibly be more interesting than yours?"

He reached out and touched her chin. "Somehow, Miss Hotchkiss, I have a feeling that you could fascinate me endlessly if you so chose."

Elizabeth gasped and then stopped breathing altogether. No man had ever touched her so, and she was probably the worst sort of harlot for thinking so, but there was something almost hypnotic about the warmth of his hand.

"Don't you think?" he whispered.

Elizabeth swayed toward him for the barest of seconds, and then she heard Mrs. Seeton—who, by the way, sounded remarkably like Susan—in her head.

"If you end the conversation," Susan's voice whispered, "he will fantasize over what you might have said next."

And then Elizabeth, who had never felt the heady bliss

of knowing a man was interested, forced the iron back into her spine for the second time that morning and said with remarkable steadiness, "I really must go, Mr. Siddons."

He shook his head slowly, never taking his eyes off of her face. "What are your interests, Miss Hotchkiss?" he asked. "Your hobbies? Your pursuits? You strike me as an uncommonly intelligent young lady."

Oh, he was definitely bamming her. He certainly hadn't known her long enough to form an opinion on her intellect. Her eyes narrowed. He wanted to know about her pursuits, did he? Well, then, she'd tell him.

"What I really like to do," she said with wide, bright eyes, "is work in my kitchen garden."

"Your kitchen garden?" he choked.

"Oh, yes. Our primary crop this year is turnips. Lots of turnips. Do you like turnips?"

"Turnips?" he echoed.

She nodded emphatically. "Turnips. Some find them dull, rather bland, really, but a more fascinating tuber you'll never find."

James glanced right and left, looking for a means of escape. What the devil was this girl talking about?

"Have you ever grown turnips?"

"Ah . . . no, I haven't."

"That's a pity," she said with great feeling. "One can learn quite a lot about life from a turnip."

James's head fell a little forward in disbelief. This he had to hear. "Really? And what, pray tell, can one learn?"

"Uh . . ."

He knew it. She was bamming him. What was she up to? He smiled innocently. "You were saying?"

"Diligence!" she blurted out. "One can learn a great deal about diligence."

''Really? How is that?''

She sighed dramatically. ''Mr. Siddons, if you have to ask, then I'm afraid you would never understand.''

While James was trying to digest that statement, she chirped, ''Oh, look, here we are back at Danbury House. Please tell Lady Danbury that I will be in the rose garden should she need me.''

And then, without so much as a farewell, she ran off.

James just stood there for a moment, trying to make sense of what had to be the most bizarre conversation of his life. And that's when he noticed it—her shadow, hanging alongside the building.

Rose garden, his foot. The blasted chit was lurking around the corner, still spying on him. He'd find out what she was up to if it was the last thing he did.

Ten hours later, Elizabeth dragged her weary feet through the front door of the Hotchkiss cottage. Susan was, not surprisingly, waiting on the bottom step of the stairs, HOW TO MARRY A MARQUIS still clutched in her hand.

''What happened?'' Susan exclaimed, bounding to her feet. ''Tell me everything!''

Elizabeth fought the urge to collapse in a fit of mortified laughter. ''Oh, Susan,'' she said with a slow shake of her head. ''We've mastered Edict Number One. He definitely thinks I'm unique.''

Chapter 4

"Isn't it a beautiful day?"

Elizabeth looked across the breakfast table at her sister's merry visage. Susan's smile was outshone only by the sun, which promised yet another day of uncommonly good weather.

"Isn't it?" Susan persisted.

Elizabeth just ignored her and continued to stab her muffin with a knife.

"If you're not going to eat that, may I have it?" Lucas asked.

Elizabeth started to push her plate across the table.

"Wait! I'd like some more, too," Jane chimed.

Elizabeth pulled the plate back, split the brutalized muffin remains in two, and pushed it back out.

"You're rather grumpy this morning," Jane said as she grabbed her share.

"Yes. Yes, I am."

As if choreographed, all three younger Hotchkisses drew back and exchanged glances. It was rare for Elizabeth to be struck with ill temper, but when she was . . .

"I believe I shall go out and play," Lucas said, standing up so fast he knocked his chair over.

"And I believe I shall join you," Jane said, shoving the rest of the muffin in her mouth.

The two children dashed out through the kitchen door. Elizabeth leveled a rather insolent stare in Susan's direction.

"*I'm* not going anywhere," Susan said. "We have too much to discuss."

"Perhaps you noticed that I am not in a conversational mood?" Elizabeth picked up her tea and took a sip. It was lukewarm. She set it back down and got up to put more water on the stove.

Yesterday had been a total fiasco. Utter disaster. What had she been thinking? She was supposed to have been practicing her social skills and instead she'd been prattling on about turnips.

Turnips!

She hated turnips.

She'd tried to tell herself that she'd had no choice. There was more to Mr. Siddons than met the eye, and he'd clearly been playing some game of his own with her. But turnips? Why did she have to pick turnips? And why had she said they had something to do with diligence? Good Lord, how was she ever to explain that?

He had probably told all of Danbury House about her bizarre fascination with root vegetables. By the time she arrived at work that morning, the story would have probably circulated from the stables to the kitchen and back. Everyone would be laughing at her. And while she didn't much mind the loss of Mr. Siddons as a "pretend marquis," she was going to have to work with the man for months—maybe years!—to come. And he probably thought she was insane.

Elizabeth took a step toward the stairs. "I'm going to be sick."

"Oh, no, you don't!" Susan exclaimed, skidding

around the table and grabbing Elizabeth's arm. "You are going to Danbury House this morning if it kills you."

"It *is* killing me. Trust me."

Susan planted her free hand on her hip. "I've never known you to be a coward, Elizabeth Hotchkiss."

Elizabeth wrenched her arm free and glared at her sister. "I'm not a coward. I just know when a battle is unwinnable. And believe me, this one has Waterloo written all over it."

"We won at Waterloo," Susan pointed out with a smirk.

"Pretend we're French," Elizabeth snapped. "I'm telling you, Mr. Siddons is not a good choice."

"What's wrong with him?"

"What's wrong with him? What's *wrong* with him?" Elizabeth's voice rose with frustration. "There's nothing wrong with him. *Everything* is wrong with him."

Susan scratched her head. "Perhaps it is my tender years, or perhaps my brain is not as fully developed as yours—"

"Oh, *please,* Susan."

"—but I have no earthly idea what you're talking about. If there is nothing wrong with the man—"

"The man is dangerous. He was playing games with me."

"Are you certain?"

"He has seduced hundreds of women. I'm sure of it."

"An estate manager?" Susan asked dubiously. "Aren't they usually short and fat?"

"This one is handsome as sin. He—"

"Handsome as sin? Really?" Susan's eyes grew wide. "What does he look like?"

Elizabeth paused, trying not to blush as Mr. Siddons's face floated in her mind. What was it about that man that was so compelling? Something about his mouth, perhaps.

His finely molded lips had the tendency to curve ever so slightly, as if they held the key to a secret joke. But then again, maybe it was his eyes. They were a rather regular shade of brown, the same color as his hair, actually, and should have seemed ordinary, but they were so deep, and when he looked at her, she felt . . .

"Elizabeth?"

Hot. She felt hot.

"Elizabeth?"

"What?" she asked distractedly.

"What does he look like?"

"Oh. He—oh, goodness, how am I supposed to describe him? He looks like a man."

"How descriptive," Susan said in a droll tone. "Remind me never to advise you to seek work as a novelist."

"I couldn't possibly make up a story any more ridiculous than the one I'm living right now."

Susan sobered. "Is it really as bad as that?"

"Yes," Elizabeth said with a sigh that was two parts frustration and one part irritation, "it is. We are almost completely out of the money Father left, and my wages from Lady Danbury are not nearly enough to support us—especially once the lease on the cottage runs out. I have to marry, but the only available man in the district besides Squire Nevins is Lady D's new estate manager, and he, aside from being far too handsome and dangerous *and* thinking that I am completely insane, couldn't possibly earn enough to qualify as a suitable candidate. So I ask you," she added, her voice rising in pitch and volume, "since you've already pointed out that I am not going to make a fortune publishing my letters, *what* do you propose I do?"

She crossed her arms, rather pleased with her speech.

Susan merely blinked and asked, "Why does he think you're insane?"

"It doesn't matter," Elizabeth ground. "What matters is that I am in a complete bind."

"As it happens," Susan said with a slow, deep smile, "I have the answer."

Elizabeth saw her sister reach behind her back for something and felt anger explode within her. "Oh, no, don't you even dare to pull that book out again."

But Susan already had the little red book open. "Listen to this," she said excitedly. " 'Edict Number Seventeen—' "

"We're already up to seventeen?"

"Be quiet. 'Edict Number Seventeen: Life is a rehearsal until you meet the man you marry.' " Susan nodded enthusiastically. "See?"

Silence.

"Elizabeth?"

"You're joking, aren't you?"

Susan looked at the book, then looked back up at her sister. "Noooo," she said slowly, "I—"

"Give me that!" Elizabeth snatched up the book and looked down.

LIFE IS A MERE REHEARSAL UNTIL YOU MEET THE MAN YOU MARRY. THUS YOU MUST PRACTICE THESE EDICTS AT ALL TIMES, ON EVERY MAN YOU MEET. IT DOES NOT MATTER IF YOU HAVE NO INTENTION OF MARRYING A CERTAIN MAN; HE MUST BE DEALT WITH AS YOU WOULD A MARQUIS. FOR IF YOU SLIP OUT OF THE HABIT OF FOLLOWING MY EDICTS, YOU WILL FORGET WHAT YOU ARE ABOUT WHEN YOU DO MEET A MARRIAGE PROSPECT. HONE YOUR SKILLS. BE READY. YOUR MARQUIS MAY BE RIGHT AROUND THE CORNER.

"Has she gone completely mad?" Elizabeth demanded. "This is not a fairy tale. There are no marquises around the corner. And frankly, I find this all rather insulting.''

"What part?''

"All of it. To listen to this woman say it, I don't even exist until I find a husband. It's preposterous. If I'm so unimportant, then what have I been doing these past five years? How have I managed to keep this family together? Not by twiddling my thumbs and hoping some kind gentleman will deign to marry me!''

Susan's mouth parted in silent surprise. Finally she said, "I don't think she meant—''

"I know she didn't—'' Elizabeth broke off her words, a little ashamed by the violence of her outburst. "I'm sorry. I didn't mean— Please forget I said anything.''

"Are you certain?'' Susan asked, her voice quiet.

"It's nothing,'' Elizabeth said quickly, turning away and looking out the window. Lucas and Jane were playing in the garden. They'd devised some game involving a piece of blue fabric tied to a stick and were squealing with glee.

Elizabeth swallowed, love and pride brimming within her. She ran her hand through her hair, her fingers stopping in place when she reached the top of her braid. "I'm sorry,'' she said to Susan. "I shouldn't have snapped at you like that.''

"I don't mind,'' Susan said sympathetically. "You've been under a great deal of strain. I know that.''

"It's just that I'm so worried.'' Elizabeth moved her hand to her forehead and rubbed. Suddenly she felt so tired and so very old. "What good is practicing my wiles upon Mr. Siddons when there aren't even any real marriage prospects to be found?''

"Lady Danbury invites visitors all the time,'' Susan said in an encouraging voice. "Doesn't she? And you told me that all her friends are rich and titled.''

"Yes, but she grants me my free days when she entertains. She says she has no need of my company when she has guests in residence."

"You'll just have to find a way around that. Concoct some reason why you need to visit. And what about this party at the end of the month? Didn't you say she always invites you to such functions?"

"It's to be a masquerade, actually. She informed me yesterday."

"Even better! We might not know enough to sew you a fashionable ball gown, but we can certainly manage a costume. You don't need to dress up as anyone fancy."

Susan moved her hands animatedly as she spoke, and for one odd moment Elizabeth thought she was looking at herself at fourteen—back when she'd thought anything was possible. Before her father had died and left her with mountains of responsibility. Before he had died and taken the innocence of her childhood along with him.

"We look so alike, you and I," she said in a small whisper.

Susan blinked. "I beg your pardon?"

"It's nothing. It's just . . ." Elizabeth paused and gave her sister a wistful smile. "It's just that sometimes our similar looks remind me how like you I used to be."

"And you're not any longer?"

"No, not really. Sometimes, just for a little bit, though." She leaned forward impulsively and kissed her sister's cheek. "Those are my very favorite moments."

Susan blinked back something that looked suspiciously like tears before assuming her usual businesslike mien. "We need to return to the matter at hand."

Elizabeth smiled. "I'd quite forgotten what that was."

"When," Susan asked with an impatient sigh, "is Lady Danbury next entertaining visitors? Not the masquerade. Just visitors."

"Oh, that," Elizabeth said grimly. "She's expecting people at the end of this week. I believe it is to be a small garden party. More of a gathering, really, than a formal party. I wrote out the invitations."

"How many will be arriving?"

"No more than ten or twelve, I think. It is only for the afternoon. We are close enough to London, after all, that people can make the trip to and from in one day."

"You must attend."

"Susan, I am not invited!"

"Surely that is only because she does not think you will accept. If you tell her—"

"I am not going to angle for an invitation," Elizabeth said hotly. "Even I have more pride than that."

"Can't you just leave something there by accident on Friday? Then you would have to return on Saturday to fetch it." Susan made a face that was more hopeful than convincing. "Maybe you would be invited to join in the festivities."

"And you don't think Lady Danbury will find that a trifle odd?" Elizabeth scoffed. "I've been her companion for five years now, and I've never forgotten any of my belongings before."

"Perhaps she will. Perhaps she won't." Susan shrugged. "But you won't know until you try. And you certainly won't find a husband if you hide yourself here all day."

"Oh, very well," Elizabeth said with great reluctance. "I shall do it. But only after I check the guest list, and then only if I can be certain that there will be an unmarried man in attendance. I'm not going to embarrass myself in front of Lady Danbury just to find that all of her guests are married."

Susan clapped her hands together. "Excellent! And

in the meantime, you shall have to practice upon this Mr.—"

"No!" Elizabeth said loudly. "I will not."

"But—"

"I said no. I will not seek this man out."

Susan raised her brows innocently. "Fine. There is no need for you to seek him out. Mrs. Seeton says one isn't supposed to do that sort of thing anyway. But if you should just happen upon him . . ."

"That won't be likely, since I plan to avoid him as if he carried the plague."

"Just in case—"

"Susan!" Elizabeth leveled her sternest glare in her sister's direction.

"Very well, but if you—"

Elizabeth held up her hand. "Not another word, Susan. I am going to Danbury House right now, where I will attend to Lady Danbury, and only Lady Danbury. Have I made myself clear?"

Susan nodded, but she clearly didn't mean it.

"Good day, then. I am certain I shall have nothing to report when I return home." Elizabeth tramped to the front door and wrenched it open. "Today shall be so dull. Utterly, blessedly dull. I am sure of it. In fact, I probably will not see Mr. Siddons even from afar."

She was wrong. So very, very wrong. He was waiting for her at the front door.

"Miss Hotchkiss," he said, his voice so amiable that Elizabeth couldn't quite trust it, "it is a pleasure to see you again."

Elizabeth found herself torn between the desire to flee into the house and the urge to wipe his confident smile right off of his face. Pride won out. She raised one of her blond brows in a supercilious gesture she'd learned from

Lady Danbury and said, quite acidly, "Is it?"

One corner of his mouth tilted upward, but one couldn't really call it a smile. "You don't seem to believe me."

Elizabeth let out a long breath between pursed lips. What the devil was she supposed to do now? She'd sworn to herself that she wasn't going to practice any more HOW TO MARRY A MARQUIS edicts on this man. He was clearly far too well versed in the art of flirting to be taken in by any of her pathetic attempts.

And after yesterday's turnip debacle, he probably thought her a complete ninny. Which begged the question: What the devil did he want with her now?

"Miss Hotchkiss," he began, after waiting in vain for her to make a comment, "I had merely hoped that we might develop a friendship of sorts. After all, we will be working together here at Danbury House for some time to come. And we both occupy those governesslike in-between posts—a bit too well-bred to mingle with the servants, yet certainly not part of the family."

She considered his words—or, to be more precise, his tone, which was suspiciously friendly. Then she regarded his face, which appeared to be equally kind and amiable.

Except for his eyes. There was something lurking in those chocolaty depths. Something . . . knowing.

"Why are you being so nice to me?" she blurted out.

He started, letting out a little cough as he did so. "I'm sure I don't know what you mean."

She pointed her finger and wagged it slowly. "I know what you're about, so don't try to fool me."

That caused him to raise a brow, which annoyed her, because he had obviously mastered the look better than she had. He said, "I beg your pardon?"

"You're very charming, you know."

His lips parted slightly, and then, after a brief moment

of silence, he said, "I find myself with nothing to say but 'thank you.'"

"It wasn't necessarily a compliment."

"But it might have been?" he asked teasingly.

She shook her head. "You want something from me."

"Only your friendship."

"No, you want something, and you're trying to charm me into getting it."

"Is it working?"

"No!"

He sighed. "Pity. It usually does."

"You admit it, then?"

"I suppose I must." He held up his hands in defeat. "But if you want me to answer your questions, you're required to humor me and stroll the grounds with me for a few minutes."

She shook her head. Going anywhere alone with this man was a huge mistake. "I can't. Lady Danbury is expecting me."

He flipped open his pocket watch. "Not for another quarter hour."

"And how do you know that?" she demanded.

"Perhaps you recall that I was hired to manage her affairs?"

"But you're not her secretary." Elizabeth crossed her arms. "Estate managers don't set schedules for their employers."

Perhaps she was imagining it, but his eyes seemed to grow warmer and more intense. "I have always found," he said, "that there is nothing so powerful as good information. Lady Danbury is an exacting woman. It seemed prudent to acquaint myself with her schedule so as not to disrupt it."

Elizabeth pursed her lips. He was right, drat the man! The very first thing she herself had done upon entering

Lady D's employ was memorize her schedule.

"I can see you agree with me, reluctant though you are to compliment me by admitting it."

She glared at him. Really, this man was beyond arrogant.

"Come, now," he said coaxingly. "Surely you can spare a few moments to help a newcomer to the area."

"Very well," Elizabeth replied, quite unable to refuse when he phrased his request as a plea for help. She had never been able to turn away from anyone in need. "I shall walk with you. But you may only have ten minutes of my time."

"A most generous lady," he murmured, and took her arm.

Elizabeth swallowed as his hand looped around the crook of her elbow. She felt it again—that odd, breathy awareness that enveloped her whenever he was near. And the worst part was that he looked as cool and composed as ever.

"Perhaps we could take a short turn through the rose garden?" he suggested.

She nodded, quite unable to say anything else. The heat from his hand had traveled up her arm, and she seemed to have forgotten how to breathe.

"Miss Hotchkiss?"

She swallowed and found her voice. "Yes?"

"I hope I am not making you uncomfortable by seeking you out."

"Not at all," she squeaked.

"Good," James said with a smile. "It is merely that I did not know to whom else to turn." He glanced over at her. Her cheeks were stained delightfully pink.

They said nothing as their steps took them through the stone arch that led into the rose garden. James steered her to the right, past Danbury House's famous Scarlet Scotch

Roses, which bloomed in a brilliant display of pink and yellow. He leaned down to smell one, stalling for time while he figured out how best to proceed from here.

He had thought about her all night and well into the morning. She was clever, and she was definitely up to something. He had spent enough time ferreting out secret plots to know when a person was acting suspiciously. And his every instinct told him that Miss Hotchkiss had been behaving out of character the day before.

At first it had seemed odd that she should be the black-mailer. After all, she couldn't be very much older than twenty. She certainly wasn't older than Melissa, who was nearly thirty-two. So she couldn't have any firsthand knowledge of Lady Danbury's extramarital affair.

But she had lived her entire life in the region; she had said so herself. Perhaps her parents had passed on a confidence. Secrets had a way of lingering in small towns for years.

Not to mention that Miss Hotchkiss had free run of Danbury House. If Aunt Agatha had left any incriminating evidence about, no one was more likely to come across it than her companion.

No matter which way he turned, he was led back to Miss Elizabeth Hotchkiss.

But if he wanted to learn her secrets, he had to make her trust him. Or at the very least, lower her guard enough so that she might let the occasional confidence slip through those delectable pink lips of hers. It seemed to him that the best way to do this was to ask for her assistance. Her sort of woman was polite to a fault. There was no way she would say no if he asked her to help him acquaint himself with the neighborhood. Even if she was the blackmailer—and thus selfish to the core—she had appearances to maintain. Miss Elizabeth Hotchkiss, companion to the Countess of Danbury, could not afford to be seen as anything less than gracious and kind.

"Perhaps you realize that I am new to the area," he began.

She nodded slowly, her eyes wary.

"And you told me yesterday that you have lived in this village your entire life."

"Yes . . ."

He smiled warmly. "I find myself in need of a guide of sorts. Someone to show me the sights. Or, at the very least, to tell me about them."

She blinked. "You want to see the sights? What sights?"

Damn. She had him there. It wasn't as if the village were brimming with culture and history. "Perhaps 'sights' isn't the best choice of words," he improvised. "But each village has its own little quirks, and if I am to be effective as manager of the largest estate in the district, I need to be aware of such things."

"That's true," she said, nodding thoughtfully. "Of course, I'm not certain what precisely you would need to know, as I've never managed an estate. And one would think that you, also, would be at a loss, since you have never managed an estate before, either."

He looked at her sharply. "I never said that."

She stopped walking. "Didn't you? Yesterday, when you said you were from London."

"I said I hadn't been managing estates in London. I did not say that I had not done so prior to that."

"I see." She turned her head to the side and looked at him assessingly. "And where were you managing estates, if not in London?"

She was testing him, the damnable chit. Why, he wasn't certain, but she was definitely testing him. But he wasn't about to let her trip him up. James Sidwell had immersed himself in disguise more times than he could count, and he had never slipped. "Buckinghamshire," he said. "That is where I grew up."

"I have heard it is beautiful there," she said politely. "Why did you leave?"

"The usual reasons."

"Which are?"

"Why are you so curious?"

She shrugged. "I'm always curious. Ask anyone."

He paused and plucked a rose. "These are beautiful, aren't they?"

"Mr. Siddons," she said with an exaggerated sigh, "I fear there is something you do not know about me."

James felt his body tense, waiting for whatever admission was forthcoming.

"I have three younger siblings."

He blinked. What the hell did that have to do with anything?

"Hence," she continued, smiling at him in such a way that he was no longer quite so sure that she was up to anything other than amusing conversation, "I am quite proficient in recognizing when a person is evading a question. In fact, my younger siblings would call me frighteningly proficient."

"I'm sure they would," he muttered.

"However," she continued personably, "you are not one of my siblings, and you are certainly under no obligation to share your past with me. We all have a right to our private feelings."

"Er, yes," he said, wondering if maybe she was nothing more than what she seemed—a nice young country-bred miss.

She smiled up at him again. "Have you any siblings, Mr. Siddons?"

"I? No. None. Why?"

"As I said, I am endlessly curious. A person's family

can reveal a great deal about his character.''

"And what does your family reveal about your character, Miss Hotchkiss?''

"That I am loyal, I suppose. And that I would do anything for my brother and sisters.''

Including blackmail? He leaned toward her, barely an inch, but it was still enough to make her lower lip tremble. James took a primitive satisfaction in that.

She just stared at him, obviously too inexperienced to know how to handle such a predatory male. Her eyes were huge, and the clearest, darkest blue James had ever seen.

His heart began to beat faster.

"Mr. Siddons?''

His skin turned hot.

"Mr. Siddons?''

He was going to have to kiss her. That's all there was to it. It was the stupidest, most ill-advised idea he'd had in years, but there didn't seem to be anything he could do to stop himself. He moved in, closing the gap between them, savoring the anticipation of the moment his lips would land on hers, and—

"Eep!''

What the hell?

She made some sort of nervous chirping sound and jerked away, her arms flailing.

And then she slipped—in what, he didn't know, since the ground was dry as bone, but she waved her arms madly to keep from falling to the ground, and in the process smacked him under the chin. Hard.

"Ow!'' he howled.

"Oh, I'm sorry!'' she said quickly. "Here, let me see to that.''

She stepped on his toe.

"Ouch!''

"I'm sorry sorry sorry." She looked terribly concerned, and normally he would have milked this for all it was worth, but damn it, his foot *really* hurt.

"I'll be fine, Miss Hotchkiss," he said. "All I need is for you to step off of my toe, and—"

"Oh, I'm sorry!" she said, for what seemed the hundredth time. She took a step back.

He winced as he flexed his toes.

"I'm sorry," she said.

He shuddered. "Don't say that again."

"But—"

"I insist."

"At least let me see to your foot." She bent down.

"*Please* don't." There were few situations in which James thought begging appropriate, but this was one of them.

"All right," she said, straightening up. "But I should—"

Smack!

"Oh, my head!" she yelped, rubbing the top of her scalp.

"My chin," James barely managed to get out.

Her blue eyes filled with worry and embarrassment. "I'm sorry."

"Brilliant aim, Miss Hotchkiss," he said, shutting his eyes in agony. "Right where you whacked me with your hand."

He heard her gulp. "I'm sorry."

And that was when he made his fatal mistake. Never again would he keep his eyes closed around a suspiciously clumsy female, no matter how appealing she was. He didn't know how she managed it, but he heard a surprised yelp, and then somehow her entire body crashed into his, and he went tumbling toward the ground.

Well, he thought he'd hit the ground.

If it had occurred to him to hope, he would have hoped to hit the ground.

But as it turned out, he should have *prayed* he'd hit the ground. It would have been so much more pleasant than the rosebush.

Chapter 5

"**I**'m sorry!"

"Don't say that," he growled, trying to decide which bit of him hurt the worst.

"But I am!" she wailed. "Here, let me help you up."

"Don't," he yelled frantically, finishing with a somewhat quieter, "touch me. Please."

Her lips parted with mortified horror, she started blinking rapidly, and for a moment James thought she might cry. "It's perfectly all right," he forced himself to lie. "I'm not hurt." At her incredulous stare, he added, "Very much."

She swallowed. "I'm so clumsy. Even Susan refuses to dance with me."

"Susan?"

"My sister. She's fourteen."

"Ah," he said, then added under his breath, "Smart girl."

She caught her lower lip between her teeth. "Are you certain you wouldn't like a hand up?"

James, who had been quietly trying to extricate himself from his thorny prison, finally faced the truth that in one-on-one combat, the rosebush would emerge the victor. "I'm going to give you my hand," he directed, keeping his words nice and slow, "and then you are going to pull me up and out. Is that clear?"

She nodded.

"Not to the side, not forward, not—"

"I said it's clear!" she snapped. Before he even had a chance to react, she grabbed his hand and hauled him out of the rosebush.

James just stared at her for a moment, more than a little shocked by the strength hidden in her tiny frame.

"I'm clumsy," she said. "Not an idiot."

Again, he was rendered speechless. Twice in one minute had to be a new record.

"Are you injured?" she asked brusquely, picking a thorn off his jacket and then another from his sleeve. "Your hand looks scratched. You should have worn gloves."

"Too hot for gloves," James murmured, watching her as she picked more thorns off him. She had to be a complete innocent—no lady of any experience, even with mere flirtation, would stand so close, her hands running up and down his body . . .

Very well, he admitted to himself, he was letting his imagination and his libido get the better of him. She wasn't exactly running her hands up and down his body, but she might as well have been with the way he was reacting. She was so close. He could just reach out and touch her hair—see how soft it really was, and—

Oh, God, he could *smell* her.

His body hardened in a second.

She pulled her hand back and looked up, her eyes innocent and blue. "Is something wrong?"

"Why would anything be wrong?" he asked, his voice strangled.

"You stiffened."

He smiled humorlessly. If she only knew. . . .

She picked off another thorn, this one caught on the collar of his jacket. "And to be frank, you sound quite odd."

James coughed, trying to ignore the way her knuckles accidentally brushed against the side of his jaw. "Frog in my throat," he rasped.

"Oh." She stood back and examined her handiwork. "Oh, dear, I missed one."

He followed her eyes ... down to his thigh. "I'll get that one," he said quickly.

She blushed. "Yes, that would be best, but—"

"But what?"

"Another one," she said with an embarrassed cough and a pointed finger.

"Where?" he asked, just to make her blush some more.

"There. A little higher." She pointed and looked away, turning red as a beet.

James grinned. He'd forgotten how much fun it was to turn ladies' cheeks to pink. "There, now. Am I clean?"

She turned back, looked him over, and nodded. "I really am terribly sorry about the, ah, rosebush," she said with a contrite tilt of her head. "Truly very sorry."

The minute James heard the word "sorry" again, he had to fight the urge to grab her by the shoulders and shake. "Yes, I believe we have already established that."

One of her delicate hands rose to her cheek in an expression of concern. "I know, but your face is scratched, and we really should treat it with salve, and—I say, *why* are you sniffing?"

Caught. "Was I?"

"Yes."

He gave her his most boyish smile. "You smell like roses."

"No," she said with an amused smile, "*you* smell like roses."

James started to laugh. His chin hurt where she'd smacked him twice, his foot throbbed where she'd stepped on it, and his entire body felt as if he'd swum through a rosebush, which wasn't as far off the truth as it sounded. Yet still he started to laugh.

He looked over at Miss Hotchkiss, who was chewing on her lower lip and eyeing him dubiously. "I'm not going mad, if that's what worries you," he said with a jaunty smile, "although I would like to accept your offer of medical treatment."

She nodded briskly. "We'd best get you inside, then. There is a small room not very far from the kitchen where Lady Danbury keeps her medicines. I'm sure there will be some sort of salve or lotion we can apply to your wounds."

"Will you . . . ah . . . be seeing to—"

"Your scrapes?" she finished for him, her lips twisting into a self-deprecating smile. "Don't worry, even I am nimble enough to tend to those scratches without causing mortal injury. I've cleaned up far more cuts and scrapes than I care to think about."

"Those siblings of yours are younger than you, then?"

She nodded. "And adventurous. Just yesterday Lucas and Jane informed me that they plan to build an underground fort." She let out an incredulous laugh. "They told me I need to chop down our only tree to provide them with wooden support beams. Where they get these ideas, I'll never know, but— Oh, I'm sorry. How rude of me to prattle on about my family."

"No," James said, more than a bit surprised by the quickness of his reply. "I enjoy hearing about your family. They sound delightful."

Her eyes softened, and he got the impression that

her mind had drifted to somewhere very far away—somewhere, to judge by her dreamy smile, that was very very nice. "They are," she replied. "Of course we bicker and argue like all families, but— Oh, look at me. I'm doing it again. All I meant to do was assure you that I have more than enough experience with minor injuries."

"In that case," he said with great flair, "I trust you completely. Anyone who has tended to small children is experienced enough to see to these paltry wounds."

"I'm glad to hear that I meet with your approval," she said wryly.

He held out his hand. "Shall we call a truce? I may call you friend?"

She nodded. "Truce."

"Good. Then back to the house with us."

They laughed and talked as they exited the rose garden, and it was only when James was halfway back to Danbury House that he remembered that he suspected her of blackmail.

Elizabeth dipped her handkerchief in the sharp-smelling salve. "This may sting a bit," she warned.

Mr. Siddons grinned. "I think I'm man enough to— Yow! What is in that?"

"I told you it might sting."

"Yes, but you didn't tell me it had *teeth*."

Elizabeth held the jar up to her nose and sniffed. "I think there might be some sort of alcohol in here. It smells a bit like brandy. Does that make sense? Would one put brandy in such a thing?"

"Not," he muttered, "if one didn't want to make any enemies."

She sniffed at it again and shrugged. "I can't tell. It could be brandy. Or perhaps some other spirit. I didn't mix it."

"Who did?" he asked, looking as if he very much dreaded the answer.

"Lady Danbury."

He groaned. "I feared as much."

Elizabeth looked at him curiously. "Why would you fear that? You hardly know her."

"True, but our families have been friends for many years. Believe me when I tell you that she is legend among my parents' generation."

"Oh, I believe you." Elizabeth laughed. "She's legend among my generation. She has all the village children quite terrified."

"That," Mr. Siddons said dryly, "I believe."

"I didn't realize you knew Lady Danbury prior to your employment," she said, dipping her handkerchief in the salve again.

"Yes, it's"—he winced as she applied a bit to his forehead—"why she hired me, I'm sure. She probably thought I'd be more trustworthy than someone referred by an agency."

"That's odd. Before you arrived, Lady Danbury dismissed me early so that she could go over the books and memorize the numbers so she could be certain you weren't robbing her blind."

James covered up a chuckle with a cough. "She said that?"

"Mmm-hmm." She leaned forward, her eyes narrowing with concentration as she scanned his face. "But I shouldn't take it personally. She'd say that about anyone, even her own son."

"Especially her own son."

Elizabeth laughed. "You do know her well, then. She is forever complaining about him."

"Did she tell you about the time he got his head stuck—"

"At Windsor Castle? Yes." She grinned, touching her fingers to her lips as she let out a little giggle. "I've never laughed so hard."

James smiled back at her, finding her nearness disarming. He felt almost giddy. "Do you know him?"

"Cedric?" She drew back slightly so that they could converse at a more comfortable distance. "Oh, I suppose I should call him Lord Danbury now, shouldn't I?"

He lifted his shoulder in a lopsided shrug. "You can call him whatever you like in my company. I, for one, like to call him a—"

She shook her finger at him. "I think you must have a very naughty streak to you, Mr. Siddons. And you're trying to coax me into saying something I might regret."

He smiled wolfishly. "I'd much rather coerce you into *doing* something you might regret."

"Mr. Siddons," she said reprovingly.

He shrugged. "Forgive me."

"As it happens, I do know the new Lord Danbury," she said, dipping her chin as she looked at him to signal that the subject had been officially changed. "Not very well, of course. He's a bit older than I am, so we did not play together as children. But he does come back to visit his mother from time to time, so our paths do occasionally cross."

It occurred to James that should Cedric decide to visit his mama anytime soon, his disguise would be completely ruined. Even if he or Aunt Agatha managed to warn him of the situation ahead of time, Cedric absolutely could not be trusted to keep his mouth shut. The man had no notion of discretion and even less of common sense. James shook his head unthinkingly. Thank goodness stupidity didn't run in the family.

"What's wrong?" Miss Hotchkiss asked.

"Nothing. Why?"

"You shook your head."

"Did I?"

She nodded. "I probably wasn't being gentle enough. I'm terribly sorry."

He captured her hand in his and caught her in a hungry gaze. "Angels could not have been more gentle."

Her eyes widened, and for a fleeting moment locked with his before shifting to their hands. James waited for her to object, but she did not, and so he let his thumb trail along her wrist as he released her. "I beg your pardon," he murmured. "I don't know what came over me."

"It's—it's quite all right," she stammered. "You've had quite a shock. It's not every day one finds oneself pushed into a rosebush."

He said nothing, just turned his face as she ministered to a scratch near his ear.

"Here, hold still," she said in a soft voice. "I need to apply this on the deepest scratch."

He closed his mouth, and Elizabeth held her breath as she leaned in close. The cut was to the left and below his mouth, curving into the hollow under his lower lip. "There's a bit of dirt here," she murmured. "I— Oh, hold still another moment. I need to . . ."

She bit her lower lip and bent her legs so that she was right on level with his face. She put her fingers to his lip and gently stretched it upward so that the small scratch was exposed. "Here you are," she whispered as she cleaned the wound, amazed that she was able to make a sound over the pounding of her heart. She'd never stood so close to a man before, and this one in particular did the oddest things to her. She had the most absurd desire to let her fingers drift over the sculpted planes of his face, and then smooth across the elegant arch of his dark eyebrows.

She forced herself to exhale and then looked down at his face. He was staring at her with an odd expression, half amused and half something else entirely. Her fingers were still on his lips, and somehow the sight of herself touching him seemed more dangerous than the actual touch.

With a little gasp she pulled her hand away.

"Are you done?" he asked.

She nodded. "I—I hope that didn't hurt you too much."

His eyes grew dark. "I didn't feel the cut at all."

Elizabeth felt herself smile self-consciously, and she took another step back—anything to regain her equilibrium. "You're a very different patient than my brother," she said, trying to turn the conversation to tamer topics.

"He probably didn't flinch half as much as I did," Mr. Siddons joked.

"No," Elizabeth said with a breathy laugh, "but he screams much louder."

"You said his name is Lucas?"

She nodded.

"Does he look like you?"

Elizabeth's eyes, which had been studying a painting on the wall in an effort not to look at Mr. Siddons, suddenly flew to his face. "That's an odd question to ask."

He shrugged. "Like you, I'm a curious sort."

"Oh. Well, then, yes, he does. We all look alike. My parents were both very fair."

James held silent for a moment as he contemplated her words. It was hard not to notice that she'd spoken of them in the past tense. "They have passed on, then?" he said gently.

She nodded, and he couldn't help but see a slight stiffening in her face as she turned her head to the side. "It's been over five years," she said. "We're used to being on our own now, but still it's''—she swallowed—"difficult."

"I'm sorry."

She was quiet for a moment, then let out a small, forced laugh. "I thought we agreed that we weren't going to utter those words."

"No," he teased, trying to weave humor into the conversation. He respected her desire not to share her grief. "We agreed that *you* would not say them. I, on the other hand . . ."

"Very well," she said, clearly relieved that he wasn't going to pry, "if you truly wish to apologize, I shall be happy to write out a list of your transgressions."

He leaned forward, resting his elbows on his knees. "Would you, now?"

"Oh, indeed. Of course, I only have three days worth of transgressions to document, but I'm fairly certain I can at least fill a page."

"Only a page? I shall have to work harder to— Miss Hotchkiss?"

Her entire body had gone stiff and she was glaring at the door. "Get *out,*" she hissed.

James stood so that he could see over the counter. Aunt Agatha's cat was sitting in the doorway, resting on his furry haunches. "Is there a problem?" James queried.

She never once took her eyes off of the animal. "That cat is a menace."

"Malcolm?" He grinned and walked over to the cat. "He wouldn't hurt a fly."

"Don't touch him," Elizabeth warned. "He's vicious."

But James just scooped him up. Malcolm let out a loud purr and buried his face into James's neck with one long, lazy rub.

Elizabeth's mouth fell open. "That little traitor. I tried to befriend him for three years!"

"I thought you've worked here for five."

"I have. But I gave up after three. A woman can only be hissed at so many times."

Malcolm looked at her, stuck his nose in the air, and went back to showering James's neck with kitty love.

James chuckled and walked back to his chair. "I'm sure he views me as a challenge. I hate cats."

Elizabeth's head fell forward in the most sarcastic of gestures. "Odd, but you don't look like you hate cats."

"Well, I don't hate this one any longer."

"How fitting," she muttered. "A man who hates all cats save one, and a cat who hates all people save one."

"Two, if you count Lady Danbury." James grinned and sat back, suddenly feeling very satisfied with his life. He was out of London, away from the simpering debutantes and their grasping mamas, and he'd somehow found himself in the company of this delightful young woman, who *probably* wasn't blackmailing his aunt, and even if she was—well, his heart hadn't raced so much in years as when she'd touched her finger to his lips.

Considering that he hadn't managed to muster up even an ounce of interest in any of the matrimonial prospects parading about in London, that had to count for something.

And maybe, he thought with a wistful hopefulness he hadn't felt in years, if she *was* blackmailing his aunt— well, maybe she had a really good reason for it. Maybe she had an ailing relative, or was being threatened with eviction. Maybe she needed the money for an important, worthy reason, and never really intended to actually shame Agatha by spreading rumors.

He smiled at her, deciding that he'd have her in his arms by the end of the week, and if she felt as good as he thought she would, he'd start thinking about pursuing her further. "With the proper inducements," he teased, "I might put in a good word for you with our furry friend here."

"I'm no longer interested in— Oh, my heavens!"

"What?"

"What time is it?"

He pulled out his pocket watch, and much to his surprise she actually rushed over and snatched it from his fingers. "Oh, dear!" she exclaimed. "I was meant to meet Lady Danbury in her drawing room twenty minutes ago. I read to her every morning, and—"

"I'm certain she won't mind. After all"—James waved at the scratches on his face—"you have ample proof that you were attending the sick and needy."

"Yes, but you don't understand. I'm not supposed to— That is, I'm supposed to be practicing—" Her eyes filled with horrified embarrassment, and she clamped her hand over her mouth.

He stood, rising to his full height and looming over her with the sole intention of intimidation. "What were you about to say?"

"Nothing," she squeaked. "I swore I wasn't going to do that any longer."

"Swore you weren't going to do what any longer?"

"It's nothing. I swear. I'm sure I'll see you later."

And then, before he could grab hold of her, she scooted out of the room.

James stared at the doorway through which she'd disappeared for a full minute before finally springing to action. Miss Elizabeth Hotchkiss was the oddest thing. Just when she'd finally started acting like herself—and he was convinced that the gentle, kind woman with the wry and razor-sharp wit was the true Elizabeth—she'd started acting skittish and stammering and spouting off all sorts of nonsense.

What was it she'd said she had to do? Read to his aunt? She'd said something about practicing something as well, and then swearing that she wasn't going to do it any longer—what the devil had that meant?

He poked his head out into the hall and looked around. All looked quiet. Elizabeth—when had he started thinking of her as Elizabeth and not the proper Miss Hotchkiss?—was nowhere in sight, probably tucked away in the library selecting reading material for Aunt—

That was it! The book. When he'd seen her in his cottage she had been hunched over his copy of Bacon's Essays.

A flash of memory, and he saw himself trying to pick up her little red book the day he'd met her. She had panicked—practically leaped in front of him to get her hands on the little tome first. She must have thought that he'd somehow managed to get his hands on her book.

But what the hell was in the book?

Chapter 6

He watched her all day. He knew just how to trail a person, slipping around corners and hiding in empty rooms. Elizabeth, who had no reason to think that anyone might be following her, was never the wiser. He listened as she read aloud, watched as she marched back and forth across the hall, fetching unnecessary objects for his aunt.

She treated Agatha with respect and affection. James kept listening for signs of impatience or anger, but whenever his aunt acted in an unreasonable manner, Elizabeth reacted with an amused indulgence that James found enchanting.

Her restraint in the face of his aunt's whimsies was nothing short of awe-inspiring. James would have lost his temper by noon. Miss Hotchkiss was still smiling when she left Danbury House at four in the afternoon.

James watched from the window as she strolled down the drive. Her head was bobbing slightly from side to side, and he had the strangest, warmest feeling that she was singing to herself. Without thinking, he started to whistle.

"What's that tune?"

He looked up. His aunt was standing in the doorway

of her drawing room, leaning heavily on her cane.

"Nothing to which you'd want to know the words," he said with a rakish smile.

"Nonsense. If it's naughty, then I certainly want to know it."

James chuckled. "Aunt Agatha, I didn't tell you the words when you caught me humming that sailors' ditty when I was twelve, and I'm certainly not about to tell you the words to this one."

"Hmmph." She thumped her cane and turned around. "Come and keep me company while I have tea."

James followed her into the drawing room and took a seat across from her. "Actually," he began, "I'm pleased you invited me to join you. I've been meaning to talk to you about your companion."

"Miss Hotchkiss?"

"Yes," he said, trying to sound disinterested. "Petite, blond."

Agatha smiled knowingly, her pale blue eyes crafty as ever. "Ah, so you noticed."

James pretended not to understand. "That her hair is blond? It would be difficult to miss, Aunt."

"I meant that she is cute as a button and you know it."

"Miss Hotchkiss is certainly attractive," he said, "but—"

"But she isn't your sort of woman," she finished for him. "I know." She looked up. "I forget how you take your tea."

James narrowed his eyes. Aunt Agatha never forgot anything. "Milk, no sugar," he said suspiciously. "And why would you think Miss Hotchkiss isn't my sort of woman?"

Agatha shrugged delicately and poured. "She has a rather understated elegance, after all."

James paused. "I believe you may have just insulted me."

"Well, you must admit that other woman was a trifle... ah, shall we say..." She handed him his tea. "Overblown?"

"*What* other woman?"

"You know. The one with the red hair and the..." She lifted her hands to the level of her chest and started making vague, circular motions. "You know."

"Aunt Agatha, she was an opera singer!"

"Well," she sniffed. "You certainly shouldn't have introduced her to me."

"I didn't," James said tightly. "You came barreling down the street at me with all of the discretion of a cannonball."

"If you're going to insult me—"

"I tried to avoid you," he cut in. "I tried to escape, but no, you were having none of it."

She placed a dramatic hand on her breast. "Pardon me for being a concerned relative. We've been after you to marry for many years now, and I merely wondered after your companion."

James took a steadying breath, trying to unclench the muscles in his shoulders. No one had the ability to make him feel like a green boy of sixteen like his aunt. "I believe," he said firmly, "that we were discussing Miss Hotchkiss."

"Ah, yes!" Agatha took a sip of her tea and smiled. "Miss Hotchkiss. A lovely girl. And so levelheaded. Not like these flighty London misses I keep meeting at Almacks. To spend an evening there one would think that intelligence and common sense had been completely bred out of the British population."

James agreed with her completely on that point, but

now really wasn't the time to discuss it. "Miss Hotch-kiss . . . ?" he reminded her.

His aunt looked up, blinked once, and said, "I don't know where I would be without her."

"Perhaps five hundred pounds wealthier?" he suggested.

Agatha's teacup clattered loudly in its saucer. "Surely you don't suspect *Elizabeth*."

"She does have access to your personal effects," he pointed out. "Could you have saved anything that might be incriminating? For all you know, she has been snooping through your things for years."

"No," she said in a quiet voice that somehow screamed authority. "Not Elizabeth. She would never do such a thing."

"Pardon me, Aunt, but how can you be certain?"

She impaled him with a glance. "I believe you are aware that I am a good judge of character, James. As proof, that should suffice."

"Of course you're a good judge of character, Agatha, but—"

She held up a hand. "Miss Hotchkiss is all that is good and kind and true, and I refuse to listen to another disparaging word."

"Very well."

"If you don't believe me, spend a little time with the girl. You will see that I am correct."

James sat back, satisfied. "I'll do just that."

He dreamed about her that night.

She was bent over that damned red book of hers, her long blond hair loose and shimmering like moonlight. She was wearing a virginal white nightgown that covered her from head to toe, but somehow he knew exactly what she looked like underneath, and he wanted her so badly. . . .

Then she was running from him, laughing over her shoulder as her hair streamed behind her, tickling his face whenever he drew close. But every time he reached out to touch her, she eluded his grasp. And every time he thought he was close enough to read the title on her little book, the gold-leaf lettering shifted and blurred, and he found himself stumbling and gasping for air.

Which was exactly how James felt when he sat up straight in his bed, the light of morning just beginning to touch the horizon. He was vaguely dizzy, breathing hard, and he had only one thing on his mind.

Elizabeth Hotchkiss.

When Elizabeth arrived at Danbury House that morning, she was frowning. She had sworn that she wasn't going to do as much as look at the cover of HOW TO MARRY A MARQUIS, but when she'd arrived home the previous day, she'd found the book laying on her bed, its bright red binding practically daring her to open it.

Elizabeth had told herself she was just going to take one peek; all she wanted to do was see if there was something about being witty and making a man laugh, but before she knew it, she was sitting on the edge of her bed, engrossed.

And now she had so many rules and regulations floating around her head she was positively dizzy. She wasn't to flirt with married men, she wasn't supposed to try to give a man advice, but she was supposed to give a suitor the cut direct if he forgot her birthday.

"Thank heavens for small favors," she murmured to herself as she entered Danbury House's great hall. Her birthday was more than nine months away, far enough in the future so as not to disrupt courtships she might possibly—

Oh, for goodness' sake. What was she thinking? She'd told herself she wasn't going to let Mrs. Seeton tell her what to do, and here she was—

"You look rather serious this morning."

Elizabeth looked up with a start. "Mr. Siddons," she said, her voice squeaking a bit on the first syllable of his name. "How lovely to see you."

He bowed. "The feeling, I assure you, is mutual."

She smiled tightly, suddenly feeling very awkward in this man's presence. They had dealt together quite famously the day before, and Elizabeth had even felt that they might call themselves friends, but that was before . . .

She coughed. That was before she'd stayed up half the night thinking about him.

He immediately held out his handkerchief.

Elizabeth felt herself blush and prayed it wasn't too obvious. "It's not necessary," she said quickly. "I was just clearing my throat."

THUMP!

"That would be Lady Danbury," Mr. Siddons murmured, not even bothering to turn toward the sound.

Elizabeth stifled a commiserating grin and turned her head. Sure enough, Lady Danbury was at the other end of the hall, thumping her cane. Malcolm was on the floor next to her, smirking.

"Good morning, Lady Danbury," Elizabeth said, immediately making her way toward the older woman. "How are you feeling?"

"Like I'm seventy-two years old," she retorted.

"Well, that's unfortunate," Elizabeth replied with a perfectly straight face, "since I have it on the best of accounts that you are no more than sixty-seven."

"Impertinent chit. You know very well I'm sixty-six."

Elizabeth hid her smile. "Do you need assistance getting to the drawing room? Have you eaten yet this morning?"

"Had two eggs already and three pieces of toast, and I don't want to sit in the drawing room this morning."

Elizabeth blinked in surprise. She and Lady Danbury spent every morning in the drawing room. And of Lady D's many lectures, her most favorite was on the prophylactic qualities of routine.

"I have decided to sit in the garden," Lady D announced.

"Oh," Elizabeth said. "I see. That's a lovely idea. The air is quite fresh this morning, and the breeze is rather—"

"I am going to take a nap."

That announcement completely robbed Elizabeth of speech. Lady Danbury frequently dozed off, but she never admitted to it, and she certainly never used the word "nap."

"Do you need assistance walking to the garden?" Mr. Siddons asked. "I would be happy to accompany you."

Elizabeth jumped a few inches. She'd completely forgotten his presence.

"Not at all," Lady D said crisply. "I don't move very quickly these days, but I'm not dead. Come along, Malcolm." Then she hobbled away, Malcolm trotting along at her side.

Elizabeth just stared after them, one hand clapped to her cheek in shock.

"It's truly remarkable how well she's trained her cat," James said.

Elizabeth turned to him, a stunned look on her face. "Does she seem ill to you?"

"No, why?"

She waved her arms awkwardly in the direction of

Lady Danbury's retreating form, completely unable to verbalize the extent of her shock.

James regarded her with an amused expression. "Is it so very odd that she might wish to take a nap in the garden? The weather is fine."

"Yes!" she said, concern making her voice overloud. "This is very strange."

"Well, I'm sure she—"

"I tell you, it's strange." Elizabeth shook her head. "I don't like this. I don't like this one bit."

He cocked his head and gave her an assessing glance. "What do you propose we do?"

She squared her shoulders. "I'm going to spy on her."

"You're going to watch her sleep?" he asked dubiously.

"Do you have any better ideas?"

"Better than watching an elderly woman sleep? Well, yes, actually, if hard-pressed I believe I could come up with one or two pastimes that would be—"

"Oh, shush!" she said irritatedly. "I don't need your assistance, anyway."

James smiled. "Had you asked for it?"

"As you so kindly pointed out," she said with a lofty lift of her chin, "it isn't so terribly difficult to watch an old woman sleep. I'm sure you have other, more important duties. Good day."

James's lips parted in surprise as she stalked off. Hang it all, he hadn't meant to *offend* her. "Elizabeth, wait!"

She stopped and turned around, probably more surprised by his use of her given name than she was by his outburst. Hell, he had surprised himself. It was just that she had occupied his thoughts for days, and he'd begun to *think* of her as Elizabeth, and—

"Yes?" she finally said.

"I'll come with you."

She gave him a rather annoyed look. "You do know how to be quiet, don't you? I don't want her catching us spying on her."

James's lips began to twitch, and it was all he could do not to burst out laughing. "You may feel confident that I shall not give us away," he said with full gravity. "I pride myself on being a rather good spy."

She scowled. "That's an odd statement. And— I say, are you all right?"

"Right as rain, why?"

"You look as if you're about to sneeze."

He caught sight of a floral arrangement and mentally latched on to it. "Flowers always make me sneeze."

"You didn't sneeze yesterday in the rose garden."

He cleared his throat and thought fast. "Those aren't roses," he said, pointing at the vase.

"Either way, I can't take you along," she said with a dismissive nod. "There are flowers all along the perimeter of the garden. I can't have you sneezing every two minutes."

"Oh, I won't," he said quickly. "Only cut flowers do this to me."

Her eyes narrowed suspiciously. "I have never heard of such an affliction."

"Neither have I. Never met anyone else who reacts the same way. It must be something in the stem. Something that . . . ah . . . releases into the air when the stem is cut."

She gave him another dubious look, so he embellished the tale by saying, "It gives me a devil of a time when I'm courting a lady. God help me if I attempt to offer her flowers."

"Very well," she said briskly. "Come along. But if you botch this—"

"I won't," he assured her.

"If you botch this," she repeated, louder this time, "I shall never forgive you."

He let his head and shoulders dip slightly forward in a small bow. "Lead the way, Miss Hotchkiss."

She took a few steps, then stopped and turned around, her blue eyes turning just a little bit hesitant. "Earlier, you called me Elizabeth."

"Forgive me," he murmured. "I overstepped."

James watched the play of emotion across her face. She wasn't certain whether to allow him the liberty of her given name. He could see her naturally friendly nature battling with her need to keep him at arm's length. Finally she tightened the corners of her mouth and said, "It is of no great import. We servants are not terribly formal here at Danbury House. If the cook and butler call me Elizabeth, you may as well, too."

James felt his heart fill with a rather absurd satisfaction. "Then you must call me James," he replied.

"James." She tested it out on her tongue, then added, "I should never refer to you as such, of course, if someone asked after you."

"Of course not. But if we are alone, there is no need to stand on occasion."

She nodded. "Very well, Mr.—" She smiled sheepishly. "James. We should be on our way."

He followed her through a maze of hallways; she insisted on taking a circuitous route so as not to rouse Lady Danbury's suspicions. James didn't see how their presence in the ballroom, breakfast room, and hothouse all in one morning could cause anything *but* suspicion, but he kept his thoughts to himself. Elizabeth was clearly taking a quiet satisfaction in her position as leader, and besides, he was rather enjoying the view from the rear.

When they finally emerged in the open air, they were on the east side of the house, close to the front, about as far away from the garden as possible. "We could have exited through the French doors in the music room," Elizabeth explained, "but this way we can make our way behind those hedges and follow them all the way around."

"An excellent idea," he murmured, following her around the back of the hedges. The shrubbery stood twelve feet tall, completely shielding them from view of the house. To his great surprise, as soon as Elizabeth turned that corner around the back of the hedges, she started running. Well, perhaps not running, but she was certainly moving somewhere between a brisk walk and a trot.

His legs were much longer than hers, though, and all he needed to do to keep up was lengthen his stride. "Are we truly in such a rush?" he inquired.

She turned around but did not stop walking. "I'm very worried about Lady Danbury," she said, then resumed her hurried pace.

James viewed this time alone with Elizabeth as an excellent opportunity to study her, but his pragmatic sensibilities still forced him to comment, "Surely life at Danbury House is not so mundane that the oddest occurrence of the summer is a woman of six and sixty taking a nap."

She whirled around again. "I'm sorry if you find my company dull, but if you recall, you were not forced to accompany me."

"Oh, your company is anything but dull," he said, flashing her his smoothest smile. "I simply do not understand the gravity of the situation."

She skidded to a halt, planted her hands on her hips, and leveled at him her sternest stare.

"You'd make a rather good governess with a stance like that," he quipped.

"Lady Danbury never takes naps," she ground out, positively glaring at him after that comment. "She lives and breathes routine. Two eggs and three pieces of toast for breakfast. Every day. Thirty minutes of embroidery. Every day. Correspondence is sorted and answered at three in the afternoon. Every day. And—"

James held up a hand. "You've made your point."

"She never takes naps."

He nodded slowly, wondering what on earth he could possibly add to the conversation at that point.

She let out one final *hmmph*ing sound, then turned back around, charging ahead at full speed. James followed, his legs moving in a long easy stride. The distance between them widened slightly, and he had just resigned himself to having to increase his speed to an easy trot when he noticed a protruding tree root up ahead.

"Mind that—"

She landed on the ground, one arm stretched out like an elegant winged bird, the other thrust forward to break her fall.

"—root," he finished. He rushed forward. "Are you injured?"

She was shaking her head and muttering, "Of course not," but she was wincing while she said it, so he wasn't inclined to believe her.

He crouched beside her and moved toward the hand she'd used to break her fall. "How is this hand?"

"I'm fine," she insisted, pulling her hand back, and picking off the bits of dirt and gravel that had embedded in her skin.

"I'm afraid I must insist upon ascertaining that fact for myself."

"Somehow," she grumbled, "this has to be your fault."

He couldn't hold back a surprised smile. "My fault?"

"I'm not sure how or why, but if there is any fairness in this world, this is your fault."

"If it is my fault," he said with what he thought was the utmost gravity, "then I really must make amends by attending to your injuries."

"I don't have—"

"I rarely take no for an answer."

With a loud sigh, she thrust her hand forward, muttering a rather ungracious, "Here."

James flexed her wrist gently. She made no reaction until he gingerly bent her hand back. "Oh!" she blurted out, clearly irritated with herself for showing her pain.

"It didn't hurt very much," she said quickly. "I'm sure it isn't sprained."

"I'm certain you're right," he agreed. There was no indication of swelling. "But you ought to favor the other one for a day or so. And you might want to go back to the house and get some ice or a cold piece of meat to put on it."

"I haven't time," she said briskly, rising to her feet. "I must check on Lady Danbury."

"If she is indeed, as you worry, taking a nap, then I tend to think your fears for her escape are somewhat exaggerated."

Elizabeth glared at him.

"In other words," he said, as gently as he could, "there is no need for you to risk your own life and limb by rushing."

He could see her weighing her words, but she finally just shook her head and said, "You are free to make your own decisions." Then she turned on her heel and dashed away.

James let out a groan, trying to remember why he was tagging along after her, anyway. Aunt Agatha, he reminded himself. This was all about Aunt Agatha. He needed to find out if Elizabeth was the blackmailer.

His gut was telling him that she was not—anyone who exhibited the sort of concern she did for an overbearing and more often than not vastly annoying old lady surely wouldn't blackmail her.

Yet James had no other suspects, and so he trotted along after her. As she rounded another corner, he lost sight of her, but his long strides soon found her standing utterly straight and perfectly still, her back to the hedge, with her head twisted so that she could look over her shoulder.

"What do you see?" he asked.

"Nothing," she admitted, "but I do seem to have developed the most awful crick in my neck."

James held down the smile he felt bubbling up within him and kept his tone serious as he said, "Would you like me to take a look?"

She turned her head back to the front and then, with an uncomfortable grimace, tilted it to the side and back up. James winced as he heard a loud cracking sound.

She rubbed her neck. "Do you think you can do it without being seen?"

Images of his past missions—in France, in Spain, and right here in England—flew through his mind. James was an expert at not being seen. "Oh," he said offhandedly, "I think I might manage it."

"Very well." She stepped back. "But if you suspect— even for a second—that she can see you, draw back."

James grinned and saluted her. "You're the general."

In that moment, Elizabeth forgot everything.

She forgot that she had no idea how she was going to support her younger siblings.

She forgot that Lady Danbury was acting very strangely and that she feared her employer might be terribly ill.

She even forgot every blasted edict in Mrs. Seeton's little book, and most of all, she forgot that this man made her stomach flip every time he raised his eyebrows.

She forgot everything but the levity of the moment and the rascally smile on James Siddons's face. With a little laugh, she reached forward and swatted him playfully on the shoulder.

"Oh, stop," she said, barely recognizing her own voice.

"Stop what?" he asked, his expression almost ludicrously innocent.

She mimicked his salute.

"You *have* been issuing orders with great facility and frequency," he pointed out. "It is only natural that I might compare you to—"

"Just check on Lady Danbury," she interrupted.

James smiled knowingly and crept around the corner of the hedge.

"Do you see anything?" Elizabeth whispered.

He ducked back. "I see Lady Danbury."

"That's all?"

"I didn't think you were interested in the cat."

"Malcolm?"

"He's on her lap."

"I don't care what the cat is doing."

His chin dipped down as he shot her a vaguely condescending look. "I didn't think you were."

"What is Lady Danbury doing?" Elizabeth ground out.

"Sleeping."

"Sleeping?"

"That *is* what she said she'd be doing, isn't it?"

She scowled at him. "I meant, is she sleeping normally? Is her breathing fitful? Does she seem to be moving about?"

"In her sleep?" he asked doubtfully.

"Don't be a nodcock. People move about in their sleep all the—" Her eyes narrowed. "Why are you smiling?"

James coughed to try to cover up his traitorous lips, and tried to remember the last time a woman had called him a nodcock. The ladies he'd met on his recent jaunt to London had been the simpering sort, complimenting him on his clothing, his face, his form. When one had actually gone so far as to compliment the slope of his forehead, he knew it was time to get away.

He'd never guessed, however, just how amusing it would be to be insulted by Elizabeth Hotchkiss.

"Why are you smiling?" she repeated impatiently.

"Was I smiling?"

"You know you were."

He leaned in far enough to cause her to catch her breath. "Do you want the truth?"

"Er, yes. The truth is almost always preferable."

"Almost?"

"Well, if the other choice is to needlessly hurt another's feelings," she explained, "then— Wait a moment! You're supposed to be answering *my* question."

"Ah, yes, the smile," he said. "It was the nodcock comment, actually."

"You're smiling because I *insulted* you?"

He shrugged and held out his hands in what he hoped was a rather charming gesture. "I'm not often insulted by women."

"Then you've been keeping company with the wrong sort of women," she muttered.

James let out a hoot of laughter.

"Be quiet," she hissed, yanking him away from the hedge. "She'll hear you."

"She's snoring loudly enough to summon a herd of sheep," he replied. "I doubt our little antics are going to rouse her."

Elizabeth shook her head, frowning. "I don't like this. She never takes naps. She always says it's unnatural."

James flashed her a grin, preparing to tease her yet again, but he held back when he saw the deep concern in her dark blue eyes. "Elizabeth," he said softly, "what is it you really fear?"

She let out a long sigh. "She might be ill. When people suddenly grow tired . . ." She swallowed. "It can be a sign of illness."

He held silent for several moments before quietly asking, "Were your parents ill before they passed on?"

Her eyes flew to his, and he realized that she had been completely surprised by his question. "No," she said, blinking. "My mother was killed in a carriage accident, and my father . . ." She paused and looked away, her expression growing heartbreakingly strained until she finally said, "He wasn't ill."

More than anything he wanted to question her further, to find out why she wouldn't discuss her father's death. In a shocking flash, he realized he wanted to know everything about her.

He wanted to know her past, her present, *and* her future. He wanted to know if she spoke French, and did she like chocolates, and had she ever read Molière.

Most of all, he wanted to know the secrets behind every tiny smile that crossed her face.

James almost took a step back at that. Never had he felt this kind of burning need to reach into the farthest corners of a woman's soul.

Elizabeth filled the awkward silence by asking, "Are your parents still living?"

"No," James replied. "My father died quite suddenly, actually. The doctor said it was his heart." He shrugged. "Or the lack thereof."

"Oh, dear," she blurted out.

"It's nothing," he said with a dismissive twist of his hand. "He wasn't a good man. I don't miss him and I don't mourn him."

The corners of her mouth tightened, but he thought he saw a hint of something—perhaps empathy?—in her eyes.

"My mother died when I was quite young," he added abruptly, not entirely certain why he was telling her this. "I barely remember her."

"I'm sorry," Elizabeth said softly. "I do hope it wasn't painful."

James feared that he hadn't been successful in keeping the answer from his eyes, because she just swallowed and said, "I'm sorry," again. He nodded in recognition of her sympathy but didn't say anything.

Elizabeth's eyes caught his for a brief moment, and then she craned her neck to take another look at Lady Danbury. "It would kill me if Lady D were in pain. I just know she would never tell anyone. She can be insufferably proud. She'd never recognize affection and concern for what they are. All she'd see is pity."

James watched her watch his aunt and was suddenly struck by how petite Elizabeth was. The fields of Danbury Park stretched out behind her in an endless patchwork of green, and she seemed terribly small and alone against the vast expanse of land. The summer breeze lifted silky strands of blond hair from her bun, and without thinking James reached out and caught one, tucking it behind her ear.

Her breath caught, and she immediately raised a hand. Her fingers brushed against his knuckles, and he fought the most insane desire to clasp her hand in his. It would only take the tiniest movement of his fingers, and it was so exquisitely tempting, but he pulled his hand back and murmured, "Forgive me. The wind blew your hair."

Her eyes widened and her lips parted as if to say something, but in the end, she just pulled away. "Lady Danbury has been very good to me," she said, her voice catching. "There is no way I could ever repay her many kindnesses."

James had never before heard his gruff, outspoken aunt referred to as kind. The *ton* respected her, feared her, even laughed at her cutting jokes, but never before had he seen the love he felt for the woman who had quite possibly saved his soul reflected in another's eyes.

And then his body became completely foreign to him and he felt himself moving forward. He wasn't controlling the motion; it was almost as if some higher power had entered his form, causing his hand to reach out and cup the back of Elizabeth's head, his fingers sliding into the silk of her hair as he pulled her to him, closer, closer, and then . . .

And then his lips were on hers, and whatever mesmerizing force had caused him to kiss her fled, and all that was left was him—him and an overpowering need to possess her in every way a man could possess a woman.

As one hand sank ever deeper into her hair, the other snaked around her, settling into the delicate curve at the small of her back. He could feel her beginning to respond to him. She was a total innocent, but she was softening, and her heart was beginning to beat faster, and then *his* heart started to pound.

"My God, Elizabeth," he gasped, moving his mouth to her cheek, and then to her ear. "I want . . . I want . . ."

His voice must have woken up something within her, because she stiffened, and he heard her whisper, "Oh, no."

James wanted to hold on to her. He wanted to slide her to the ground and kiss her until she had lost all reason, but he must have been more honorable than he'd ever imagined, because he let her go the instant she began to pull away.

She stood across from him for several seconds, looking more shocked than anything else. One tiny hand was clasped over her mouth, and her eyes were wide and unblinking. "I never thought . . ." she murmured into her hand. "I can't believe . . ."

"You can't believe what?"

She shook her head. "Oh, this is awful."

That was a bit more than his ego could bear. "Well, now, I wouldn't say—"

But she had already run off.

Chapter 7

Elizabeth arrived at Danbury House the following morning with one overriding goal in mind: to stay as far away from James Siddons as humanly possible.

He had kissed her. He had actually kissed her. Worse, she had let him. And even worse, she had run off like a coward—all the way home. Only once in all her years as Lady Danbury's companion had she ever cried off work early, and that was when she'd had a lung fever. Even then, she had tried to remain at her post, leaving only when Lady Danbury had threatened to care for her herself.

But this time all it took was one kiss from one handsome man, and she was sniveling like a ninny. Elizabeth had been so mortified by her actions that she'd sent Lucas back to Danbury House with a note for Lady D explaining that she was feeling quite ill. It wasn't entirely a lie, Elizabeth reasoned. She'd been hot and flushed, and her stomach had felt altogether queer.

Besides, the alternative to lying was death by mortification. All in all, it took Elizabeth very little time to decide that her little fib was entirely justified.

She'd spent the evening holed up in her room, obsessively poring over HOW TO MARRY A MARQUIS. There weren't too many references to kissing. Mrs. Seeton obviously thought that anyone who'd been smart enough to purchase her book was smart enough to know that one was not supposed to kiss a gentleman to whom one did not have a deep and potentially lasting connection.

And one certainly shouldn't enjoy it.

Elizabeth groaned, remembering all this. So far the day was progressing like any other, except for the fact that she had looked over her shoulder so many times that Lady Danbury had asked if she had developed a nervous tic.

Embarrassment forced her to stop twisting her neck, but she still jumped a little every time she heard footsteps.

She tried to tell herself that it shouldn't be terribly difficult to avoid him. Mr. Siddons must have a thousand duties as estate manager, nine hundred of which required his presence outside. So if Elizabeth just barricaded herself in Danbury House, she ought to be safe. And if he decided to pursue the odd task that took him indoors . . . well, then, she was certain she could find some reason to leave the house and enjoy the warm English sunshine.

And then it started to rain.

Elizabeth's forehead fell against the glass of the sitting room window with a dull thud. "This can't be happening," she muttered. "This simply cannot be happening."

"What can't be happening?" Lady Danbury asked briskly. "The rain? Don't be a nodcock. This is England. Hence, it must be raining."

"But not today," Elizabeth sighed. "It was so sunny this morning when I walked over."

"Since when has that ever made a difference?"

"Since . . ." She shut her eyes and swallowed a groan. Anyone who'd lived her whole life in Surrey ought to know that one could not depend on a sunny morning. "Oh, never mind. It's not important."

"Are you worried about getting home? Don't be. I'll have someone drive you home. You shouldn't expose yourself to the elements so soon after an illness." Lady Danbury's eyes narrowed. "Although I must say you look remarkably recovered."

"I don't feel remarkably recovered," Elizabeth said, quite honestly.

"What did you say was wrong with you?"

"My stomach," she mumbled. "I think it was something I ate."

"Hmmph. No one else fell sick. Can't imagine what you ate. But if you spent the afternoon casting up your accounts—"

"Lady Danbury!" Elizabeth exclaimed. She certainly hadn't spent the previous afternoon casting up her accounts, but still, there was no need to discuss such bodily functions.

Lady D shook her head. "Too modest by half. When did women get to be so prissy?"

"When we decided that vomit wasn't a pleasant topic of conversation," Elizabeth retorted.

"That's the spirit!" Lady Danbury chortled, clapping her hands together. "I declare, Elizabeth Hotchkiss, you sound more and more like myself every day."

"God help me," Elizabeth groaned.

"Even better. Exactly what I would have said." Lady Danbury sat back, tapped her index finger to her forehead, and frowned. "Now, then, what was I talking about? Oh, yes, we wanted to make sure that you wouldn't have to walk home in the rain. Don't fear, we'll find someone to drive you. My new estate manager, if need be. Lord knows he won't be able to get anything done in this weather."

Elizabeth gulped. "I'm certain the rain will let up soon."

Lightning forked through the sky—just to spite her, she was sure—followed by a clap of thunder so loud Elizabeth jumped a foot. "Ow!" she yelped.

"What did you do to yourself now?"

"Just my knee," she replied with a patently false smile. "Doesn't hurt a bit."

Lady Danbury snorted her disbelief.

"No, really," Elizabeth insisted. "Funny how I never noticed that end table there, though."

"Oh, that. Moved it there yesterday. Mr. Siddons suggested it."

"That figures," Elizabeth muttered.

"Beg pardon?"

"Nothing," she said, a little too loudly.

"Hmmph," was Lady Danbury's reply. "I'm thirsty."

Elizabeth immediately warmed to the prospect of having something to do besides stare out the window and worry that Mr. Siddons was going to make an appearance. "Would you care for tea, Lady Danbury? Or perhaps I can have Cook prepare some lemonade."

"Too early in the morning for lemonade," Lady D barked. "Too early for tea, as a matter of fact, but I'll have some anyway."

"Didn't you take tea with breakfast?" Elizabeth pointed out.

"That was *breakfast* tea. Different entirely."

"Ah." Someday, Elizabeth thought, she would receive a sainthood for this.

"Make sure Cook puts biscuits on the tray. And don't forget to ask her to fix something for Malcolm." Lady D craned her head this way and that. "Where *is* that cat?"

"Plotting his latest scheme to torture me, no doubt," Elizabeth muttered.

"Eh? What was that?"

Elizabeth turned toward the door, still looking over her

shoulder at Lady Danbury. "Nothing at all, Lady Danbury. I'll just—"

Anything else she might have said was lost as her shoulder bumped into something large, warm, and decidedly human.

Elizabeth groaned. Mr. Siddons. It had to be. She had never been a particularly lucky woman.

"Steady, there," she heard him say, a split second before his hands gently grasped her upper arms.

"Mr. Siddons!" Lady Danbury trilled. "How lovely to see you so early in the morning."

"Indeed," Elizabeth muttered.

"Won't you join us for tea?" Lady D continued. "Elizabeth was just off to fetch a tray."

Elizabeth was still refusing—on principle, although she wasn't entirely certain *which* principle—to look at his face, but she felt his wolfish smile nonetheless.

"I'd be delighted," he said.

"Excellent," Lady Danbury replied. "Elizabeth, off with you, then. We'll need tea for three."

"I can't go anywhere," Elizabeth ground out, "while Mr. Siddons is holding on to my arms."

"Was I doing that?" he said guilelessly, releasing his grip. "Didn't even realize it."

If she'd had any sort of fortune, Elizabeth decided grimly, she'd have bet it then and there that he was lying.

"I did have a few questions for our dear Miss Hotchkiss," Mr. Siddons said.

Elizabeth's lips parted in surprise.

"They can wait until she returns, I'm sure," he murmured.

Elizabeth's head darted back and forth between Mr. Siddons and Lady Danbury as she tried to comprehend the oddly quiet tension in the room. "If you're sure," she said. "I'd be happy to—"

"He thinks you're blackmailing me," Lady Danbury said bluntly.

"He thinks I'm doing *what*?" Elizabeth nearly screeched.

"Agatha!" Mr. Siddons burst out, sounding very much as if he wanted to curse the old lady to perdition. "Haven't you ever heard of the word 'subtlety'?"

"Hmmph. Has never worked for me."

"I'll say," he muttered.

"Did you just call her Agatha?" Elizabeth asked. She looked over at Lady Danbury in surprise. She'd been tending to the countess for five years and had never presumed to use her given name.

"I knew Mr. Siddons's mother," Lady Danbury said, as if that explained everything.

Elizabeth planted her hands on her hips and glowered up at the handsome estate manager. "How dare you think I would blackmail this sweet old lady!"

"Sweet?" Mr. Siddons echoed.

"Old?" Lady Danbury hollered.

"I would never stoop so low," Elizabeth said with a sniff. "Never. And shame on you for thinking so."

"That's what I told him," Lady D said with a shrug. "You do need the money, of course, but you're not the sort to—"

Mr. Siddons's hand closed around her arm again. "You need money?" he demanded.

Elizabeth rolled her eyes. "Doesn't everyone?"

"I have plenty," Lady D said.

Her two employees whipped their heads around in unison and glared at her.

"Well, it's the truth," she said, *hmmph*ing loudly.

"Why do you need money?" Mr. Siddons asked softly.

"That is none of your concern!"

But Lady Danbury obviously thought it was, because she said, "It all started when—"

"Lady Danbury, *please*!" Elizabeth shot her a pleading look. It was hard enough to be so pressed for funds. To have the countess shame her in front of a stranger . . .

Lady Danbury seemed to realize—for once—that she had overstepped herself and closed her mouth.

Elizabeth closed her eyes and let out a breath. "Thank you," she whispered.

"I'm thirsty," Lady D stated.

"Right," Elizabeth said, mostly to herself, although her words were loud enough for everyone to hear. "The tea."

"What are you waiting for?" Lady Danbury demanded, thumping her cane.

"A sainthood," Elizabeth muttered under her breath.

Mr. Siddons's eyes widened. Oh, *blast*, he'd heard her. She'd grown so used to being alone with Lady Danbury that she'd forgotten to watch what she whispered to herself.

But Mr. Siddons, to her great surprise, abruptly let go of her arm and started to cough. And then, just when any normal person would have ceased, he doubled over, collapsed against the wall, and started coughing even more violently.

Elizabeth's antagonism gave way to concern as she leaned down. "Are you all right?"

He nodded hurriedly, without removing his hand from his mouth.

"Has he something stuck in his throat?" Lady Danbury yelled.

"I can't imagine what," Elizabeth replied. "He wasn't eating anything."

"Whack his back," Lady D said. "Whack it hard."

Mr. Siddons shook his head and dashed out of the room.

"Perhaps you should follow," Lady Danbury suggested. "And don't forget to whack him."

Elizabeth blinked twice, shrugged her shoulders, and quit the room, thinking that whacking him on the back might prove to be a rather satisfying endeavor. "Mr. Siddons?" She looked left and right but didn't see him. "Mr. Siddons?"

And then she heard it. Great big roars of laughter coming from around the corner. She shut the door with alacrity.

By the time she rounded the corner, Mr. Siddons was sitting on a cushioned bench, gasping for air.

"Mr. Siddons? James?"

He looked up, and suddenly he didn't seem quite as dangerous as he had the day before. "A sainthood," he squeaked. "Good God, yes, we all deserve one."

"Well, you've only been here a few days," Elizabeth pointed out. "You've a couple more years in her company, I think, before you could even be considered for martyr."

Mr. Siddons tried to hold back his laughter, but it burst out of him in a great big rush of air. When he regained control of himself he said, "It's the quiet ones like you who are the most dangerous and cunning."

"Me?" Elizabeth asked in disbelief. "I'm not the least bit quiet."

"Perhaps not, but you do choose your words carefully."

"Well, yes," she said with an unconscious tilt of her head. "I'm clumsy enough in body without tossing my mouth into the mixture."

James decided then and there that she couldn't possibly be the blackmailer. Oh, he knew that he hadn't gathered enough facts to make this pronouncement, but his instincts had been telling him for days that she had to be innocent. He just hadn't been smart enough to listen.

He regarded her for a moment, then asked, "Shall I help you fetch the tea?"

"Surely you have more important things to do than accompanying a lady's companion to the kitchen."

"I have often noticed that ladies' companions are the ones most in need of companionship."

Her lips curved into a reluctant smile. "Now, now, Lady Danbury is a good sort."

James watched her mouth with unabashed interest. He wanted to kiss her, he realized. This wasn't surprising in and of itself—he'd thought of very little in the past day *besides* kissing her. What was odd was that he wanted to do it right then and there in the hall. He was usually much more discreet.

"Mr. Siddons?"

He blinked, a touch embarrassed to have been caught staring at her.

"Who is blackmailing Lady Danbury?"

"If I knew that, I'd hardly have been accusing you."

"Hmmph. Don't think I've forgiven you for that."

"Good God," he said, startled. "You're beginning to sound like her."

Elizabeth's eyes widened in horror. "Lady Danbury?"

He nodded and *hmmph*ed in a perfect imitation of Elizabeth imitating Lady D.

She gasped. "I didn't do that, did I?"

He nodded again, his eyes dancing with amusement.

She groaned. "I'm going to get the tea."

"Then you've forgiven me for suspecting you of blackmail?"

"I suppose I must. It's not as if you knew enough of my character to clear me immediately."

"Very broad-minded of you."

She shot him a look that told him she didn't much appreciate his flip comment. "But what I don't understand is, what on earth could Lady Danbury have done to warrant blackmail?"

"That is not for me to say," he said quietly.

Elizabeth nodded. "I'll get the tea."

"I'll come with you."

She put up a hand. "No. You won't."

He took her fingers and kissed the very tips. "Yes. I will."

Elizabeth stared down at her hand. Dear Lord, the man had kissed her again! Right there in the hall. Too stunned to pull her hand back, she looked right and left, terrified that a servant might stumble upon them.

"You had never been kissed before yesterday," he murmured.

"Of course not!"

"Not even on the hand." He let her fingers drop, then took her other hand and kissed her knuckles.

"Mr. Siddons!" she gasped. "Are you mad?"

He smiled. "I'm glad you haven't been kissed before."

"You are mad. Utterly mad. And," she added defensively, "of course I've been kissed on the hand."

"Your father doesn't count."

More than anything, Elizabeth wanted to find a hole in the ground and jump in it. She felt her cheeks burn, and she knew that she didn't have to say a word for him to know that he was right. There weren't very many unmarried men in her little village, and certainly none of them was urbane enough to kiss her on the hand.

"Who are you?" she whispered.

He looked at her oddly, his brown eyes narrowing. "James Siddons. You know that."

She shook her head. "You've never been an estate manager before. I'd bet my life on it."

"Would you like to see my references?"

"You carry yourself wrong. A servant would—"

"Ah, but I am not precisely a servant," he interrupted. "As you are not. I understand you're of the local gentry."

She nodded.

"Mine is an old family, as well," he continued. "Our pride, unfortunately, was not lost with our money."

"Unfortunately?"

One corner of his mouth turned up. "It makes for awkward moments."

"Like this one," Elizabeth said firmly. "You must return to the drawing room this instant. Lady Danbury is in there, wondering, I'm sure, why the devil I shut the door, and what we are doing, and while I don't profess to know *your* mind, *I* do not wish to make explanations."

James just stared at her, wondering why he suddenly felt as if he'd been dressed down by his governess. He grinned. "You're good at that."

Elizabeth had managed to take three steps toward the kitchen. She let out a frustrated breath and turned around. "At what?"

"At speaking to a grown man as if he were a child. I feel quite put in my place."

"You do not," she retorted, waving her hand toward him. "Just look at you. You don't look the least bit contrite. You're grinning like an idiot."

He cocked his head. "I know."

Elizabeth threw up her hands. "I have to go."

"You make me smile."

His words, soft and intense, stopped her in her tracks. "Turn around, Elizabeth."

There was some sort of connection between the two of

them. Elizabeth knew nothing of love, but she knew she could fall in love with this man. She felt it deep in her heart, and it terrified her. He wasn't a man she could marry. He had no money; he'd said so himself. How was she to send Lucas to Eton with an estate manager as a husband? How was she to feed and clothe Susan and Jane? Susan was only fourteen now, but soon she'd want to make her debut. London was out of the question, but even a small local debut would cost money.

And that was the one thing that neither Elizabeth nor the man standing in front of her—possibly the only man who could ever capture her heart—had.

Dear God, she'd thought that life had treated her unfairly before, but this . . . this was nothing short of agony.

"Turn around, Elizabeth."

She kept walking. It was the hardest thing she'd ever done.

Late that night, Susan, Jane, and Lucas Hotchkiss huddled together on the cold floor of the upstairs hall, directly outside their older sister's bedchamber.

"I think she's crying," Lucas whispered.

"Of course she's crying," Jane hissed. "Any fool could tell she's crying."

"The question is," Susan cut in, "*why* is she crying?"

No one had an answer to that.

They flinched a moment later when they heard a slightly louder than usual sob, then swallowed uncomfortably when it was followed by a loud sniffle.

"She has been very worried about money of late," Lucas said hesitantly.

"She's always worried about money," Jane retorted.

"It's only natural," Susan added. "People who don't have money always worry about it."

The two younger Hotchkisses nodded in agreement.

"Do we really have nothing?" Jane whispered.

"I'm afraid so," Susan said.

Lucas's eyes began to glisten. "I'm not going to get to go to Eton, am I?"

"No, no," Susan said quickly, "of course you will. We just have to economize."

"How can we economize when we have nothing?" he asked.

Susan didn't reply.

Jane nudged her in the ribs. "I think one of us should comfort her."

Before Susan could do so much as nod, they heard a loud crash, followed by the unbelievably astonishing sound of their proper older sister yelling, "Goddamn you to hell!"

Jane gasped.

Susan's mouth fell open.

"I can't believe she said that," Lucas breathed reverently. "I wonder who she was damning."

"It's not something to be proud of," Jane snapped, poking in the soft spot above his collarbone.

"Ow!"

"And don't say 'damn,' " Susan added.

"It is so something to be proud of. Even I have never said that."

Jane rolled her eyes. "Men."

"Stop bickering," Susan said distractedly. "I think I had better go in and see her."

"Yes," Jane replied, "as I was just saying—"

"Why does everything have to be your idea?" Lucas said sullenly. "You always—"

"This *was* my idea!"

"Quiet!" Susan practically barked. "Downstairs, the both of you. And if I find out that either one of you has disobeyed me, I shall overstarch your undergarments for a month.''

The two small children nodded and ran down the stairs. Susan took a deep breath and knocked on Elizabeth's door.

No answer.

Susan knocked again. "I know you're in there."

Footsteps, followed by a vicious yanking open of the door. "Of course you know I'm in here," Elizabeth snapped. "They can probably hear me all the way to Danbury House."

Susan opened her mouth, closed it, and then reopened it again to say, "I was going to ask if something is wrong, but then I realized how ridiculous that sounded, so instead perhaps I might ask *what* is wrong?"

Elizabeth's reply was not verbal. Instead, she turned her head and glared at a red object laying in the corner.

"Dear God!" Susan exclaimed, scurrying across the room. "Was this the thud I heard?"

Elizabeth glanced disdainfully at HOW TO MARRY A MARQUIS, carefully held in her sister's hands.

"This book belongs to Lady Danbury!" Susan said. "You yourself made me promise not to even crack the spine. And you threw it across the room?"

"My priorities have changed. I don't care if that book burns. I don't care if Mrs. Seeton burns."

Susan's mouth formed a perfect circle. "Were you damning Mrs. Seeton to hell?"

"Perhaps I was," Elizabeth said in an insolent voice.

Susan clapped a hand to her face in shock. "Elizabeth, you don't sound like yourself."

"I don't feel like myself."

"You must tell me what has happened to make you so upset."

Elizabeth let out a short, shallow breath. "That book has ruined my life."

Susan blinked. "You have never been given to melodrama."

"Perhaps I've changed."

"Perhaps," Susan said, clearly growing a little irritated with her sister's evasions, "you would care to expound upon how this book has ruined your life."

Elizabeth looked away so Susan couldn't see how badly her face was trembling. "I wouldn't have flirted with him. I would never have approached him if I hadn't gotten it into my head to—"

"Dear God!" Susan cut in. "What did he do to you? Did he dishonor you in any way?"

"No!" Elizabeth cried out. "He would never."

"Then what happened?"

"Oh, Susan," Elizabeth replied, silent tears streaming down her face. "I could love him. I could truly love him."

"Then what's wrong?" Susan asked in a gentle whisper.

"Susan, he hasn't two coins to rub together! He's an estate manager!"

"But couldn't you be happy with a simple life?"

"Of course I could," Elizabeth snapped. "But what about Lucas's education? And your debut? And Jane's watercolors? Haven't you been listening to a word I've said this last week? Did you think I was looking for a husband for the fun of it? We need money, Susan. Money."

Susan couldn't even bring herself to look into her sister's eyes. "I'm sorry if you feel you have to sacrifice yourself."

"The funny part is, I didn't think it was such a sacrifice. Lots of women marry men they don't love. But now . . ." She paused and wiped her eyes. "Now it's just hard. That's all it is. Hard."

Susan swallowed and softly said, "Maybe you should return the book."

Elizabeth nodded. "I'll do it tomorrow."

"We can—we can decide how to proceed later. I'm sure you can find a husband without having to practice on—"

Elizabeth held up a hand. "Let's not talk about it now."

Susan nodded, then smiled weakly as she held up the book. "I'll just go dust this off. You can return it tomorrow."

Elizabeth didn't move as she watched her sister leave the room. Then she crawled onto her bed and started to cry. But this time she held the pillow over her head, muffling the sounds of her sobs.

The last thing she wanted was more sympathy.

Chapter 8

Elizabeth arrived at Danbury House earlier than usual the following morning, hoping to sneak into the library and replace the book before Lady Danbury finished breaking her fast. All she wanted was to get the dratted thing out of her sight and out of her possession forever.

She had played out the scene in her mind a hundred times. She would slide How to Marry a Marquis back onto the bookshelf and shut the library door firmly behind her. And that, she prayed, would be that.

"You have caused me nothing but grief," she whispered into her satchel.

Dear Lord, she was turning into the veriest idiot. She was talking to a book. A book! It didn't have any powers, it wasn't going to change her life, and it certainly wasn't going to answer her when she was stupid enough to send words in its direction.

It was just a book. An inanimate object. The only power it held was what she chose to give it. It could only be important in her life if she made it such.

Of course, that didn't explain why she half expected it to glow in the dark every time she peered into her satchel.

She tiptoed down the hall, for once in her life blessedly thankful for Lady Danbury's firm adherence to routine.

The countess would be about one-quarter of the way through breakfast right now, which meant that Elizabeth would have at least twenty more minutes before her employer appeared in the drawing room.

Two minutes to slip the book back into the library, and eighteen to calm herself down.

Elizabeth had her hand in her satchel and was clutching the book as she rounded the corner. The library door was ajar. Perfect. The less noise she made, the less likely it would be that anyone would stumble upon her. Not that there was much activity in this part of the house before Lady D finished her breakfast, but still, one couldn't be too careful.

She slid sideways through the door's opening, her gaze firmly fixed on the shelf where she'd found the book earlier that week. All she had to do was cross the room, put the book back, and leave. No detours, no unnecessary stops.

She pulled the book out, her eyes focused on the shelf. Two more steps, and—

"Good morning, Elizabeth."

She screamed.

James drew back slightly in surprise. "My deepest apologies for startling you."

"What are you doing here?" she demanded.

"You're shaking," he said in a concerned voice. "I really did startle you, didn't I?"

"No," she said, her voice overly loud. "It's just that I wasn't expecting anyone. The library is usually vacant this time of the morning."

He shrugged. "I like to read. Lady Danbury told me I may make free use of her collection. I say, what's that in your hand?"

Elizabeth followed his eyes to her hand and gasped. Good God, she was still holding the book. "It's nothing," she blurted out, trying to shove it back into her satchel. "Nothing." But her nerves made her fingers clumsy, and the book tumbled to the ground.

"It's that book you were trying to hide from me the other day," he said with a triumphant gleam in his eye.

"It's not!" she practically yelled, dropping to the floor to cover it. "It's just a silly novel I borrowed, and—"

"Is it any good?" he drawled. "I might like to read it."

"You'd hate it," she said quickly. "It's a romance."

"I like romance."

"Of course everybody likes romance," she blathered, "but do you really want to read about it? I think not. It's very melodramatic. You'd be bored silly."

"You think?" he murmured, one corner of his mouth rising into a rather knowing sort of half-smile.

She nodded frantically. "When all is said and done, it's really a book for women."

"That's rather discriminatory, don't you think?"

"I'm just trying to save you some time."

He crouched down. "That's very thoughtful of you."

She shifted so that she was sitting squarely on the book. "It's good to be thoughtful."

He moved closer, his eyes glowing. "That's one of the things I like best about you, Elizabeth."

"What?" she squeaked.

"Your thoughtfulness."

"You couldn't possibly," she returned, practically jumping on his words. "Just yesterday you thought I was blackmailing Lady Danbury. How thoughtful is *that*?"

"You're trying to change the subject," he scolded, "but just for the record, I had already decided you weren't the blackmailer. It is true that you were the initial suspect—after all, you do have rather free access into Lady Danbury's belongings—but one doesn't require very much time in your company to make an accurate assessment of your character.''

''How thoughtful of you,'' she said acerbically.

''Get off the book, Elizabeth,'' he ordered.

''No.''

''Get off the book.''

She groaned audibly. Her life couldn't have possibly come to this. ''Mortification'' couldn't even begin to describe the state of her mind. And ''beet'' couldn't begin to describe the state of her cheeks.

''You're only making it worse.'' He reached down, and somehow managed to grab the corner of the book.

She immediately hunkered down. ''I'm not moving.''

He leered at her and wiggled his fingers. ''I'm not moving my hand.''

''You lecher,'' she breathed. ''Fondling a lady's backside.''

He leaned in. ''If I were fondling your backside, you'd be wearing a decidedly different facial expression.''

She smacked him on the shoulder. It was probably no less than he deserved, James thought, but he was damned if he was leaving the library without getting a good look at her little red book.

''You can insult me all you want,'' she said in a lofty voice, ''but it will have no effect. I am not moving.''

''Elizabeth, you resemble nothing so much as a hen trying to hatch a book.''

''If you were any kind of a gentleman—''

''Ah, but there's a time and place for gentlemanly behavior, and this isn't one of them.'' He jammed his fingers farther under her, getting a few more inches of the book under his hand. One more shove, and he ought to be able to hook his thumb around the edge of the book, and then it would be his!

Her jaw clenched. "Get your hand out from under me," she ground out.

He did the opposite, lurching his fingers forward yet another half inch. "A remarkable feat, really, saying all that between your teeth."

"James!"

He held up his free hand. "Just one moment, if you will. I'm concentrating."

As she glared at him, he hooked his thumb around the top edge of the book. His mouth spread into a lethal smile. "You're sunk now, Miss Hotchkiss."

"What do you— Aaaaaaaaccccccck!"

With one big heave, he yanked the book out from under her, sending her sprawling.

"Nooooooooooo!" she yelled, sounding as if the very fate of the world rested in her ability to retrieve her book.

James raced across the room, triumphantly holding the book high in the air. Elizabeth was a full foot shorter than he was; she'd never be able to reach.

"James, *please*," she begged.

He shook his head, wishing he didn't feel like quite so much of a cad; the expression on her face was rather heartwrenching. But he'd been wondering about her book for days, and he'd come this far, so he twisted his head up, turned over the book, and read the title.

HOW TO MARRY A MARQUIS

He blinked. Surely she didn't know . . . no, she couldn't possibly know his true identity.

"Why did you do that?" she said in a choked voice. "Why did you have to do that?"

He tilted his head toward her. "What's this?"

"What does it look like?" she snapped.

"I . . . ah . . . I don't know." Still holding the book

aloft, he opened it up and flipped through a few pages. "It looks rather like a guidebook, actually."

"Then that's what it is," she shot back. "Now please give it back. I have to return this to Lady Danbury."

"This belongs to my—to Lady Danbury?" he asked in disbelief.

"Yes! Now give it back."

James shook his head, looking back up at the book, then returning his gaze to Elizabeth. "But why would she need a book like this?"

"I don't know," she nearly wailed. "It's old. Maybe she purchased it before she married Lord Danbury. But please, let me just put it back on the shelf before she comes back from breakfast."

"In a moment." He turned another page and read:

> YOU MUST NEVER SEPARATE YOUR LIPS WHEN YOU SMILE. A CLOSE-LIPPED SMILE IS INFINITELY MORE MYSTERIOUS, AND YOUR JOB IS TO FASCINATE YOUR MARQUIS.

"Is that why they always do that?" he murmured. He glanced over at Elizabeth. "Edict Number Twelve explains a lot."

"The book," she growled, holding out her hand.

"Just in case you're interested," he said with an expansive wave of his hand, "I myself prefer a woman who knows how to smile. This"—he stretched his lips out in a tight mockery of a smile—"is really quite unbecoming."

"I don't think Mrs. Seeton meant for you to do *this*." She returned his strained expression with one of her own. "I think you're supposed to do *this*." This time she curved her lips into a delicate half-smile, one that sent a shiver down his spine right to his—

"Yes," he said with a cough, "that's considerably more effective."

"I cannot believe I'm discussing this with you," she said, more to herself than to him. "Can we please just put the book back?"

"We've at least ten more minutes before Lady Danbury finishes her breakfast. Don't worry." He returned his attention to the little red book. "I'm finding this fascinating."

"I'm not," she ground out.

James turned his attention back to Elizabeth. She was standing as stiff as a board, her hands fisted at her side. Her cheeks were stained with two angry splotches of red. "You're angry with me," he said.

"Your perceptiveness is astounding."

"But I was only poking fun at you. You must know it was never meant to be insulting."

Her eyes grew a little harder. "Do you see me laughing?"

"Elizabeth," he said placatingly, "it was all in good fun. Surely you don't take this book seriously."

She didn't answer. The silence in the room grew thick, and James saw a flash of pain in those sapphire eyes of hers. The corners of her lips quivered, then tightened, and then she looked away. "Oh, God," he breathed, little knives of guilt stabbing at his midsection. "I'm so sorry."

She lifted her chin, but he could see her face working with suppressed emotion as she said, "Can we stop this now?"

Silently, he lowered his arms and handed her the book. She didn't thank him, just took it back and held it close to her chest.

"I didn't realize you were looking for a husband," he said softly.

"You don't know anything about me."

He gestured awkwardly at the book. "Has it been helpful?"

"No."

The flatness in her voice was a punch to his gut. Somehow, James suddenly realized, he was going to have to make this better. He had to take away the dead expression in her eyes, return the lilt to her voice. He had to hear her laugh, to hear himself laugh at some little joke of hers.

He didn't know why. He just knew it was something he had to do.

He cleared his throat and asked, "Is there any way I might be of assistance?"

"I beg your pardon?"

"Can I help you in any way?"

She looked at him suspiciously. "What do you mean?"

James's lips parted slightly as he tried to figure out how the devil to reply. "Just that . . . well, I happen to know a thing or two about finding a husband—or rather, in my case, a wife."

Her eyes bugged out. "You're married?!"

"No!" he said, surprising even himself with the force of his reply.

She relaxed visibly. "Oh, thank goodness. Because you . . . you . . ."

"Because I kissed you?"

"Yes," she muttered, her cheeks turning pink around the already present red splotches.

He reached out and tucked his fingers under her chin, forcing her to look up at him. "If I were married, Elizabeth, you can be certain I would not dally with another female."

"How . . . thoughtful of you."

"All I meant to say was that if you are truly looking for a husband, I would be happy to assist you in any way possible."

Elizabeth just stared at him, unable to believe the irony of the moment. Here she was, standing before the man she'd spent the entire previous night crying over, and he was offering to help her find another man to marry? "This can't be happening," she said to herself. "This just can't be happening."

"I don't see why not," he said smoothly. "I consider you a friend, and—"

"How on earth could you possibly help me?" she asked, wondering what devil was possessing her to even pursue the subject. "You're new to the district. You couldn't possibly introduce me to any suitable candidates. And," she added, gesturing toward him, "you clearly are not well-versed in the art of fashion."

He lurched backward. "I beg your pardon!"

"They're perfectly nice clothes, but they are several years past their prime."

"So are yours," he said with a smirk.

"I know," she shot back. "That's why I need help from someone who knows what he's talking about."

James tilted his head tensely to the side and then brought it back up, trying to suppress a retort. The impertinent chit ought to see his closet in London. Clothing galore, all in the first stare of fashion, and none of those ridiculous dandified stripes and frills. "Why are you so keen to marry?" he asked, deciding that it was more important to assess her situation than it was to defend his attire.

"That's none of your concern."

"I disagree. If I'm to aid you, it must be my concern."

"I haven't agreed to *allow* you to help me," she retorted.

His eyes fell on the book. "Does it have to be a marquis?"

She blinked, uncomprehending. "I beg your pardon?"

"Does it have to be a marquis?" he repeated. "Must you have a title? Is it so very important?"

She took a step back at his strident tone. "No."

James felt his muscles relax. He hadn't even realized how tense he'd been, or just how important her negative answer was to him. For his entire life, he'd been made painfully aware that it was his position that mattered, not his character. His father had never called him his son, only his heir. The previous marquis hadn't known how to relate to a child; he'd treated James as a miniature adult. Any childhood transgression was viewed as an insult to the title, and James had quickly learned to keep his normally exuberant personality cloaked under a mask of serious obedience—at least when he was in his father's compay.

At school he'd been popular—boys of his charm and athletic ability usually were—but it had taken some time to weed out the true friends from those who saw him as a means to a better life and position.

And then in London—good God! He could have had two heads and the trunk of an elephant for all those ladies cared. "The marquis, the marquis," he'd heard whispered. "He's a marquis. He has a fortune. He lives in a castle." His looks and youth he'd heard referred to as a boon, but never once had he heard anyone make mention of his wit, his sense of humor, or even his smile.

When it came right down to it, Elizabeth Hotchkiss was the first woman he'd met in a long while who seemed to like him for himself.

He looked back at her. "No marquis?" he murmured. "Why, then, the book?"

Her fisted hands shook at her sides, and she looked as

if she might stamp her foot at any moment. "Because it was *here*. Because it wasn't called How to Marry an Untitled Gentleman of Some Fortune and Reasonable Good Humor. I don't know."

James had to smile at that.

"But I doubt I could attract a titled gentleman in the first place," she added. "I have no dowry, and I'm certainly not a diamond of the first water."

They disagreed there, but he suspected she wouldn't believe him even if he said so. "Do you have any candidates in mind?" he asked.

She paused for a long, telling moment before saying, "No."

"Then you *do* have a man in mind," he said with a grin.

Again, she remained silent for several seconds before saying, in a tone that told him his life would be in danger if he pursued the topic further, "He isn't suitable."

"And what constitutes suitable?"

She sighed wearily. "I don't want to be beaten, I'd rather not be abandoned—"

"My, my, we're aiming high."

"Forget I said anything," she snapped. "I don't know why I'm sharing this with you, anyway. You obviously have no idea how it feels to be desperate, to lack choices, to know that no matter what you do—"

"Elizabeth," he said softly, reaching out and grasping her fingers. "I'm sorry."

"He has to have money," she said dully, staring down at her hand in his. "I need money."

"I see."

"I doubt you do, but it's probably enough for you to know that I'm destitute."

"Lady Danbury doesn't pay you enough to support yourself?" he asked quietly.

"She does, but it isn't enough to support my younger siblings. And Lucas *must* go to Eton."

"Yes," he said distractedly, "a boy should. He's a baronet, you say?"

"No, I didn't say, but yes, he is."

"Lady Danbury must have told me."

She shrugged and let out an exhale mixed with self-mocking laughter. "It's common knowledge. We're the district's official example of impoverished gentry. So you see, I'm not precisely marriageable. All I have to offer is my family's bloodlines. And even those aren't terribly impressive. It's not as if I spring from nobility."

"No," he mused, "but one would think that many a man would wish to marry into the local gentry, especially a titled branch. And you have the added bonus of being quite beautiful."

She looked up sharply. "Please don't patronize me."

He smiled in disbelief. She clearly had no idea of her charms.

"I've been told I'm reasonably pretty—" she began.

Well, perhaps some idea.

"—but beautiful is quite a stretch."

He waved his hand, dismissing her protest. "You'll have to trust me on this measure. As I was saying, I'm certain there must be several men in the district who'd like to marry you."

"There's one," she said distastefully. "A local squire. But he's old, fat, and mean. My younger sister has already said that she will run away to a workhouse if I marry him."

"I see." James rubbed his chin, searching for a solution to her dilemma. It seemed a crime that she would have to marry some disgusting old squire twice her age. Perhaps there was something he could do. He had enough money to send her brother to Eton a thousand times over.

Or rather, the Marquis of Riverdale did. James Siddons, a Mere Mister, wasn't supposed to have anything other than the clothes on his back.

But perhaps he could arrange for some sort of anonymous gift. Surely Elizabeth wouldn't be so proud as to ignore an unexpected windfall. He didn't doubt that she'd refuse a gift for her own sake, but not when the welfare of her family was at stake.

James made a mental note to contact his solicitor as soon as possible.

"So," she said with an uncomfortable laugh, "unless you've a fortune tucked away, I really don't see how you can help me."

"Well," he said, avoiding an outright lie, "I'd thought to aid you in a different manner."

"What do you mean?"

He chose his words carefully. "I know a bit about the art of flirtation. Before I sought employment, I was . . . not precisely active, but I did participate in the social scene."

"In London?" she asked dubiously. "With the *ton*?"

"I will never understand the complexities of a London season," he said, quite emphatically.

"Oh. Well, that's no matter, I suppose, as I lack the funds for a season." She looked back up and offered him a rueful smile. "And even if I didn't, it would all go toward Lucas's education, anyway."

He stared at her, taking in the sight of that delicate oval face and big blue eyes. She had to be the least selfish person he'd ever met. "You're a good sister, Elizabeth Hotchkiss," he said quietly.

"Not really," she said in a sad voice. Sometimes I feel so resentful. If I were a better person I'd—"

"Nonsense," he interrupted. "There is nothing wrong with anger over injustice."

She laughed. "It's not injustice, James, it's just poverty. I'm sure you understand."

In his entire life, James had never had to do without. When his father had been alive, he'd been granted a monstrously huge allowance. And then, upon gaining the title, he'd inherited an even more monstrously huge fortune.

Elizabeth tilted her head and gazed out the window, where a soft breeze was ruffling the leaves of Lady Danbury's favorite elm. "Sometimes," she whispered, "I wish . . ."

"What do you wish?" James asked intently.

She gave her head a little shake. "It doesn't matter. And I really do have to see to Lady Danbury. She'll be arriving at the sitting room any minute now and is sure to need me."

"*Elizabeth!*" came the loud bellow from across the hall.

"See? Do you see how well I know her?"

James inclined his head respectfully and murmured, "Most impressive."

"ELIZABETH!"

"Heavens above," Elizabeth said, "what can she possibly need?"

"Company," James replied. "That's all she really needs. Company."

"Where is that ridiculous cat when I need it?" She turned and made to leave.

"Elizabeth!" James called out.

She turned back. "Yes?"

"The book." He pointed at the small red volume, still tucked under her arm. "You don't want to take that to the drawing room, do you?"

"Oh! No!" She shoved it into his hands. "Thank you. I'd completely forgotten that I was holding it."

"I'll put it back for you."

"It goes on that shelf over there," she said, pointing across the room. "Sideways. Facedown. You need to make sure you leave it exactly as I say."

He smiled indulgently. "Would you feel better if you put it back yourself?"

She paused, then said, "Yes, actually, I would," and grabbed the book back. James watched as she dashed across the room and carefully placed the book on the proper shelf. She inspected her handiwork for a moment, then tapped it on the bottom, moving it slightly to the left. Twisting her mouth in thought, she regarded it for another moment, then tapped it back to the right.

"I'm certain Lady Danbury won't notice if the book is an inch or so off."

But she ignored him, dashing across the room with only an "I'll have to see you later" in his direction.

James poked his head out the door, watching as she disappeared into Agatha's sitting room. Then he shut the library door, crossed the room, picked up the book, and began to read.

Chapter 9

"**Y**ou want to do *what*?"

Elizabeth stood in front of Lady Danbury, her mouth hanging open in surprise.

"I told you, I'm going to take a nap."

"But you never take naps."

Lady Danbury raised a brow. "I took one just two days ago."

"But—but—"

"Close your mouth, Elizabeth. You're beginning to resemble a fish."

"But you have told me," Elizabeth protested, "time and again, that the hallmark of civilization is routine."

Lady D shrugged and made a fussy little chirping sound. "A lady cannot take it upon herself to occasionally change her routine? All routines need periodic readjustment."

Elizabeth managed to shut her mouth, but she still couldn't believe what she was hearing.

"I may take a nap every day," Lady Danbury stated, crossing her arms. "I say, what the devil are you looking for?"

Elizabeth, who had been tossing bewildered glances around the room, replied, "A ventriloquist. These words

141

couldn't possibly be coming from your mouth.''

"I assure you they are. I'm finding afternoon naps to be prodigiously refreshing.''

"But the one you took the other day—your single previous nap since childhood, I might add—was in the morning.''

"Hmmph. Maybe it was. Maybe it wasn't.''

"It was.''

"It would have been better in the afternoon.''

Elizabeth had no idea how to argue against such illogic, so she just threw up her arms and said, "I'll leave you to your sleep, then.''

"Yes. Do that. And shut the door behind you. I'm certain I'll need absolute silence.''

"I can't imagine you'd require anything less.''

"Sly girl. Where is all this cheek coming from?''

Elizabeth threw her employer a scolding look. "You know very well it comes from you, Lady Danbury.''

"Yes, I'm doing a rather good job of molding you, aren't I?''

"God help me,'' Elizabeth muttered.

"I heard that!''

"I don't suppose there is any chance that your hearing will be the first of your senses to go.''

Lady Danbury laughed out loud at that one. "You do know how to entertain an old lady, Elizabeth Hotchkiss. Don't think I don't appreciate that. I do care for you a great deal.''

Elizabeth blinked in surprise at Lady D's uncharacteristic show of sentimentality. "Why, thank you.''

"I'm not always a complete churl.'' Lady Danbury regarded the small watch she wore around her neck on a chain. "I believe I'd like to be roused in seventy minutes.''

"Seventy minutes?" Where on earth did Lady D come up with these odd numbers?

"An hour really isn't enough, but I'm far too busy to waste an hour and a half. Besides," Lady Danbury added with a sly look, "I like to keep you on your toes."

"Of that," Elizabeth muttered, "I have no doubt."

"Seventy minutes, then. And not a moment sooner."

Elizabeth shook her head in amazement as she walked to the door. Before she exited, though, she turned around and asked, "Are you sure you're feeling well?"

"Every bit as well as a fifty-eight-year-old woman has a right to."

"Which is really quite a blessing," Elizabeth said wryly, "since you're sixty-six."

"Impertinent chit. Get out of here before I dock your wages."

Elizabeth arched her brows. "You wouldn't dare."

Lady Danbury smiled to herself as she watched her companion shut the door behind her. "I am doing a good job," she said to herself, her tone filled with tenderness— and perhaps just a hint of self-congratulation. "She's becoming more like me every day."

Elizabeth let out a long breath and plopped down on a cushioned bench in the hall. What was she supposed to do with herself now? If she'd known that Lady Danbury was going to take to napping on a regular basis, she would have brought along some mending, or perhaps the household accounts. The Lord knew the Hotchkiss finances could always use some shuffling.

Of course there was always How to Marry a Marquis. She'd sworn she wasn't going to look at the blasted book again, but maybe she should just peek in the library to make certain that James hadn't moved it, or turned it over, or ruffled the pages, or—or, well, done *anything* to it.

No, she told herself firmly, clutching the maroon velvet of the bench seat to keep herself from rising. She was not going to have anything more to do with Mrs. Seeton and her edicts. She was going to sit here, attached to this bench like glue, until she decided how to spend her seventy minutes.

Without entering the library. Whatever she did, she was not going to enter the library.

"Elizabeth?"

She looked up to see James—or rather, James's head, poking out of the doorway to the library.

"Could you join me for a moment?"

She stood. "Is there a problem?"

"No, no. Quite the opposite, actually."

"That sounds promising," she murmured. It had been a long time since someone had summoned her for *good* news. *Could you join me for a moment?* tended to be the polite way of saying, *Your account is past due and if you don't pay immediately I shall have to notify the authorities.*

He motioned to her with his hand. "I need to speak with you."

She joined him in the library. So much for her latest resolution. "What is it?"

He held up How TO MARRY A MARQUIS and frowned. "I've been reading this."

Oh, *no*.

"It's really quite fascinating."

She groaned and clapped her hands over her ears. "I don't want to hear it."

"I'm convinced I can help you."

"I'm not listening."

He grabbed her hands and pulled until she was

stretched out like a starfish. "I can help you," he said again.

"I'm beyond help."

He chuckled, the rich sound warming Elizabeth right to her very toes. "Now, now," he said, "don't be pessimistic."

"*Why* are you reading that?" she asked. Heavens above, what could this or any handsome, charming man possibly find interesting in such a book? If one wanted to put the plainest face possible on it, it was a treatise for desperate women. And didn't men tend to equate desperate women with hemlock, food poisoning, and the bubonic plague?

"Call it my insatiable curiosity," he replied. "How could I resist, after being forced to go to such heroic lengths to retrieve the book earlier this morning?"

"Heroic lengths?" she exclaimed. "You yanked it out from under me!"

"The word 'heroic' is always open to interpretation," he said blithely, flashing her yet another of those dangerously masculine smiles.

Elizabeth closed her eyes and let out a weary and bewildered sigh. This had to be the strangest conversation of her life, and yet somehow it seemed quite natural.

The most bizarre part was that she didn't really feel embarrassed. Oh, certainly her cheeks were a bit pink, and she couldn't quite believe some of the words coming from her mouth, but by all rights, she should have perished of acute mortification by now.

It was James, she realized. Something about him put her at ease. He had such an easy smile, a comforting laugh. He might have a dangerous and downright mysterious side to him, and sometimes he did look at her in an oddly hot sort of way that made the air positively thick, but other than that it was nearly impossible to feel uncomfortable in his company.

"What are you thinking about?" she heard him ask.

She opened her eyes. "I was thinking that I cannot remember the last time I felt so ridiculous."

"Don't be silly."

"Sometimes," she said with a self-deprecating shake of her head, "I just can't help it."

He ignored her comment and held up the book, shaking it with little flips of his wrist. "This has problems."

"HOW TO MARRY A MARQUIS?"

"Many problems."

"I'm thrilled to hear it. I must say it seems prodigiously difficult to live up to her edicts."

James began to pace back and forth, his warm brown eyes clearly lost in thought. "It is obvious to me," he announced, "that Mrs. Seeton—if that is indeed her real name—never once consulted a *man* when drawing up her edicts."

Elizabeth found this so interesting she sat down.

"She can offer as many rules and regulations as she likes," he expounded, "but her methodology is flawed. She asserts that if you follow her edicts, you will marry a marquis—"

"By 'marquis,' I think she merely meant an eligible gentleman," Elizabeth interrupted. "I imagine she was just aiming for alliteration in the book title."

He shook his head. "It makes no difference. Marquis, eligible gentleman—we're all men."

"Yes," she said slowly, just barely resisting the urge to verify this fact by letting her gaze wander up and down his form, "one would hope."

James leaned in, staring intently at her face. "I ask you this: How, pray tell, is Mrs. Seeton—if that is indeed her real name—to judge whether or not her rules are appropriate?"

"Well," Elizabeth stalled, "I suppose she might have chaperoned a few young ladies and—"

"Faulty logic," he interrupted. "The only person who can truly judge whether or not her rules are appropriate is a marquis."

"Or an eligible gentleman," she put in.

"Or an eligible gentleman," he conceded with a slightly sideways nod of his head. "But I can assure you, as a moderately eligible gentleman, if a woman approached me, following all of these edicts—"

"But she wouldn't approach you," Elizabeth cut in. "Not if she was following Mrs. Seeton's instructions. It would be against the rules. A lady must wait until a gentleman approaches her. I can't remember which edict that is, but I know it's in there."

"Which only goes to show how asinine most of this is. The point I was trying to make, however, is that if I met a protégée of our dear Mrs. Seeton—if that is indeed her real name—"

"Why do you keep saying that?"

James thought about that for a moment. Must have been all those years as a spy. All he said, however, was, "I haven't the foggiest. But as I was saying, if I met one of her protégées, I would run screaming in the other direction."

There was a beat of silence, and then Elizabeth said, with a hint of a mischievous smile, "You didn't run from me."

James's head snapped up. "What do you mean?"

Her smiled widened, and she looked almost feline in her pleasure at having unnerved him. "Didn't you read the edict about practicing the edicts?" She leaned forward to peer into the pages of How to Marry a Mar-

QUIS, through which he was now rifling, looking for the aforementioned edict. "I think it's number seventeen," she added.

He stared at her in disbelief for a full ten seconds before asking, "You practiced on me?"

"It sounds rather cold-blooded, I know, and I did have a twinge or two of guilt about it, but I really didn't have any choice. After all, if not you, who?"

"Who, indeed," James muttered, not precisely certain why he was irritated. It wasn't because she'd been practicing upon him; that was rather amusing, actually. Rather, he thought it might be that he hadn't *realized* she'd been practicing upon him.

For a man who prided himself on his instinct and perception, that was rather galling, indeed.

"I shan't do it any longer," she promised. "It was probably rather unfair of me."

He set to pacing, tapping his finger against his jaw as he tried to decide how best to turn this situation to his advantage.

"James?"

Aha! He whipped around in a blur of motion, his eyes lit with the thrill of a new idea. "Who were you practicing for?"

"I don't understand."

He sat down across from her and let his forearms rest on his thighs as he leaned in. Earlier that morning he'd sworn to himself that he would rid the look of desperation from her eyes. In all truth, that look wasn't there now, but he knew it would return just as soon as she remembered her three hungry siblings at home. And now he'd found a way to help her and have a brilliant time doing it.

He was going to tutor her. She wanted to snare some unsuspecting man into marriage—well, no one could know more about such traps than the Marquis of River-dale. He'd had every trick sprung on him, from giggling debutantes following him into dark corners, to shockingly explicit love letters, to naked widows showing up in his bed.

It seemed to stand to reason that if he'd learned so well how to avoid marriage, he ought to be able to apply his knowledge in the opposite direction. With a little work, Elizabeth ought to be able to catch any man in the land.

It was that bit—the "work" part of it—that had his pulse quickening, and certain less-mentionable parts of his anatomy thickening. For any tutoring lesson would have to involve at least a cursory examination of the amorous arts. Nothing, of course, that would compromise the girl, but—

"Mr. Siddons? James?"

He looked up, aware that he'd been woolgathering. Good God, but she had the face of an angel. He found it nearly impossible to believe she thought she needed help in finding a husband. But she did think it, and that gave him the most splendid opportunity. . . .

"When you were practicing on me," he asked in a low, focused voice, "who was your ultimate goal?"

"You mean to marry?"

"Yes."

She blinked and her mouth moved slightly before she said, "I—I don't know, actually. I hadn't gotten quite that far in my thinking. I was merely hoping to attend one of Lady Danbury's gatherings. It seemed as good a place as any to find an eligible gentleman."

"Has she one scheduled soon?"

"A gathering? Yes. It is to be Saturday, I believe. A small garden party."

James sat back. Damn. His aunt hadn't told him she was expecting company. If any of her guests were acquaintances of his, he'd have to make himself very scarce very fast. The last thing he needed was some London dandy slapping him on the back in front of Elizabeth and calling him Riverdale.

"I don't believe anyone is planning to stay the night, however," she added.

James nodded thoughtfully. "Then this will be an excellent opportunity for you."

"I see," she said, not sounding nearly as excited as he would have expected.

"All you need to do is determine which men are unmarried and choose the best of the lot."

"I have already looked over the guest list, and there are several unattached gentlemen expected. But"—she let out a frustrated laugh—"you've forgotten one thing, James. The gentleman in question must also choose me."

He waved off her protest. "Failure is not a possibility. By the time we're through with you—"

"I don't like the sound of that."

"—you'll be impossible to resist."

One of Elizabeth's hands unconsciously rose to her cheek as she stared at him in amazement. Was he offering to *train* her? To render her marriageable? She didn't know why she should be so surprised by this—after all, he had never made an indication—save for one sweet kiss—that he was interested in her for himself. And besides, she had made it clear that she could not marry a penniless estate manager.

So then why was she so depressed that he seemed so eager to marry her off to a wealthy, well-connected gentleman—exactly what she told him she wanted and needed out of life?

"What does this training entail?" she asked suspiciously.

"Well, we haven't much time," he mused, "and

there's nothing we can do about your wardrobe.''

"How kind of you to point that out," she muttered.

He shot her a vaguely remonstrating look. "If I recall, you had no compunction about insulting my wardrobe earlier.''

He had her there, she allowed. Good manners forced her to say, somewhat grudgingly, "Your boots are very nice.''

He grinned and regarded his footwear, which, though old, appeared very well-made. "Yes, they are, aren't they?''

"If a bit scuffed," she added.

"I shall polish them tomorrow," he promised, his somewhat superior look telling her that he refused to rise to her bait.

"I'm sorry," she said quietly. "That was uncalled for. Compliments should be freely given, without restrictions or qualifications.''

He looked at her with an oddly assessing expression for a moment before asking, "Do you know what I like about you, Elizabeth?''

She couldn't even possibly imagine.

"You're as kind and good a person as they come," he continued, "but unlike most kind and good people, you don't preach or cloy, or try to make everyone else kind and good.''

Her mouth dropped open. This was the most unbelievable speech.

"And underneath all that kindness and goodness, you seem to possess a wicked sense of humor, no matter how hard you occasionally try to suppress it.''

Oh, dear Lord, if he said anything more, she was going to fall in love with him on the spot.

"There's no harm in poking fun at a friend as long as you intend no malice," he said, his voice melting into a soft caress. "And I don't think you would know how to be malicious if someone offered you a dissertation on the subject."

"Then I suppose that makes us friends," she said, her voice catching slightly.

He smiled at her, and her heart stopped beating. "You really have no choice but to be friends with me," he said, leaning closer. "After all, I know all of your most embarrassing secrets."

A nervous giggle escaped her lips. "A friend who is going to find me a husband. How quaint."

"Well, I should think I could do a better job than Mrs. Seeton. If that is indeed—"

"Don't say it," she warned.

"Consider it not said. But if you want some help . . ." He looked at her closely. "You do want help, don't you?"

"Er, yes." *I think.*

"We will need to begin right away."

Elizabeth glanced over at an ornate table clock Lady Danbury had had imported from Switzerland. "I'm due back in the drawing room in less than an hour."

He flipped through a few pages of HOW TO MARRY A MARQUIS, shaking his head as he scanned the words. "Hmm, that's not very much time, but—" He looked up sharply. "How did you manage to escape Lady Danbury at this time of day?"

"She's taking a nap."

"Again?" His face showed his surprise clearly.

She shrugged. "I found it just as unbelievable as you do, but she insisted. She demanded absolute silence and told me not to rouse her for seventy minutes."

"Seventy?"

Elizabeth grimaced. "That's to keep me on my toes. I'm quoting her on that, by the way."

"Somehow that does not surprise me." James drummed his fingers on the library's main table, then looked up. "We can start after you finish with her this afternoon. I'll need some time to devise a lesson plan, and—"

"A lesson plan?" she echoed.

"We need to be organized. Organization renders any goal reachable."

Her mouth fell open.

He frowned. "Why are you looking at me like that?"

"You sound *exactly* like Lady Danbury. In fact, she says that very same phrase."

"Is that so?" James coughed, then cleared his throat. Damn, but he was slipping up. Something about Elizabeth and those angel-blue eyes of hers made him forget that he was working undercover. He should never have used one of Aunt Agatha's favorite maxims. They'd been drummed into his head so frequently as a child that they were now his maxims as well.

He'd forgotten that he was talking to the one person who knew every single one of Agatha's quirks as well as he did. "I'm certain it's just a coincidence," he said, keeping his tone firm. It was his experience that people tended to believe whatever he said as long as he sounded as if he knew what he was talking about.

But not, apparently, Elizabeth. "She says it at least once a week."

"Well, then, I'm sure I must have heard her at some point."

She seemed to accept that explanation, for she let the matter drop and instead said, "You were saying something about lesson plans . . ."

"Right. I will need the afternoon to plan, but perhaps we might meet when you are done with Lady Danbury. I will walk you home, and we can begin en route."

She smiled weakly. "Very well. I shall meet you at the front gate at thirty-five minutes past four. I am dismissed at half four," she explained, "but it will take me five minutes to walk to the gate."

"Can we not simply meet here?"

She shook her head. "Not unless you want every gossip at Danbury House talking about us."

"An excellent point. The front gate it is, then."

Elizabeth nodded and left the room, her wobbly legs just managing to make it back to the cushioned bench. Dear Lord, what on earth had she gotten herself into?

Meow.

She looked down. Malcolm the demon cat was sitting at her feet, staring at her as if she were a kitchen rat.

"What do you want?"

The cat shrugged. Elizabeth hadn't known that a cat could shrug, but then again, she hadn't thought she'd ever find herself sitting in Danbury House's great hall, talking to her feline nemesis.

"You think I'm ridiculous, don't you?"

Malcolm yawned.

"I've agreed to let Mr. Siddons train me to find a husband."

The cat's ears perked forward.

"Yes, I know you like him better than me. You like everyone better than me."

The cat shrugged again, clearly unwilling to contradict her statement.

"You think I can't do it, don't you?"

Malcolm made a rolling motion with his tail. Elizabeth was at a complete loss to translate this, but given the cat's well-documented distaste for her, she tended to believe it meant, "*I* have a better chance of finding a husband than you do."

"Elizabeth?"

She turned beet-red and jerked her head to the side. James had poked his head through the library door and was regarding her quizzically.

"Are you talking to the cat?"

"No."

"I could have sworn I heard you talking to the cat."

"Well, I'm not."

"Oh."

"Why would I talk to the cat? He hates me."

His lips twitched. "Yes. So you said."

She tried to pretend she didn't realize that her cheeks were burning. "Don't you have something to do?"

"Ah, yes, the lesson plans. I shall see you a bit after half four."

Elizabeth waited until she heard the library door click shut. "Dear God," she breathed. "I have gone insane. Completely insane."

Adding insult to injury, the cat nodded.

Chapter 10

J ames arrived at the front gate at a quarter past four, knowing he was ridiculously early, but somehow unable to stop his feet from carrying him to the appointed meeting site. He had felt restless all afternoon, constantly drumming his fingers on tables and pacing across rooms. He had tried to sit down and write out the lesson plan he had bragged about, but the words would not come.

He had no experience in training a young lady for society. The only young lady he really *knew* was the wife of his best friend, Blake Ravenscroft. And Caroline hadn't precisely been trained for society herself. As for all of his other female acquaintances—they were just the sort Mrs. Seeton was trying to mold Elizabeth into. Just the sort that had prompted his overwhelming relief at leaving London.

What was it *he* wanted in a woman? His quest to help Elizabeth seemed to beg the question. What was it he wanted in a wife? He had to marry; there was no arguing fate in that respect. But it had been so damned hard to imagine spending the rest of his life with a shy flower who was afraid to express an opinion.

Or worse, a shy flower who didn't even *possess* an opinion.

And the final twist of the bayonet was that those opinionless young ladies invariably came with *extremely* opinionated mothers.

He wasn't being fair, he forced himself to concede. He'd met a few young ladies who were interesting. Not many, but a few. One or two of them he even could have married without fearing that he was ruining his life. It wouldn't have been a love match, and there would have been no grand passion, but he could have been passably content.

So what was it these ladies—the ones who had fleetingly caught his attention—had possessed? It was a certain joie de vivre, a love for life, a smile that seemed real, a light in the eyes. James was fairly certain he wasn't the only man who had seen these things—all of the young ladies in question had been quickly snapped up into marriage, usually by men whom he liked and respected.

Love for life. Maybe that was what this was all about. He'd spent the morning reading HOW TO MARRY A MARQUIS, and with each edict, he'd pictured a little bit more of that incomparable sapphire light melting away from Elizabeth's eyes.

He didn't want her molded into some predetermined ideal of young English womanhood. He didn't want her walking with her eyes downcast, trying to be mysterious and demure. He just wanted her to be herself.

Elizabeth shut the door to Danbury House behind her and set off down the main drive. Her heart was racing, her hands were clammy, and while she didn't feel precisely embarrassed that James had discovered her desperate secret, she was as nervous as could be.

She had spent all afternoon berating herself for accepting his offer. Hadn't she spent the previous night sobbing herself to sleep, all because she thought she could love him—a man she could never marry? And now she was purposely putting herself in his company, allowing him to tease her, to flirt with her, and—

Good God, what if he wanted to kiss her again? He said he was going to train her to attract other men. Did that entail kissing? And if it did, should she let him do it?

She groaned. As if she'd be able to stop him. Every time they were in the same room together, her eyes wandered to his mouth, and she remembered what it felt like to have those lips on hers. And God help her, she wanted that again.

A final glimpse of bliss. Maybe that was what this was all about. She was going to have to marry someone she didn't love, maybe even someone she didn't much like. Was it so wrong to want a few last days of laughter, of secret glances, of that heady tingle of newborn desire?

As she walked toward the front gate she suspected that she was courting heartbreak by agreeing to meet James, but her heart wouldn't let her do anything else. She'd read enough Shakespeare to trust the Bard, and if he said it was better to have loved and lost than never to have loved at all—she believed him.

He was waiting for her, just out of sight of Danbury House, and his eyes lit up when he saw her.

"Elizabeth," he called out, striding toward her.

She paused, content to just watch him approach, the light breeze ruffling his dark hair. She'd never met anyone who seemed more comfortable in his skin as James Siddons. He had such an easy stride, a smooth gait. She thought about the innumerable times she'd tripped over a rug or swung her hand into a wall and sighed in envy.

He reached her side and said simply, "You're here."

"Didn't you think I would be?"

"I had thought you might have second thoughts."

"Of course I have second thoughts. This is quite the most irregular thing I've ever done."

"How admirable of you," he murmured.

"But it wouldn't matter if I'd had second, third, or even fourth thoughts." She smiled helplessly. "I have to walk right by here to get home, so I couldn't avoid you if I tried."

"How fortunate for me."

"I have a feeling that fortune often smiles upon you."

He cocked his head. "Now, why would you say that?"

She shrugged. "I don't know. You just seem the sort who always lands on his feet."

"I suspect you are a survivor, too."

"In a certain sense, I suppose. I could have given up on my family years ago, you know. Relatives did offer to take in Lucas."

"But not the rest of you?"

She smiled wryly. "The rest of us aren't in possession of titles."

"I see." He took her arm and motioned to the south. "Is it this way?"

She nodded. "Yes, about a mile down the road, then about a quarter of a mile down the side lane."

They walked for a few paces, and then he turned to her and said, "You said you were a survivor 'in a certain sense.' What did you mean by that?"

"It's easier for a man to be a survivor than a woman."

"That makes no sense."

She gave him a faintly pitying look. He would never understand what she had to say, but she supposed she owed it to him to try to explain nonetheless. "When a man falls on hard times," she said, "there are quite a number of things he may do, options he may pursue, to reverse his situation. He may join the army, or sign on to a pirate ship. He may look for work, as you have done.

He may use his charm and looks"—she shook her head and smiled reluctantly—"as I imagine you have also done."

"And a woman may not do these things?"

"A woman looking for work does not have many options if she does not wish to leave her home. A governess post might pay marginally better than a lady's companion, but I doubt many employers would look too kindly upon my bringing Susan, Jane, and Lucas with me to live in the servants' wing."

"Touché," he said with an understanding nod.

"And as for charm and looks, well, a woman can use those for three things. She can go into the theater, she can become a man's mistress, or she can marry. As for me, I have no inclination or talent for acting and no wish to shame my family by entering into an illicit relationship." She looked up at him and shrugged. "My only choice is marriage. That, I suppose, is what it means for a woman to be a survivor."

She paused, and the corners of her mouth quivered as if they didn't know whether to attempt a smile or a frown. "Rather distasteful, don't you think?"

James didn't answer her for several moments. He liked to think of himself as a broad-minded individual, but he had never once taken the time to imagine what it must be like in the tight, pinching shoes of a woman. He had taken his life, with its myriad choices, for granted.

She tilted her head. "Why are you looking at me so intently?"

"Respect."

She drew back in surprise. "I beg your pardon?"

"I admired you before. You seemed an uncommonly intelligent and amusing young woman. But now I realize that you deserve my respect as well as my admiration."

"Oh. I—I—" She blushed, clearly at a loss for words.

He shook his head. "I didn't mean to make you uncomfortable."

"You didn't," she replied, the squeak in her voice proving her a liar.

"Yes, I did, and I certainly didn't mean for this to be such a serious afternoon. We have work to do, but there is no reason it shouldn't be entertaining."

She cleared her throat. "What did you have in mind?"

"We haven't much time, so we are forced to prioritize," he said. "We must focus upon only the very most important skills."

"Which are?"

"Kissing and boxing."

Elizabeth dropped her satchel.

"You seem surprised."

"I couldn't possibly imagine which of those two surprises me more."

He swooped down and picked up her bag for her. "It makes perfect sense when you think on it. A gentleman is going to want to kiss a lady before he tenders an offer of marriage."

"Not if he respects her," she pointed out. "I have it on the best authority that men don't kiss unmarried women whom they respect."

"I kissed you."

"Well . . . that was . . . different."

"And I believe we have made it clear that I respect you. But enough of that." He waved her protests away. "You must trust me when I tell you that no gentleman with an ounce of sense in his head is going to marry a woman without testing the waters first."

"Put that way," she muttered, "it's positively poetic."

"However, that can put you in an awkward position."

"Oh, you realize that?" she asked sarcastically.

He shot her a look, clearly irritated by her constant interruption. "Some gentlemen lack basic common sense and judgment, and might not break off the kiss at an appropriate time. That is why we must teach you to box."

"And you're going to do all of this in one afternoon?"

He pulled out his pocket watch and flipped it open, his face a perfect picture of nonchalance. "No, I had thought just the kissing for this afternoon. We can see to the boxing tomorrow."

"And you are trained in the sport of pugilism?"

"Of course."

She eyed him suspiciously. "Aren't lessons terribly expensive? I had heard that there were only a handful of instructors in London who are considered of superior quality."

"There are always ways to obtain what one needs," he said. He looked over at her with a raised eyebrow. "I believe you said I am the sort who always lands on his feet."

"I suppose now you are going to tell me you are the sort who lands on his feet with his arms primed and ready to box?"

He laughed and made a few jabs in the air. "There is nothing like it to keep the blood flowing."

She frowned dubiously. "It doesn't look a very feminine pursuit."

"I thought we had decided we weren't going to subscribe to Mrs. Seeton's view of femininity."

"We're not," she retorted, "but we are trying to find me a husband."

"Ah, yes, your husband," he said darkly.

"I cannot imagine there is a man in England who wants to marry a lady pugilist."

"You don't need to be a pugilist. You just need to be

able to punch well enough to show that you cannot be taken advantage of.''

She shrugged and made a fist. "Like this?"

"God, no. Don't tuck your thumb in. You're sure to break it."

Elizabeth moved her thumb to the outside of her fist. "Like this?"

He nodded approvingly. "Exactly. But we were going to study kissing today."

"No, let's save that." She thrust her arm forward a few times. "I'm rather enjoying myself."

James groaned, not quite sure what was bothering him more—that he had to put off kissing her another day or that she had the weakest punch he'd ever seen. "No, no, not like that," he said, positioning himself behind her. He let her bag fall to the ground as he put his hand on her elbow and readjusted the angle of her shoulder. "You punch like a girl."

"I *am* a girl."

"Well, that much I've always found obvious, but you don't have to punch like one."

"And how," she asked, mocking a deep male voice, "does a *man* punch?"

"Girls, I've learned, punch like this." He made a fist and moved his arm forward and back, his elbow never straying far from his side. "Men, on the other hand, put a little swing into it."

"Do please demonstrate."

"Very well. Back off, then. I shouldn't like to injure you."

Elizabeth offered him a dry smile and took a few steps back. "Is that enough room for a *man*?"

"Don't mock. Just watch." He drew his arm back. "I shall have to show you this at half the usual speed since

I'm not actually punching anything but air. The momentum is likely to take me with the punch.''

"By all means, then," she said with a magnanimous wave of her hand. "Half speed."

"Pay attention. You're watching a master."

"Of that," she said dryly, "I have no doubt."

He moved his entire arm forward, the motion beginning at the center of his back and surging through his shoulder to his fist. If he had been moving at full speed, and if there were someone standing in front of him, James rather thought he might have knocked him out. "What do you think?" he asked, thoroughly pleased with himself.

"Do it again."

He raised his brows but complied, putting even more swing into it this time. He looked up to her face; she had her eyes narrowed and was studying him as if he were a prized piece of livestock.

Looking up briefly, she asked, "One more time?"

"Are you paying attention or just trying to make me look like an idiot?"

"Oh, I'm definitely paying attention. If you look like an idiot it has nothing to do with me."

James pulled his arm back one last time. "To recap," he said, "a woman punches forward from the shoulder, without using the muscles of her middle back."

Elizabeth imitated his female punch. "Like this."

"Precisely. A man, on the other hand, utilizes the strength of his back as well as his arm."

"These muscles here?" She lifted up her right arm and used her left hand to motion to the muscles wrapping around her right rib cage.

His mouth went dry. Her dress was tightening around her in most unusual places.

"Here, James?" she demanded, poking her back. "Or

here?'' This time she poked his back, except that she missed, and got him more in the side, rather close to his waist.

"Right the first time," he said, darting away from her finger. If she missed his back by another inch or two in the southerly direction, he wouldn't be held responsible for his actions.

"So it's a little like this." She threw a half-speed punch, moving only marginally faster than he had while doing it.

"Yes. But you need a little bit more lateral movement. Watch me one more time." He threw another punch. "See?"

"I think so. Would you like me to give it a go?"

"Yes." He crossed his arms. "Punch me."

"Oh, no, I couldn't."

"No, I want you to."

"I couldn't possibly. I've never intentionally hurt another person before."

"Elizabeth, the entire purpose of this lesson is so you can injure another person if the need arises. If you cannot bring yourself to punch a human being, this has been a total waste of time."

She looked doubtful. "If you insist."

"I do."

"Very well." With barely a moment for either of them to prepare, she drew back and let fly. Before James had any idea what was happening, he was sprawled on the ground, and his right eye socket was throbbing.

Elizabeth, rather than displaying any sort of worry or concern over his health, was jumping up and down, squealing with glee. "I did it! I really did it! Did you see it? Did you see it?"

"No," he muttered, "but I felt it."

She planted her hands on her hips and beamed, looking

as if she had just been crowned queen of the world. "Oh, that was brilliant! Let's do it again."

"Let's not," he grumbled.

She stopped grinning and leaned down. "I didn't hurt you, did I?"

"Not at all," he lied.

"I didn't?" She sounded disappointed.

"Well, maybe just a little bit."

"Oh, good, I—" She choked back whatever it was she was planning to say. "I didn't mean that the way it sounded. I swear. I don't want you to be injured, but I did put all of my strength into that punch, and—"

"I shall be showing the effects tomorrow, have no fear."

She gasped with gleeful horror. "I gave you a black eye?"

"I thought you didn't want me to be injured."

"I don't," she said quickly, "but I must confess I've never done anything remotely like this before, and it's rather satisfying to have done it right."

James didn't think his eye was going to sport quite as splendid a bruise as she obviously hoped, but he was rather irritated with himself nonetheless for so seriously underestimating her. She was such a tiny thing; he'd never dreamed she'd get it right on the first punch. And even then, he'd figured she couldn't possibly possess enough strength to do more than stun her opponent. All he'd really been hoping for was to teach her enough to temporarily disarm a man while she made her escape.

But, he thought ruefully, giving his eye a gingerly pat, it appeared that her punches were anything but temporary. He looked up at her; she looked so damned proud of herself he had to smile and say, "I have created a monster."

"Do you think?" Her face lit up even more, which

James hadn't thought possible. It was as if the very sun were pouring from her eyes.

Elizabeth started jabbing her fists in the air. "Perhaps you could teach me some advanced techniques."

"You're quite advanced enough, thank you."

She stopped jumping about, her face sobering. "Should we put something on that eye? It might not swell and bruise if we put something cooling on it."

James almost refused. His eye truly wasn't that bad off—it had been surprise more than anything that had knocked him to the ground. But Elizabeth had just invited him into her home, and this was an opportunity not to be missed. "Something cooling would be just the thing," he murmured.

"Follow me, then. Do you need a hand?"

James regarded her outstretched hand with a bit of chagrin. How feeble-bodied did she think he was? "You punched me in the eye," he said in a dry voice. "The rest of me works quite well, thank you."

She pulled her hand back. "I had merely thought— You did hit the ground rather hard, after all."

Damn. Another opportunity lost. His pride was getting deuced annoying. He could have leaned on her the entire way home. "Why don't I try it on my own and we'll see how it goes?" he suggested. Maybe he could sprain an ankle in twenty yards or so.

"That sounds a good idea. But be careful not to overtax yourself."

James took a few careful steps, trying to remember which side it was that had hit the ground. It wouldn't do to limp on the wrong side.

"Are you sure you're not in pain?

He had to be a complete cad to take advantage of the concern in her eyes, but clearly his conscience had departed for destinations unknown, because James sighed and said, "I think it's my hip."

She glanced down at his hip, which caused other, nearby regions to feel a bit of pain. "Is it bruised?"

"That is all I can think," he replied. "I'm sure it's nothing but—"

"But it hurts to walk," she said with a maternal nod. "You'll probably feel better by morning, but it does seem silly to overexert yourself." She scrunched her brow in thought. "Perhaps it would be best if you simply returned to Danbury House. If you walk to my cottage, you'd have to walk back, and—"

"Oh, I'm sure it's not as bad as that," he said quickly. "And I did say I would walk you home."

"James, I do walk home by myself every day."

"Nonetheless, I must keep my promises."

"I'm happy to release you from this one. After all, you could hardly have expected to be knocked to the ground."

"Truly, it's not that painful. I just cannot walk with my usual speed."

She looked uncertain.

"Besides," he added, thinking that he needed to reinforce his position, "we still have much to discuss concerning Lady Danbury's garden party on Saturday."

"Very well," she said reluctantly. "But you must promise to tell me if the pain becomes overwhelming."

A promise easily kept, since he wasn't in any pain at all. Well, not of the sort to which she referred.

They'd taken only a few steps before Elizabeth turned to him and asked, "Are you all right?"

"Perfectly," he assured her. "But now that you have mastered the art of self-defense, I do think we should move on to other aspects of your education."

She blushed. "You mean . . ."

"Precisely."

"Don't you think it would be wise to begin with flirting?"

"Elizabeth, I don't think you have anything to worry about on that score."

"But I haven't the slightest clue how to go about it!"

"I can only say that you are a natural."

"No!" she said forcefully. "I'm not. I haven't the faintest idea what to say to men."

"You seemed to know what to say to me. That is," he amended, "when you weren't trying to adhere to Mrs. Seeton's edicts."

"You don't count."

He coughed. "And why not?"

"I don't know," she said with a little shake of her head, "you just don't. You're different."

He coughed again. "Not so very different from the other members of my gender."

"If you must know, you're much easier to talk to."

James considered that. Prior to meeting Elizabeth, he'd prided himself on being able to render sniveling debutantes and their grasping mamas utterly speechless with one well-placed stare. It had always been a most effective tool—one of the only truly useful things he had ever learned from his father.

Out of curiosity, he fixed his most supercilious, I-am-the-Marquis-of-Riverdale stare on her—the one that routinely sent grown men scurrying into corners—and said, "What if I looked upon you like this?"

She burst out laughing. "Oh, stop! Stop! You look ridiculous."

"I beg your pardon?"

"Stop, James. Oh, you must. You look like a little boy pretending to be a duke. I know, because my younger brother tries the same stunt on me all the time."

Pride stung, he said, "And how old is your brother?"

"He's eight, but—" Whatever she had meant to say was lost in her laughter.

James couldn't remember the last time someone had laughed at him, and he didn't particularly enjoy being compared to an eight-year-old boy. "I can assure you," he said, his voice pure ice, "that—"

"Don't say any more," she said, laughing. "Really, James, one shouldn't strut like an aristocrat if one cannot carry it off."

Never, in his entire career as an agent for the War Office, had he been more tempted to reveal his identity. He was itching to grab her and shake her and yell, "I'm a damned marquis, you little fool! I can be a perfectly good snob when I've a mind for it."

But on the other hand, there was something rather charming about her artless laughter. And when she turned to him and said, "Oh, please don't be insulted, James. It's a compliment, really. You're far too nice a person to be an aristocrat," he decided that this might actually be the most enchanting moment of his life.

His gaze was fixed upon an unremarkable patch of dirt, so she had to duck to move herself to his line of vision. "Forgive me?" she teased.

"I might find it in my heart. . . ."

"If you don't forgive me, then I might have to practice my pugilism again."

He winced. "In that case, I definitely forgive you."

"I thought you might. Let's go home."

And he wondered why, when she said the word "home," he actually thought it might apply to him as well.

Chapter 11

E lizabeth was surprised how unconcerned she was about the state of her home when she and James arrived at her doorstep. The green damask drapes were faded, and the moldings in need of a new coat of paint. The furniture was well-made but well-worn, with pillows strategically placed over the areas most in need of recovering. All in all, the house had a slightly spare look. There were precious few knickknacks; anything of any value had already made its way to pawnbroker or traveling peddler.

Usually she felt the need to explain how her family had fallen on hard times, and to make it clear that they had lived in a much bigger house before her parents died. Lucas was a baronet, after all, and it was embarrassing that they should be reduced to such circumstances.

But with James she simply opened her door with a smile, certain he would see her little cottage the way she did—as a warm, comfortable home. He'd alluded to a well-born background himself, but he'd also said that his family had lost whatever fortunes they had once possessed, so he would understand her inability to purchase new things, her need to economize.

The house was—thankfully!—tidy, and the air smelled

173

of warm biscuits. "You're in luck today," Elizabeth said with a smile. "Susan must have decided to do some baking."

"It smells delicious," James said.

"Ginger biscuits. Here, why don't you follow me into the kitchen? We're terribly informal here, I'm afraid." She pushed open the door to the kitchen and ushered him in. When he didn't immediately seat himself, she scolded him and said, "You mustn't stand on attention on my account. Your hip is bruised and must pain you terribly. Besides, it's silly for you to stand there while I prepare tea."

He pulled out a chair and sat down, then asked, "Are those your siblings in the garden?"

Elizabeth pushed aside a curtain and peered out the window. "Yes, those are Lucas and Jane. I'm not certain where Susan is, although she must have been here recently. These biscuits are still warm." With a smile, she deposited a plateful in front of him. "I'll call Lucas and Jane. I'm sure they will want to meet you."

James watched with interest as she knocked three times on the windowpane. Within seconds, the kitchen door flew open and two little urchins appeared.

"Oh, it's you, Elizabeth," the little boy said. "I thought you were Susan."

"No, it's just me, I'm afraid. Have you any idea where she's gone off to?"

"She went to the market," the little boy replied. "With any luck someone will give us some meat for those turnips."

"Pity is more like it," the little girl muttered. "Why anyone would give up a perfectly good piece of meat for a perfectly wretched turnip is quite beyond me."

"I hate turnips," James said.

All three Hotchkisses turned their blond heads in his direction.

He added, "A friend of mine once told me that one can learn quite a bit about diligence from a turnip, but I never could figure out what she meant."

Elizabeth started choking on air.

"That sounds like a lot of rubbish to me," the little girl said.

"Lucas, Jane," Elizabeth interrupted loudly. "I would like you to meet Mr. Siddons. He is my friend, and he also works at Danbury House. He is Lady Danbury's new estate manager."

James stood and shook Lucas's hand with all the gravity he would afford the prime minister. He then turned to Jane and kissed her hand. Her entire face lit up, but more importantly, when he looked up at Elizabeth for approval, she was beaming.

"How do you do?" he murmured.

"Very well, thank you," Lucas said.

Jane didn't say anything. She was too busy gazing at the hand he'd kissed.

"I have invited Mr. Siddons for tea and biscuits," Elizabeth said. "Would the two of you like to join us?"

Normally James would have regretted the loss of this time alone with Elizabeth, but there was something positively heartwarming about sitting here in the kitchen with this little threesome who so obviously knew what it meant to be a family.

Elizabeth handed a biscuit to each of her siblings and asked, "What did you two do all day? Did you finish the lessons I laid out for you?"

Jane nodded. "I helped Lucas with his arithmetic."

"You did not!" Lucas sputtered, crumbs flying from his mouth. "I can do it all by myself."

"Maybe you can," Jane said with a superior shrug, "but you didn't."

"Elizabeth!" Lucas protested. "Did you hear what she said to me?"

But Elizabeth ignored the question, instead sniffing the air with obvious distaste. "What on earth is that smell?"

"I went fishing again," Lucas replied.

"You must go wash yourself immediately. Mr. Siddons is our guest, and it isn't polite to—"

"I don't mind a bit of a fishy smell," James interrupted. "Did you catch anything?"

"I almost had one that was thiiiiiissss big," Lucas said, spreading his arms nearly as wide as they would go, "but he got away."

"Isn't that always the case," James murmured sympathetically.

"I did catch two medium-sized ones, though. I left them in a bucket outside."

"They're quite disgusting," Jane put in, having lost interest in her hand.

Lucas turned on her in an instant. "You don't say that when you get to eat them for supper."

"When I eat them for supper," she shot back, "they don't have eyes."

"That's because Lizzie chops off their heads, you nodcock."

"Lucas," Elizabeth said loudly, "I really think you should go outside and wash off some of that smell."

"But Mr. Siddons—"

"—was just being polite," Elizabeth cut in. "Do it now, and change your clothing while you're about it."

Lucas grumbled, but he did as he was told.

"He's such a trial sometimes," Jane said with a world-weary sigh.

James had to cough to keep from laughing.

Jane took this as agreement and further explained, "He is only eight."

"And how old are you?"

"Nine," she replied, as if that made all the difference in the world.

"Jane," Elizabeth said from over at the hearth, where she was putting water on for tea, "may I speak with you for a moment?"

Jane politely excused herself and moved to her sister's side. James pretended not to watch as Elizabeth leaned down and whispered something in her sister's ear. Jane nodded and ran off.

"What was that all about?" he had to ask.

"I thought she might do with a washing up as well, but I didn't want to embarrass her by asking in front of you."

He cocked his head. "Do you really think she would have been embarrassed by that?"

"James, she's a nine-year-old girl who thinks she's fifteen. You're a handsome man. Of course she'd be embarrassed."

"Well, you would know better than I," he replied, trying not to let his pleasure show at her having complimented his looks.

Elizabeth motioned to the plate of biscuits. "Aren't you going to try one?"

He took one and bit into it. "Delicious."

"Aren't they? I don't know what Susan does with them. I've never managed to make mine come out as nice." She took one and bit into it.

James stared up at her, unable to tear his eyes away from the sight of her nibbling away. Her tongue darted out to catch an errant crumb, and—

"I'm back!"

He sighed. One of life's most unexpected erotic moments, interrupted by an eight-year-old boy.

Lucas grinned up at him. "Do you like to fish?"

"It's one of my favorite sports."

"I should like to hunt, but Elizabeth won't let me."

"Your sister is a very wise woman. A boy your age should not handle a gun without the proper supervision."

Lucas pulled a face. "I know, but that's not why she doesn't let me do it. It's because she's too softhearted."

"If not wanting to watch you mangle a poor, innocent rabbit," Elizabeth cut in, "means that I am too softhearted, then—"

"But you eat rabbit," Lucas argued. "I've seen you."

Elizabeth crossed her arms and grumbled, "It's different when it has ears."

James laughed. "You sound like young Jane with her aversion to fish eyes."

"No, no, no," Elizabeth insisted, "it's entirely different. If you recall, I am the one who always cuts off the fish heads. So clearly I am not squeamish."

"Then what's the difference?" he prodded.

"Yes," Lucas said, crossing his arms and cocking his head in a perfect imitation of James, "what's the difference?"

"I don't have to answer this!"

James turned to Lucas and said behind his hand, "She knows she hasn't a leg to stand on."

"I heard that!"

Lucas just giggled.

James exchanged a very male glance with the little boy. "Women do tend to get annoyingly sentimental when it comes to small, furry creatures."

Elizabeth kept her eyes on the stove, pretending to fix the tea. It had been so long since Lucas had met a man he could look up to and admire. She worried constantly that she was depriving him of something important by raising him herself, with only sisters for company. If she'd allowed any of her relations to take him in, he still wouldn't have had a father, but at least he would have had an adult male in his life.

"What's the biggest fish you've ever caught?" Lucas asked.

"On land or on sea?"

Lucas actually poked him in the arm when he said, "You can't catch a fish on land!"

"I meant on a pond."

The little boy's eyes grew wide. "You've fished on the sea?"

"Of course."

Elizabeth looked at him with a bemused glance. His tone was so matter-of-fact.

"Were you on a ship?" Lucas asked.

"No, it was more of a sailboat."

A sailboat? Elizabeth shook her head as she pulled some dishes out of the cupboard. James must have well-connected friends.

"How big was the fish?"

"Oh, I don't know. Maybe about this big." James measured a length of about two feet with his hands.

"Hells bells!" Lucas yelled.

Elizabeth nearly dropped a saucer. "Lucas!"

"I'm sorry, Elizabeth," Lucas said without much thought, and without even turning to face her. His attention never wavered from James as he asked, "Did he put up a fight?"

James leaned down and whispered something in Lucas's ear. Elizabeth arched her neck and strained her ears, but she couldn't make out what he said.

Lucas nodded somewhat glumly, then stood up, crossed the room to Elizabeth, and gave her a little bow. Elizabeth was so surprised that this time she did drop what she was holding. Thankfully, it was just a spoon.

"I'm sorry, Elizabeth," Lucas said. "It isn't polite to use such language in front of a lady."

"Thank you, Lucas." She looked over at James, who offered her a secret smile. He tilted his head toward the boy, so she leaned down, handed Lucas a plate of biscuits, and said, "Why don't you and Jane go and find Susan? And you may eat these biscuits on the way to town."

Lucas's eyes lit up at the sight of the biscuits, and he quickly grabbed them and left the room, leaving Elizabeth openmouthed in his wake. "What did you say to him?" she asked in amazement.

James shrugged. "I can't tell you."

"But you must. Whatever it was, it was terribly effective."

He sat back, looking terribly pleased with himself. "Some things are best left between men."

Elizabeth frowned playfully, trying to decide whether she ought to press him further, when she noticed a darkening stain near his eye. "Oh, I completely forgot!" she blurted out. "Your eye! I must find something to put on that."

"It will be fine, I'm sure. I've had far worse injuries with far less attention paid to them."

But she wasn't listening, as she shuffled hurriedly through her kitchen in search of something cool.

"You needn't go to any trouble," he tried again.

She looked up, which surprised him. He'd thought she was far too involved in her search to be listening, let alone responding to him.

"I won't argue with you about this," she stated. "So you might as well save your breath."

James realized she spoke the truth. Elizabeth Hotchkiss wasn't the sort to leave projects unfinished or responsibilities unmet. And if she insisted upon tending to his bruised eye, there was very little he—a peer of the realm, a man twice her size—could do to stop her.

"If you must," he murmured, trying to sound at least a little bit put out by her ministrations.

She twisted her hands around something in the sink, then turned around and held it out to him. "Here."

"What is that?" he asked suspiciously.

"It's just a wet cloth. What did you think—that I was going to slap Lucas's catch of the day on your face?"

"No, you're not angry enough today for that, although—"

She raised her brows as she covered his bruised eye with the cloth. "Are you intimating that you think you might someday anger me enough so that—"

"I'm not saying anything of the kind. God, I hate being fussed over. You merely— No, it's a bit to the right."

Elizabeth adjusted the cloth, leaning forward as she did so. "Is that better?"

"Yes, although it seems to have grown quite warm."

She jerked back a few inches and straightened. "I'm sorry."

"It's just the cloth," he said, not nearly noble enough to pull his gaze off of what was directly in front of him.

He wasn't sure if she realized he was staring at her breasts, but she let out a little "Oh!" and jumped away. "I can cool this off again." She did so, then held out the wet cloth. "You had better do this yourself."

He moved his gaze to her face, his expression as innocent as a puppy dog. "But I like it when you do it."

"I thought you didn't like to be fussed over."

"I didn't think I did."

That earned him a half-beleaguered, half-sarcastic, one-hand-on-hips pose. She looked rather ridiculous, and somehow at the same time amazing, standing there with a dishrag hanging from her hand. "Are you trying to convince me that I am your angel of mercy, come from heaven to—"

His mouth spread into a slow, hot smile. "Precisely."

She threw the cloth at him, leaving a wet spot in the middle of his shirt. "I don't believe you for one second."

"For an angel of mercy," he muttered, "you have a rather short temper."

She groaned. "Just put the cloth on your eye."

He did as she asked. Far be it from him to disobey her when she was in such a temper.

They stood regarding each other for a moment, and then Elizabeth said, "Take that off for one second."

He took his hand away from his eye. "The cloth?"

She nodded once.

"Didn't you just order me to put it back on my eye?"

"Yes, but I want to get a look at the extent of the bruising."

James saw no reason not to comply, so he leaned forward, lifting his chin and tilting his face so that she could easily look at his eye.

"Hmmm," she said. "It's not nearly as purple as I would have expected."

"I told you it wasn't a serious injury."

She frowned. "I *did* knock you to the ground."

He arched his neck a little farther, silently daring her to put her mouth within kissing distance again. "Perhaps if you looked closer."

She wasn't falling for it. "I'm going to be able to see the color of your bruise better by moving closer? Hmmph. I don't know what you're up to, but I'm far too smart for your tricks."

That she was too innocent to realize he was trying to sneak a kiss both amused and delighted him. After a moment of thought, however, he realized that it horrified him as well. If she was that ignorant to his true motives, what the hell was she going to do when faced with libertines whose aims were considerably less noble than his?

And she would, he knew. He might possess a rake's reputation, but he tried to live his life with a certain modicum of honor, which was more than he could say for much of the *ton*. And Elizabeth, with that moonbeam hair of hers, not to mention those eyes, and that mouth, and—

Hell, he hadn't meant to sit here and total up her attributes. The point was, she had no powerful family to defend her, and thus gentlemen *would* try to take advantage of her, and the more he thought about it, the less convinced he was that she would be able to make it to the altar with her purity—and her soul—intact.

"We're going to have to have another boxing lesson tomorrow," he blurted out.

"I thought you said—"

"I know what I said," he snapped, "but then I started thinking."

"How very industrious of you," she murmured.

"Elizabeth, you must know how to defend yourself. Men are cads. Scoundrels. Idiots, one and all."

"Yourself included?"

"Especially me! Do you have any idea what I was trying to do right then when you were inspecting my eye?"

She shook her head.

His eyes grew hot with fury and need. "If you'd given me one more second, just one more blessed second, I would have had my hand behind your neck, and before you could count to one, you would have been in my lap."

She made no comment, which, for some asinine reason he couldn't quite define, infuriated him. "Do you understand what I'm saying?" he demanded.

"Yes," she said coolly. "And I shall regard this lesson

as a critical part of my education. I'm far too trusting.''

''You're damned right about that,'' he grumbled.

''Of course, it does present an interesting dilemma for tomorrow's lesson.'' She crossed her arms and regarded him with an assessing look. ''After all, you told me that I must study the more, er, amorous aspects of courtship.''

James had a feeling he wasn't going to like what was coming next.

''You tell me I must learn to kiss, *and*''—here she shot him a look that was dubious in the extreme—''you tell me that you must be the one to teach me.''

James couldn't think of any words that might possibly present him in a flattering light, so he kept his mouth shut and tried to maintain his dignity by glowering at her.

''Now you tell me,'' she continued, ''that I should trust no one. So why should I trust you?''

''Because *I* have your best interests at heart.''

''Ha!''

As set-downs went, it was short, to the point, and remarkably effective.

''Why are you helping me?'' she whispered. ''Why have you made this bizarre offer of your services? Because it *is* bizarre, you know. Surely you must realize that.''

''Why have you accepted?'' he countered.

Elizabeth paused. There was no way to answer his question. She was a terrible liar, and she certainly couldn't tell him the *truth*. Oh, he'd have a fine time with that—learning that she wanted to spend one last week, or if she was lucky a whole fortnight, in his company. She wanted to hear his voice, and breathe his scent, and catch her breath when he drew too near. She wanted to fall in love and pretend it could last forever.

No, the truth was not an option.

"It doesn't matter why I've accepted," she finally replied.

He stood. "Doesn't it?"

Without even realizing it, she took a step back. It was so much easier to fake bravado when he was sitting down. But at his full height, he was the most intimidating male specimen she'd ever come across, and all her recent ramblings about feeling so comfortable in his presence seemed rather foolish and premature.

It was different now. He was here. He was close. And he wanted her.

That easy feeling had fled—the one that allowed her to be so true to herself in his company, to say whatever was on her mind without fear of embarrassment. It had been replaced by something infinitely more thrilling, something that stole her breath and her reason and her very soul.

His eyes never left hers. The rich brown color smoldered and darkened as he closed the distance between them. She couldn't blink, she couldn't even breathe as he drew ever nearer. The air grew hot, and then electric, and then he stopped.

"I'm going to kiss you now," he whispered.

She couldn't make a sound.

One of his hands settled at the hollow in the small of her back. "If you don't want me to, tell me now, because if you don't . . ."

She didn't think she moved, but her lips parted in silent assent.

His other hand slid behind her head, and she thought she heard him murmur something as his fingers sank into the silk of her hair. His lips brushed against hers, once, twice, then moved to the corner of her mouth, where his tongue teased the sensitive skin of the edge of her lips until she was forced to gasp her pleasure.

And all the time, his hands were moving, caressing her back, tickling the nape of her neck. His mouth moved to her ear, and when he whispered, she felt it every bit as much as she heard it.

"I'm going to pull you closer." His breath, and his words, were hot against her skin.

Some barely conscious part of Elizabeth realized that he was according her an uncommon respect, and she managed to find her voice long enough to say, "Why are you asking me?"

"To give you the chance to say no." His gaze—hot, heavy, and very male—swooped down over her face. "But you won't say no."

She hated that his confidence was not misplaced, hated that she could refuse him nothing when he held her in his arms. But she loved the crackling awareness that washed over her—a strange sense that for the first time in her life, she understood her own body.

And when he pulled her close, she loved that his heart was racing every bit as fast as hers.

His heat seared her, and she felt nothing but him, heard nothing but the rushing of her own blood, and a softly worded, "Damn."

Damn?

He pulled away.

Damn. Elizabeth stumbled backward, plopping into a chair that got in her way.

"Do you hear that?" James whispered.

"What?"

A murmur of voices. "*That*," he hissed.

Elizabeth shot up like a bullet. "Oh, no," she groaned. "It's Susan. And Lucas and Jane. Do I look presentable?"

"Er, almost," he lied. "You might want to . . ." He made vague "fixing" motions around his head.

"My hair?" She gasped. "My hair! What did you do to my hair?"

"Not as much as I would have liked," he muttered.

"Oh dear oh dear oh dear." She scurried over to the sink, pausing only to look over her shoulder to say, "I have to set an example. I swore to God five years ago I would set an example. And look at me."

He'd been doing little else all afternoon, James thought glumly, and all it had gotten him was frustration.

The front door slammed. Elizabeth jumped. "Does my hair truly look mussed?" she asked frantically.

"Well, it doesn't look as it did when we arrived," he conceded.

She patted her head with quick, nervous movements. "I can't possibly fix it in time."

He chose not to answer. It was his experience that wise men did not interrupt a lady's toilet.

"There's only one thing to do," she said.

James watched with interest as she dunked her hands in a small pot of water that had been sitting on the counter. It was the same pot she'd used to wet the cloth for his eye.

The children's voices drew closer.

And then Elizabeth, whom he had previously considered a reasonably sober and rational human being, heaved her hands upward, splashing water all over her face, her bodice, and in all truth, all over him.

Her sanity, he decided as he slowly shook the water from his boots, was a question that clearly needed revisiting.

Chapter 12

"**H**eavens to St. Peter," Susan exclaimed. "What happened to you?"

"Just a small accident," Elizabeth replied. Her lying must have been improving, because Susan didn't immediately roll her eyes and snort her disbelief. Flinging the water had been a flawed plan, but certainly inspired. If she couldn't make her hair look any better, she might as well make it look worse. At least then no one would suspect that her disarray was due to James's fingers.

Lucas's small blond head turned this way and that as he surveyed the damage. "It looks as if we've been visited by the great flood."

Elizabeth tried not to scowl at his interference. "I was preparing a wet cloth for Mr. Siddons, who injured his eye, and then I knocked over the pot, and—"

"How come the pot is still standing up?" he asked.

"Because I righted it," Elizabeth snapped.

Lucas blinked, and actually took a step back.

"I should probably be on my way," James said.

Elizabeth glanced in his direction. He was shaking the water from his hands, and looked remarkably patient, considering that she'd just doused him without a moment's notice.

189

Susan cleared her throat. Elizabeth ignored her. Susan cleared her throat again.

"If I might have a towel first?" James murmured.

"Oh, yes, of course."

Susan cleared her throat again, a great big hacking sound that made one wish for a doctor, a surgeon, and a clean, well-lighted hospital. Not to mention a quarantine room.

"What is it, Susan?" Elizabeth hissed.

"You might introduce me?"

"Oh, yes." Elizabeth felt her cheeks grow warm at this obvious lapse of protocol. "Mr. Siddons, may I present my younger sister, Miss Susan Hotchkiss. Susan, this is—"

"Mr. Siddons?" Susan gasped.

He smiled and inclined his head in a most urbane manner. "You sound as if you know of me."

"Oh, not at all," Susan replied, so quickly that the veriest fool could tell she was lying. She smiled—a touch too broadly, in Elizabeth's opinion—and then quickly changed tack. "Elizabeth, have you done something new with your hair?"

"It's wet," Elizabeth ground out.

"I know, but it still looks—"

"It's *wet*."

Susan shut her mouth, then somehow managed to say, "Sorry," without moving her lips.

"Mr. Siddons must be on his way," Elizabeth said desperately. She jolted forward and grabbed his arm. "I'll see you to the gate."

"It was a pleasure meeting you, Miss Hotchkiss," he said to Susan over his shoulder—he couldn't have done it any other way, since Elizabeth had hauled him past all three younger Hotchkisses and was presently maneuvering him through the door to the hall. "And you, as well,

Lucas!" he called out. "We must go fishing someday!"

Lucas squealed with glee and ran into the hall after them. "Oh, thank you, Mr. Siddons. Thank you!"

Elizabeth had James practically to the front steps when he ground to a halt and said, "There is one more thing I have to do."

"What more could you possibly have to do?" she demanded. But he'd already wrenched free of her grip and strode back to the kitchen door. When she thought he was out of earshot, she mumbled, "It seems to me we've already done everything today."

He threw a wicked grin over his shoulder. "Not everything."

She sputtered and spluttered, trying to come up with an appropriately scathing retort, when he completely ruined the moment by melting her heart.

"Oh, Jane," he called out, leaning against the doorframe.

Elizabeth couldn't see into the kitchen, but she could picture the scene perfectly as her baby sister lifted her head, her dark blue eyes wide and wondrous.

James blew a kiss into the kitchen. "Goodbye, sweet Jane. I do wish you were a little more grown up."

Elizabeth let out a beatific sigh and sank into a chair. Her sister would be dreaming on that kiss for the rest of her girlhood.

The speech was overrehearsed, but the sentiment was certainly sincere. Elizabeth knew that she would have to confront James about their scandalous behavior, and she'd played out conversations in her head all night and into the following morning. She was still reciting her words as she tramped her way through the mud—it had rained the previous night—to Danbury House.

This plan—this strange, bizarre, incomprehensible plan

which was supposed to deposit her on the altar of marriage—it needed rules. Dictums of behavior, guidelines, that sort of thing. Because if she didn't have some idea what she was supposed to expect in James Siddons's company, she was liable to go mad.

For example, her behavior the previous afternoon was clearly the mark of a highly distracted mind. She had flung water all over herself in a fit of panic. Not to mention her wanton reaction to James's kiss.

She was going to have to assume a certain modicum of control. She refused to be some sort of charity case for his entertainment. She was going to insist upon repaying him for his services, and that was that.

Furthermore, he couldn't grab her and sweep her into his embrace when she wasn't expecting it. As silly as it sounded, his kisses were going to have to remain purely academic. It was simply the only way she was going to emerge from this episode with her soul intact.

As for her heart—well, that was probably already a lost cause.

But no matter how many times she tried to rehearse the little speech she'd prepared, it sounded wrong. First too bossy, then too weak. Too strident, and then too cajoling. Where on earth was a woman supposed to look for advice?

Maybe she should take just one more peek into HOW TO MARRY A MARQUIS. If it was rules and edicts she wanted, she'd certainly find them there. Perhaps Mrs. Seeton had included something about how to convince a man that he was wrong without mortally insulting him. Or how to get a man to do what you wanted while making him think it had all been *his* idea from the very beginning. Elizabeth was certain she'd seen something to that effect in her readings.

And if there wasn't, there sure as heaven ought to be.

Elizabeth couldn't imagine a more useful skill. It had been one of the few pieces of feminine advice her mother had passed on to her before she died. "Never take the credit," Claire Hotchkiss had told her. "You'll accomplish far more if you let him think he is the smartest, bravest, most powerful man in creation."

And from what Elizabeth had observed, it had worked. Her father had been utterly besotted with her mother. Anthony Hotchkiss hadn't been able to see anything else— including his children—when his wife walked in the room.

Unfortunately for Elizabeth, however, when her mother had been dispensing advice about *what* to do with a man, she had never seen fit to explain *how* to carry out that advice.

Maybe these things were intuitive to some women, but certainly not to Elizabeth. Good heavens, if she had been forced to consult a guidebook just to tell her what to say to a man, she certainly wouldn't know how to make him believe that her ideas were actually his.

She was still trying to master the most basic lessons of courtship. That seemed an advanced technique indeed.

Elizabeth stamped the mud from her feet on the outer steps to Danbury House, then let herself in the front door and scurried down the hall to the library. Lady D was still at breakfast, this area of the house was quiet, and that blasted little book was waiting. . . .

She kept her feet on the elegant runner carpet that extended much of the length of the hall. Something about the silence struck her as sacred—of course that may have had something to do with the endless bickering she suffered through during breakfast when Lucas and Jane had fought over whose turn it was to clean up. The second her feet touched the floor, there was a horrible clatter, echoing through the hall, and jangling her already frayed nerves.

She dashed into the library, inhaling the scent of the polished wood and old books. How she savored these brief moments of privacy. With a careful and quiet motion, she shut the door behind her and scanned the shelves. There it was, sitting sideways on the shelf where she'd found it days earlier.

Just one peek couldn't hurt. She knew it was a silly book, and that most of it was stuff and nonsense, but if she could find just one little scrap of advice that would help with her current dilemma . . .

She picked up the book and leafed through it, her fingers nimbly flipping the pages as she skimmed Mrs. Seeton's words. She bypassed the bit about wardrobes, and the nonsense about practicing. Maybe there was something toward the end—

"*What are you doing?*"

She looked up, painfully aware that her expression was one of a deer staring down the barrel of a hunter's rifle. "Nothing?"

James strode across the room, his long legs carrying him to intimidating closeness in only five steps. "You're reading that book again, aren't you?"

"Not reading, precisely," Elizabeth stammered. She was a complete ninny to be so embarrassed, but she couldn't help feeling like she had just been caught doing something most unsavory. "It was more of a browse."

"I find myself remarkably uninterested in the difference between the two."

Elizabeth quickly decided that the best course of action was a change of subject. "How did you know I was here?"

"I heard your footsteps. Next time, if you want to engage in acts of subterfuge, walk on the carpet."

"I did! But the carpet ends, you know. One has to step on the floor for a few paces to enter the library."

His brown eyes took on a strange, almost academic light, as he said, "There are ways to muffle— Oh, never mind. That is *not* the matter at hand." He reached out and snatched How to Marry a Marquis away from her. "I thought we had agreed that this was nothing but nonsense. A collection of drivel and claptrap designed to turn women into brainless, sniveling idiots."

"I was under the impression that men *already* thought we were brainless, sniveling idiots."

"Most are," he grunted in agreement. "But you don't have to be."

"Why, Mr. Siddons, you shock me. I think that might have been a compliment."

"And you say you don't know how to flirt," he grumbled.

Elizabeth couldn't contain the smile that welled up within her. Of all his compliments, the reluctant ones touched her the most.

He scowled at her, his expression turning almost boyishly petulant as he jammed the book back on the shelf. "Don't let me catch you looking at that again."

"I was only looking for a bit of advice," she explained.

"If you need advice, *I'll* give it to you."

Her lips pursed for a brief second before she answered with, "I don't think that's appropriate in this case."

"What the hell does that mean?"

"Mr. Siddons—"

"James," he snapped.

"James," she amended. "I don't know what has propelled you into such a temper, but I do not appreciate your language. Or your tone."

He let out a long exhale, appalled at the way his body

shuddered as he did so. His gut had been twisted in knots for nearly twenty-four hours, and all over this little slip of a female. She barely reached his shoulder, for God's sake.

It had started with that kiss. No, he thought grimly, it had started long before that, with the anticipation, the wondering, the dreaming of what it would be to feel her mouth beneath his.

And of course it hadn't been enough. It hadn't been nearly enough. He'd managed to fake nonchalance fairly well the previous afternoon—with the help of her pot of well-aimed water, which had certainly taken the edge off of his need.

But the night had left him all alone with his imagination. And James had a vivid imagination.

"I am in a temper," he finally answered her, avoiding an outright lie by adding, "because I did not sleep well last night."

"Oh." She seemed surprised by the simplicity of his answer. She opened her mouth as if to interrogate him further, then closed it.

Good for her, he thought harshly. If she expressed so much as a vague interest in why he didn't sleep well, he swore he'd tell her. He'd describe his dreams in every last explicit detail.

"I'm sorry that you suffer insomnia," she finally said, "but I do think we need to discuss your offer to aid me in finding a husband. I'm sure you realize that it is highly irregular."

"I thought we had decided that we weren't going to let that guide our actions."

She ignored him. "I need a certain measure of stability in my life, Mr. Siddons."

"James."

"James." She repeated his name, the word coming out

on a sigh. "I cannot be constantly on my guard, watching for you to pounce on me at any second."

"Pounce?" One corner of his mouth tilted up in a hint of a smile. He rather liked the image *pouncing* brought to mind.

"And it certainly cannot be beneficial for us to be so, ah . . ."

"Intimate?" he supplied, just to annoy her.

It worked. The look she threw at him could have shattered a window. "The point is," she said loudly, as if that could drown out his interference, "our aim is to find me a husband, and—"

"Don't worry," he said grimly. "We'll find you a husband." But even as he said the words, he became vaguely aware of a strange distaste in his mouth. He could picture his tutoring lessons with Elizabeth—picture each and every perfect little minute—but the thought of her actually achieving her stated goal of marriage left him slightly sick.

"This brings me to another point," she said.

James crossed his arms. One more point and he might have to muzzle her.

"About this work, and your willingness to help me find a husband—I'm not sure I'm comfortable being in your debt."

"You won't be."

"Yes," Elizabeth said firmly, "I will. And I insist upon paying you back."

The smile he gave her was so potently masculine it turned her ankles to water. "And how," he drawled, "do you intend to pay me back?"

"Blackmail."

He blinked in surprise. She took a little pride in that. "Blackmail?" he echoed.

"Lady Danbury told me that you are helping to uncover her blackmailer. I should like to assist you."

"No."

"But—"

"I said *no*."

She glared at him, and then, when he didn't say anything further, she said, "Why not?"

"Because it might be dangerous, that's why not."

"You're doing it."

"I'm a man."

"Oh!" she exclaimed, fisting her hands at her side. "You are such a hypocrite! Everything you said yesterday about respecting me, and thinking I'm more intelligent than the average female—was that just a heap of nonsense to get me to trust you so you could—so you could—"

"Respect has nothing to do with this, Elizabeth." He planted his hands on his hips, and she actually took a step back at the strange expression in his eyes. It was almost as if he'd become another man right there in the space of five seconds—one who'd done dangerous things, known dangerous people.

"I'm leaving," she said. "You can stay here for all I care."

He caught her by the sash of her dress. "I don't think we've concluded this conversation."

"I'm not so certain I want your company."

He let out a long, frustrated breath. "Respect doesn't mean that I am willing to put you in danger."

"I find it difficult to believe that Lady Danbury's nemesis is a dangerous individual. It's not as if she's being blackmailed for state secrets or the like."

"How can you be sure of that?"

She gaped at him. "She is?"

"No, of course not," he snapped. "But you hardly know that, do you?"

"Of course I do! I've worked for her for over five years. Do you really think Lady Danbury could be carrying on in a suspicious manner without my noticing it? Good gracious, just look how I reacted when she started napping."

He glared at her, his dark eyes brooking no argument. "You are not joining the blackmail investigation, and that is final."

She crossed her arms in return and said nothing.

"Elizabeth?"

A more cautious woman might have heeded the hard warning in his voice, but Elizabeth wasn't feeling terribly prudent at that moment. "You cannot stop me from trying to help Lady Danbury. She has been as a mother to me, and—" She choked on her words as he backed her up against a table, his hands closing around her upper arms with stunning intensity.

"I will bind you, I will gag you. I'll tie you to a damn tree if that's what it takes to keep your meddling nose where it belongs."

Elizabeth gulped. She'd never seen a man so furious. His eyes were flashing, his hand was shaking, and his neck was held so tensely that it seemed the tiniest tap could snap his head right off.

"Well, now," she squeaked, trying to pry his fingers loose. He didn't seem to have any concept of how tightly he was holding her—or even that he was holding her at all. "I didn't say I would meddle exactly, just aid you in certain, completely safe endeavors, and—"

"Promise me, Elizabeth." His voice was low and intent, and it was nearly impossible not to melt at the ferocity of feeling in those three little words.

"I—ah—" Oh, where was Mrs. Seeton when she needed her? Elizabeth had tried cajoling him out of his temper—she was fairly certain that was included in Edict

Number Twenty-six—but it hadn't had the least effect. James was still furious, his hands were still closed around her arms like twin vises, and God help her, but Elizabeth couldn't seem to take her eyes off his mouth.

"Promise me, Elizabeth," he repeated, and all she could do was watch his lips as he formed the words.

His hands tightened around her arms, and that, combined with some heavenly force, jolted her out of a trance, and she jerked her eyes up to meet his. "I won't do anything without consulting you first," she whispered.

"That's not good enough."

"It's going to have to be." She winced. "James, you're hurting me."

He looked down at his hands as if they were foreign objects, then abruptly released her. "I'm sorry," he said distractedly. "I didn't realize."

She took a step backward, rubbing her arms. "It's all right."

James stared at her for a long moment before swearing under his breath and turning away. He had been tense, and he had been frustrated, but he had never anticipated the violent flood of emotion she had unleashed. The merest hint of Elizabeth in danger, and he turned into a blithering idiot.

The irony was exquisite. Just last year he had laughed at his best friend when he'd been in a similar situation. Blake Ravenscroft had come completely unhinged when his future wife had attempted to take part in a War Office operation. James had found the entire situation vastly amusing. It had been clear to him that Caroline wouldn't be facing any real danger, and he'd thought Blake a besotted ass for raising such a fuss.

James could look at the present situation with enough objectivity to know that Elizabeth was facing even less danger here at Danbury House. And yet his blood coursed with fear and fury at the very mention of her involvement in the blackmail affair.

He had a feeling this was not a good sign.

This had to be some sort of sick obsession. He'd done nothing but think about Elizabeth Hotchkiss since he'd arrived at Danbury House earlier in the week. First he'd had to investigate her as a possible blackmailer, then he'd found himself thrust in the unlikely position of courtship tutor.

Actually, he'd thrust himself in that role, but he chose not to dwell on that point.

The fact was, it was only natural that he'd fear for her safety. He'd been cast as her protector of sorts, and she was such a tiny little thing; any man would feel protective.

And as for this need—the one that was raking his gut and firing his pulse—well, he was a man, after all, and she was a woman, and she was here, and she was really quite beautiful, in his opinion at least, and when she smiled it did strange things to his—

"Damn it all," he muttered, "I'm going to have to kiss you."

Chapter 13

Elizabeth had time to catch one short breath before his arms closed around her. His mouth met hers with a stunning mix of power and tenderness, and she melted—positively *melted*—into his embrace.

In fact, her last rational thought was that the word "melted" seemed to be popping up in her mind with increasing regularity. Something about this man did that to her. One of those heavy-lidded stares—the kind that hinted of things dark and dangerous, things she knew nothing about—and she was lost.

His tongue darted between her lips, and she felt her mouth opening under his. He explored her fully, caressed her deeply, made her breath his own.

"Elizabeth," he rasped. "Tell me you need this. Tell me."

But she was beyond words. Her heart was racing, her knees shaking, and some dim part of her knew that if she said the words, there could be no turning back. So she took the coward's way out, and arched her neck for another kiss, silently inviting him to continue his sensual exploration.

His mouth moved to the line of her jaw, then teased her ear, then moved to the tender skin of her neck, and all the while his hands were moving. One slid down to the curve of her buttocks, cupping it with exquisite tenderness as he gently pressed her hips against his arousal. And the other was moving up, over her rib cage, toward . . .

Elizabeth stopped breathing. Every nerve in her body was quivering with anticipation, aching with a clawing need she had never even imagined existed.

When his hand closed over her breast, it didn't matter that there were two layers of fabric between her skin and his. She felt burned, branded, and she knew that no matter what happened, part of her soul would belong to this man forever.

James was murmuring things, words of love and need, but she comprehended nothing other than the stark desire in his voice. And then she felt herself slowly falling. His hand at her back supported her, but she was descending to the soft carpet of the library floor.

He moaned something—it sounded like her name—and it was more of a plea than anything else. And then she was on her back, and he was covering her. The weight of him was thrilling, his heat breathtaking. But then he arched his hips forward and she felt the true extent of his desire for her, and her sensual trance was broken.

"James, no," she whispered. "I can't." If she didn't stop this now, it wouldn't stop. She didn't know how she knew this, but it was as true as her name.

His lips stilled, but his breathing was ragged, and he didn't move off of her.

"James, I can't. I wish—" She caught herself at the last second. God above, had she nearly told him that she wished she could? Elizabeth colored with shame. What sort of woman was she? This man was not her husband and he never would be.

"Just one moment," he said hoarsely. "I need a moment."

They both waited while his breathing steadied. After a few seconds, he lifted himself to his feet and, always the gentleman (even under the most trying of circumstances), held out his hand.

"I'm sorry," she said, allowing him to help her up, "but if I'm to marry—my husband will expect—"

"Don't say it," he snarled. "Don't say a damned word." He let her hand drop and turned forcefully away. Christ. He'd had her on the floor. He'd been within an inch of making love to her, of taking her innocence forever. He'd known it was wrong, known it was beyond wrong, but he hadn't been able to stop himself. He'd always prided himself on being able to control his passions, but now—

Now it was different.

"James?" Her voice came from behind him, soft and hesitant.

He said nothing, not trusting himself to speak. He felt her indecision; even though his back was to her, he could feel her trying to decide whether or not to say anything further.

But God help him, if she mentioned the word "husband" one more time . . .

"I hope you're not angry with me," she said with quiet dignity. "But if I must marry a man for his money, the least I can do in return is come to him as an innocent." A short burst of laughter welled in her throat; it was a bitter sound. "It makes all this a bit less sordid, don't you think?"

His voice was low and as steady as he could make it when he said, "I will find you a husband."

"Maybe that isn't the best idea. You—"

He whirled around and snapped, "I said I'd find you a damned husband!"

Elizabeth took a few steps backward to the door. Her mother had always said that there was no reasoning with a man in a temper, and come to think of it, she rather thought Mrs. Seeton had written the very same thing. "I'll just speak with you later on the subject," she said quietly.

He let out a long, shaky exhale. "Please accept my apologies. I didn't mean to—"

"It's all right," she said quickly. "Truly. Although perhaps we ought to cancel our lessons for the day, considering . . ."

He shot her a glance when she let her words trail off. "Considering what?"

Blast the man, he was going to make her say it. Her cheeks turned warm as she replied, "Considering that I've done all the kissing that could possibly be appropriate prior to marriage." When he didn't make a comment, she muttered, "Probably more."

He gave her a curt nod. "Have you the list of guests arriving tomorrow?"

She blinked, startled by the sudden change of subject. "Lady Danbury has it. I could bring it to you later in the afternoon."

"I'll get it myself."

His tone didn't invite further comment, so she left the room.

James had spent the entire morning scowling. He'd scowled at the servants, he'd scowled at Malcolm, he even scowled at the damned newspaper.

His normally easy stride was punctuated by stamps and tromps, and when he returned to Danbury House after a couple of hours in the fields, his boots made enough noise to wake the dead.

What he really needed was his aunt's bloody cane. It was childish of him, he knew, but there was something rather satisfying about taking out his frustration on the floor. But stamping his feet just wasn't enough. With the cane, he could pound a damned hole through the floor.

He barreled through the great hall, his ears unwillingly pricking up as he passed the slightly open door to the drawing room. Was Elizabeth in there? And what was she thinking as he stamped by? She had to know that he was there. She'd have to be stone cold deaf to miss the noise he was making.

But instead of Elizabeth's musical lilt of a voice, he heard his aunt's froggy boom. "James!"

James let out a nearly silent groan. If his aunt was calling him James, it meant that Elizabeth was not with her. And if Elizabeth was not with her, it meant that Agatha wanted to Speak With Him. Which never boded well.

He took a couple of steps backward and poked his head into the doorway. "Yes?"

"I need to speak with you."

How he managed not to groan he never knew. "Yes, I imagined as much."

She thumped her cane. "You needn't sound as if you're on your way to an execution."

"That depends on whose execution we're talking about," he muttered.

"Eh? What'd you say?" Thump thump thump.

He entered the room, his eyes doing a quick scan for Elizabeth. She wasn't there, but Malcolm was, and the cat quickly hopped off the windowsill and trotted to his side.

"I said," James lied, "that I want one of those canes."

Agatha's eyes narrowed. "What's wrong with your legs?"

"Nothing. I just want to make some noise."

"Couldn't just slam a door?"

"I've been outside," he said in a bland voice.

She chuckled. "Bad mood, eh?"

"The worst."

"Care to share why?"

"Not if you had a gun pointed at my heart."

That caused her to raise her brows. "You should know better than to raise my curiosity like that, James."

He smiled at her humorlessly and sat down in a chair opposite her. Malcolm followed and settled at his feet. "Did you need something, Agatha?" James asked.

"The pleasure of your company isn't enough?"

He wasn't in the mood to play games, so he stood back up. "If that's all, then I'll be going. I have duties I must carry out as your erstwhile estate manager."

"*Sit!*"

He sat. He always obeyed his aunt when she used that tone of voice. Some habits were very hard to break.

Agatha cleared her throat—never a good sign. James resigned himself to a long lecture.

"My companion has been acting very oddly of late," she said.

"Oh?"

She tapped the pads of her fingertips together. "Yes, quite unlike herself. Have you noticed?"

There was no way he was explaining the events of the past few days to his aunt. No way in hell. "I cannot say that I know Miss Hotchkiss very well," he replied, "so I cannot offer an opinion."

"Really?" she asked, her tone suspiciously casual. "I had thought the two of you had developed a friendship of sorts."

"We have. Of sorts. She's a most amiable young lady." The tips of his ears started to feel hot. If the blush spread to his cheeks, he decided, he'd have to leave the country. He hadn't blushed in a decade.

But then again, he hadn't been interrogated by his aunt in nearly that long.

"However," he continued, shaking his head slightly so that his hair would cover his ears, "it has been only a few days. Certainly not long enough to make a judgment on her behavior."

"Hmmph." There was an interminable moment of silence, and then Agatha's expression made an abrupt change and she asked, "How is your investigation proceeding?"

James blinked only once. He was well used to his aunt's sudden changes of subject. "It's not," he said bluntly. "There's little I can do until the blackmailer makes another demand. I've already spoken to you about your servants, and you assure me that they are all either too loyal or too illiterate to have hatched this scheme."

Her icy blue eyes narrowed. "You don't still hold Miss Hotchkiss in question, do you?"

"You will be happy to learn that I have eliminated her as a suspect."

"What else have you done?"

"Nothing," James admitted. "There is nothing to do. As I said, I'm afraid the next move is the blackmailer's."

Lady Danbury tapped the ends of her fingers together. "So what you're telling me is that you're forced to remain here at Danbury House until the blackmailer makes another demand?"

James nodded.

"I see." She settled deeper into her chair. "Then it seems all you can do is stay busy as my estate manager so no one guesses your true identity."

"Agatha," he said in a forbidding voice, "you didn't lure me here just to get an estate manager for free?" At her offended look, he added, "I know how tightfisted you can be."

"I cannot believe you would think that of me," she sniffed.

"That and more, dear aunt."

She smiled too sweetly. "It is always nice to have one's intelligence respected."

"Your cunning is one thing I would never underestimate."

She laughed. "Ah, I raised you well, James. I do love you."

He sighed as he rose to his feet again. She was a crafty old thing, and she had no compunction about meddling in his life and occasionally turning it into a living hell, but he did love her. "I'll return to my duties, then. We wouldn't want anyone thinking I'm an incompetent estate manager."

She shot him a look. Agatha never did appreciate sarcasm from persons other than herself.

James said, "You'll have to alert me if you receive another note from the blackmailer."

"The instant I get it," she assured him.

He paused at the door. "I understand you're having a gathering tomorrow?"

"Yes, a small garden party, why?" But before he could answer, she said, "Oh, of course. You don't want to be recognized. Here, let me get you the guest list." She pointed across the room. "Fetch me that box of papers on the desk."

James did as she bid.

"Good thing I made you change your name, eh? Wouldn't do for one of the servants to mention Mr. Sidwell."

James nodded as his aunt rifled through her papers. He was generally known as Riverdale, and had been since he'd ascended to the title at age twenty, but his family name was common enough knowledge.

Agatha let out an "Aha!" and pulled out a sheet of cream-colored paper. Before she handed it over, she scanned it, murmuring, "Oh dear. I can't imagine you don't know at least one of these people."

James read over the names, allowing his aunt to believe that his interest in the list lay with his desire to keep his identity a secret. The truth, however, was that he wanted to see the pool of men from whom he was supposed to choose a bloody husband for Elizabeth.

> *Sir Bertram Fellport.* Drunk.
>
> *Lord Binsby.* Inveterate gambler.
>
> *Daniel, Lord Harmon.* Married.
>
> *Sir Christopher Gatcombe.* Married.
>
> *Dr. Robert Gifford.* Married.
>
> *Mr. William Dunford.* Too rakish.
>
> *Captain Cynric Andrien.* Too military.

"This won't do," James growled, just barely resisting the urge to crumple the paper into a pathetic little ball.

"Is there a problem?" Agatha inquired.

He looked up in surprise. He'd completely forgotten that Agatha was in the room. "Do you mind if I make a copy of this?"

"I can't see why you would want to."

"Just for my records," he improvised. "It is very important to keep accurate records." In actuality, James was of the belief that the less put into writing, the better. There was nothing like written documents to incriminate a person.

Agatha shrugged and held out a piece of paper. "You'll find a quill and ink in the desk near the window."

A minute later, James had neatly copied the guest list and was waiting for the ink to dry. He walked back to his aunt, saying, "There is always the possibility that the blackmailer is among your guests."

"I find that highly doubtful, but you are the expert."

That caused him to raise his brows in amazement. "You're actually deferring to my judgment on a matter? Will wonders never cease."

"Sarcasm doesn't become you, m'boy." Agatha craned her neck to look at the paper in his hands. "Why did you leave off the women's names?"

More improvisation. "They are less likely as suspects."

"Hogwash. You yourself spent the first few days panting after Miss Hotchkiss, thinking—"

"I was *not* panting after her!"

"I was speaking metaphorically, of course. I merely intended to point out that you did originally suspect Miss Hotchkiss, so I do not understand why you should now eliminate all other women as suspects."

"I'll get to them once I go through the men," James muttered irritably. No one had the ability to corner him like his aunt. "I really need to get back to work."

"Go, go." Agatha waved her hand in the air dismissively. "Although it's a shock to see the Marquis of Riverdale tending to menial labor with such diligence."

James just shook his head.

"Besides, Elizabeth is due back any moment now. I'm sure she will be better company than you have been."

"No doubt."

"Go."

He went. In all truth, he didn't much relish the thought

of running into Elizabeth just then, anyway. He wanted time to go over the list first, to prepare his arguments concerning the unsuitability of most—that is, of *all*—the men.

And that was going to take a bit of work, since two of them were men James had always called friends.

Elizabeth was walking home later that afternoon when she bumped into James, who was leaving his little cottage. She had been tempted to take an alternative route to the main drive but had dismissed that as cowardly. She *always* walked past the estate manager's cottage when she walked home, and she wasn't going to go out of her way on the *off* chance that James *might* be at home instead of in the fields or visiting a tenant, or doing one of the thousand duties he was contracted to perform.

And then there he was, opening the front door of his cottage, just as she walked on by.

Elizabeth made a mental note never again to depend upon luck.

"Elizabeth," he practically barked. "I've been looking for you."

She took one look at his thundercloud expression and decided that now was an excellent time to develop a life-or-death emergency at home. "I'd love to chat," she said, trying to breeze past him, "but Lucas is ill, and Jane—"

"He didn't look ill yesterday."

She tried to smile sweetly, but it was a difficult maneuver while her teeth were gritted together. "Children can fall ill so quickly. If you'll excuse me."

He grabbed her arm. "If he were truly ill, then you would not have come to work today."

Oh, blast. He had her there. "I didn't say he was desperately ill," she ground out, "but I'd like to tend to him, and—"

"If he isn't desperately ill, then surely you can spare two minutes for me." And then, before she had a chance even to yelp, he'd grabbed her by the elbow and yanked her into his cottage.

"Mr. Siddons!" she shrieked.

He kicked the door shut. "I thought we'd gotten past 'Mr. Siddons.' "

"We've regressed," she hissed. "Let me out."

"Stop acting like I'm about to ravish you."

She glared at him. "I don't see why that seems such an impossibility."

"Good God," he said, raking his hand through his hair. "When did you develop these termagant tendencies?"

"When you forced me into your cottage!"

"I certainly wouldn't have done so if you hadn't started lying about your brother."

Her mouth fell open, and she let out a little huff of outrage. "How dare you accuse me of lying!"

"Aren't you?"

"Well, yes," she admitted testily, "but that is only because you are a rude, arrogant boor who refuses to accept no for an answer."

"Refusing to accept the negative usually guarantees a positive result," he replied, his voice so condescending that Elizabeth had to grab on to her skirt just to keep from smacking him.

Her voice and her eyes pure ice, she said, "It appears my only escape is allowing you to speak your piece. What was it you desired to say?"

He shook a piece of paper in front of her. "I obtained this from Lady Danbury."

"Your notice of termination, I hope," she muttered.

He let that one pass. "It's Lady Danbury's guest list. And I regret to inform you that none of these gentlemen is acceptable."

"Oh, and I suppose you know them all personally," she scoffed.

"As a matter of fact, I do."

She yanked the paper out of his hand, ripping a small corner off in the process. "Oh, please," she said derisively. "There are two lords and a sir. How could you know all of them?"

"Your brother is a sir," he reminded her.

"Yes, well, your brother is not," she shot back.

"You don't know that."

Her head jerked up. "*Who are you?*"

"My brother isn't a sir," he said in an annoyed voice. "I don't even *have* a brother. I was merely pointing out that you have the unfortunate habit of leaping to assumptions without sorting through your facts."

"What," she said, so slowly that he knew her temper was hanging by a frayed thread, "is wrong with these men?"

"Three of them are married."

Her jaw shook, probably from grinding her teeth together. "What is wrong with the unmarried guests?"

"Well, for one thing, this one"—he pointed to Sir Bertram Fellport—"is a drunk."

"Are you certain?"

"I could not in all conscience allow you to marry a man who abuses spirits."

"You didn't answer my question."

Damn, but she was tenacious. "Yes, I'm certain he's a drunk. And a mean one, at that."

She looked back down at the torn paper in her hand. "What about Lord Binsby?"

"He gambles."

"Excessively?"

James nodded, beginning to enjoy himself. "Excessively. And he's fat."

She started to point again. "What about——"

"Married, married, and married."

She looked up sharply. "All three of them?"

He nodded. "One of them even happily."

"Well, that certainly bucks tradition," she muttered.

James declined to comment.

Elizabeth let out a long exhale, and he noticed that her sighs were bridging the gap from annoyed to weary. "That still leaves Mr. William Dunford and Captain Cynric Andrien. I suppose one is deformed and the other a simpleton?"

He was sorely tempted to agree with her, but one look at Dunford and the captain and she'd know he'd been bamming her. "They are both considered to be handsome and intelligent," he admitted.

"Then what is the problem?"

"Dunford's a rake."

"So?"

"He's certain to be unfaithful."

"I'm hardly a prize, James. I can't expect perfection."

His eyes glowed hot. "You should expect fidelity. You should *demand* it."

She stared at him in disbelief. "It would be lovely, I'm sure, but it hardly seems as important as——"

"Your husband," he growled, "will remain faithful to you or he will answer to me."

Elizabeth's eyes bugged out, her mouth fell open, and then she collapsed into a fit of giggles.

James crossed his arms and glared at her. He was not accustomed to having his shows of gallantry laughed at.

"Oh, James," she gasped, "I'm so sorry, and that was very sweet of you. Almost"—she wiped her eye—

"sweet enough for me to forgive you for abducting me."

"I didn't abduct you," he said sullenly.

She waved her hand. "How on earth do you expect to defend my honor once I'm married?"

"You're not marrying Dunford," he muttered.

"If you say so," she said, so seriously and so carefully that he knew she was dying to laugh again. "Now, then, why don't you tell me what is wrong with Captain Andrien?"

There was a long pause. A really long pause. Finally James blurted out, "He stoops."

Another pause. "You're ruling him out because he stoops?" she asked incredulously.

"It's a sign of inner weakness."

"I see."

James realized that Andrien was going to have to do more than stoop. "Not to mention," he added, stalling while he tried to think up a suitable fib, "that I once saw him yell at his mother in public."

Elizabeth clearly couldn't manage a reply. Whether that was due to suppressed laughter or utter stupefaction, James didn't know.

And he wasn't entirely certain he wanted to find out.

"Er, it was most disrespectful," he added.

Without warning, she reached out and touched his forehead. "Do you have a fever? I think you have a fever."

"I don't have a fever."

"You're acting like you have a fever."

"Are you going to put me to bed and tend to me with loving kindness if I have a fever?"

"No."

"Then I don't have a fever."

She took a step back. "In that case, I had better go."

James sagged against the wall, utterly worn out. She did this to him, he realized. If he wasn't grinning like an idiot, he was furious. If he wasn't furious, he was overcome with lust. If he wasn't overcome with lust—

Well, that was a moot question, wasn't it?

He watched her as she swung the door open, mesmerized by the delicate curve of her gloved hand.

"James? James?"

Startled, he lifted his head.

"Are you certain Captain Andrien stoops?"

He nodded, knowing he'd be proven a liar the next day but hoping he could devise another, more clever lie to patch up this one.

She pursed her lips.

His gut clenched, then did a flip.

"Doesn't that seem odd to you? A military man who stoops?"

He shrugged helplessly. "I told you not to marry him."

She made a funny little sound from the back of her throat. "I can improve his posture."

He could only shake his head. "You're a remarkable woman, Elizabeth Hotchkiss."

She gave him a nod, then walked out the door. Before she shut it, however, she poked her head back in. "Oh, James?"

He looked up.

"Stand up straight."

Chapter 14

The following afternoon found Elizabeth skulking near the front gates of Danbury House, cursing at herself first for her idiocy, then for her cowardice, and finally just because.

She'd followed Susan's advice and left her notebook—the one in which she scribbled all of her household accounts—at Danbury House the day before. Since the notebook was so essential to everyday life, she was required to retrieve it during the garden party.

"There is nothing suspicious about my presence here," she said to herself. "I forgot my notebook. I need my notebook. I can't possibly survive until Monday without it."

Of course that didn't explain why she had brought the notebook—which had never before left the Hotchkiss cottage—with her in the first place.

She'd waited until nearly four, when the guests would probably be outside enjoying the warm country sunshine. Lady Danbury had mentioned tennis and tea on the south lawn. It wasn't precisely on the route Elizabeth would need to take in order to retrieve her notebook, but there was no reason that she could not make a special trip to find Lady Danbury to ask her if she'd seen the notebook.

No reason except her pride.

God, Elizabeth hated this. She felt so desperate, so grasping. Every time the wind blew, she was certain it was her parents up in heaven, retching as they watched her debase herself. How horrified they would be to see her this way, making up flimsy excuses just to attend a party to which she had not been invited.

And all this just to make the acquaintance of a man who probably stooped.

She groaned. She'd been standing at the front gate, leaning her head against the bars for twenty minutes. If she waited here much longer, she was liable to slip through and get her head stuck, just like Cedric Danbury at Windsor Castle.

There could be no more putting it off. Holding her chin up and shoulders back, she marched forward, purposefully skirting the area near James's cottage. The last thing she needed right now was an audience with him.

She slipped through the front door of Danbury House, her ears perked for party noise, but all she heard was silence. The notebook was in the library, but she was pretending she didn't know that, so she moved through the house to the French doors leading out to the back terrace.

Sure enough, a dozen or so stylishly clad ladies and gentlemen were milling about on the lawn. A couple of them were holding tennis racquets, some were sipping punch, and they all were laughing and chattering away.

Elizabeth bit her lip. Even their voices sounded elegant.

She nudged out onto the terrace. She had a feeling she looked as timid as a mouse, but that was really of no matter. No one would expect Lady Danbury's companion to stride brazenly into the party.

Lady D was holding court at the far side of the terrace,

sitting in an overstuffed chair that Elizabeth recognized as belonging to the blue room. The velvet-covered monstrosity was the only piece of indoor furniture that had been removed to the terrace, and it definitely played the part of a throne, which Elizabeth imagined was Lady D's intention. Two ladies and a gentleman sat with her. The ladies were nodding attentively at every word, the gentleman's eyes were glazed over, and no one seemed to think it odd that Malcolm was laying on Lady D's lap, belly up with his paws splayed out like an X. He looked like a little kitty corpse, but Lady Danbury had assured Elizabeth time and again that his spine was fantastically flexible and that he actually liked the position.

Elizabeth edged a little closer, trying to make out Lady D's words so that she could interrupt at the least disruptful moment. It wasn't very difficult to follow the conversation; it was more of a monologue than anything else, with Lady Danbury as the star player.

She was just about to step forward and try to catch Lady Danbury's attention when she felt someone grasp her elbow. Whirling around, she found herself face-to-face with the most beautiful man she'd ever seen. Golden hair, cerulean eyes—"handsome" was far too rugged an adjective to describe him. This man had the face of an angel.

"More punch, if you please," he said, handing her his cup.

"Oh, no, I'm sorry, you don't understand. I—"

"Now." He smacked her on the rump.

Elizabeth felt her color rise, and she thrust his punch glass back at him. "You are mistaken. If you'll excuse me."

The blond man's eyes narrowed dangerously, and Elizabeth felt a wary shiver scoot down her spine. This wasn't a man to cross—although one had to think that even the most ill-tempered sorts couldn't get that upset over a glass of punch.

With a little shrug, she dismissed the incident from her mind and made her way to Lady Danbury, who looked up at her in surprise. "Elizabeth!" she exclaimed. "Whatever are you doing here?"

Elizabeth schooled her features into what she hoped was a winsome, apologetic sort of smile. After all, she had an audience. "I'm terribly sorry to disturb you, Lady Danbury."

"Nonsense. What is the matter? Is there a problem at home?"

"No, no, it's nothing so dreadful." She stole a glance at the gentleman at Lady Danbury's side. His coloring was rather like James's, and they seemed to be of a similar age, but his eyes somehow looked years younger.

James had seen things. Dark things. It was there in his eyes, when he thought she wasn't watching him.

But she had to stop fantasizing about James. There was nothing wrong with this gentleman here. Looking at him objectively, she had to admit that he was devastatingly handsome. And he definitely didn't stoop.

He just wasn't James.

Elizabeth gave her head a mental shake. "I fear I've left my notebook here," she said, looking back at Lady Danbury. "Have you seen it? I do require it before Monday."

Lady D shook her head as she sank her hand into Malcolm's copious ecru fur and rubbed his belly. "I cannot say that I have. Are you certain you brought it? I've never known you to bring that sort of thing before."

"I'm certain." Elizabeth swallowed, wondering why the truth felt so much like a lie.

"I wish I could help you," Lady Danbury said, "but I do have guests. Perhaps you would like to conduct a search on your own. There cannot be more than five or six rooms where you are likely to find it. And the servants know you have free rein of the house.''

Elizabeth straightened and nodded. She'd been dismissed. ''I'll go look right now.''

Suddenly the man standing next to Lady Danbury jumped forward. ''I'd be happy to assist.''

''But you can't leave,'' one of the ladies whined.

Elizabeth watched the tableau with interest. It was clear why the ladies had been so interested in remaining at Lady D's side.

''Dunford,'' Lady Danbury barked, ''I was just telling you about my audience with the Russian countess.''

''Oh, I've met her already,'' he said with a wicked grin.

Elizabeth's mouth fell open. She'd never met anyone who couldn't be cowed into submission by Lady Danbury. And that smile—good God, she'd never seen anything like it. This man had clearly broken *many* hearts.

''Besides,'' he continued, ''I rather fancy a good treasure hunt.''

Lady Danbury frowned. ''I suppose I had better introduce you, then. Mr. Dunford, this is my companion, Miss Hotchkiss. And these two ladies are Miss and Mrs. Corbishley.''

Dunford looped his arm through Elizabeth's. ''Excellent. I'm sure we shall find that errant notebook in no time.''

''You really needn't—''

''Nonsense. I cannot resist a damsel in distress.''

''It's hardly distress,'' Miss Corbishley said in a waspish voice. ''She lost her notebook, for goodness' sake.''

But Dunford had already whisked Elizabeth away, through the terrace doors and into the house.

Lady Danbury frowned.

Miss Corbishley glared at the terrace doors as if she were trying to set the house on fire.

Mrs. Corbishley, who rarely saw reason to hold her tongue, said, "I'd dismiss that woman, were I you. She's far too forward."

Lady Danbury fixed her with a scathing glance. "And on what do you base that assumption?"

"Why, just look at the way—"

"I have known Miss Hotchkiss longer than I have known you, Mrs. Corbishley."

"Yes," she replied, the corners of her mouth pinching in a most unattractive manner, "but I am a Corbishley. You know my people."

"Yes," Lady Danbury snapped, "and I never liked your people. Hand me my cane."

Mrs. Corbishley was too shocked to comply, but her daughter had the presence of mind to grab the cane and thrust it into Lady Danbury's hands.

"Well, I never!" Mrs. Corbishley sputtered.

Thump! Lady Danbury rose to her feet.

"Where are you going?" Miss Corbishley asked.

When Lady Danbury answered, her voice sounded distracted. "I have to talk with someone. I have to talk with someone right away."

And then she hobbled off, moving faster than she had in years.

"You do realize," Mr. Dunford said, "that I shall be in your debt until the day I die?"

"That's a very long promise to make, Mr. Dunford," Elizabeth replied, her voice tinged with amusement.

"Just Dunford, if you please. I haven't been called Mister in years."

She couldn't help but smile. There was something uncommonly friendly about this man. It had been Elizabeth's experience that those blessed with amazingly good looks tended to be cursed with amazingly bad temperaments, but Dunford seemed to be the exception that proved the rule. He'd make a fine husband, she decided, if she could get him to ask her.

"Very well, then," she said. "Just Dunford. And who were you trying to escape? Lady Danbury?"

"Good God, no. Agatha is always good for an entertaining evening."

"Miss Corbishley? She did seem interested. . . ."

Dunford shuddered. "Not half so interested as her mother."

"Ah."

He quirked a brow. "I gather you're acquainted with the type."

A little burst of horrified laughter escaped her lips. Good God, she *was* that type.

"I'd give an entire guinea for *those* thoughts," Dunford said.

Elizabeth shook her head, not certain whether to continue laughing or dig a hole—and jump in it. "Those thoughts are far too expensive for—" Her head jerked. Was that James's head she'd seen poking out from the blue room?

Dunford followed her stare. "Is something wrong?"

She waved an impatient hand at him. "Just one moment. I thought I saw—"

"What?" His brown eyes grew sharp. "Or who?"

She shook her head. "I must be mistaken. I thought I saw the estate manager."

He looked at her with a blank expression. "Is that so very odd?"

Elizabeth gave her head a little shake. There was no way she was even going to *try* to explain her situation. "I . . . ah . . . believe I might have left the notebook in the sitting room. That is where Lady Danbury and I usually spend our days together."

"Lead on, then, my lady."

He followed her into the sitting room. Elizabeth made great pretense of opening drawers and the like. "A servant might have confused it with Lady Danbury's things," she explained, "and put it away."

Dunford stood by as she searched, clearly too much of a gentleman to pry too deeply into Lady Danbury's belongings. It didn't matter much if he did look, Elizabeth thought wryly. Lady D kept all of her important possessions locked away, and he certainly wasn't going to find the notebook, which was tucked away in the library.

"Perhaps it's in another room," Dunford suggested.

"It might be, although—"

A discreet knock at the open door interrupted her. Elizabeth, who'd had no idea how she was going to finish her sentence, gave swift and silent thanks to the servant standing in the doorway.

"Are you Mr. Dunford?" the footman asked.

"I am."

"I have a note for you."

"A note?" Dunford reached out one hand and took the cream-colored envelope. As his eyes scanned the words, his lips settled into a frown.

"Not bad news, I hope," Elizabeth said.

"I must return to London."

"Immediately?" Elizabeth wasn't able to keep the disappointment from her voice. He didn't make her blood rush like James, but Dunford was certainly marriage material.

"I'm afraid so." He shook his head. "I'm going to kill Riverdale."

"Who?"

"The Marquis of Riverdale. A rather good friend of mine, but he can be so vague. Look at this!" He shook it in the air, not giving her any opportunity to look. "I can't tell if this is an emergency or if he wants to show me his new horse."

"Oh." There didn't seem to be much else to say.

"And how he found me, I'd like to know," Dunford continued. "The man dropped out of sight last week."

"It sounds serious," Elizabeth murmured.

"It will be," he said, "once I strangle him."

She gulped to keep from laughing, which she sensed would be *very* inappropriate.

He looked up, his eyes focusing on her face for the first time in several minutes. "I trust you can continue without me."

"Oh, of course." She smiled wryly. "I've done so for more than twenty years already."

Her comment caught him by surprise. "You're a good sort, Miss Hotchkiss. If you'll excuse me."

And then he was gone. "A good sort," Elizabeth mimicked. "A good sort. A bloody good sort." She groaned. "A boring good sort."

Men didn't marry "good sorts." They wanted beauty and fire and passion. They wanted, in the words of the infernal Mrs. Seeton, someone utterly unique.

Well, not too unique.

Elizabeth wondered if she'd go to hell for burning Mrs. Seeton in effigy.

"Elizabeth."

She looked up to see James, grinning at her from the doorway.

"What are you doing?" he asked.

"Reflecting upon the sweet hereafter," she muttered.

"A noble pursuit, to be sure."

She looked up sharply. His voice struck her as a little too amiable. And why was it that *his* smile made her heart stop, when Dunford's—which, objectively speaking, had to be the most startling combination of lips and teeth in all creation—made her want to give him a sisterly pat on the arm?

"If you don't open your mouth soon," James said in an annoyingly bland voice, "you're going to grind your teeth to powder."

"I met your Mr. Dunford," she said.

He murmured, "Did you, now?"

"I found him quite pleasant."

"Yes, well, he's a pleasant sort."

Her arms straightened into two angry sticks at her sides. "You told me he was a rake," she accused.

"He is. A pleasant rake."

Something was wrong here. Elizabeth was certain of it. James seemed a bit too unconcerned that she'd met Dunford. She wasn't sure what sort of reaction she'd been expecting, but complete dispassion was definitely not it. Her eyes narrowing, she asked, "You're not acquainted with the Marquis of Riverdale, are you?"

He started choking.

"James?" She rushed to his side.

"Just a bit of dust," he gasped.

She gave him a pat on the back, then crossed her arms, too lost in her own ponderings to spare him any more sympathies. "I think this Riverdale fellow is a relation of Lady Danbury's."

"You don't say."

She tapped her finger against her cheek. "I'm sure she's mentioned him. I want to say he's her cousin, but maybe he's actually a nephew. She has scads of siblings."

James forced one corner of his mouth into a smile, but he doubted it was convincing.

"I could ask her about him. I probably *should* ask her about him."

He had to change the subject, and fast.

"After all," Elizabeth continued, "she'll want to know why Dunford left so suddenly."

James doubted that. Agatha was the one who'd hunted him down and demanded he get Dunford—that unscrupulous rake, she'd called him—away from Elizabeth.

"Perhaps I ought to find her right now."

Without even a second's pause, he starting coughing again. The only other way to keep her from leaving the room was to grab her and ravish her on the floor, and he had a feeling she wouldn't consider that appropriate behavior.

Well, perhaps that wasn't the only other way, but it was certainly the one that held the most appeal.

"James?" she asked, concern clouding her sapphire eyes. "Are you certain you're all right?"

He nodded, wrenching out a few more coughs.

"You really don't sound well." She laid a warm, gentle hand on his cheek.

James sucked in his breath. She was standing close, far too close, and he could feel his body growing tight.

She moved her hand to his forehead. "You look rather queer," she murmured, "although you don't feel warm."

He said, "I'm fine," but it came out halfway on a gasp.

"I could ring for tea."

He shook his head quickly. "Not necessary. I'm—" He coughed. "I'll be fine." He smiled weakly. "See?"

"Are you sure?" She drew her hand back and studied

him. With each blink, that cloudy, unfocused look disappeared from her eyes, to be replaced with a brisk air of utter competence.

Pity. The cloudy, unfocused look was a much better prelude to a kiss.

"You're well?" she reiterated.

James nodded.

"Well, if that's the case," she said, her voice exhibiting what he thought was a remarkable lack of concern, "I'm going home."

"So soon?"

One of her shoulders rose and fell in an oddly endearing shrug. "I'm not about to accomplish anything more today. Mr. Dunford has been called back to London by this mysterious marquis, and I doubt I'm going to wring a proposal from the blond Adonis who mistook me for a serving wench."

"Adonis?" Good God, was that his voice? He'd never known he could sound so peevish.

"Face of an angel," she elaborated. "Manners of an ox."

He nodded, feeling much better. "Fellport."

"Who?"

"Sir Bertram Fellport."

"Ah. The one who drinks too much."

"Precisely."

"How *do* you know these people?"

"I told you, I used to mix in higher circles."

"If you're such good friends with these people, don't you want to say hello?"

It was a good question, but James had a good answer. "And let them see how far I've fallen? Absolutely not."

Elizabeth sighed. She knew precisely how he felt. She'd endured all the village whispers, the pointed fingers and titters. Every Sunday she brought her family to church, and every Sunday she sat ramrod straight, trying to act as if she *wanted* to dress her siblings in outdated frocks and breeches that were perilously worn in the knees. "We have a lot in common, you and I," she said softly.

Something flickered in his eyes, something that looked like pain, or maybe shame. Elizabeth realized then that she *had* to leave, because all she wanted to do was wrap her arms around his shoulders and comfort him—as if a tiny woman like herself could somehow shield this big, strong man from the worries of the world.

It was ludicrous, of course. He didn't need her.

And she needed not to need him. Emotion was a luxury she couldn't afford at this point in her life.

"I'm going," she said quickly, horrified by the tang of huskiness she heard in her voice. She hurried past him, wincing as her shoulder brushed his arm. For the barest of seconds she thought he might reach out and stop her. She sensed him hesitate, felt him move, but in the end he just said, "I shall see you Monday?"

She nodded, and hurried out the door.

James stared at the empty doorway for several minutes. Elizabeth's scent still hung in the air, a vague mix of strawberries and soap. Innocent stuff, to be sure, but it was enough to set his body tightening and make him ache for the feel of her in his arms.

In his arms, hell. Who was he trying to fool? He wanted her under him, surrounding him. He wanted her on top of him, beside him.

He just wanted her. Period.

What the *hell* was he going to do about her?

He'd already arranged to have a bank draft forwarded

to her family—anonymously, of course. Elizabeth would never accept it otherwise. That ought to stop all this nonsense about her marrying the first able-bodied—and able-walleted—man she could get to propose.

But it would do nothing about the muddle *he* was in. When his aunt had chased him down earlier that afternoon and told him that Elizabeth had gone off with Dunford, he'd felt a rush of jealousy unlike anything he'd ever dreamed possible. It had squeezed around his heart, pounded through his blood, and left him half irrational, unable to think of anything other than getting Dunford out of Surrey and back to London.

London, hell. If he could have figured out a way to send Dunford to Constantinople he would have done it.

He was through trying to convince himself that she was just another woman. The thought of her in another man's arms made him physically ill, and he was not going to be able to carry off this charade of finding her a husband much longer. Not when every time he saw her he was nearly overcome with the desire to haul her off into a closet and ravish her.

James groaned with resignation. It was becoming clearer to him every day that he was going to have to marry the chit. That was certainly the only avenue that would offer his mind and body any measure of peace.

But before he could marry her, he was going to have to reveal his true identity, and he couldn't do that until he'd taken care of this blackmail business for Agatha. He owed his aunt this much. Surely he could put aside his own needs for one measly fortnight.

And if he couldn't solve this riddle within a fortnight— well, then, he didn't know what the hell he was going to do. He sincerely doubted he could last much longer than two weeks in his current state of distress.

With a loud and unapologetic curse, he turned on his heel and strode outside. He needed some fresh air.

Elizabeth tried not to think of James as she scooted past his cozy little cottage. She wasn't successful, of course, but at least she didn't have to worry about stumbling over him this afternoon. He was back in the sitting room, presumably laughing over the way she'd fled the scene.

No, she admitted to herself, he wasn't laughing at her. It would make things so much easier if he were. Then she could hate him.

As if the day weren't bad enough, Malcolm had apparently decided that torturing Elizabeth was more fun than listening to Lady Danbury lecture the Corbishleys, and the immense cat was presently trotting alongside her, hissing at regular intervals.

"Is this truly necessary?" Elizabeth demanded. "To follow me out just to hiss at me?"

Malcolm's reply was another hiss.

"Beast. No one believes you hiss at me, you know. You only do it when we're alone."

The cat smirked. Elizabeth would swear to it.

She was still arguing with the blasted cat when she drew alongside the stables. Malcolm was growling and hissing with complete abandon, and Elizabeth was jabbing her finger at him and demanding silence, which was probably why she did not hear the approaching footsteps.

"Miss Hotchkiss."

Her head jerked up. Sir Bertram Fellport—the blond Adonis with the face of an angel—was standing in front of her. Rather too close, in her opinion. "Oh, good day, sir." She took a discreet and, she hoped, inoffensive step back.

He smiled, and Elizabeth half expected a gaggle of cherubs to appear about his head, singing of angels on high. "I am Fellport," he said.

She nodded. She knew that already, but she saw no reason to inform him of this. "I am pleased to make your acquaintance."

"Did you find your notebook?"

He must have been listening to her conversation with Lady Danbury. "No," she replied, "I did not. But I am certain it shall turn up. These things always do."

"Yes," he murmured, his sky-blue eyes regarding her with uncomfortable intensity. "Have you worked for Lady Danbury long?"

Elizabeth inched back another baby step. "Five years."

He reached out and stroked her cheek. "It must be a lonely existence."

"Not at all," she said stiffly. "If you'll excuse me."

His hand shot out and wrapped around her wrist with painful force. "I don't excuse you."

"Sir Bertram," she said, somehow keeping her voice even over the pounding of her heart, "may I remind you that you are a guest in Lady Danbury's home?"

He tugged on her wrist, forcing her to move closer to him. "And may I remind you that you are in Lady Danbury's employ, and thus obligated to see to her guests' comfort?"

Elizabeth looked up at those stunningly blue eyes and saw something very ugly and cold. Her stomach knotted, and she realized that she had to get away *now*. He was pulling her toward the stables, and once he had her out of sight, there would be no escape.

She let out a scream, but it was cut short by the vicious clamping of his hand over her mouth. "You're going to do what I say," he hissed in her ear, "and afterward, you're going to say, 'Thank you.' "

And then all of Elizabeth's worst fears were realized as she felt herself being dragged into the stables.

Chapter 15

James had his hands shoved in his pockets as he made his way to the stables. He was indulging in a rare fit of sulkiness; it wasn't often that he had to deny himself anything he truly wanted, and putting off his pursuit of Elizabeth had left him in a bad mood.

The fresh air hadn't helped much, so he decided to take that idea to the next level and go for a ride. A breakneck, hell-for-leather, wind-whipping-one's-hair-into-knots-and-tangles sort of ride. As Agatha's estate manager he had free run of the stables, and if it was irregular for such a person to be galloping about like a wild man—well, James intended to be moving far too fast for anyone to recognize him.

But when he arrived at the stables, Malcolm was on his hind legs, clawing madly at the door and screeching like a banshee.

"Good God, cat. What has gotten into you?"

Malcolm howled, backed up a few steps, and head-butted the door.

That was when James noticed that the stable doors were closed, which was odd for this time of day. Even though the guests' horses had long since been rubbed down, and the grooms had probably all removed to the

Bag of Nails for a pint, one would think that the doors would have remained open. It was a warm day, after all, and the horses could use whatever breeze filtered in.

James heaved the doors open, wincing at the loud creaking of a rusty hinge. He supposed it was his job to take care of things like that. Or at least to see to it that someone else got it done. He tapped his gloved hand against his thigh for one moment, then headed for the supply closet to find something to grease the hinge. It wouldn't take too long to fix, and besides, he rather thought a bit of messy manual labor would do him good just now.

As he reached for the closet door, however, he heard the oddest sound.

No more than a rustle, really, but something about it didn't sound like it originated from a horse.

"Is anyone here?" James called out.

More rustling ensued, and it was faster and more frantic this time, accompanied by a strange panicked grunting noise.

James's blood ran cold.

There were dozens of stalls. The noise could be coming from any of them. And yet somehow he knew. His feet carried him to the stall in the farthest corner, and with a savage cry that was ripped from his very soul, he tore the stall door off its hinges.

Elizabeth knew what hell looked like. It had blue eyes and blond hair, and a vicious, cruel smile. She fought Fellport with everything she had, but at a hair over seven stone, she might as well have been a feather for all the effort he needed to drag her across the stables.

His mouth ground against hers, and she fought to keep her lips closed. He might be stealing her dignity and her control, but she would keep at least one part of herself from him.

He pulled his head away and pressed her up against a post, his fingers biting her upper arms. "I just kissed you, Miss Hotchkiss," he said in an oily voice. "Thank me."

She stared at him mutinously.

He yanked her toward him, then shoved her back against the post, grinning when her head cracked against the hard, splintered wood. "I believe you had something to say to me," he cooed.

"Go to hell," she spat. She knew she shouldn't provoke him; doing so would only cause him to lash out at her, but goddamn him, she would not allow him control over her words.

He glared at her, and for one blessed moment, Elizabeth thought he might not punish her for her insult. But then, with a furious grunt, he heaved her away from the post and threw her into an empty stable stall. She landed sprawled on the hay and tried to scramble to her feet, but Fellport was too quick, and too large, and he landed on her with a force that knocked the breath from her body.

"Leave me alone, you—"

His hand clamped over her mouth, and her head was twisted painfully to the side. She sensed the crisp hay digging into her cheek, but she felt no pain. She felt . . . nothing. She was leaving her body, her mind somehow sensing that the only way to get through this horror was to pull away, watch it from above, make that body—the one being abused by Fellport—not her own.

And then, just when the separation was almost complete, she heard a noise.

Fellport heard it, too. His hand tightened over her mouth and he went utterly still.

It was the creaking of the stable door. The head groomsman had meant to fix it yesterday, but he'd been called away on some silly errand, and everyone had been so busy today with so many guests.

But the creak meant that someone was here. And if someone was here, then Elizabeth had a chance.

"Is anyone here?"

James's voice.

Elizabeth thrashed as she'd never thrashed before. She found strength she'd never dreamed she possessed, grunting and squeaking under Fellport's hand.

What happened next was a blur. There was a loud cry—it didn't even sound human—and then the stall door crashed open. Fellport was lifted from her, and Elizabeth scrambled toward the corner, clutching at the ragged pieces of her dress.

James was a man possessed. He pummeled Fellport with brutal fists, and his eyes held a wild, feral look as he shoved the man's face into the hay.

"Do you like the taste of hay?" James hissed. "How do you like having your face pressed to the ground?"

Elizabeth stared at the two men in horrified fascination.

"Does it make you feel strong to hold her down, to abuse someone half your size? Is that it? You get to do whatever you want just because you're bigger and stronger?" James shoved Fellport's head farther down, grinding his face into the hay and dirt. "Ah, but I'm bigger and stronger than you. How does it feel, Fellport? How does it feel to be at my mercy? I could break you in two."

There was a harsh silence, punctuated only by James's ragged, uneven breathing. He was staring intently at Fellport, but his eyes looked strangely distant as he whispered, "I've waited for this moment. I've been waiting years to pay you back."

"Me?" Fellport squeaked.

"All of you," James ground out. "Every last one of

you. I couldn't save——'' He choked on his words, and no one breathed as the muscles of his face jerked.

"I can save Elizabeth," he whispered. "I won't let you take her dignity."

"James?" Elizabeth whispered. Dear God, he was going to kill him. And Elizabeth, God save her soul, wanted to watch. She wanted James to tear the man in two.

But she didn't want to see James hang, which would almost certainly be the outcome. Fellport was a baronet. An estate manager couldn't kill a baronet and get away with it. "James," she said, more loudly, "you must stop."

James paused, just long enough for Fellport to get a good look at his face. "You!" Fellport grunted.

James's body was shaking, but he held his voice low and steady as he said, "Apologize to the lady."

"That whore?"

Fellport's head slammed against the ground.

"Apologize to the lady."

Fellport said nothing.

And then, in a whir of movement so quick that Elizabeth couldn't quite believe her eyes, James pulled out a gun.

Elizabeth's breath caught, and her quivering hand flew up to cover her mouth.

There was a loud click, and James pressed the muzzle of the gun to Fellport's head.

"Apologize to the lady."

"I——I——'' Fellport began to shake uncontrollably, and he couldn't get the words out.

James moved the gun slowly, almost lovingly, against Fellport's temple.

"Apologize to the lady."

"James," Elizabeth said, terror evident in her voice, "you must stop. It's all right. I don't need——"

"It's not all right!" he roared. "It will never be all right! And this man will apologize or I'll—"

"I'm sorry!" The words exploded from Fellport's mouth, high-pitched and panicked.

James grabbed Fellport's shirt collar and hauled him off the floor. Fellport gasped as the fabric bit into his skin. "You will be leaving this party," James said in a deadly voice.

Fellport just made a choking sound.

James turned to Elizabeth, never once loosening his grip on Fellport. "I will be right back."

She nodded tremulously, clutching her hands together in an effort to stem their shaking.

James dragged Fellport outside, leaving Elizabeth alone in the stall. Alone with a thousand questions.

Why had James been carrying a gun? And where had he learned to fight with such deadly precision? James's punches hadn't been influenced by friendly, sporting pugilism; they had been designed to kill.

And then there were the scarier questions, the ones that wouldn't allow her heart to stop racing, her body to stop trembling. What if James hadn't come across them in time? What if Fellport had turned brutal? What if . . . ?

Life couldn't be lived according to "what ifs?" and Elizabeth knew she was only prolonging her misery by dwelling on what might have happened rather than what did, but she couldn't stop replaying the attack over and over in her mind. And whenever she got to the point where James had saved her, he didn't appear, and Fellport pushed further, tearing off her clothes, bruising her skin, taking her—

"Stop," she said aloud, pressing her fingers into her temples as she sank to the ground. Her tremors began to widen into shakes, and the sobs she hadn't allowed herself to feel began to well in her throat. She took deep breaths, trying to keep her traitorous body under control, but she wasn't strong enough to hold back the tears.

Her head fell into her hands, and she began to cry. And then she felt the oddest thing. Malcolm crawled onto her lap and began to lick away her tears. And for some reason that made her cry all the more.

James's interview with Sir Bertram Fellport was brief. It didn't require many words to explain what would happen to the baronet if he ever again set foot on Lady Danbury's property. And while Fellport was shaking with fear and resentment, James amended his threat to include Fellport's ever coming within twenty yards of Elizabeth, no matter her location.

After all, if James followed through with his plans to make her his wife, they would undoubtedly cross paths in London.

"Do we understand each other?" James asked, his voice terrifyingly calm.

Fellport nodded.

"Then get the hell off the property."

"I need to gather my things."

"I'll have them sent to you," James bit off. "Did you bring a carriage?"

Fellport shook his head. "I came with Binsby."

"Good. The town is barely a mile away. You can hire someone to take you back to London from there."

Fellport nodded.

"And if you breathe a word of this to anyone," James said in a deadly voice, "if you so much as mention my presence here, I will kill you."

Fellport nodded again, looking as if he wanted nothing more than to follow James's orders and leave, but James still had him by the collar.

"One more thing," James said. "If you mention me,

I will, as I said, kill you, but if you mention Miss Hotch-kiss . . ."

Fellport soiled himself.

"I will do it slowly."

James let go of Fellport's collar, and the baronet stumbled a few steps before running off. James watched him disappear over the gentle rise of the hill, then strode back into the stables. He hadn't liked leaving Elizabeth alone after such a traumatic experience, but he'd had no choice. He had to deal with Fellport, and he didn't think that Elizabeth wanted to be in the same room as the scoundrel for one moment longer than was necessary.

Not to mention that Fellport could have revealed James's true identity at any moment.

The minute James stepped into the stables, he heard her crying.

"Damn," he whispered, stumbling for half a step as he went to her. He didn't know how to comfort her, didn't have the slightest idea what to do. All he knew was that she needed him, and he prayed to God that he didn't fail her.

He reached the corner stall, the door still hanging drunkenly from its hinges. Elizabeth was huddled against the far wall, her arms wrapped around her legs, her forehead resting against her knees. The cat had somehow wedged itself into the hollow space between Elizabeth's thighs and torso, and, much to James's amazement, appeared to be trying to comfort her.

"Lizzie?" James whispered. "Oh, Lizzie."

She was swaying slightly from side to side, and he could see her shoulders rise and fall with each shuddering breath.

He knew that sort of breath. It was the one you drew when you were trying so hard to keep your feelings inside, but you just weren't strong enough.

He moved swiftly to her side, settling down next to her in the hay. Laying his arm around her slender shoulders, he whispered, "He's gone."

She said nothing, but he felt her muscles tense.

James looked down at her. Her clothing was dirty but not torn, and though he was fairly certain that Fellport had not managed to rape her, he prayed that his attack had not gone beyond a brutal kiss.

Kiss? He nearly spat out the word. Whatever Fellport had done to her, however much he had forced his mouth against hers, it had not been a kiss.

James's eyes wandered over the top of her head. Her white-gold hair was matted with straw, and even though he could not see her face, she looked so forlorn.

His hand clenched. It was rushing back—that familiar feeling of helplessness. He could feel her terror. It shook through him, coiled in his belly. "Please," he whispered. "Tell me what I can do."

She made no sound, but she huddled closer to his side. James tightened his embrace.

"He won't bother you again," he said fiercely. "I promise you."

"I try so hard to be strong," she gasped. "Every day, I try so hard. . . ."

James turned and grasped her by the shoulders, forcing her to lift her teary eyes to his. "You *are* strong," he said. "You're the strongest woman I know."

"I try so hard," she said again, as if trying to reassure herself of this. "Every day. But I wasn't strong enough. I wasn't—"

"Don't say that. This wasn't your fault. Men like Fellport . . ." James paused to gather a ragged breath. "They hurt women. It's the only way they know how to feel strong."

She didn't say anything, and he could see her struggling to hold back the sobs gathering in her throat.

"This—this violence . . . it is due to a defect in his person, not yours." He shook his head and squeezed his eyes shut for the barest of moments. "You didn't ask him to do this to you."

"I know." She shook her head, and her lips quivered into the saddest smile he'd ever seen. "But I couldn't stop him."

"Elizabeth, he is twice your size!"

She let out a long breath and pulled away from him, slumping back against the wall. "I'm tired of being strong. I'm so tired of it. Since the day of my father's death . . ."

James stared at her, searched her eyes as they went blank, and a very queer, foreboding feeling squeezed around his heart. "Elizabeth," he asked carefully, "how did your parents die?"

"My mother was killed in a carriage accident," she replied, her voice hollow. "Everybody saw it. The mangled carriage. They covered her body, but everyone saw how she died."

He waited for her to say something about her father, but she didn't. Finally, he whispered, "And your father?"

"He killed himself."

James's lips parted in surprise, and he was struck by a fierce and uncontrollable anger. He had no idea what had happened to make Elizabeth's father feel so desperate, but Mr. Hotchkiss had taken the coward's way out, leaving his eldest daughter to care for his family.

"What happened?" he asked, trying to keep the anger out of his voice.

Elizabeth looked up, a bitter, fatalistic sound escaping her lips. "It was six months after Mama's accident. He always—'' She choked on her words. "He always did love her best.''

James started to say something, but words were spilling from Elizabeth's lips with the speed of rushing water. It was as if he'd broken through a dam, and now she couldn't stem the flow of emotion.

"He just couldn't go on,'' she said, her eyes growing bright with anger. "Every day he'd slip further and further into some secret place that none of us could reach. And we *tried*! God, I swear to you, we tried.''

"I know you did,'' he murmured, squeezing her shoulder. "I know you. I know you tried.''

"Even Jane and Lucas. They would scramble onto his lap, just like before, but he'd push them away. He wouldn't hug us. He wouldn't touch us. And toward the end, he wouldn't even speak to us.'' She took a deep, sucking breath, but it did little to calm her. "I always knew he'd never love us as he did her, but you'd think he'd love us *enough*.''

Her fingers curled into a tight fist, and James watched with helpless sorrow as she pressed it hard against her mouth. He reached out and touched her fingers, feeling oddly relieved when they wrapped around his hand.

"You'd think,'' she said, her voice the saddest, tiniest whisper, "that he'd have loved us enough to *live*.''

"You don't have to say anything more,'' James whispered, knowing he'd be haunted forever by this moment. "You don't need to tell me.''

"No.'' She shook her head. "I want to. I've never said the words.''

He waited while she gathered her courage.

"He shot himself,'' she said, the words barely audible. "I found him in the garden. There was so much blood.'' She swallowed convulsively. "I've never seen so much blood.''

James held silent, wanting so much to say something to comfort her, but knowing there were no words to help.

She laughed bitterly. "I tried to tell myself it was his last act of caring, shooting himself in the garden. I made so many trips to the well, but at least the blood washed right into the ground. If he'd shot himself in the house, the Lord only knows how I would have cleaned it up."

"What did you do?" he asked softly.

"I made it look like a hunting accident," she whispered. "I dragged his body out to the woods. Everybody knew he was a hunter. No one suspected it was anything else, or if they did, they never said anything."

"You dragged him?" he asked in disbelief. "Was your father a small man? I mean, you're quite petite, and—"

"He was about your height, although a bit thinner. I don't know where I got the strength," she said, shaking her head. "Born of pure terror, I suppose. I didn't want the children to know what he'd done." She looked up, the expression in her eyes suddenly unsure. "They still don't know."

He squeezed her hand.

"I've tried not to speak ill of him."

"And you've been shouldering this burden for five years," he said softly. "Secrets are heavy, Elizabeth. They're hard to carry alone."

Her shoulders rose and fell in a weary shrug. "Maybe I did the wrong thing. But I panicked. I didn't know what else to do."

"It sounds as if you did exactly what needed to be done."

"He was buried in consecrated ground," she said in a flat voice. "According to the church—according to everyone but me—it wasn't a suicide. Everyone kept offering condolences, calling it such a tragedy, and it was all I could do not to scream out the truth."

She twisted her head to face him. Her eyes were wet and glistening, the exact color of violets. "I hated that he was made to sound a hero. I was the one to hide his suicide, and yet I wanted to tell everyone that he was a coward, that he had left me to pick up his pieces. I wanted to shake them and shake them and shake them and make them stop saying what a *good* father he was. Because he wasn't." Her voice grew low and fierce. "He wasn't a good father. We were nuisances. He only wanted Mama. He never wanted us."

"I'm sorry," James whispered, taking her hand.

"It's not your fault."

He smiled, trying to coax one from her in return. "I know, but I'm still sorry."

Her lips quivered—almost a smile, but not quite. "Isn't it ironic? You'd think that love is a good thing, wouldn't you?"

"Love *is* a good thing, Elizabeth." And he meant it. He meant it more than he ever could have dreamed he would.

She shook her head. "My parents loved too much. There simply wasn't enough left over for the rest of us. And when Mama was gone—well, we just couldn't take her place."

"That is not your fault," James said, his eyes searching hers with mesmerizing intensity. "There's no limit on love. If your father's heart wasn't big enough for his whole family, that means *he* was flawed, not you. If he'd been any sort of a man, he would have realized that his children were miraculous extensions of his love for your mother. And he would have had the strength to go on without her."

Elizabeth digested his words, letting them sink slowly into her heart. She knew he was right, knew that her father's weaknesses were his weaknesses, not hers. But it was so damned hard to accept it. She looked up at James, who was staring at her with the kindest, warmest eyes she'd ever seen. "Your parents must have loved each other very much," she said softly.

James drew back in surprise. "My parents . . ." he said slowly. "Theirs was not a love match."

"Oh," she said softly. "But maybe that's for the best. After all, my parents—"

"What your father did," James interrupted, "was wrong and weak and cowardly. What my father did . . ."

Elizabeth saw the pain in his eyes and squeezed his hands.

"What my father did," he whispered savagely, "should earn him a place in hell."

Elizabeth felt her mouth go dry. "What do you mean?"

There was a long silence, and when James finally spoke, his voice was very strange. "I was six when my mother died."

She held silent.

"They told me she fell down the stairs. Broke her neck. Such a tragedy, they all said."

"Oh, no." The words slipped from Elizabeth's lips.

James turned his head abruptly to face her. "She always tried to tell me she was clumsy, but I'd seen her dance. She used to hum as she waltzed partnerless through the music room. She was the most beautiful, graceful woman I've ever seen. Sometimes she'd pick me up and waltz with me resting on her hip."

Elizabeth tried to comfort him with a smile. "I used to do that with Lucas."

James shook his head. "She wasn't clumsy. She never walked into a sconce or knocked over a candle. He hurt her, Elizabeth. He hurt her every damned day."

She swallowed, her lower lip catching between her

teeth. Suddenly his uncontrollable rage at Fellport made a touch more sense. The anger was more than two decades old. It had been simmering far too long.

"Did he—did he hurt you?" she whispered.

He gave his head a little shake. "Never. I was the heir. He used to remind her of that all the time. She was worthless now that she'd given him me. She may have been his wife, but I was his blood."

A shiver rushed down Elizabeth's spine, and she knew he was quoting words he'd heard far too many times.

"And he used me," James continued. His eyes had grown flat, and his large, strong hands were trembling. "He used me to further his rages against her. He never agreed with her methods of parenting. If he saw her hugging me or comforting me when I cried, he flew into a fury. She was coddling me, he would yell. She would turn me into a weakling."

"Oh, James." Elizabeth reached out and stroked his hair. She couldn't help herself. She'd never known anyone so in need of human comfort.

"And so I learned not to cry." He shook his head despairingly. "And after a while I pulled away from her embraces. If he couldn't catch her hugging me, maybe he would stop hitting her."

"But he didn't stop, did he?"

"No. There was always a reason she needed to be put in her place. And eventually—" His breath whooshed out on a raw and shaky exhale. "Eventually he decided her place was at the bottom of the stairs."

Elizabeth felt something hot on her cheeks, and it was only then that she realized she was crying. "What happened to you?"

"That," James replied, his voice growing slightly stronger, "is perhaps the only bright spot in the story. My aunt—my mother's sister—came and snatched me away. I think she'd always suspected that my mother was mistreated, but she'd never dreamed it was as bad as it was. Much later, she told me that she would be damned if she was going to let my father start in on me."

"Do you think he would have?"

"I don't know. I was still valuable. His only heir. But he needed someone to abuse, and with Mama gone . . ." He shrugged.

"Your aunt must be a very special woman."

He looked over at her, wanting more than anything to tell her the truth, but he couldn't. Not yet. "She is," he said, his voice husky with emotion. "She saved me. As sure as if she pulled me from a burning building, she saved me."

Elizabeth touched his cheek. "She must have taught you how to be happy."

"She kept trying to hug me," he said. "That first year, she tried to show me love, and I kept pulling away. I thought my uncle would beat her if she held me." He raked his hand through his hair, a short, angry laugh escaping his lips. "Can you believe that?"

"How could you have thought anything else?" Elizabeth asked quietly. "Your father was the only man you knew."

"She taught me how to love." He let out a short, staccato breath. "I'm still not up to snuff at forgiveness, but I do know love."

"Your father doesn't deserve forgiveness," she said. "I have always tried to follow God's sermons, and I know that we're meant to turn the other cheek, but your father doesn't deserve it."

James was silent for a moment, and then he turned to her and said, "He died when I was twenty. I didn't attend the funeral."

It was the ultimate insult a child could aim at a parent.

Elizabeth nodded with grim approval. "Did you see him as you were growing up?"

"I had to on occasion. It was unavoidable. I was his son. Legally, my aunt hadn't a leg to stand on. But she was strong, and she cowed him. He'd never met a woman who stood up to him before. He had no idea how to deal with her."

Elizabeth leaned forward and pressed a gentle kiss to his forehead. "I shall include your aunt in my prayers tonight." Her hand drifted to his cheek, and she gazed at him with wistful regret, wishing there was some way she could turn back the clock, some way to hold that long-ago little boy and show him that the world could be a safe and loving place.

He turned his face into her hand. His lips pressed against her palm, seeking the warmth of her skin and honoring the warmth of her heart. "Thank you," he whispered.

"For what?"

"For being here. For listening. For just being you."

"Thank you, then," she whispered back. "For all the same things."

Chapter 16

As James walked Elizabeth home, he felt his life fall into focus. Since he had been forced out of the War Office, he had been floating more than actually living. He had been caught by malaise, knowing he had to move forward with his life but dissatisfied with the options that had presented themselves. He knew he needed to marry, but his response to the women in London had been almost uniformly lukewarm. He needed to take a more active interest in his lands and estates, but it was difficult to call Riverdale Castle home when he saw his father's shadow in every corner.

But in the space of a week, his life had assumed a new direction. For the first time in over a year, he wanted something.

He wanted someone.

He wanted Elizabeth.

He had been bewitched before this afternoon, enchanted and obsessed to the point where he'd decided he'd marry her. But something very strange and magical had occurred in the stable stall when he'd tried to comfort Elizabeth.

He'd found himself telling her things he'd held secret for years. And as the words had poured forth, he'd felt a hollow within him filling up. And he knew that he wasn't bewitched by Elizabeth. He wasn't enchanted, and he wasn't obsessed.

He needed her.

And he knew that he wouldn't find peace until he made her his, until he knew every inch of her body and every corner of her soul. If this was love, he gave himself up to it willingly.

But he could not abandon his responsibilities, and he would not break his promise to his aunt. He'd solve the mystery of this damned blackmailer. After all Agatha had done for him as a child, he'd solve this mystery for her.

Elizabeth loved Agatha. She would understand.

But that didn't mean that he would sit on his hands. He'd told Agatha that the best way to find the blackmailer was to wait for another note, and that was true, but he was tired of waiting.

He looked over at Elizabeth's face, took in those endless blue eyes and flawless skin, and made his decision. "I have to go to London tomorrow," he said abruptly.

Her head turned toward his in an instant. "London?" she echoed. "Why?"

"Some unpleasant family business," he replied, hating that he could not tell her the whole truth, but taking some comfort in the fact that his words were not precisely a lie.

"I see," she said slowly.

Of course she didn't see, he thought angrily. How could she? But he could not tell her. It was unlikely that Agatha's blackmailer might turn violent, but James could not completely discount that possibility. The only way to fully safeguard Elizabeth was to leave her in the dark.

"I'll be back soon," he said. "I hope within a week."

"You're not planning to pursue Fellport, are you?"

she asked, worry creasing her brow. "Because if you are—"

He pressed his index finger gently against her soft lips. "I'm not planning to pursue Fellport."

Her expression remained uncertain. "If you attack him again, you will hang," she persisted. "Surely you know—"

James silenced her with a kiss that was brief and yet full of promise. "Don't worry over me," he murmured against the corner of her mouth. He drew back, taking both of her hands in his. "There are things I need to do, items I need to take care of before . . ."

His words trailed off, and he saw the silent question resting in her eyes. "We will be together," he vowed. "I promise you."

In the end, he had to kiss her one last time. "The future looks very bright," he whispered, the words soft and sweet against her lips. "Very bright indeed."

Elizabeth held those words close to her heart ten days later, when there was still no sign of James. She wasn't certain why she was so optimistic about the future; she was still a lady's companion and James was still an estate manager, and neither of them possessed a cent, but somehow she trusted in his abilities to make the future, as he had put it, bright.

Maybe he was expecting an inheritance from a distant relative. Maybe he knew one of the masters at Eton and could arrange for Lucas to attend at a reduced rate. Maybe . . .

Maybe maybe maybe. Life was full of maybes, but suddenly "maybe" held a lot more promise.

After so many years of shouldering responsibility, she felt almost giddy at abandoning her constant sense of worry. If James said he could solve her problems, she

believed him. Maybe she was foolish, thinking a man
could swoop into her life and make everything perfect.
After all, her father hadn't exactly been a model of de-
pendability and rectitude.

But surely she deserved a little bit of magic in her life.
Now that she had found James, she couldn't bring herself
to look for pitfalls and dangers. Her heart felt lighter than
it had in years, and she refused to think that anything
might steal that bliss away.

Lady Danbury confirmed that James had been granted
a brief leave to visit his family. It was a singular boon
for an estate manager, but Elizabeth assumed that James
was given greater latitude and consideration due to his
family's slight connection to the Danburys.

What was odd, however, was Lady Danbury's near-
constant state of irritability. She may have given James
time to tend to his business, but she clearly had not done
so with great grace and charity. Elizabeth could not count
the number of times she'd caught Lady D grumbling
about his absence.

Lately, though, Lady Danbury had been too preoccu-
pied with her upcoming masquerade ball to defame
James. It was to be the largest ball held at Danbury House
in years, and the entire staff—plus the fifty extra servants
brought in just for the event—was buzzing with activity.
Elizabeth could barely make it from the sitting room to
the library (which was only three doors down) without
tripping over someone or other, racing to Lady Danbury
with questions about the guest list, or the menu, or the
Chinese lanterns, or the costumes, or . . .

Yes, costumes. Plural. Much to Elizabeth's shock,
Lady Danbury had arranged for two costumes. Queen
Elizabeth for herself, and a shepherdess girl for Elizabeth.

Elizabeth was not amused.

"I am not going to carry that crook around with me all night," she swore.

"Crook, ha. That's nothing," Lady D chortled. "Just wait until you see the sheep."

"*Whaaaat?*"

"I'm only kidding. Good heavens, girl, you must develop a better sense of humor."

Elizabeth spluttered a great deal of nonsense before finally managing to get out, "I beg your pardon!"

Lady D waved her hand dismissively. "I know, I know. Now you're going to tell me that anyone who has survived five years working for me must be in possession of an excellent sense of humor."

"Something like that," Elizabeth muttered.

"Or perhaps that if you didn't have a stellar sense of humor you'd by now have been killed by the torture of serving as my companion."

Elizabeth blinked. "Lady Danbury, I think you might be developing a sense of humor yourself."

"Euf. At my age one has to have a sense of humor. It's the only way to make it through the day."

Elizabeth only smiled.

"Where's my cat?"

"I have no idea, Lady Danbury. I haven't seen him this morning."

Lady D twisted her head this way and that, speaking as she scanned the room for Malcolm. "Still," she pontificated, "one would think I would receive at least a token more respect."

"I certainly don't know what you mean by such a comment."

Lady Danbury's expression was wry. "Between you and James, I shall never be allowed to grow too big for my britches."

Before Elizabeth could reply, Lady D turned back

around and said, "At my age it's my *right* to be too big for my britches."

"And what age would that be today?"

Lady D wagged her finger. "Don't be sly. You know very well how old I am."

"I do my best to keep track of it."

"Hmmph. Where's my cat?"

Since she had already replied to that question, Elizabeth instead asked, "When, ah, do you expect Mr. Siddons to return?"

Lady Danbury's eyes were far too perceptive when she asked, "My errant estate manager?"

"Yes."

"I don't know, drat the man. We're falling into complete ruin here."

Elizabeth glanced through the window at the endless pristine lawns of Danbury House. "You might be overstating slightly."

Lady D started to say something, but Elizabeth held up her hand and said, "And don't tell me that at your age it's your prerogative to exaggerate."

"Well, it is. Hmmph. Malcolm!"

Elizabeth's eyes flicked to the door. The king of Danbury House was padding into the sitting room, his fat paws moving silently across the carpet.

"There you are, sweetie," Lady Danbury cooed. "Come to Mama."

But Malcolm didn't even flick his café au lait tail at her. While Lady D watched in horror, her cat trotted straight to Elizabeth and hopped up on her lap.

"Good kitty," Elizabeth purred.

"What is going on here?" Lady D demanded.

"Malcolm and I have come to a rapprochement of sorts."

"But he hates you!"

"Why, Lady Danbury," Elizabeth said, pretending to be shocked. "All these years you have insisted that he's a perfectly friendly kitty."

"He's certainly a perfect kitty," Lady D muttered.

"Not to mention all the times you told me this was all in my head."

"I lied!"

Elizabeth slapped a hand against her cheek in mock disbelief. "No!"

"I want my cat back."

Elizabeth shrugged. Malcolm flipped over onto his back and stretched out with his paws over his head.

"Miserable traitorous feline."

Elizabeth smiled down at the cat as she rubbed the fur under his chin. "Life is good, eh, Malcolm? Life is very, very good."

Malcolm purred in agreement, and Elizabeth knew it had to be true.

Back in London, James was frustrated as hell. He'd spent well over a week investigating Agatha's life and had come up with nothing. He couldn't find a soul who even knew of anyone with a grudge against his aunt. Oh, plenty of people had plenty to say about her acerbic wit and direct manner, but no one truly hated her.

Furthermore, there was nary a hint of a whisper of scandal surrounding her past. As far as London was concerned, Agatha, Lady Danbury, had led an exemplary life. Upstanding and true, she was lauded the prime example of proper English womanhood.

Truth be told, he couldn't remember ever pursuing an investigation that was quite so boring.

He'd known that it was unlikely he'd find anything substantive; after all, the blackmailer had sought out his aunt in Surrey. But he'd unearthed no clues at Danbury

House, and London had seemed the logical next step. If Agatha's enemy had learned of her secret past through the *ton*'s brilliantly efficient gossip mill, then it stood to reason that someone in London would know *some*thing.

James had been bitterly disappointed.

There was nothing to do now except return to Danbury House and hope that the blackmailer had made another demand. This seemed unlikely, however; surely his aunt would have notified him if she'd received another threatening note. She knew where to reach him; he'd told her exactly where he was going and what he hoped to accomplish.

Agatha had argued bitterly against his leaving. She had been convinced that her blackmailer would be found in Surrey, skulking in the shadows of Danbury House. By the time James exited through the front door, Agatha had been in fine form, grumpy and sullen, more irritable than her cat.

James winced when he thought of poor Elizabeth, stuck in his aunt's surly company for the past week. But if anyone could draw Agatha out of her temper, he was convinced it was Elizabeth.

Three more days. He would devote no more time to his London investigation. Three days and then he would return to Danbury House, announce his failure to his aunt and his intentions to Elizabeth.

Three more days and he could begin his life anew.

By Friday afternoon, Danbury House was under siege. Elizabeth locked herself in the library for a full hour just to get away from the swarms of servants readying the mansion for that night's masquerade celebration. There was no escape from the frenzied activity, however; Lady Danbury had insisted that Elizabeth make her preparations at Danbury House. It was a sensible proposal, eliminating the need for Elizabeth to travel home and then return in full costume. But it also made it impossible for her to slip away for a few minutes of peace.

The time in the library didn't count. How could it count when no less than five servants banged on the door, requesting her opinion on the most inane of matters. Finally Elizabeth had to throw up her hands and yell, "Ask Lady Danbury!"

When the first of the carriages rolled down the drive, Elizabeth fled upstairs to the room Lady Danbury had assigned to her for the evening. The dreaded shepherdess costume hung in the wardrobe, accompanying crook leaning against the wall.

Elizabeth flopped onto the bed. She had no desire to arrive early. She fully expected to spend most of the evening by herself. She didn't mind her own company, but the last thing she wanted was to be *noticeably* by herself. Arriving while the party was a true crush meant that she could blend into the crowd. By then, Lady Danbury's guests ought to be too involved in their own conversations to pay attention to her.

But the guests arrived in a flood rather than a trickle, and Elizabeth knew Lady Danbury well enough to know that the countess would drag her downstairs by the hair if she put off her appearance much longer. So she donned the shepherdess costume, affixed the feathered mask Lady D had also purchased for her, and stood in front of the mirror.

"I look ridiculous," she said to her reflection. "Utterly ridiculous." Her white dress was a mass of tucks and frills, adorned with more lace than any shepherdess could afford, and the bodice, while certainly not indecent, was cut lower than anything she'd ever worn before.

"As if any shepherdess could run through the fields wearing this," she muttered, tugging at the dress. Of course it was unlikely a shepherdess would be wearing a feathered mask, either, but that seemed neither here nor there compared to the expanse of bosom she was showing.

"Oh, I don't care," she declared. "No one will know who I am, anyway, and if anyone tries anything untoward, at least I have this blasted crook."

With that, Elizabeth grabbed the crook and jabbed it in the air like a sword. Satisfactorily armed, she marched out of the room and down the hall. Before she reached the stairs, however, a door swung open, and a woman dressed as a pumpkin came dashing out—right into Elizabeth.

They both hit the carpet with a thud and a flurry of apologies. Elizabeth clambered to her feet, then looked back down at the pumpkin, who was still sitting on her behind.

"Do you need a hand up?" Elizabeth asked.

The pumpkin, who was holding her green mask in her hand, nodded. "Thank you. I'm a bit ungainly these days, I'm afraid."

It took Elizabeth a couple of blinks, but then she realized what the pum—the lady! she had to stop thinking of her as a pumpkin—meant. "*Oh, no!*" Elizabeth said, dropping to her knees beside her. "Are you all right? Is your . . ." She motioned to the lady's middle, although it was difficult to tell what was the middle under the pumpkin costume.

"I'm fine," the lady assured her. "Only my pride is bruised, I assure you."

"Here, let me help you up." It was difficult to maneuver the costume, but eventually Elizabeth managed to get the lady to her feet.

"I am terribly sorry for crashing into you," the lady apologized. "It's just that I was running so late, and

I know my husband is downstairs tapping his foot, and—"

"It was no trouble, I assure you," Elizabeth said. And then, because the lady was such a friendly pumpkin, she added, "I'm rather grateful to you, actually. This might be the first time I haven't been the cause of such an accident. I'm terribly clumsy."

Elizabeth's new friend laughed. "Since we are so well-acquainted, please allow me to be terribly forward and introduce myself. I am Mrs. Blake Ravenscroft, but I would be most insulted if you called me anything but Caroline."

"I am Miss Elizabeth Hotchkiss, Lady Danbury's companion."

"Good gracious, really? I had heard she could be quite a dragon."

"She's really very sweet underneath. But I shouldn't like to get on her bad side."

Caroline nodded and patted her light brown hair. "Am I mussed?"

Elizabeth shook her head. "No more mussed than one would expect of a pumpkin."

"Yes, I suppose pumpkins can be allowed greater latitude in neatness of coiffure."

Elizabeth laughed again, liking this woman immensely.

Caroline held out her arm. "Shall we go down?"

Elizabeth nodded, and they made their way toward the stairs.

"My stem is definitely off to you," Caroline said with a laugh, lifting her green mask in salute. "My husband spent quite a bit of time here as a child, and he assures me that he is still terrified of Lady Danbury."

"Was your husband friends with her children?"

"Her nephew, actually. The Marquis of Riverdale. I

hope to see him this evening, actually. He must be invited. Have you met him?"

"No. No, I haven't. But I heard a bit about him last week."

"Really?" Caroline began to step carefully down the stairs. "What is he up to? I haven't heard from him in over a month."

"I don't know, actually. Lady Danbury held a small garden party last week, and he sent a note asking one of the guests to meet him in London immediately."

"Oooh. How intriguing. And how very like James."

Elizabeth smiled at the mention of the name. She had her own James, and she couldn't wait to see him again.

Caroline stopped on a step and turned to Elizabeth with a very sisterly, and very nosy expression. "What is that about?"

"What?"

"That smile. And don't say you weren't. I saw it."

"Oh." Elizabeth felt her cheeks grow warm. "It's nothing. I have a suitor whose name is also James."

"Really?" Caroline's aquamarine eyes held the gleam of a born matchmaker. "You must introduce us."

"He isn't here, I'm afraid. He is Lady Danbury's new estate manager, but he was recently called to London. Some sort of family emergency, I believe."

"That's a pity. I already feel that we are the truest of friends. I should have liked to have met him."

Elizabeth felt her eyes grow misty. "That was such a lovely thing to say."

"Do you think so? I'm so glad you don't think me too forward. I wasn't raised in society, and I have the most appalling habit of speaking without thinking first. It drives my husband mad."

"I'm sure he adores you."

Caroline's eyes glowed, and Elizabeth knew that hers

had been a love match. "I'm so late he's likely to bite my head off," Caroline admitted. "He can be such a worrier."

"Then we had best be on our way."

"I cannot wait to introduce you to Blake."

"That would be lovely. But first I must find Lady Danbury and make certain she doesn't need anything."

"Duty calls, I suppose. But you must promise that we shall meet up again later this evening." Caroline smiled wryly and motioned to her costume. "I'm fairly easy to spot."

Elizabeth reached the bottom of the steps and unlinked her arm from Caroline's. "It's a promise." Then, with a smile and a wave, she dashed away from the ballroom. Lady Danbury would be out front receiving her guests, and it would be easier to scoot outside the house than to try to battle the crowds within.

"What the hell?" James followed that query with considerably darker and louder curses as he steered his horse around the crush of carriages slowly rolling toward Danbury House.

The masquerade ball. The bloody, annoying, inconvenient masquerade ball. He'd forgotten all about it.

He'd planned the evening to the last detail. He was going to go to his aunt, tell her that he'd failed, that he hadn't been able to flush out her blackmailer, and promise her that he would continue to try, but that he could not put his life on hold while doing so.

Then he would ride out to Elizabeth's cottage and ask her to marry him. He'd been grinning like an idiot the entire ride home, planning his every word. He had thought to take Lucas aside and ask him for his sister's hand. Not that James planned to let an eight-year-old dictate his life, but somehow the thought of including the little boy left his heart warm.

Plus he had a feeling that Elizabeth would be charmed by the gesture, which was probably his true motive in the entire affair.

But he was not going to be able to escape Danbury House this evening, and he certainly wasn't going to be able to gain a private audience with his aunt.

Frustrated with the clog of carriages, he nudged his horse off of the main road and cut through the lightly forested field that ran alongside the main lawn of Danbury House. The moon was full, and enough light spilled through the many windows of the mansion to light his trail, so he didn't have to slow down overmuch as he made his way to the stables.

He took care of his horse and trudged into his little cottage, smiling as he remembered the time he'd caught Elizabeth snooping there weeks earlier. He still hadn't told her about that. No matter; he'd have a lifetime to share and make memories with her.

He tried to ignore the sounds of the party, preferring the peace and seclusion of his temporary home, but he could not ignore the rumblings of his empty stomach. He'd rushed back to Surrey, eager to see Elizabeth, and hadn't stopped for so much as a bite of bread. His cottage, of course, held nothing edible, so he allowed himself one loud curse, and then trudged back outside. With any luck, he could make it to the kitchen without being recognized or waylaid by a drunken reveler.

He kept his head down as he weaved through the crowds spilling out onto the lawns. If he acted like a servant, Agatha's guests would see a servant and, with luck, leave him alone. Lord knew, they wouldn't expect the Marquis of Riverdale to be quite so dusty and rumpled.

He'd passed the edge of the crowd, and was about halfway to his destination, when out of the corner of his eye he saw a blond shepherdess trip over a rock, wave her left arm wildly for balance, and then finally right herself by jamming her crook into the ground.

Elizabeth. It had to be. No other blond shepherdess could be quite so enchantingly clumsy.

She seemed to be scooting along the perimeter of Danbury House, heading for the front. James changed tack slightly and headed in her direction, his heart soaring with the knowledge that she would soon be in his arms.

When had he grown into such a romantic fool?

Who knew? Who cared? He was in love. He had finally found the one woman who could complete his heart, and if that made him a fool, so be it.

He crept up behind her as she scurried toward the front of the house, and before she could hear his footsteps crunching along the gravel, he reached out and grasped her wrist.

She whirled around with a shocked gasp. James watched with delight as her eyes melted from panic to joy.

"James!" she cried out, her free hand reaching out to grab his. "You're back."

He lifted her hands to his lips and kissed them in turn. "I couldn't stay away."

Their time apart had made her shy, and she didn't quite meet his eyes when she whispered, "I missed you."

Propriety be damned. He gathered her into his arms and kissed her. And then, when he could actually force himself to tear his lips from hers, he whispered, "Come with me."

"Where?"

"Anywhere."

She went.

Chapter 17

❦

The night was hung with magic. The moon glowed bright, the air was dusted with the delicate scent of wildflowers, and the wind was a romantic whisper against the skin.

Elizabeth thought she must be a princess. The woman tearing across the field, hair streaming like a golden ribbon, could not be plain and ordinary Elizabeth Hotchkiss. For one night, she was transformed. For one night, her heart held no worries, no burdens. She was bathed in laughter and passion, enveloped by pure joy.

Hand in hand, they ran. Danbury House dipped out of sight, although the sounds of the party still drifted through the air. The trees around them grew more dense, and finally James stopped, his breathing heavy from exertion and excitement.

"Oh, my goodness," Elizabeth gasped, nearly crashing into him. "I haven't run so fast since—"

His arms snaked around her, and her breath stopped. "Kiss me," he ordered.

Elizabeth was lost to the night's enchantment, and any hesitations she might have had, any notions of what was proper and what was scandal, melted away. She arched her neck, offering him her lips, and he took them, his

271

mouth capturing hers in the sweetest mix of tenderness and primitive need.

"I won't take you. Not now—not yet," he vowed against her skin. "But let me love you."

Elizabeth didn't know what he meant, but her blood ran hot and fast in her veins, and she could deny him nothing. She looked up, saw the fire in his chocolate eyes, and made her decision. "Love me," she whispered. "I trust you."

James's fingers trembled as he brought them reverently to the smooth skin of her temples. Her hair was golden silk beneath his fingers, and she looked so achingly small and fragile beneath his large, suddenly awkward hands. He could break her, he realized. She was tiny and fine, and his to protect. "I'll be gentle," he whispered, barely recognizing his own voice. "I will never hurt you. Never."

She trusted him. It was a powerful, soul-changing gift.

He let his fingers trail lightly down the planes of her cheeks to the bare skin of her neck. Her costume was like nothing she'd worn before, teasing him with the hint of her bare shoulders, threatening to slip over and off with just the slightest nudge. He could hook his finger around the soft white fabric and reveal one delicate shoulder, and then the other, and then he could pull the gown ever downward, baring her—

Blood pooled in his groin. Good God, if he was growing this hard just *thinking* about undressing her, what the hell was going to happen when he actually had her naked and willing in his arms? How would he ever manage to make love to her with the gentleness and care she deserved?

His breath burning in his lungs, he slowly slid her gown over one shoulder, never taking his eyes off the skin he bared. She glowed in the moonlight like the rarest pearl, and when he lowered his head to nuzzle the warm, seductive curve where her neck met her shoulder, it was like coming home.

As he kissed her, his hand worked the same magic to the other side of her dress, and he heard her gasp as the fabric inched down, revealing the gentle swell of the tops of her breasts. She murmured something—he thought it might be his name—but she didn't say no, and so he undid the single button nestled between her breasts, loosening the neckline of her dress just enough to allow it to fall away.

Her hands rose up to cover herself, but he caught them in his and held them away as he leaned forward to press one feather-light kiss on her lips. "You're beautiful," he whispered, the heat of his voice entering her mouth. "So beautiful."

Still holding both her hands in one of his, he reached out and gently cupped one of her breasts, allowing it to fill his palm. She was surprisingly lush and full, and he could not stop his groan of pleasure as he felt her nipple pucker in the hollow of his palm.

He looked up at her face, needing to see her expression, needing to know that she loved his touch. Her lips were parted and glistening as if she had just wet them with her tongue. Her eyes were dazed and unfocused, and her breath was coming in tiny fast gasps.

He slid one of his hands to cup her bottom, supporting her as they sank to the ground. The grass was a soft, cool carpet beneath them, Elizabeth's hair spreading out like a priceless golden fan. James just stared at her for a moment, murmuring a soft thanks to whatever god had led him to this moment, and then he lowered his head to her breast, making love to her with his mouth.

Elizabeth let out a startled "Oh!" as his lips closed around her nipple. His breath felt hot on her breast, and her blood felt hot beneath it. Her body became utterly foreign, feeling almost as if she were growing too big for her skin. She was overcome by the need to move, to point her toes and rub the soles against the grass, to flex her hands and then sink them into his thick brown hair.

She arched her back beneath him, consumed by some passionate devil urging her to reach for whatever it was he was offering. "James," she gasped, and then she whispered it again. His name was the only word that came to her lips, and it sounded like a plea and a prayer.

Her dress had been pulled down as far as it could go, and so one of his hands moved to her leg, stealing over her calf before sliding up to the outside of her knee. And then, so slowly she ached from the anticipation, his hand slid over her knee to squeeze the soft skin of her lower thigh.

His name passed over her lips again, but his mouth was on hers, and so her words were lost in his kiss. His hand traveled farther along her leg, moving to the softer skin of her inner thigh. She stiffened, sensing that she was nearing the edge of something, traveling to some secret place from which there was no return.

James lifted his head to look at her. She had to blink several times before she could even focus on his beloved features, and then, a rakish smile adorning his lips, he asked, "More?"

Heaven help her, she nodded, and she saw his smile widen just before his mouth lowered to the underside of her chin, nudging it up until his lips could explore the entire expanse of her neck.

And then his hand moved higher.

He was nearly at the top of her thigh now, so close to the very core of her privacy and womanhood. The proximity was unnerving, and her legs began to tremble in anticipation.

"Trust me," he whispered. "Just trust me. I'll make this good for you. I promise."

Her trembling didn't stop, but her legs parted slightly, allowing him to settle his body between her thighs. She hadn't realized until that moment that he had been holding himself away from her, using his powerful arms to support his weight.

But all of that changed as he lowered his body onto hers. The weight of him was thrilling, the length, the heat. He was so much larger than she; she'd never understood the full extent of his power and strength until it was pressed up so intimately against her.

His hand spanned the entire breadth of her thigh, his thumb coming dangerously close to the curls shielding her womanhood. He squeezed, he teased.

And then he touched her.

Elizabeth was completely unprepared for the bolt of pure electricity that shot up her spine. She'd never known she could feel so hot, so tingly, so desperate for the touch of another human being.

His fingers tickled her until she was certain she could take no more, and then he did it some more. His hot breath teased her ear until she was certain it would burn right off, and then he kept on whispering—words of love and words of passion. Every time she was certain she had reached her limit, he lifted her higher, rushing her to a new level of passion.

She tore at the grass, afraid that if she wrapped her arms around James she'd rend his shirt in two. But then, as his finger slid into her, he whispered, "Touch me."

Tentatively, afraid of her own passion, she brought her hands to the collar of his shirt. The top button was undone; the second quickly slipped through its loophole in her haste to touch his skin.

"My God, Elizabeth," he gasped. "You kill me."

She stopped, her eyes flying to his.

"No," he said, laughing despite himself. "That's good."

"Are you sure? Because— Ohhhhhhhhh!"

She had no idea what he did, how exactly he moved his fingers, but the pressure that had been building within her suddenly exploded. Her body tensed, then arched, then shook, and when she finally shuddered to the ground, she was certain she must be in a thousand pieces.

"Oh, James," she sighed. "You make me feel so good inside."

His body was still hard as a rock, and he was tense with desire that he knew must go unfulfilled that night. His arms began to quiver under the weight of his body, so he rolled onto his side, fitting himself alongside her on the grass. He propped his head up on one elbow, taking in the exquisite sight of her face. Her eyes were closed, her lips parted, and he was certain he'd never seen anything quite as beautiful in his life.

"There is so much I need to tell you," he whispered, smoothing her hair away from his forehead.

Elizabeth's eyes fluttered open. "What?"

"Tomorrow," he promised, gently drawing up her bodice. It seemed a shame to cover such perfect beauty, but he knew she was still self-conscious about her nakedness. Or at least she *would* be, once she remembered that she was naked.

She blushed, proving his theory that, in the aftermath of passion, she had forgotten her undressed state. "Why can't you tell me tonight?" she asked.

It was a good question. It was on the tip of his tongue to blurt out his true identity and ask her to marry him, but something was holding him back. He was only going to propose marriage once in his life, and he wanted it to be perfect. He had never dreamed he'd find a woman who so totally captured his soul. She deserved roses and diamonds, and him on bended knee.

And he felt he owed it to Agatha to tell her that he was ending his charade before he actually ended it.

"Tomorrow," he promised again. "Tomorrow."

That seemed to satisfy her, for she sighed and sat up. "I suppose we must be getting back."

He shrugged and grinned. "I have no pressing appointments."

That earned him a friendly scowl. "Yes, but I am expected. Lady Danbury spent all week nagging me to attend her masquerade. If I do not make an appearance, I will never hear the end of it." She shot him a wry, sideways sort of look. "She is so close to driving me mad as it is. An endless lecture about my not attending is likely to send me right over the edge."

"Yes," James murmured, "she is rather handy with guilt."

"Why don't you come with me?" Elizabeth asked.

The very worst of ideas. Any number of people might recognize him. "I'd love to," he lied, "but I cannot."

"Why?"

"Er, I'm quite dusty from the road, and—"

"We'll brush you off."

"I have no costume."

"Bah! Half the men refuse to wear costumes. I'm certain we can find you a mask."

In desperation, he blurted out, "I simply cannot mix among people in my current state."

That caused her to snap her mouth shut on whatever reply she'd been forming. After several seconds of awkward silence, she finally asked, "What state do you mean?"

James groaned. Had no one explained the workings of men and women to her? Probably not. Her mother had died when she was only eighteen, and he found it difficult to imagine his aunt taking on the delicate task. He looked over at Elizabeth. Her eyes were expectant. "I don't suppose you'll let me tell you that I'd like to jump in a lake and leave it at that," he said.

She shook her head.

"I didn't think so," he muttered.

"You didn't . . . ah . . ."

He jumped on her words. "Exactly! I didn't."

"The problem," she said, not meeting his eyes, "is that I'm not precisely certain what you didn't do."

"I'll show you later," he promised. "God help me, if I don't show you later, I'll be dead before the month is out."

"A whole month?"

A month? Was he insane? He was going to have to get a special license. "A week. Definitely a week."

"I see."

"No, you don't. But you will."

Elizabeth coughed and blushed. "Whatever it is you're talking about," she mumbled, "I have a feeling it's rather naughty."

He lifted her hand to his lips. "You're still a virgin, Elizabeth. And I'm frustrated as hell."

"Oh! I . . . " She smiled sheepishly. "Thank you."

"I'd tell you it was no trouble at all," he said, taking her arm, "except that would be a blatant lie."

"And I suppose," she added mischievously, "that you would also be lying if you said it was your pleasure."

"That would be a *huge* lie. Of proportions immense."

She laughed.

"If you don't start according me the proper respect," he muttered, "I may have to toss you in the lake along with me."

"Surely you can take a bit of teasing."

"I rather think I've taken all the teasing my body can stand already this evening."

She let out another peal of giggles. "I'm sorry," she gasped. "I don't mean to laugh at you, but—"

"Yes, you do." He tried not to grin, but he wasn't successful.

"All right, yes, I do, but it's only because—" She stopped walking and reached up to touch his beloved face. "It's only because you make me so happy and free. I cannot remember the last time I felt so able to simply laugh."

"What about when you're with your family?" he asked. "I know you adore them."

"I do. But even when we are laughing and joking and having the loveliest of times, there is always a cloud hanging over me, constantly reminding me that it all could be taken away. That it all *would* be taken away the moment I found myself unable to support them."

"You will never have to worry about that again," he said, his voice a fierce vow. "Never."

"Oh, James," she said wistfully. "You're very sweet to say so, but I don't see how you can—"

"You'll have to trust me," he interrupted. "I have a few tricks up my sleeve. Besides, I thought you said that when you were with me that pesky gray cloud disappeared."

"When I'm with you I forget about my worries, but that doesn't mean they're gone."

He patted her hand. "I may surprise you yet, Elizabeth Hotchkiss."

They walked toward the house in companionable silence. As they drew near, the sounds of the party grew louder—music, mixed with chatter, and the occasional roar of raucous laughter.

"It sounds like quite a crush," Elizabeth commented.

"Lady Danbury would accept no less," James replied. He glanced at the stately stone mansion, which had come into view. Guests had spilled out onto the lawn, and he knew he was going to have to make his exit immediately.

"Elizabeth," he said, "I must leave now, but I will call upon you tomorrow."

"No, please let's stay." She smiled up at him, her dark blue eyes heartbreakingly huge. "We've never danced."

"I promise you that we shall." He kept his eye on the closest members of the crowd. He didn't see anyone he knew, but one could never be too careful.

"I'll find you a mask, if that's your worry."

"No, Elizabeth, I just can't. You must accept that."

She frowned. "I don't see why you must—"

"It's simply the way it must be. I— Ooof!" Something very large and padded crashed into James's back. Clearly they were not quite as far from the crowds as he'd thought. He turned around to dress down the clumsy partygoer—

And found himself staring straight into the aquamarine eyes of Caroline Ravenscroft.

Elizabeth watched the scene that unfolded with an increasing sense of disbelief and horror.

"James?" Caroline asked, her eyes growing round with delight. "Oh, James! It's so lovely to see you!"

Elizabeth's eyes flew from James to Caroline, trying to figure out how these two people knew each other. If Caroline knew James, surely she would have known he was the estate manager Elizabeth had mentioned earlier that evening.

"Caroline," James responded, his voice impossibly tight.

Caroline tried to throw her arms around him, but her

pumpkin costume rendered hugs difficult. "Where have you been?" she demanded. "Blake and I are most displeased. He has been trying to reach you for— Elizabeth?"

James froze. "How do you know Elizabeth?" he asked, his words slow and careful.

"We met this evening," Caroline replied, giving him a dismissive wave before turning to her new best friend. "Elizabeth, I have been looking for you all night. Where did you disappear to? And how do you know James?"

"I—I—" Elizabeth couldn't get the words out, couldn't possibly verbalize what was becoming increasingly obvious.

"When did you meet Elizabeth?" Caroline flipped around to face James, her light brown braid clipping him in the shoulder. "I told her about you this afternoon and she said she didn't know you."

"You told me about him?" Elizabeth whispered. "No, you didn't. You didn't mention James. The only person you told me about was—"

"James," Caroline cut in. "The Marquis of Riverdale."

"No," Elizabeth said in a shaky voice, her mind suddenly filled with images of a little red book and endless edicts. How to Marry a Marquis. No, it was impossible. "This isn't—"

Caroline turned to James. "James?" Her eyes grew wide as she realized that she had unwittingly destroyed a secret. "Oh, no. I'm sorry. I never dreamed you would be working in disguise here at Danbury House. You told me you were through with all that."

"With all what?" Elizabeth asked, her voice slightly shrill.

"This isn't about the War Office," James bit off.

"What, then?" Caroline asked.

"The Marquis of Riverdale?" Elizabeth echoed. "You're a marquis?"

"Elizabeth," James said, all but ignoring Caroline. "Give me a moment to explain."

A marquis. James was a marquis. And he must have been laughing at her for weeks. "You bastard," she hissed. And then, using every boxing lesson he'd ever given her, plus quite a bit of sheer instinct, she drew back her right arm and swung.

James stumbled. Caroline shrieked. Elizabeth stalked away.

"Elizabeth!" James boomed, striding after her. "Get back here this instant. You will listen to me."

His hand closed around her elbow. "Let go of me!" she cried out.

"Not until you listen to me."

"Oh, you must have had so much fun with me," she choked out. "So much fun pretending to teach me how to marry a marquis. You bastard. You filthy bastard."

He nearly flinched at the venom in her voice. "Elizabeth, I never once—"

"Did you laugh about me with your friends? Did you laugh about the poor little lady's companion who thought she might be able to marry a marquis?"

"Elizabeth, I had my reasons for keeping my identity a secret. You're jumping to conclusions."

"Don't patronize me," she spat out, trying to yank her arm free of his grip. "Don't ever even speak to me again."

"I will not let you run off without hearing me out."

"And I let you touch me," she whispered, her horror showing clearly on her face. "I let you touch me and it was all a lie."

He caught hold of her other arm and pulled her up against him until her breasts were flattened against his ribs. "Don't you ever," he hissed, "call that a lie."

"Then what was it? You don't love me. You don't even respect me enough to tell me who you are."

"You know that's not true." He looked up and saw that a small crowd had begun to form near Caroline, who was still standing openmouthed about ten yards away. "Come with me," he ordered, pulling her around the corner of Danbury House. "We'll discuss this in private."

"I'm not going anywhere with you." She dug her heels in, but she was no match for his greater strength. "I'm going home, and if you ever attempt to speak with me again, I shall not answer to the consequences."

"Elizabeth, you are being irrational."

She snapped. Whether it was his voice or his words, she never knew, but she just snapped. "Don't you tell me what I am!" she yelled, pounding her fists against his chest. "Don't you tell me anything!"

James just stood there, letting her hit him. He stood so still that eventually her arms, sensing no resistance, had to stop.

She pulled away, her body wracked by deep and violent breaths as she stared up at his face. "I hate you," she said in a low voice.

He said nothing.

"You have no idea what you've done," she whispered, shaking her head in disbelief. "You don't even think you've done anything wrong."

"Elizabeth." He'd never dreamed it could take such strength just to call forward one simple word.

Her eyes grew faintly pitying, as if she'd suddenly realized that he must be beneath her, that he would never be worthy of her love and respect. "I'm going home. You may inform Lady Danbury that I have resigned."

"You can't resign."

"And why not?"

"She needs you. And you need the—"

"The money?" she spat out. "Is that what you were going to say?"

He felt his cheeks grow warm, and he knew she could see his answer in his eyes.

"There are some things I won't do for money," she told him, "and if you think I'm going to come back here and work for your aunt— Oh, my God!" she gasped, as if just realizing what she'd said. "She's your aunt. She must have known. How could she do this to me?"

"Agatha had no knowledge of what was happening between us. Whatever blame you choose to assign, none can be heaped upon her shoulders."

"I trusted her," she whispered. "She was like a mother to me. Why would she let this happen?"

"James? Elizabeth?"

They both turned to see a very tentative pumpkin poking her head around the corner, followed by a somewhat irritable black-haired pirate, who was waving his arms in the opposite direction, yelling, "Go away! All of you! There is nothing to see."

"This is not a good time, Caroline," James said, his words clipped.

"Actually," Caroline said softly, "I fear it might be just the right time. Perhaps we could all adjourn inside? Somewhere private?"

Blake Ravenscroft, Caroline's husband and James's best friend, stepped forward. "She's right, James. Gossip is already flying. Half the party is going to be creeping around this corner within minutes."

Caroline nodded. "I'm afraid there is going to be a terrible scandal."

"I'm sure there already is one," Elizabeth retorted.

"Not that I care. I'm sure I will never see any of these people again."

James felt his fingernails bite into his palms. He was getting heartily sick of Elizabeth's stubbornness. Not once had she given him the opportunity to state his case. What was all that nonsense she'd said about trusting him? If she'd really trusted him, she might have let him get a word in edgewise.

"You *will* see these people again," he said in a dangerous voice.

"Oh, and when would that be?" she taunted. "I'm not of your ilk, as you have so capably—if rather underhandedly—pointed out."

"No," he said softly, "you're better."

That startled her into silence. Her mouth trembled, and her voice shook when she finally said, "No. You can't do this. What you did is unforgivable, and you can't use sweet words as absolution."

James gritted his teeth and took a step toward her, heedless of the way Caroline and Blake were gaping at him. "I will give you one day to get over your anger, Elizabeth. You have until this time tomorrow."

"And then what happens?"

His eyes grew hot as he leaned forward, purposefully intimidating her with his size. "And then you marry me."

Chapter 18

Elizabeth punched him again, this time catching him so off guard that he tumbled to the ground.

"That is a terrible thing to say!" she cried out.

"Elizabeth," Caroline said, grabbing her wrist and yanking her to her side. "I think he just asked you to marry him. That's a *nice* thing to say. A nice thing." She turned to her husband, who was looking at James and trying not to laugh. "Isn't that a nice thing?"

"He doesn't mean it," Elizabeth snapped. "He's only saying that because he feels guilty. He knows what he did was wrong and—"

"Wait a moment," Blake interjected. "I thought you said he didn't even know he'd done anything wrong."

"He didn't. He doesn't. I don't know!" Elizabeth swung around, her eyes narrowing on the darkly handsome gentleman. "And you weren't even there. How do you know what I said? Were you eavesdropping?"

Blake, who had worked with James at the War Office for many years, simply shrugged. "Second nature, I'm afraid."

"Well, it's a despicable habit. I—" She stopped short, motioning toward him with an impatient gesture. "Who *are* you?"

"Blake Ravenscroft," he said with a polite bow.

"My husband," Caroline supplied.

"Ah, yes, the one who has been friends with *him*"—Elizabeth jerked her hand toward James, who was sitting on the ground, holding his nose—"for years. Pardon me if that connection does not recommend you."

Blake only smiled.

Elizabeth shook her head, feeling oddly off-kilter. Her world was crashing down around her with dizzying speed, everyone was talking at once, and the only thing she seemed able to hold on to for any length of time was her anger for James. She shook her finger at him, still glaring at Blake. "He's an aristocrat. A bloody marquis."

"Is that so bad?" Blake asked, raising his brows.

"He should have told me!"

"James," Caroline said, kneeling down next to him as far as her costume would let her. "Are you bleeding?"

Bleeding? Elizabeth hated that she cared, but she couldn't stop her gasp, and she immediately turned to James. She would never forgive him for what he'd done, and she certainly never wanted to see him again, but she didn't want him to be *hurt*.

"I'm not bleeding," James muttered.

Caroline looked up at her husband and said, "She hit him twice."

"Twice?" Blake grinned. "Really?"

"It's not funny," Caroline said.

Blake looked down at James. "You let her hit you twice?"

"Hell, I taught her."

"That, good friend, shows an incredible lack of foresight on your part."

James scowled at him. "I was trying to teach her to protect herself."

"From whom? You?"

"No! From— Oh, for the love of God, what does it matter, I—" James looked up, saw Elizabeth carefully inching away, and bounded to his feet. "You're not going anywhere," he growled, grabbing at the sash at the waist of her costume.

"Let me go! Ouch—oh—James!" She wiggled like a fish out of water, unsuccessfully trying to turn around so that she could glare at him. "Let. Me. GO!"

"Not in a million years."

Elizabeth looked at Caroline pleadingly. Surely another woman would be sympathetic to her plight. "Please tell him to let me go."

Caroline glanced from James to Blake and then back at Elizabeth. Clearly torn between her allegiance to her old friend and her sympathy for Elizabeth, she stammered, "I—I don't know what's going on, except he didn't tell you who he was."

"Isn't that enough?"

"Well," Caroline hedged, "James rarely tells people who he is."

"What?" Elizabeth squeaked, whirling around so she could shove James in his aristocratic shoulder. "You have done this before? You despicable, amoral—"

"Enough!" James roared.

Six costumed heads peeked out from around the corner.

"I really think we ought to move inside," Caroline said weakly.

"Unless you *prefer* an audience," Blake added.

"I want to go home," Elizabeth stated, but no one was listening to her. She didn't know why this surprised her; no one had been listening to her all night.

James nodded curtly at Blake and Caroline and then motioned to the house with a quick jerk of his head. His grip tightened on the sash of Elizabeth's dress, and when he started to walk inside the house, there was nothing she could do but follow.

A few moments later she found herself in the library, the cruelest stroke of irony. HOW TO MARRY A MARQUIS was still laying on the shelf, just where she'd left it.

Elizabeth suppressed an irrational urge to laugh. Mrs. Seeton had been right; there *was* a marquis around every corner. Nobility everywhere, just laying in wait to humiliate poor, unsuspecting women.

And that was what James had done. Every time he'd given her a lesson on how to catch a husband—a *marquis*, damn him—he'd humiliated her. Every time he'd tried to teach her how to smile or flirt, she'd been demeaned. And when he'd kissed her, pretending to be nothing more than a humble estate manager, he'd soiled her with his lies.

If James hadn't been holding on to her sash, she probably would have grabbed the damned book and heaved it out the window—and then pushed him right along after it.

Elizabeth felt his eyes on her face, burning into her skin, and when she looked up at him, she realized that he had followed her gaze to Mrs. Seeton's book.

"Don't say anything," she whispered, painfully aware of the presence of the Ravenscrofts. "Please don't mortify me like that."

James nodded curtly, and Elizabeth felt her entire body go limp with relief. She didn't know Blake, and she hardly knew Caroline, but she couldn't bear for them to know she'd been so pathetic as to turn to a guidebook to find a husband.

Blake shut the library door behind him, then looked up at the room's occupants with a blank expression. "Er," he said, his eyes darting back and forth between Elizabeth and James, "would you like us to leave?"

"Yes," James bit off.

"No!" Elizabeth practically yelled.

"I think we should go," Blake said to his wife.

"Elizabeth wants us to stay," Caroline pointed out, "and we can't leave her here alone with him."

"It wouldn't be proper," Elizabeth hastened to add. She didn't want to be alone with James. If they were alone, he would wear her down, make her forget her anger. He'd use soft words and gentle touches, and she'd lose sight of what was true and what was right. She knew he had that power, and she hated herself for it.

"I think we're well past propriety," James retorted.

Caroline sank against the edge of a table. "Oh, dear."

Blake gave her an amused glance. "Since when have you been so concerned with propriety?"

"Since— Oh, be quiet." And then, in a hushed voice she added, "Don't you want them to marry?"

"I didn't even know she existed until ten minutes ago."

"I'm not going to marry him," Elizabeth declared, trying not to notice that her voice broke on her words. "And I'd appreciate it if the two of you would not speak as if I weren't in the room."

Caroline's eyes slid to the floor. "Sorry," she mumbled. "I hate it when people do that to me."

"I want to go home," Elizabeth said yet again.

"I know, dear," Caroline murmured, "but we really should sort this out, and—"

Someone started banging on the door.

"Go away," Blake yelled.

"You'll feel much better in the morning if we sort this out now," Caroline continued. "I promise you that—"

"*QUIET!*"

James's voice shook the room with so much power that Elizabeth sat down. Unfortunately, his hand was still wrapped around her sash, so she found herself gasping for air as it cut into her ribs. "James," she wheezed, "let go."

He did, although probably more out of his desire to shake his fist at everyone than anything else. "For the love of God," he thundered, "how is a man meant to *think* with all of this noise? Can we possibly conduct a single conversation? Just one, that we all may follow?"

"Actually," Caroline put in, probably unwisely, "if one wants to place a fine point upon it, we *were* discussing a single topic. Of course we were all talking at *once*—"

Her husband yanked her to his side with enough authority to force out a little yelp. She made no sound after that.

"I need to speak with Elizabeth," James said. "Alone."

Elizabeth's response was sure and swift. "No."

Blake started walking toward the door, dragging Caroline after him. "It's time we left, darling."

"We can't leave her here against her will," Caroline protested. "It isn't right, and in all conscience, I cannot—"

"He's not going to hurt her," Blake interrupted.

But Caroline just hooked one of her feet around the leg of a table. "I'm not leaving her," she ground out.

Elizabeth mouthed a heartfelt "thank you" from across the room.

"Blake . . ." James said, flicking his eyes over at Caroline, who had thrown her orange pumpkin arms around a wing chair.

Blake shrugged. "You'll soon learn, James, that there are times one just can't argue with one's wife."

"Well, he can learn that with some other wife," Elizabeth declared, "because I'm not marrying him."

"Fine!" James exploded, waving an angry arm at Blake and Caroline. "Stay and listen. You're likely to listen against the door, anyway. And as for *you* . . ." He turned his furious gaze on Elizabeth. "You *will* listen to me and you *will* marry me."

"See?" Caroline whispered to Blake. "I knew he'd come around and let us stay."

James turned slowly around, his neck held so tightly that his jaw was shaking. "Ravenscroft," he said to Blake, his voice dangerously controlled, "don't you ever get the urge to strangle her?"

"Oh, all the time," Blake said cheerfully. "But for the most part, I'm glad she married me instead of you."

"What?" Elizabeth screeched. "He asked her to marry him?" Her head snapped back and forth for several seconds before she managed to stop moving and fix her eyes on Caroline. "He asked you to marry him?"

"Yes," Caroline replied with a dismissive shrug. "But he wasn't serious."

Elizabeth turned hard eyes to James. "Are you in the habit of extending insincere marriage proposals?"

James turned even harder eyes to Caroline. "You are *not* improving the situation."

Caroline turned limpid eyes to her husband.

"Don't look to me for help," he said.

"He would have married me if I'd said yes," Caroline explained with a loud sigh. "But he only asked to goad Blake into proposing. It was really quite thoughtful of him. He'll make you a wonderful husband, Elizabeth. I promise."

Elizabeth stared at the three of them in disbelief. Watching them interact was exhausting.

"We're confusing you, aren't we?" Caroline asked.

Elizabeth was quite without words.

"It's really a rather remarkable story," Blake said with

a shrug. "I'd write a book about it, except no one would believe me."

"Do you think?" Caroline asked, her eyes lighting with delight. "What would you call it?"

"Not sure," Blake said, scratching his chin. "Perhaps something about catching oneself an heiress."

James shoved his furious face up close to Blake. "Why not HOW TO DRIVE YOUR FRIENDS COMPLETELY AND IRREVOCABLY *INSANE*?"

Elizabeth shook her head. "You're *all* mad. I'm sure of it."

Blake shrugged. "I'm sure of it half the time, too."

"May I please have a word with Elizabeth?" James snapped.

"So sorry," Blake said in a voice that was clearly designed to annoy. "I'd quite forgotten why we were here."

James sank his left hand into the hair right above his forehead and pulled; it seemed the only way to keep from wrapping his hand around Blake's neck. "I'm starting to realize," he growled, "why courtships are best conducted in private."

Blake raised a brow. "Meaning?"

"Meaning that you have ruined everything."

"Why?" Elizabeth countered. "Because he inadvertently revealed your identity?"

"I was going to tell you everything tomorrow."

"I don't believe you."

"I don't care if you believe me!" James shouted. "It's the truth."

"Pardon my interruption," Caroline put in, "but shouldn't you care if she believes you? After all, you did ask her to be your wife."

James started to shake, desperate to strangle someone in the room but not certain with whom he was the most furious. There was Blake, with his mocking stares; Caroline, who had to be the meddlingist woman in all creation; and *Elizabeth* . . .

Elizabeth. Yes, she had to be the one he really wanted to light into, because just the thought of her name made his temperature rise by several degrees. And this was not due merely to passion.

He was furious. Bone-shaking, teeth-rattling, muscles-about-to-jump-from-his-skin furious. And his three current companions clearly did not realize what danger they were courting each time they cracked another asinine joke.

"I am going to speak now," he said, keeping his voice painfully slow and steady. "And the person who interrupts me will be tossed out the window. Is that clear?"

No one said anything.

"*Is that clear?*"

"I thought you wanted us to be quiet," Blake said.

Which turned out to be all the incentive Caroline needed to open her mouth and say, "Do you think he realizes that the window isn't open?"

Elizabeth clapped her hand over her mouth. James glared at her. God help her if she laughed.

He drew a deep breath and stared hard into her blue eyes. "I did not tell you who I was because I was called here to investigate the blackmail of my aunt."

"Someone is blackmailing your aunt?" Caroline breathed.

"Good God!" Blake exclaimed. "The cretin must have a death wish." He looked over at Elizabeth. "I, for one, am terrified by the old dragon."

James looked at the Ravenscrofts, then looked markedly at the window, then looked back at Elizabeth. "It would not have been prudent to inform you of my true purposes here at Danbury House, because, if you recall, *you* were the prime suspect.''

"You suspected Elizabeth?" Caroline interrupted. "Are you completely insane?"

"He did," Elizabeth affirmed. "And he is. Insane, I mean."

James took a steadying breath. He was about two steps away from spontaneous combustion. "I quickly cleared Elizabeth of suspicion," he ground out.

"That's when you should have told me who you were," Elizabeth said. "Before—" She cut herself off and stared purposefully at the ground.

"Before what?" Caroline asked.

"The window, my dear," Blake said, patting his wife on the arm. "Remember the window."

She nodded and turned back to James and Elizabeth, her expression expectant.

James purposefully ignored her, focusing his entire being on Elizabeth. She was sitting in a chair, her back ramrod straight, and her face looked so tense he thought that the merest caress might cause her to shatter. He tried to remember what she'd looked like just an hour earlier, flushed with passion and delight. To his great horror, he could not.

"I did not reveal myself to you at that time," he continued, "because I felt that my first duty must be to my aunt. She has been . . ." He fought for words that might explain the depth of his devotion for the crotchety old lady, but then he remembered that Elizabeth knew of his past. In fact, she was the only person to whom he'd ever told the entire story of his childhood. Even Blake knew only bits and pieces.

"She has been very important to me over the years," he finally said. "I couldn't—"

"You don't have to explain your love for Lady Danbury," Elizabeth said quietly, not raising her eyes to meet his.

"Thank you." He cleared his throat. "I did not know—I still do not know—the identity of her blackmailer. Furthermore, I have no way of determining whether or not this individual might prove dangerous. I saw no reason to draw you into the matter any further."

Elizabeth looked up suddenly, and the expression in her eyes was heartbreaking. "Surely you know that I would never have done anything to harm Lady Danbury."

"Of course not. Your devotion to her is obvious. But the fact remains that you are not experienced in such matters, and—"

"And I suppose you are?" she asked, her sarcasm evident but not obnoxious.

"Elizabeth, I have spent most of the last decade of my life working for the War Office."

"The gun," she whispered. "The way you attacked Fellport. I knew something was not right."

James swore under his breath. "My altercation with Fellport had nothing to do with my experience in the War Office. For God's sake, Elizabeth, the man had attacked you."

"Yes," she replied, "but you seemed far too familiar with violence. It was too easy for you. The way you drew your gun . . . You'd had far too much experience with it."

He leaned forward, his eyes burning into hers. "What I felt in that moment was far from familiar. It was rage, Elizabeth, pure and primitive, and quite unlike anything that's ever before coursed through my veins."

"You've—you've never felt rage before?"

He shook his head slowly. "Not like that. Fellport dared to attack what was mine. He's lucky I let him live."

"I'm not yours," she whispered. But her voice lacked confidence.

"Aren't you?"

From across the room, Caroline sighed.

"James," Elizabeth said. "I can't forgive you. I just can't."

"What the hell can't you forgive me for?" he snapped. "For not telling you I had a bloody title? I thought you said you didn't want a damned marquis."

She pulled back from his anger, whispering, "What do you mean?"

"Don't you remember? It was in this very room. You were holding the book, and——"

"Don't mention that book," she said, her voice low and furious. "Don't you ever mention it."

"Why not?" he taunted, his anger and pain making him mean. "Because you don't want to be reminded of how desperate you'd become? Of how grasping and greedy?"

"James!" Caroline exclaimed. "Stop it."

But he was too hurt, too far gone. "You're no better than me, Elizabeth Hotchkiss. You preach about honesty, but you were going to trap some poor, unsuspecting fool into marriage."

"I was not! I would never have married someone without making sure he knew my situation first. You know that."

"Do I? I don't recall your mentioning such noble principles. In fact, all I recall is your practicing your wiles upon me."

"You asked me to!"

"James Siddons, estate manager, was good enough to be teased," he sneered, "but not good enough to marry. Was that it?"

"I loved James Siddons!" she burst out. And then,

horrified by what she'd said, she jumped to her feet and raced for the door.

But James was too quick. He blocked her path, whispering. "You loved me?"

"I loved *him*," she cried out. "I don't know who you are."

"I am the same man."

"No, you're not. The man I knew was a lie. He wouldn't have taunted a woman the way you did me. And yet—" Her voice broke, and a horrified laugh escaped her lips. "And yet, he did. Didn't he?"

"For God's sake, Elizabeth, what the hell did I do that was so evil and base?"

She stared at him in disbelief. "You don't even know, do you? You disgust me."

The muscles in his throat twitched with rage, and it took every ounce of his restraint not to grab her shoulders and shake her until she saw sense. His anger and pain were so raw, so close to the surface that he feared one tiny show of emotion would unleash the whole, horrifying flood of fury. Finally, exerting a self-control he could barely believe he possessed, he managed to bite off two clipped words: "Explain yourself."

She stood utterly still for a moment, and then, with a stamp of her foot, she stalked across the room and yanked out the copy of How to Marry a Marquis that had been resting on the shelf. "Do you remember this?" she yelled, shaking the little red book in the air. "Do you?"

"I believe you asked me not to mention that book in front of the Ravenscrofts."

"It doesn't matter. You've humiliated me so thoroughly in front of them, anyway. I might as well finish off the job."

Caroline laid a comforting hand on Elizabeth's arm. "I

think you're quite brave," she said softly. "Please don't think you've been shamed in any way."

"Oh, you don't think so?" Elizabeth lashed out, choking on every word. "Well, then, look at *this*!" She thrust the book into Caroline's hands.

The book was face-down, so Caroline murmured her incomprehension until she turned it over and read the title. A small cry of alarm escaped her lips.

"What is it, dear?" Blake asked.

Silently, she handed him the book. He regarded it, flipping it over in his hands a few times. Then they both looked up at James.

"I'm not certain what happened," Caroline said carefully, "but my imagination is devising all sorts of disasters."

"He found me with that," Elizabeth said. "I know it's a ridiculous book, but I had to marry and I didn't have anyone to whom to turn for advice. And then he found me with it, and I was afraid he'd mock me. But he didn't." She paused for breath, then hastily wiped away a tear.

"He was so kind. And then he—and then he offered to *tutor* me. He agreed that I could never hope to marry a marquis—"

"I never said that!" James said hotly. "You said that. Not I."

"He offered to help me interpret the book so that—"

"I offered to burn the book, if you recall. I told you it was utter nonsense." He glared at her, and when that didn't cause her to quake in her shoes, he glared at Blake and Caroline. That also seemed to have no effect, so he turned back to Elizabeth and yelled, "For the love of God, woman, there's only one rule in that bloody book worth following."

"And that is?" Elizabeth asked disdainfully.

"That you marry your damned marquis!"

She was silent for a long moment, her blue eyes holding his, and then, in a movement that sliced his gut in two, she turned away.

"He said he would help me learn how to catch a husband," she said to the Ravenscrofts. "But he never told me who he was. He never told me he was a bloody *marquis*."

No one made a response, so Elizabeth just let out a bitter breath and said, "And now you know the entire tale. How he poked fun at me and my unfortunate circumstances."

James crossed the room in a heartbeat. "I never laughed at you, Elizabeth," he said, his eyes intent upon her face. "You must believe that. I never intended to hurt you."

"Well, you did," she said.

"Then marry me. Let me spend a lifetime making it up to you."

A fat tear squeezed out of the corner of her eye. "You don't want to marry me."

"I have asked you repeatedly," he said with an impatient exhale. "What more proof do you need?"

"Am I not allowed to have my pride? Or is that an emotion reserved for the elite?"

"Am I such a terrible person?" The question was punctuated by a vaguely bewildered exhale. "So I didn't tell you who I was. I'm sorry. Excuse me for enjoying— no, reveling—in the fact that you fell in love with *me*, not my title, not my money, not my anything. Just me."

A choking sound emerged from her throat. "It was a test?"

"No!" he practically yelled. "Of course it wasn't a test. I told you, I had very important reasons for concealing my identity. But . . . but . . ." He fought for words, having no idea how to express what was in his heart. "But it still felt good. You have no idea, Elizabeth. No idea at all."

"No," she said quietly, "I don't."

"Don't punish me, Elizabeth."

His voice was thick with emotion, and Elizabeth felt that warm baritone all the way down to her soul. She had to get out of here, had to escape before he spun any more lies around her heart.

Yanking her hands away from his, she hurried toward the door. "I have to go," she said, panic rising in her voice. "I can't be with you right now."

"Where are you going?" James asked, slowly following her.

"Home."

His arm came out to prevent her from leaving. "You are not walking home by yourself. It is dark, and the district is full of drunken revelers."

"But—"

"I don't care if you hate me," he said in a voice that brooked no protest. "I will not permit you to leave this room by yourself."

She looked entreatingly at Blake. "Then you can do it. Will you see me home? Please?"

Blake stood, and his eyes met with James's for a brief moment before nodding. "I would be honored."

"Take care of her," James said gruffly.

Blake nodded again. "You know I will." He took Elizabeth's arm and escorted her out of the room.

James watched them go, then leaned against the wall, his body shaking with all the emotion he'd been trying to keep in check all evening. The fury, the pain, the exasperation, even the damned frustration—after all, he had not found his own pleasure in the woods with Elizabeth.

They all rocked within him, eating him up, making it difficult to breathe.

He heard a little clucking sound and looked up. Blast, he'd completely forgotten that Caroline was still in the room.

"Oh, James," she sighed. "How could you?"

"Save it, Caroline," he snapped. "Just save it."

And then he stormed off, crashing heedlessly through the crowds in the hall. There was a bottle of whiskey in his cottage that promised to be the evening's best companion.

Chapter 19

❦

It didn't take long for Elizabeth to decide that Blake Ravenscroft—despite his being bosom bows with James—was a very wise man. He didn't, as he drove her home, attempt to make conversation, or ask prying questions, or do anything other than offer her a comforting pat on the arm and say, "If you need someone, I'm certain Caroline would be happy to talk with you."

It took a smart man indeed to know when to keep his mouth shut.

The drive home was conducted in silence, save for Elizabeth's occasional directions to her home.

As they drove up to the Hotchkiss cottage, however, Elizabeth was surprised to see the small structure ablaze with light. "Heavens," she murmured. "They must have lit every candle in the house."

And then, of course, habit kicked in, and she began to mentally tally the cost of those tapers and pray that they hadn't used any of the expensive beeswax candles she normally reserved for company.

Blake took his eyes off the road to look at her. "Is something wrong?"

"I hope not. I can't imagine—"

The curricle drew to a halt, and Elizabeth jumped down

without waiting for assistance from Blake. There was no reason why the Hotchkiss cottage should be so abuzz with activity, no reason whatsoever. There was enough noise spilling from the house to wake the dead, and while it sounded like a raucous, happy sort of noise, Elizabeth could not stem the panic rising in her chest.

She burst through the door and followed the loud squeals and laughter into the sitting room. Susan, Jane, and Lucas were holding hands and spinning in a circle, laughing and singing bawdy songs at the top of their lungs.

Elizabeth was completely dumbstruck. She'd never seen her siblings act this way. She liked to think that she'd managed to shoulder most of their worries for the past five years, and that they'd had a lovely and reasonably carefree childhood, but she'd never seen them so completely drunk with happiness.

She felt Blake standing at her side, and when he whispered, "Do you know what happened?" she couldn't even formulate a reply.

After about five seconds, Susan caught sight of her sister standing in the doorway and gaping at them, and she yanked the dancing circle to a halt, causing Jane and Lucas to crash into each other in a laughing tangle of skinny arms and blond hair.

"Elizabeth!" Susan exclaimed. "You're home."

Elizabeth nodded slowly. "What is going on? I didn't expect you to be still awake."

"Oh, Elizabeth!" Jane cried out. "The most brilliant thing has happened. You'll never believe!"

"Wonderful," Elizabeth replied, her emotions still too battered to put much feeling into the word. But she tried. She didn't know what had happened to bring such bliss to her siblings, but she owed it to them to wipe some of the pain from her eyes and at least attempt to look excited.

Susan rushed over, holding a piece of paper she'd retrieved from a writing table. "Look what arrived while you were out. A messenger brought it."

"A *liveried* messenger," Jane added. "He was terribly handsome."

"He was a servant," Lucas told her.

"That doesn't mean he wasn't handsome," she retorted.

Elizabeth felt herself smile. Listening to Lucas and Jane bicker was so wonderfully *normal*. Not like the rest of this god-awful evening. She took the paper from Susan and looked down.

And then her hands began to shake.

"Isn't it brilliant?" Susan asked, her blue eyes lighting with wonder. "Who would have thought?"

Elizabeth said nothing, trying to fight the rising tide of nausea in her stomach.

"Who do you think it could be?" Jane asked. "It must be someone so very lovely. The kindest, loveliest person in all the world."

"May I?" Blake murmured.

Silently, she handed him the paper. When she looked up, Susan, Jane, and Lucas were staring at her with bewildered expressions.

"Aren't you happy?" Jane whispered.

Blake gave her back the paper and she looked down again, as if another reading would somehow change the offending message.

Sir Lucas Hotchkiss,
Miss Hotchkiss,
Miss Susan Hotchkiss,
Miss Jane Hotchkiss,

It gives me great pleasure to inform you that your family is the recipient of this charitable anonymous bank draft, in the amount of £5000.

Further arrangements have been made by your benefactor for Sir Lucas to attend Eton. He should report to the school at the beginning of the next term.

> Sincerely,
> Geo. Shillingworth
> Shillingworth and Son, Solicitors

It was from James. It had to be. She turned to Blake, unable to keep the hardness from her eyes.

"He only meant to help you," Blake said softly.

"It's insulting," she just barely managed to say. "How can I accept this? How could I possibly—"

He placed his hand on her arm. "You're overwrought. Perhaps if you consider this in the morning—"

"Of course I'm overwrought! I—" Elizabeth caught sight of her siblings' stricken faces and covered her mouth with her hand, horrified by her outburst.

Three pairs of blue eyes were darting between her face and that of Mr. Ravenscroft, whom they didn't even *know*, and—

Mr. Ravenscroft. She should introduce him to the children. They had to be upset enough over her reaction, and at the very least they should know who was standing in their parlor.

"Susan, Jane, Lucas," she said, trying to keep her voice even, "this is Mr. Ravenscroft. He is a friend of—" She swallowed. She'd almost said "Mr. Siddons," but that wasn't even his real name, was it? "He is a friend of Lady Danbury's," she finished. "And he was kind enough to see me home."

Her siblings mumbled their greetings, and Elizabeth turned to Blake and said, "Mr. Ravenscroft, these are—" She broke off, eyes narrowing. "I say, it is *Mr.* Ravenscroft, isn't it? You're not hiding some sort of title as well, are you?"

Blake shook his head, a hint of a smile touching the corners of his lips. "A mere mister, I'm afraid, although if full disclosure is necessary, my father is a viscount."

Elizabeth wanted to smile, knowing his comments were meant to amuse, but she just couldn't summon one up. Instead, she turned to her siblings, and with a heavy heart, said, "We can't accept this."

"But—"

"We can't." Elizabeth didn't even know which of her siblings had voiced the objection, she jumped in so fast over the protest. "It is too much. We can't accept that kind of charity."

Jane apparently disagreed. "But don't you think whomever gave us the money wanted us to have it?"

Elizabeth swallowed against the lump in her throat. Who knew what James had intended? Was this all part of some grand scheme to mock her? After what he'd already done, who knew how his mind worked?

"I'm sure he did," she said carefully, "else it wouldn't be our names at the top of the letter. But that is irrelevant. We cannot accept this sort of money from a stranger."

"Maybe it's not a stranger," Susan said.

"Then that's even worse!" Elizabeth retorted. "My God, can you imagine? Some horrid person treating us like puppets, pulling our strings, thinking he can control our destiny? It's sick. Sick."

There was silence, followed by the most awful sound. Lucas, fighting back tears. He looked up at Elizabeth, his eyes heartbreakingly huge. "Does that mean I won't get to go to Eton?" he whispered.

Elizabeth's breath caught in her throat. She tried to tell Lucas that he couldn't go, knew she *had* to tell him that they could not accept James's money, but the words just wouldn't come out.

She stood there, looking at her brother's trembling face. He was trying so hard to keep his upper lip stiff and not show his disappointment. His little arms were rigid sticks at his sides, and his chin was jutted out, as if keeping his jaw still would somehow stem his tears.

Elizabeth looked at him and saw the price of her pride.

"I don't know about Eton," she said, leaning down to embrace him. "Maybe we can still make it work."

But Lucas pulled back. "We can't afford it. You try so hard to hide it, but I know the truth. I can't go. I'm never going to be able to go."

"That's not true. Maybe this"—she motioned vaguely to the letter—"means something different." She smiled weakly. Her words were utterly without conviction, and even an eight-year-old—*especially* an eight-year-old— could tell she was lying.

Lucas's eyes fixed on hers for the most agonizing, longest moment of her life. And then he just swallowed and said, "I'm going to bed."

Elizabeth didn't even try to stop him. There was nothing she could say.

Jane followed without a word, her little blond braid somehow looking decidedly limp.

Elizabeth looked at Susan. "Do you hate me?"

Susan shook her head. "But I don't understand you."

"We can't accept this, Susan. We'd be indebted to our benefactor for the rest of our lives."

"But why does it matter? We don't even know who he is!"

"I won't be indebted to him," Elizabeth said fiercely. "I won't."

Susan drew back a step, her eyes growing wide. "You know who it is," she whispered. "You know who sent this."

"No," Elizabeth said, but they both knew she was lying.

"You do. And that's why you won't accept it."

"Susan, I won't discuss this further."

Susan backed away, grasping the doorframe when she reached the hall. "I'm going to comfort Lucas," she said. "He needs a shoulder to cry on."

Elizabeth winced.

"A rather direct hit," Blake murmured, once Susan was up the stairs.

Elizabeth turned. She'd completely forgotten he was there. "I beg your pardon?"

He shook his head. "It doesn't bear repeating."

She sank against the back of the sofa, her legs refusing to hold her up a single second longer. "It seems you've been privy to all my private moments this evening."

"Not all."

She smiled humorlessly. "I suppose you're going to go back to the marquis and tell him everything."

"No. I'll tell my wife everything, but not James."

Elizabeth looked at him with confusion. "Then what *will* you tell him?"

Blake shrugged as he headed for the door. "That he's an idiot if he lets you go. But I suspect he knows that already."

Elizabeth woke up the following morning, *knowing* it was going to be a hideous day. There was no one she wanted to see, absolutely no one she had any desire to speak to, and that included herself.

She didn't want to face her siblings and their disappointed faces. She didn't want to see the Ravenscrofts—

total strangers who had witnessed her utter and complete humiliation. She refused to visit Lady Danbury; she didn't think she could spend the day in the countess's company without breaking down in tears and asking her how she could have participated in James's deception.

And she certainly didn't want to see James.

She rose, dressed, then just sat on her bed. A strange malaise had come over her. The previous day had been so exhausting in every way; her feet, her mind, her heart—everything refused to work now. She'd be happy if she could just sit there on the bed, not seeing anyone, not doing anything, for a week.

Well, not happy. Happy was a stretch. But what she was feeling was certainly better than what she'd be feeling if someone knocked on the door and—

Knock-knock.

Elizabeth looked up. "Just once," she grumbled at the ceiling, "just once couldn't You grant me one small favor?" She stood, took a step, then looked up again, her features slipping into a decidedly disgruntled expression. "As favors go, this one would have been very small."

She yanked open the door. Susan was standing in the hall, her hand raised to knock again. Elizabeth didn't say anything, mostly because she had a feeling she wouldn't be proud of her tone of voice if she did.

"You've a visitor," Susan said.

"I don't want to see him."

"It's not a 'him.'"

Elizabeth's entire face jutted forward in surprise. "It's not?"

"No." Susan held out a creamy white calling card. "She seems a rather nice lady."

Elizabeth looked down, absently noticing that the card was made of the finest, most expensive of papers.

Mrs. Blake Ravenscroft

"I assume she's the wife of the man we met yesterday?" Susan asked.

"Yes. Her name is Caroline." Elizabeth ran her hand through her hair, which she hadn't even managed to pin up yet. "She's a very nice person, but truly, I'm not up to visitors just now, and—"

"Pardon," Susan interrupted, "but I don't think she'll leave."

"I'm sorry?"

"I believe her exact words were, 'I imagine she doesn't want visitors, but I'm happy to wait until she feels otherwise.' Then she sat down, pulled out a book—"

"Dear God, it wasn't How to Marry a Marquis, was it?"

"No, it was black, actually, and I think it must have been some sort of journal because she started to write in it. But as I was saying," Susan added, "then she looked up at me and said, 'You needn't worry. I can entertain myself.'"

"She said that?"

Susan nodded and shrugged. "So I'm not worrying. She seems perfectly happy to scribble in her book. I did put a pot of tea on, though, just for good manners."

"She's really not going to leave, is she?"

Susan shook her head. "She seems a most stubborn woman. I don't think she's going to leave until she sees you. I wouldn't be surprised if she brought a change of clothing."

"I suppose I had better dress my hair and go down," Elizabeth said with a sigh.

Susan reached over to Elizabeth's small vanity table and picked up a hairbrush. "I'll help you."

Elizabeth assumed this was a ploy to get information out of her; Susan had never offered to dress her hair before. But the bristly brush felt so nice on her scalp, Elizabeth decided just to go along with it. It was a rare moment indeed when someone waited upon her.

Elizabeth counted the swipes the brush made through her hair before Susan started asking questions. One swipe, two swipes, three swipes, four—ah, she paused slightly before the fifth, she must be getting ready for something. . . .

"Does Mrs. Ravenscroft's visit have anything to do with the events of last night?" Susan asked.

Five swipes. Elizabeth was impressed. She'd never thought Susan would last past three.

Susan pulled the brush through Elizabeth's hair again. "Lizzie? Did you hear me?"

"I'm sure I don't know the reason for Mrs. Ravenscroft's visit," Elizabeth lied.

"Hmmph."

"Ow!"

"Sorry."

"Give me that!" Elizabeth snatched the brush away from her sister. "And the hairpins, too. I don't trust you with any sharp objects."

Susan stepped back, crossed her arms, and frowned.

"It's difficult to concentrate with you glowering at me like that," Elizabeth muttered.

"Good."

"Susan Mary Hotchkiss!"

"Don't talk to me like you're my mother."

Elizabeth let out a long, weary breath, rubbing her hand over her brow. The morning only needed this. "Susan," she said quietly, "I will tell you what you need to know when I am able."

Susan stared at her for several moments, apparently weighing her words.

"That's the best I can do," Elizabeth added, jabbing the last hairpin into her coiffure. "So you might as well exhibit a bit of grace and try to understand my position."

Susan nodded, her eyes darkened with a touch of contrition. She stepped out of the way as Elizabeth exited the room, then she followed her down the stairs.

Caroline was perched on the sofa in the sitting room, scribbling away in a leather-bound notebook when Elizabeth entered.

At the sound of footsteps, Caroline looked up. "You're not terribly surprised to see me, I expect."

Elizabeth smiled very slightly. "I wasn't expecting you, but now that you're here, no, I cannot say I'm surprised."

Caroline snapped her book shut. "Blake told me everything."

"Yes, he said he would. I—" Elizabeth stopped, twisted her neck to look over her shoulder, and glared at Susan, who was loitering in the doorway. Susan made haste to depart after such a glower, but Elizabeth turned to her guest nonetheless and said, "Would you care to walk along the lane? I can't anticipate the nature of your conversation, but if you desire privacy, I strongly suggest we adjourn outside."

Caroline laughed. "I love families. They're so perfectly nosy." She stood, supporting her lower back as she did so. "I'm sure you wish yours in Greece right now—or farther!—but I never had a family growing up, and I can tell you it's lovely to have someone so interested that they want to eavesdrop."

"I suppose that depends on one's mood," Elizabeth allowed.

Caroline patted her stomach. "It's part of the reason

I'm so looking forward to this child. I haven't a family behind me, so I might as well create one for the future.''

They walked out the front door and strolled away from the house, Caroline still holding onto her little black book. When they were out of sight of the cottage, Caroline turned to Elizabeth and said, ''I hope you do not feel insulted by James's actions regarding the bank draft.''

''I don't see how else I might feel.''

Caroline looked as if she had a suggestion, but she closed her mouth, gave her head a tiny shake, and then continued in a different vein. ''Perhaps he arranged for the bank draft because he didn't want you to feel forced into marrying against your heart.''

Elizabeth said nothing.

''I'm sure I don't know the entire story,'' Caroline continued, ''but I've been trying to piece it together as best as I am able, and I believe that you felt you had to marry well to support your family.''

Elizabeth nodded sadly. ''We have nothing. I can barely feed them.''

''I'm certain James just wanted to give you the freedom to choose whom you wanted. Maybe even to choose a lowly estate manager.''

Elizabeth's head whipped around to face her. ''No,'' she said in a low, shaking voice, ''he never wanted that.''

''Didn't he? When I spoke to you before the party, it sounded as if you and your estate manager were nearing an agreement.''

Elizabeth caught her lower lip between her teeth. When James had been plain Mr. Siddons, he had never mentioned marriage, but he *had* vowed that they would find a way to be together. Elizabeth had assumed his words were sincere, but how was she to trust such words when his very identity had been a lie?

Caroline cleared her throat. "I don't think you should accept James's charity."

"Then you understand how I feel—"

"I think you should marry him."

"He made a fool of me, Caroline."

"I don't think that was his intention."

"It was certainly the outcome."

"Why do you think that?" And then before Elizabeth could answer, Caroline added, "I don't think you're a fool. I know Blake doesn't. And James certainly—"

"May we *please* stop talking about James?"

"Very well. I suppose we might as well return to your home, then." Caroline reached behind her and placed a supporting hand on her lower back. "I don't seem to have my usual energy these days." Then she held out her black book, asking, "Would you mind holding this?"

"Certainly. Is it a journal?"

"Of a sorts. It's my personal dictionary. When I come across a new word, I like to jot it down, along with its definition. Then, of course, I must use it in context, or I will certainly forget it."

"How interesting," Elizabeth murmured. "I should give it a try."

Caroline nodded. "I wrote about you last night."

"You did?"

She nodded again. "It's right there on the last page. The last page I've written on, that is. Go ahead. I don't mind if you've a look at it."

Elizabeth flipped through the pages until she reached the last entry. It read:

in•ex•or•a•ble (adjective). Relentless; unyielding; implacable.

I fear that James will prove inexorable *in his pur-suit of Miss Hotchkiss.*

"I fear it, too," Elizabeth muttered.

"Well, 'I fear' was really just a phrase," Caroline has-tened to explain. "I certainly don't fear it. In fact, if I am to be completely honest, I should have written that I *hoped* James would prove inexorable."

Elizabeth looked at her new friend and fought the urge to groan. "Maybe we should just go home."

"Very well, but if I might make one last point—"

"If it has to do with James, I'd really rather you didn't."

"It does, but I promise it's the last. You see . . ." Car-oline paused to scratch her chin, smiled sheepishly, then said, "I do this when I'm stalling for time."

Elizabeth motioned with her hand toward the road home, and they began to walk. "I'm sure you're going to tell me that James is a perfectly lovely man, and—"

"No, I wasn't going to say that at all," Caroline in-terrupted. "He's perfectly insufferable, but you will have to trust me when I tell you that that is the best sort of man."

"The kind you can't live with?"

"No, the kind you can't live without. And if you love him—"

"I don't."

"You do. I can see it in your eyes."

"I don't."

Caroline waved her protest away. "You do. You just don't realize it yet."

"Caroline!"

"What I was trying to say is that even though James did a perfectly awful thing by not telling you his true identity, he did have his reasons, and none of them had anything to do with humiliating you. Of course," Caroline added with a nod of her head, "I realize that is easy for me to say, since I am not the one who took marquis-marrying lessons from a marquis. . . ."

Elizabeth winced.

"But his intentions were honorable, I am sure of it. And once you get over your anger—your very valid and well-deserved anger"—Caroline looked over at Elizabeth to make certain she heard that part—"you will realize that you will be miserable without him in your life."

Elizabeth tried to ignore her words, because she had a sinking suspicion that they were more accurate than she would have liked.

"Not to mention," Caroline continued blithely, "that *I* will be miserable without you in *my* life. I know no females my age besides Blake's sister, and she's off in the West Indies with her husband."

Elizabeth couldn't help but smile, but she was saved from further reply when she noticed that the front door of her cottage was open. She turned to Caroline and asked, "Didn't we shut that behind us?"

"I thought we did."

It was then they heard the thump.

Followed by the bellow for tea.

Followed by a decidedly feline howl.

"Oh, no," Elizabeth groaned. "Lady Danbury."

Chapter 20

❧

Lady Danbury rarely traveled without her cat.

Malcolm, unfortunately, had difficulty appreciating the finer aspects of life outside of Danbury House. Oh, he made the occasional trip to the stables, usually in search of a big fat mouse, but having been raised among the nobility, he clearly considered himself one of their ilk, and he did not enjoy being wrenched out of his cushy surroundings.

Much to Lucas's and Jane's fascination, Malcolm chose to express his ire with a mournful, rather accusatory whine. He repeated this at two-second intervals, with a regularity that would have been impressive had the sound not been quite so monstrously annoying.

"Maw," he moaned.

"What is that sound?" Caroline asked.

THUMP.

"The whine or the thump?" Elizabeth returned, letting her forehead fall into her hand.

"Maw."

"Both."

THUMP.

Elizabeth waited for Malcolm's next "Maw," and re-

321

plied, "That was Lady Danbury's cat, and"—THUMP—
"*that* was Lady Danbury."

Before Caroline could reply, they heard another sound,
that of feet scurrying very quickly through the house.

"That, I imagine," Elizabeth said dryly, "was my sister Susan, fetching tea for Lady Danbury."

"I've never met Lady Danbury," Caroline said.

Elizabeth grabbed her by the arm and hauled her forward. "Then you are in for a treat."

"Elizabeth!" Lady D boomed from the sitting room.
"I hear you!"

"She hears everything," Elizabeth muttered.

"I heard that, too!"

Elizabeth lifted her brows and mouthed, "See?" in
Caroline's direction.

Caroline opened her mouth to say something, then
stopped with a panicked glance toward the sitting room.
She grabbed her notebook out of Elizabeth's hands,
snatched a quill off the writing table that sat in the hall,
and scribbled something.

Elizabeth looked down and read:

She terrifies me.

She nodded. "She does that to most people."

"*Elizabeth!*"

"Maw."

Elizabeth shook her head. "I can't believe she brought
her cat."

"*ELIZABETH!*"

"I think you had better go in and see to her," Caroline
whispered.

Elizabeth sighed, walking toward the sitting room with
the slowest steps possible. Lady Danbury would surely
have an opinion on the humiliating events of the previous

evening, and Elizabeth would surely have to sit still while she gave it. Her only consolation was that she was dragging Caroline along with her.

"I'll wait here," Caroline whispered.

"Oh, no, you don't," Elizabeth shot back. "I listened to your lecture. Now you have to listen to hers."

Caroline's mouth dropped open in consternation.

"You're coming with me," Elizabeth ground out, clamping her hand around Caroline's arm, "and that is final."

"But—"

"Good day, Lady Danbury," Elizabeth said, smiling though clenched teeth as she poked her head into the sitting room. "This is certainly a surprise."

"Where have you been?" Lady Danbury demanded, shifting her weight in Elizabeth's favorite threadbare chair. "I have been waiting for hours."

Elizabeth raised a brow. "I've only been gone for fifteen minutes, Lady Danbury."

"Hmmph. You grow cheekier every day, Elizabeth Hotchkiss."

"Yes," Elizabeth said with a hint of a smile, "I do, don't I?"

"Hmmph. Where's my cat?"

"Maaaaaaawwwwwwww!"

Elizabeth turned around to see a flash of ecru fur streak down the hall, followed by two squealing children. "I believe he's currently occupied, Lady Danbury."

"Hmmph. Bother the cat. I'll deal with him later. I need to speak with you, Elizabeth."

Elizabeth yanked Caroline into the room. "Have you met Mrs. Ravenscroft, Lady Danbury?"

"That Blake fellow's wife, eh?"

Caroline nodded.

"Nice enough fellow, I suppose," Lady D allowed.

"Friends with my nephew. Came to visit as a child."

"Yes," Caroline replied. "He's terrified of you."

"Hmmph. Smart man. You should be, too."

"Oh, absolutely."

Lady Danbury's eyes narrowed. "Are you funning me?"

"As if she would dare," Elizabeth cut in. "The only one you don't terrify is me, Lady Danbury."

"Well, I'm going to give it my best attempt right now, Elizabeth Hotchkiss. I need to speak with you, and it's urgent."

"Yes," Elizabeth said warily, perching on the edge of the sofa. "I feared as much. You've never called upon our cottage before."

As Lady Danbury cleared her throat, Elizabeth let out a long exhale, waiting for the lecture she was sure to receive. Lady Danbury had an opinion on everything, and Elizabeth was certain that the events of the previous night were no exception. Since James was her nephew, she would surely take his side, and Elizabeth would be forced to endure a long list of his many positive attributes, punctuated by the occasional mention of Lady Danbury's positive attributes.

"You," Lady D said dramatically, pointing her finger in Elizabeth's direction, "did not attend my masquerade ball last night."

Elizabeth's jaw dropped. "*That's* what you wanted to ask me about?"

"I'm most displeased. You"—she jabbed her finger in Caroline's direction—"I saw. The pumpkin, yes? A most barbaric fruit."

"I believe it's a vegetable," Caroline murmured.

"Nonsense, it's a fruit. If it has seeds in the fleshy bit, it's a fruit. Where did you learn your biology, girl?"

"It's a gourd," Elizabeth ground out. "May we leave it at that?"

Lady Danbury waved her hand dismissively. "Whatever it is, it doesn't grow in England. Therefore I have no use for it."

Elizabeth felt herself begin to slouch. Lady Danbury was exhausting.

The countess in question whipped her head around to face her. "I'm not through with you, Elizabeth."

Elizabeth would have groaned, had she had time before Lady D sharply added, "And sit up straight."

Elizabeth stood.

"Now, then," Lady Danbury continued, "I worked very hard to convince you to attend my party. I obtained a costume for you—a very becoming costume, I might add—and you repay me by not even paying your respects in the receiving line? I was most insulted. Most—"

"Maaaaaawwwwwwww!"

Lady Danbury looked up in time to see Lucas and Jane run screaming down the hall. "What are they doing to my cat?" she demanded.

Elizabeth craned her neck. "I'm not certain if they are chasing Malcolm or if *he* is chasing *them*."

Caroline perked up. "I'd be happy to go and investigate."

Elizabeth let one of her hands land heavily on Caroline's arm. "Please," she said too sweetly, "stay."

"Elizabeth," Lady Danbury barked, "are you going to answer me?"

Elizabeth blinked in confusion. "Had you asked me a question?"

"Where were you? Why did you not attend?"

"I . . . I . . ." Elizabeth floundered for words. She certainly couldn't tell the *truth*—that she'd been out being seduced by her nephew.

"Well?"

Knock knock knock.

Elizabeth shot out of the room like a bullet. "Must answer the door," she called out over her shoulder.

"You'll not escape me, Lizzie Hotchkiss!" she heard Lady Danbury yell. She also thought she heard Caroline mutter the word "traitor" under her breath, but by then Elizabeth was already consumed with worry that it might be James standing on the other side of the heavy oak door.

She took a deep breath. If he was there, there was nothing she could do about it. She swung open the door.

"Oh, good day, Mr. Ravenscroft." Now, why did she feel so disappointed?

"Miss Hotchkiss." He nodded. "Is my wife here?"

"Yes, in the sitting room with Lady Danbury."

Blake winced. "Perhaps I'll come back later. . . ."

"Blake?" they heard Caroline call out—in a rather desperate sort of a voice. "Is that you?"

Elizabeth nudged Blake in the arm. "Too late."

Blake shuffled into the sitting room, the expression on his face precisely that of an eight-year-old boy about to be scolded for a prank involving a frog and a pillowcase.

"Blake." Caroline's voice practically sang with relief.

"Lady Danbury," he murmured.

"Blake Ravenscroft!" Lady Danbury exclaimed. "I haven't seen you since you were eight years old."

"I've been hiding."

"Hmmph. All of you are growing far too cheeky in my old age."

"And how are you faring these days?" Blake inquired.

"Don't try to change the subject," Lady D warned.

Caroline turned to Elizabeth and whispered, "Is there a subject?"

Lady Danbury narrowed her eyes and shook her finger at Blake. "I still haven't finished talking to you about the time you put that frog in poor Miss Bowater's pillowcase."

"She was a terrible governess," Blake replied, "and besides, it was all James's idea."

"I'm sure it was, but you should have had the moral rectitude to—" Lady Danbury cut herself off rather suddenly, and shot an uncharacteristically panicked glance at Elizabeth, who then remembered that her employer didn't know that she had discovered James's true identity.

Elizabeth, not wanting to touch *that* as a potential source of conversation, turned and studied her fingernails assiduously. After a moment, she looked up, blinked, feigned surprise, and asked, "Were you speaking to me?"

"No," Lady D replied in a puzzled voice. "I didn't even mention your name."

"Oh," Elizabeth said, thinking she might have overdone the not-paying-attention act. "I saw you looking at me, and—"

"No matter," Lady Danbury said quickly. She turned back to Blake and opened her mouth, presumably to scold him, but nothing came out.

Elizabeth bit her lip to keep from laughing. Poor Lady Danbury wanted so desperately to scold Blake for some two-decades-old schoolboy prank, but she couldn't, because that would lead to a mention of James, about whom she *thought* Elizabeth didn't know the truth, and—

"Tea, anyone?" Susan staggered into the room under the weight of an overloaded tea service.

"Just the thing!" Lady Danbury looked ready to vault out of her chair in her haste to have the subject changed.

This time Elizabeth did laugh. Dear God, when had

she managed to develop a sense of humor about this fiasco?

"Elizabeth?" Caroline whispered. "Are you laughing?"

"No." *Cough.* "I'm coughing."

Caroline muttered something under her breath that Elizabeth did not interpret as a compliment.

Susan set the tea service down on a table with a loud clatter, then was cut off by Lady Danbury, who yanked her chair closer in and announced, "I will pour."

Susan stepped back, bumping into Blake, who then sidled up to his wife and whispered, "All this charming tableau needs is James."

"Bite your tongue," Elizabeth muttered, making no apologies for eavesdropping.

"Lady Danbury doesn't know that Elizabeth knows," Caroline whispered.

"What are you three whispering about?" Lady D barked.

"Nothing!" It would have been difficult to discern which of the threesome yelled the word the loudest.

Silence reigned as Lady Danbury handed a cup of tea to Susan, then Blake leaned over and whispered, "Did I hear a knock?"

"Stop your teasing," Caroline scolded.

"It was the cat," Elizabeth said firmly.

"You have a cat?" Blake asked.

"It's Lady Danbury's cat."

"Where *is* my cat?" Lady D asked.

"She hears everything," Elizabeth muttered.

"I heard *that*!"

Elizabeth rolled her eyes.

"You seem in rather good spirits today," Blake commented.

"It is far too exhausting to be distraught. I have decided to return to my previous custom of making the best of the worst.''

"I'm glad to hear that," Blake murmured, "because I just saw James ride up."

"What?" Elizabeth whipped around to look out the window. "I don't see him."

"He already rode past."

"What are you three *talking* about?" demanded Lady Danbury.

"I thought you said she heard everything," Caroline mentioned.

Lady Danbury turned to Susan and said, "Your sister looks as if she's about to suffer an apoplectic fit."

"She's looked like that since last night," Susan said.

Lady D hooted with laughter. "I like your sister, Elizabeth. If you ever up and get married on me, I want *her* for my new companion."

"I'm not getting married," Elizabeth said, more out of habit than anything else.

Which caused both Ravenscrofts to turn and look at her with dubious expressions.

"I'm not!"

That was when the pounding began on the door.

Blake raised a brow. "And you say you're not getting married," he murmured.

"Elizabeth!" Lady Danbury barked. "Shouldn't you be answering the door?"

"I had considered ignoring it," Elizabeth mumbled.

Lucas and Jane chose that moment to appear in the doorway.

"Do you want me to answer the door?" Jane asked.

"I think I lost Lady Danbury's cat," Lucas added.

Lady D dropped her teacup. "Where is my poor Malcolm?"

"Well, he ran into the kitchen, and then out into the

garden, and then behind the turnip patch, and—''

''I could waltz to the doorknob,'' Jane added. ''I need to practice.''

''Malcolm!'' Lady D howled. ''Here, kitty kitty!''

Elizabeth turned around to scowl at Caroline and Blake, both of whom were shaking with uncontrollable silent laughter.

Lucas said, ''I don't think he's going to hear you from here, Lady Danbury.''

The banging grew louder. Apparently Jane had decided to circle around the hall before angling off to the front door.

Then James started to bellow Elizabeth's name, followed by a rather irritated, ''Open this door at once!''

Elizabeth sagged onto a cushioned bench, fighting the absurd impulse to laugh. If the temperature in the room were only a few degrees hotter, she'd swear she was in hell.

James Sidwell, Marquis of Riverdale, was not in a good mood. His temperament couldn't even be classified as passably polite. He had been climbing the walls all morning, practically chaining himself to his bed to keep from going to Elizabeth.

He'd wanted to call upon her first thing, but no, both Caroline and Blake had insisted that he give her a little time. She was overwrought, they'd said. Better to wait until her emotions weren't running quite so high.

So he'd waited. Against his better judgment, and, more importantly as pertained to his temper, against his natural instinct, he'd waited. And then, when he'd finally gone to the Ravenscrofts' room to ask them if they thought he'd waited long enough, he'd found a note from Caroline to Blake, explaining that she'd gone out to the Hotchkiss cottage.

And then he'd found a note from Blake to himself, saying much the same thing.

And then, to add insult to injury, as he'd dashed through Danbury House's great hall, the butler had stopped him to mention that the countess had gone out to the Hotchkiss cottage.

The only damned creature who hadn't made the mile-long journey was the blasted cat.

"Elizabeth!" James bellowed, pounding his fist against the surprisingly well-made and sturdy door. "Let me in this instant or I swear I'll—"

The door abruptly swung open. James looked out into nothingness, then redirected his gaze several inches down. Little Jane Hotchkiss was standing in the doorway, beaming up at him. "Good day, Mr. Siddons," she chirped, extending her hand. "I'm learning to waltz."

James reluctantly faced the fact that he couldn't barrel past a nine-year-old girl and live with his conscience. "Miss Jane," he replied. "It's fine to see you again."

She wiggled her fingers.

He blinked.

She wiggled them again.

"Oh, right," he said quickly, leaning down to kiss her hand. Apparently once you'd kissed a little girl's hand, you were obligated to repeat the gesture for the rest of her childhood.

"It's a fine day, don't you think?" Jane asked, affecting her most grown-up accent.

"Yes, I . . ." His words trailed off as he glanced past her shoulder, trying to catch a glimpse of whatever was causing such a commotion in the sitting room. His aunt was bellowing about something, Lucas was yelling something else, and then Susan came tearing out, scooting across the hall and into the kitchen.

"I found him!" Susan yelled.

Then, much to James's astonishment, an obese ball of fur trotted out of the kitchen, crossed the hall, and sauntered into the sitting room.

Damn. Even the bloody cat had managed to get here before he had.

"Jane," he said with what he thought was a heroic measure of patience, "I really need to speak with your sister."

"Elizabeth?"

No, Susan. "Yes, Elizabeth," he said slowly.

"Oh. She's in the sitting room. But I should warn you"—Jane cocked her head flirtatiously—"she's very busy. We've had a lot of guests this afternoon."

"I know," James muttered, waiting for Jane to move so that he wouldn't run her over on his way to the sitting room.

"Maw!"

"That cat is not very well-behaved," Jane said primly, showing no signs of moving now that she had a new topic of conversation. "He has been whining like that all day."

James noticed that his hands had balled into impatient fists. "Really?" he asked, as politely as he was able. If he used a tone of voice that reflected how he was really feeling, the little girl would probably run screaming in the other direction.

And the path to Elizabeth's heart definitely did not include reducing her younger sister to tears.

Jane nodded. "He is a terrible cat."

"Jane," James said, squatting down to her level, "could I speak with Elizabeth now?"

The little girl swept aside. "Of course. You should have asked."

James resisted the urge to comment further. Instead, he thanked Jane, kissed her hand again for good measure, and then strode off to the sitting room, where, much to his great surprise and slight amusement, he found Elizabeth on her hands and knees.

"Malcolm," Elizabeth hissed, "you get out from under that cabinet right now."

Malcolm sniffed.

"Right now, you miserable little kitty."

"Do *not* refer to my cat as a miserable little kitty," Lady Danbury boomed.

Elizabeth reached out and tried to grab the recalcitrant furball. The recalcitrant furball replied with a claw-filled swipe of his paw.

"Lady Danbury," Elizabeth announced without lifting her head, "this cat is a monster."

"Don't be ridiculous. Malcolm is nature's perfect kitty, and you know it."

"Malcolm," Elizabeth muttered, "is the spawn of the devil."

"Elizabeth Hotchkiss!"

"It's true."

"Just last week you said he was a wonderful cat."

"Last week he was being nice to me. If I recall, *you* called him a traitor."

Lady Danbury sniffed as she watched Elizabeth try to grab the cat again. "He is clearly overset because those beastly children were chasing him around the house."

That was *it*! Elizabeth hauled herself to her feet, fixed a deadly stare in Lady Danbury's direction, and growled, "*No one* calls Lucas and Jane beasts but me!"

What ensued wasn't quite utter silence. Blake was audibly laughing under his hand, and Lady Danbury was sputtering about, making strange gurgling noises, and blinking so hard that Elizabeth would swear she could hear her eyelids clamp shut.

But nothing would have prepared her for the sound of

slow clapping coming from behind her. Elizabeth turned slowly around, twisting to face the doorway.

James. Standing there with an impressed half-smile and an arched eyebrow. He cocked his head at his aunt, saying, "I can't remember the last time I heard anyone speak to you that way, Aunt."

"Except you!" Lady D retorted. Then, realizing he'd just called her "aunt," she started sputtering anew, jerking her head in Elizabeth's direction.

"It's all right," James said. "She knows everything."

"Since when?"

"Since last night."

Lady Danbury turned to Elizabeth and snapped, "And you didn't tell me?"

"You didn't ask!" Then Elizabeth turned back to James and growled, "How long have you been standing there?"

"I saw you crawling under the cabinet, if that's what you're asking."

Elizabeth fought an inner groan. She'd managed to grab hold of Jane and beg her to stall James, and she'd been hoping that Jane would have kept him in the hall at least until she'd managed to return the blooming cat to Lady Danbury.

She hadn't really wanted James's first view of her after last night's debacle to be of her swishing behind.

When she got her hands on that cat . . .

"Why," Lady Danbury shrilled, "did no one inform me of the change in James's public identity?"

"Blake," Caroline said, tugging on her husband's arm, "this might be our cue to leave."

He shook his head. "I wouldn't miss this for the world."

"Well, you're going to have to," James said forcefully. He crossed the room and grabbed hold of Elizabeth's hand. "You are all welcome to stay and enjoy your tea, but Elizabeth and I are leaving."

"Wait a moment," she protested, making an unsuccessful attempt to retrieve her hand. "You can't do this."

He stared at her blankly. "I can't do what?"

"This!" she retorted. "You have no rights over me—"

"I will," he said, flashing her a very confident, very male smile.

"Bad strategy on his part," Caroline whispered to Blake.

Elizabeth clawed her hands, trying desperately to contain her anger. "This is my house," she ground out. "If anyone is going to invite my guests to enjoy themselves, it will be I."

"Then do it," James returned.

"And you cannot order me to leave with you."

"I didn't. I told your assorted guests—all of whom I gather were uninvited—that we were leaving."

"He's bungling this badly," Caroline whispered to Blake.

Elizabeth crossed her arms. "I'm not going anywhere."

James's expression became positively menacing.

"If he'd only asked her nicely . . ." Caroline whispered to Blake.

"Blake," James said, "muzzle your wife."

Blake laughed, which earned him a rather solid punch in the arm from his wife.

"And *you*," James said to Elizabeth. "I've had all that my patience will allow. We need to talk. We can either do it outside or do it here, in front of my aunt, your siblings, and"—here he jerked a hand toward Caroline and Blake—"these two."

Elizabeth swallowed nervously, frozen with indecision.

James leaned in closer. "You decide, Elizabeth."

She did nothing, strangely unable to make her mouth form words.

"Very well, then," James snapped. "I'll decide for you." And then, without further ado, he grabbed Elizabeth around the waist, threw her over his shoulder, and hauled her out of the room.

Blake, who had been watching the unfolding drama with an amused smile on his face, turned to his wife and said, "Actually, darling, I'd have to disagree. All things considered, I think he handled that rather well."

Chapter 21

~~~OQC~~~

By the time James had her out the front door, she was wiggling like an eel. An angry eel. But James had been modest when he'd described his pugilistic pursuits; his experience was extensive, and he'd had considerably more than a ''few lessons.'' When in London, he made daily excursions to Gentleman Jackson's Boxing Establishment, and when out of London, he frequently alarmed and amused his servants by hopping gracefully from foot to foot and punching at bales of hay. As a result, his arm was strong, his body was hard, and Elizabeth, for all her squirming, wasn't going anywhere.

''Put me down!'' she squealed.

He saw no reason to reply.

''My lord!'' she said in protest.

''James,'' he snapped, widening their distance from the cottage with long, purposeful strides. ''You've used my given name often enough.''

''That was when I thought you were Mr. Siddons,'' she shot back. ''And put me down.''

James kept walking, his arm a vise under her ribs.

''James!''

He grunted. ''That's more like it.''

Elizabeth bucked a little harder, forcing him to wrap a

second arm around her. She stilled almost immediately.

"You finally realize that escape is impossible?" James asked mildly.

She scowled at him.

"I'll interpret that as a yes."

Finally, after another minute of silent journey, he set her down near an enormous tree. Her back was to the trunk, and her feet were boxed in by thick, gnarled roots. James stood in front of her, his stance wide and his arms crossed.

Elizabeth glared up at him and crossed her arms in return. She was perched on the raised ground that sloped into the tree trunk, so the difference between their heights was not as great as usual.

James shifted his weight slightly but did not say anything.

Elizabeth jutted her chin forward and tightened her jaw.

James raised a brow.

"Oh, for heaven's sake!" Elizabeth burst out. "Just say what you came here to say."

"Yesterday," he said, "I asked you to marry me."

She swallowed. "Yesterday I refused."

"And today?"

It was on the tip of her tongue to say, "You haven't asked me today," but the words died before they could cross her lips. That was the sort of remark she might have made to the man she'd known as James Siddons. This man—this marquis—was someone else entirely, and she had no idea how she was meant to act around him. It wasn't that she was unfamiliar with the idiosyncrasies of the nobility; she'd spent years in the company of Lady Danbury, after all.

She felt as if she were trapped in some strange little farce, and she didn't know the rules. All her life she'd been taught how to behave; every gently bred English girl was taught such things. But no one had ever told her what to do when one fell in love with a man who changed identities the way other people changed their clothes.

After a long minute of silence, she said, "You shouldn't have sent that bank draft."

He winced. "It arrived?"

"Last night."

He swore under his breath, muttering something about "bloody bad timing."

Elizabeth blinked back the moisture forming in her eyes. "Why would you do such a thing? Did you think I wanted charity? That I was some pathetic, helpless—"

"I thought," he cut in forcefully, "that it was a crime you should have to marry some gout-ridden old lecher to support your siblings. Futhermore, it nearly broke my heart watching you bend over backwards to try to live up to Mrs. Seeton's vision of womanhood."

"I don't want your pity," she said in a low voice.

"This isn't pity, Elizabeth. You don't need those damned edicts. All they did was smother your spirit." He raked a weary hand through his hair. "I couldn't bear it if you lost that spark that makes you so special. That quiet fire in your eyes or the secret smile when you're amused—she would have beaten that out of you, and I couldn't watch."

She swallowed, uncomfortable with the kindness of his words.

He stepped forward, halving the distance between them. "What I did, I did out of friendship."

"Then why the secrecy?" she whispered.

His brows lifted over a doubtful stare. "Are you telling me you would have accepted?" He waited only a second before adding, "I thought not. Besides, I was still supposed to be James Siddons. Where was an estate manager meant to find that sort of money?''

''James, do you have any idea how demeaned I felt last night? When I came home, after all that had happened, to find an *anonymous* bank draft?''

''And how,'' he countered, ''would you have felt if it had arrived two days earlier? Before you knew who I was. Before you had any reason to suspect I might have sent it.''

She bit her lip. She probably would have been suspicious, but also elated. And she certainly would have accepted the gift. Pride was pride, but her siblings needed to eat. And Lucas needed to go to school. And if she accepted James's proposal . . .

''Do you have any idea how selfish you are?'' he demanded, thankfully cutting into her thoughts, which were leading her in a most dangerous direction.

''Don't you dare,'' she shot back, her voice shaking with rage. ''Don't you dare call me that. I'll accept other insults as possibly true, but not that.''

''Why, because you've spent the past five years slaving away for your family's well-being? Because you've passed every windfall on to them and taken nothing for yourself?''

His voice was mocking, and Elizabeth was too furious to reply.

''Oh, you've done all that,'' he said with cruel grandeur, ''but the one chance you have to truly better your situation, the single opportunity to end your worries and give them the life I know you think they deserve, you throw it all away.''

''I have my pride,'' she ground out.

James laughed harshly. ''Yes, you do. And it's quite clear that you value it more than you do the well-being of your family.''

She raised her hand to slap him, but he caught it easily. "Even if you didn't marry me," he said, trying to ignore the slash of pain that simple sentence struck in his chest. "Even if you didn't marry me, you could have taken the money and locked me out of your life."

She shook her head. "You would have had too much control over me."

"How? The money was yours. A bank draft. I had no way to take it back."

"You would have punished me for taking it," she whispered. "For taking it and not marrying you."

He felt something in his heart turn cold. "Is that the sort of man you think I am?"

"I don't know what sort of man you are!" she burst out. "How could I possibly? I don't even know who you are."

"Everything you need to know about the sort of man I am and the husband I'd be, you know already." He touched her cheek, allowing every emotion, every last bit of love to rise to the surface. His soul was laid bare in his eyes, and he knew it. "You know me better than anyone, Elizabeth."

He saw her hesitation, and in that instant, he hated her for it. He'd offered her everything, every shred of his heart, and all she could do was *hesitate*?

He swore under his breath and turned to leave. But he'd only taken two steps when he heard Elizabeth call out, "Wait!"

Slowly, he turned around.

"I'll marry you," she blurted out.

His eyes narrowed. "Why?"

"Why?" she echoed dumbly. "Why?"

"You've refused me repeatedly for two days," he pointed out. "Why the change of heart?"

Elizabeth's lips parted, and she felt her throat close up

in panic. She couldn't get a word out, couldn't even form a thought. Of all things, she'd never expected him to question her acceptance.

He moved forward, the heat and strength of his body overwhelming even though he made no move to touch her. Elizabeth found herself backed up against the tree, breathless as she stared up into his dark eyes, which were gleaming with anger.

"You—you asked me," she just barely managed to say. "You asked me and I said yes. Isn't that what you wanted?"

He shook his head slowly and leaned his hands against the tree, one on her left, one on her right. "Tell me why you accepted."

Elizabeth tried to sink farther into the tree trunk. Something about his quiet, deadly resolve terrified her. If he'd been yelling, or scolding, or anything else she might have known what to do. But this calm fury was unnerving, and the tight prison made by his arms and the tree made her blood burn in her veins.

She felt her eyes widen, and knew that the expression he must see there would brand her a coward. "You—you made some very good arguments," she said, trying to hold on to her pride—the one emotion he accused her of overindulging. "I—I can't give my siblings the life they deserve, and you can, and I was going to have to marry, anyway, and it might as well be someone I—"

"Forget it," he spat out. "The offer is rescinded."

The breath left her body in a short, violent *whoosh*. "Rescinded?"

"I won't have you that way."

Her ankles grew wobbly, and she held on to the wide trunk of the tree behind her for support. "I don't understand," she whispered.

"I won't be married for my money," he vowed.

"Oh!" she burst out, her energy and outrage returning in full force. "Now who is the hypocrite? First you tutor me so that I might marry some other poor, unsuspecting fool for his money, then you berate me for not using your money to support my siblings. And now . . . now you have the gall to rescind your offer of marriage—a highly ungentlemanly act, I might add—because I had the honesty to say that I need your wealth and position for my family. Which," she bit off, "is exactly what you've been using to try to get me to marry you in the first place!"

"Are you done?" he asked in an insolent voice.

"No," she retorted. She was angry and hurt, and she wanted him to hurt, too. "You were going to be married for your money eventually. Isn't that the way things work among your set?"

"Yes," he said with chilling softness, "I was probably always destined for a marriage of fortunes. It's what my parents had, and theirs before them, and theirs before them. I can tolerate a cold marriage based on pound notes. I've been bred for it." He leaned forward until his lips were just a breath away from hers. "But I can't tolerate one like that with you."

"Why not?" she whispered, unable to pull her eyes from his.

"Because we have *this*."

He moved quickly, his large hand cupping the back of her head as his lips found hers. In her last coherent second before he crushed her against him, she thought that this would be a kiss of anger, a furious embrace. But even though his arms held her tightly in place, his mouth moved across hers with stunning, melting gentleness.

It was the kind of kiss a woman died for, the sort that one wouldn't break if the flames of hell were licking at one's feet. Elizabeth felt her insides quicken, and her arms tore from his firm grasp to wrap around his body. She touched his arms, his shoulders, and his neck, her hands finally coming to rest in his thick hair.

James whispered words of love and desire across her cheek until he reached her ear. He tickled the lobe, murmuring his satisfaction as her head lolled back, revealing the long, elegant arch of her throat. There was something about a woman's neck, about the way her hair drew softly from her skin, that had never failed to arouse him.

But this was Elizabeth, and she was different, and James was completely undone. Her hair was so blond that it seemed almost invisible where it met her skin. And the scent of her was tantalizing, a gentle mix of soap and roses, and something else—something that was uniquely this woman.

He trailed his mouth down the neck, stopping to pay homage to the delicate line of her collarbone. The top buttons of her frock were undone; he had no memory of slipping them open, but he must have, and he reveled in the small strip of skin that was bared to him.

He heard her breathing, felt it whisper across his hair as he moved back up to kiss the underside of her chin. She was gasping now, moaning between breaths, and James's body tightened even more at the evidence of her desire. She wanted him. She wanted him more than she could ever understand, but he knew the truth. This was one thing she could not hide.

Reluctantly, he pulled away, forcing himself to set a foot of space between them even as his hands rested on her shoulders. They were both shaking, breathing hard, and still needed the support of each other. James wasn't certain he trusted his own balance, and she looked no better.

His eyes raked over her, taking in every inch of her dishevelment. Her hair had escaped the confines of her bun, and each strand seemed to tease him, begging to be drawn over his lips. His body was drawn into a tight coil, and it took every ounce of James's control not to pull her back against him.

He wanted to tear the clothes from her body, lay her down on the soft grass, and claim her as his own in the most primitive way possible. And then when he was done, when she could have no doubt that she belonged completely and irrevocably to him, he wanted to do it again, this time slowly, exploring every inch of her with his hands, and then with his lips, and then, when she was hot and arching with need—

Abruptly, he yanked his hands away from her shoulders. He couldn't touch her when his mind was racing into such dangerous territory.

Elizabeth sagged against the tree, raising huge blue eyes to meet his. Her tongue darted out to wet her lips, and James felt that little flick straight in his gut.

He took another step away. With each move she made, each tiny, barely audible breath, he lost another piece of his control. He no longer trusted his hands; they itched to reach for her.

"When you admit that *this* is why you want me," he bit off, his voice hot and intense, "*then* I'll marry you."

Two days later, the memory of that last kiss still made Elizabeth shake. She had stood by the tree, dazed and stunned, and watched him walk away. Then she had remained in place for another ten minutes, her eyes fixed on the horizon, staring blankly at the last spot where she'd seen him. And then, when her mind had finally woken from the passionate shock of his touch, she had sat down and cried.

She had been dishonest when she had tried to convince herself that she wanted to marry him because he was a wealthy marquis. It was ironic, really. She'd spent the last month resigning herself to the fate of marrying for money, and now she'd fallen in love, and he was wealthy enough to give her family a better life, but everything was all wrong.

She loved him. Or rather, she loved a man who looked just like him. Elizabeth didn't care what Lady Danbury or the Ravenscrofts told her; humble James Siddons could not be the same man inside as the lofty Marquis of Riverdale. It simply wasn't possible. Everyone had his place in British society; this was something people were taught early, especially people like Elizabeth, daughters of minor gentry who lived on the fringes of the *ton*.

It seemed that she could solve all of her problems by going to him and telling him she wanted him, not his money. She'd be married to the man she loved, with ample resources to support her family. But she could not shake the nagging suspicion that she did not know him.

The pragmatist inside reminded her that she probably wouldn't know any man she chose to marry, or at least that she would not know him well. Men and women rarely conducted courtships beyond the most superficial of levels.

But with James, it was different. Just as he said he could not tolerate a marriage of convenience with her, she did not think she could withstand a union without trust. Maybe with someone else, but not with him.

Elizabeth squeezed her eyes shut and lay back upon her bed. She'd spent much of the past few days holed up in her room. After the first few attempts, her siblings had given up on trying to talk with her and had taken to leaving trays of food outside her door. Susan had prepared all of Elizabeth's favorite dishes, but most of the food had gone untouched. Heartbreak, apparently, did little to build an appetite.

A tentative knock sounded at the door, and Elizabeth turned her head to look out the window. Judging from the level of the sun, it was about the right time for the evening meal. If she ignored the knock, they would just leave the tray and go away.

But the knock persisted, and so Elizabeth sighed and forced herself to her feet. She crossed the small room in three steps and pulled open the door, revealing all three younger Hotchkisses.

"This came for you," Susan said, holding out a creamy envelope. "It's from Lady Danbury. She wants to see you."

Elizabeth raised a brow. "You've taken to reading my correspondence?"

"Of course not! The footman she sent over told me."

"It's true," Jane put in. "I was there."

Elizabeth reached out and took the envelope. She looked at her siblings. They looked back.

"Aren't you going to read it?" Lucas finally said.

Jane nudged her brother in the ribs. "Lucas, don't be rude." She glanced up at Elizabeth. "Are you?"

"Now who's being rude?" Elizabeth countered.

"You might as well open it," Susan said. "If nothing else, it will take your mind off of—"

"Don't say it," Elizabeth warned.

"Well, you certainly cannot wallow in self-pity forever."

Elizabeth made a *sheesh*ing sound on top of a sigh. "Aren't I entitled to at least a day or two?"

"Of course," Susan said conciliatorily. "But even by that schedule, your time is up."

Elizabeth groaned and tore open the envelope. She wondered how much her siblings knew of her situation. She had told them nothing, but they were little ferrets when it came to uncovering secrets, and she'd wager they knew over half the story by now.

"Aren't you going to open it?" Lucas asked excitedly.

Elizabeth raised her brows and looked over at her brother. He was actually jumping up and down. "I can't imagine why you're so excited to hear what Lady Danbury has to say," she said.

"I can't imagine, either," Susan growled, slamming a hand down on Lucas's shoulder to keep him still.

Elizabeth just shook her head. If the Hotchkisses were bickering, then life must be returning to normal, and that had to be a good thing.

Ignoring the grunts of protest Lucas was making at being manhandled by his sister, Elizabeth slipped the paper from the envelope and unfolded it. It took her eyes mere seconds to scan the lines, and a surprised "Me?" escaped her lips.

"Is something wrong?" Susan asked.

Elizabeth shook her head. "Not precisely. But Lady Danbury wants me to come see her."

"I thought you weren't working for her any longer," Jane said.

"I'm not, although I imagine I shall have to eat crow and ask for my position back. I don't see how else we're to have enough money to eat."

When Elizabeth looked up, all three younger Hotchkisses were chewing on their lower lips, obviously dying to point out that (A) Elizabeth could have married James or (B) she could have at least deposited the bank draft instead of tearing it into four neat pieces.

Elizabeth dropped to her hands and knees to grab her boots from under the bed, where she'd kicked them the day before. She found her reticule sitting beside it, and she snatched that up as well.

"Are you leaving right now?" Jane asked.

Elizabeth nodded as she sat on the braided rug to pull on her boots. "I shouldn't wait up for me," she said. "I don't know how long I'll be. I imagine Lady Danbury will have a carriage bring me home."

"You might even stay the night," Lucas said.

Jane walloped him in the shoulder. "Why would she do that?"

"It might be easier if it's dark," he returned with a glare, "and—"

"Either way," Elizabeth said loudly, finding the entire conversation somewhat bizarre, "you needn't wait up."

"We won't," Susan assured her, herding Lucas and Jane out of the way as Elizabeth stepped out into the hall. They watched as she dashed down the stairs and yanked open the front door. "Have a good time!" Susan called out.

Elizabeth threw her a sarcastic look over her shoulder. "I'm sure I won't, but thank you for the sentiment."

She pulled the door shut behind her, leaving Susan, Jane, and Lucas standing at the top of the stairs. "Oh, you might just be surprised, Elizabeth Hotchkiss," Susan said with a grin. "You might just be surprised yet."

The past few days would not rank among James Sidwell's finest. To deem his temper foul would be a gross understatement, and Lady Danbury's servants had long since started taking circuitous routes around the house just to avoid him.

His first inclination had been to get good and drunk, but he'd already done that once, on the night Elizabeth had discovered his true identity, and all it had left him with was a blistering hangover. And so the glass of whiskey he'd poured when he'd returned home from her cottage still sat on the desk in the library, sipped at no more than twice. Ordinarily, his aunt's well-trained servants would have swept away the half-filled glass; nothing upset their sensibilities more than a stale glass of liquor laying directly upon a polished tabletop. But James's ferocious expression the first time anyone had dared to knock on the locked library door had ensured his privacy, and now his haven—and his stale glass of whiskey— remained his own.

He was, of course, wallowing in self-pity, but it seemed to him that a man deserved a day or two of antisocial behavior after what he'd been through.

It would have been easier if he could have decided with whom he was more angry: Elizabeth or himself.

He picked up the glass of whiskey for the hundredth time that day, looked at it, and set it down. Across the room, HOW TO MARRY A MARQUIS sat on the shelf, its red leather spine silently daring him to look at anything else. James glared at the book, just barely suppressing the urge to hurl the whiskey at it.

Let's see . . . if he doused it with whiskey, then tossed it into the fireplace . . . the resulting inferno would be most satisfying.

He was actually considering it, trying to gauge how high the flames would reach, when a knock sounded at the door, this one considerably more forceful than the servants' paltry attempts.

"James! Open this door at once."

He groaned. Aunt Agatha. He rose to his feet and crossed the room to the door. He might as well get this over with. He knew that tone of voice; she'd pound the door until her fist turned bloody.

"Agatha," he said too sweetly, "how lovely to see you."

"You look like hell," she barked, then pushed past him to settle into one of the library's wing chairs.

"Still as tactful as ever," he murmured, leaning against a tabletop.

"Are you drunk?"

He shook his head and motioned to the whiskey. "Poured a glass but never drank it." He looked down at the amber liquid. "Hmmm. The surface is beginning to get dusty."

"I didn't come here to discuss spirits," Agatha said haughtily.

"You did inquire as to my sobriety," he pointed out.

She ignored his comment. "I hadn't realized you had become friendly with young Lucas Hotchkiss."

James blinked and stood up straight. Of all the non sequiturs his aunt might have chosen—and she was a master at changing the subject with no warning whatsoever—he certainly never expected *this*. "Lucas?" he echoed. "What about Lucas?"

Lady Danbury held out a folded piece of paper. "He sent you this letter."

James took it from her, noting the childish smudges on the paper. "I suppose you read this," he said.

"It was not sealed."

He decided not to press the matter and unfolded the paper. "How odd," he murmured.

"That he wants to see you? I don't think it's the least bit odd. The poor boy has not had a man in his life since he was three and his father died in that hunting accident."

James looked up sharply. Apparently Elizabeth's ruse had worked. If Agatha hadn't managed to discover the truth about Mr. Hotchkiss's death, then the secret was safe.

"He probably has a question for you," Agatha continued. "Something he'd be too embarrassed to ask his sisters. Boys are like that. And I'm sure he's confused about all that has happened in the past few days."

James looked at her with curious eyes. His aunt was displaying a remarkable sensitivity to the little boy's plight.

And then Agatha said, softly, "He reminds me of you when you were that age."

James caught his breath.

"Oh, don't look so surprised. He is, of course, much happier than you were at the time." She reached down and gathered up her cat, who had slunk into the room. "But he has that lost expression boys get when they reach a certain age and they don't have a man to guide them." She stroked Malcolm's thick fur. "We women are, of course, extremely capable and, for the most part, far wiser than men, but even I must admit there are some things we cannot do."

While James was comprehending the fact that his aunt had actually admitted that there existed a task beyond her capabilities, she added, "You *are* going to see him, aren't you?"

James was insulted that she would even ask. Only an unfeeling monster could ignore such a request. "Of course I'm going to see him. I'm rather curious, however, about his choice of locale."

"Lord Danbury's hunting lodge?" Agatha shrugged. "It's not as odd as you'd think. After he died, no one had any use for it. Cedric isn't fond of hunting, and since he never leaves London, anyway, I offered it to Elizabeth. She refused, of course."

"Of course," James murmured.

"Oh, I know you're thinking her too proud, but the truth is, she has a five-year lease on her cottage, so the move wouldn't have saved her any money. And she didn't want to uproot her family." Lady Danbury lifted Malcolm up into a standing position on her lap and let him kiss her nose. "Isn't he just the most darling cat?"

"Depends on your definition of 'darling,' " James said, but only to needle his aunt. He owed the cat eternal gratitude for leading him to Elizabeth when Fellport had attacked her.

Lady D scowled at him. "As I was saying, Elizabeth refused, but she allowed that they might move there once her rent came due, so she brought the entire family out for a visit. Young Lucas was quite taken with it." She frowned thoughtfully. "I think it was the hunting trophies. Young boys love that sort of thing."

James glanced at a clock that was being used as a bookend. He'd need to leave in about a quarter of an hour if he wanted to be prompt for Lucas's requested meeting.

Agatha sniffed the air and stood, letting Malcolm vault onto an empty bookshelf. "I'll leave you to your own company," she said, leaning on her cane. "I'll tell the servants not to expect you for supper."

"I'm sure this won't take long."

"One never knows, and if the boy is troubled, you might need to spend some time with him. Besides"—she paused as she reached the doorway and turned around— "it's not as if you've graced the table with your illustrious presence these past few days, anyway."

A cutting comeback would spoil her magnificent exit, so James just smiled wryly and watched her walk slowly down the hall, her cane thumping softly in time with her footsteps. He'd long since learned that everyone was happier if Agatha got to have the last word at least half the time.

James walked slowly back into the library, picked up the whiskey glass, and tossed contents through the open window. Setting the glass back down on the table, he glanced around the room, and his eyes fell upon the little red book that had been haunting him for days.

He strode to the bookshelf and picked it up, tossing

the slim volume from hand to hand. It weighed almost nothing, which seemed ironic, since it had done so much to change his life. And then, in a split-second decision he would never quite understand, he slipped it into his coat pocket.

Much as he detested the book, it somehow made him feel closer to *her*.

Chapter 22

~~~~

As Elizabeth approached the late Lord Danbury's hunting lodge, she chewed nervously on her lower lip, and paused to reread Lady Danbury's unexpected missive.

Elizabeth—

As you are aware, I am being blackmailed. I believe you might have information that will unearth the villain who has chosen me as his target. Please meet me at Lord Danbury's hunting lodge at eight this evening.

Yrs,
Agatha, Lady Danbury

Elizabeth couldn't imagine why Lady Danbury would think she possessed any pertinent information, but she had no reason to be suspicious of the note's authenticity. She knew Lady D's handwriting as well as her own, and this was no forgery.

She purposefully had not shared the note with her younger siblings, preferring to tell them that Lady Danbury needed to see her and leave it at that. They knew nothing of the blackmail plots, and Elizabeth hadn't wanted to worry them, especially since Lady D wanted to meet at such a late hour. It was still quite light out at eight, but unless the countess could conduct her business in mere minutes it would be dark when Elizabeth had to return home.

Elizabeth paused with her hand on the doorknob. There was no carriage in sight, and Lady Danbury's health did not allow her to walk such distances. If the countess had not yet arrived, then the door was probably locked, and . . .

The knob turned in her hand.

"How odd," she murmured, and entered the house.

There was a fire blazing in the hearth, and an elegant supper was laid on the table. Elizabeth walked farther into the room, turning in a slow circle as she took in the preparations. Why would Lady Danbury . . .

"Lady Danbury?" she called out. "Are you here?"

Elizabeth sensed a presence in a doorway behind her and whirled around.

"No," James said. "Only me."

Elizabeth's hand flew to her mouth. "What are you doing here?" she gasped.

His smile was lopsided. "The same as you, I imagine. Did you receive a note from your brother?"

"Lucas?" she asked, startled. "No, from your aunt."

"Ah. Then they are all conspiring against us. Here . . ." He held out a crumpled piece of paper. "Read this."

Elizabeth unfolded the note and read:

My lord—

Before you leave the district, I beg of you to grant me an audience. There is a matter of some sensi-

*tivity about which I should like to ask your advice.
It is not something a man would like to discuss with
his sisters.*

*Unless I hear otherwise, I shall expect to meet
you at Lord Danbury's hunting lodge at eight this
evening.*

*Sincerely,
Sir Lucas Hotchkiss*

Elizabeth barely stifled a horrified giggle. "It's Lucas's handwriting, but the words are straight from Susan's mouth."

James smiled. "I thought it sounded a touch precocious."

"He is very bright, of course—"

"Of course."

"—but I cannot quite hear him use the phrase 'matter of some sensitivity.' "

"Not to mention," James added, "that at the age of eight, it is unlikely that he should even *have* a matter of some sensitivity."

Elizabeth nodded. "Oh! I'm sure you shall want to read this." She handed him the letter she'd received from Lady Danbury.

He scanned it, then said, "I'm not surprised. I arrived a few minutes before you did and found these." He held out two envelopes, one marked, *Read immediately* and one marked *Read after you've reconciled.*

Elizabeth choked back horrified laughter.

"My reaction precisely," he murmured, "although I doubt I looked half so fetching."

Her eyes flew to his face. He was staring at her with a quiet, burning intensity that robbed her of breath. And then, without diverting his gaze from hers, even for a second, he asked, "Shall we open them?"

It took Elizabeth a few moments to realize what he was talking about. "Oh, the envelopes. Yes, yes." She licked her lips, which had gone quite dry. "But both?"

He held up the one marked *Read after you've reconciled* and shook it slightly in the air. "I can save it, if you think we will have cause to read it shortly."

She swallowed convulsively and avoided the question by saying, "Why don't we open the other one and see what it says?"

"Very well." He nodded graciously and slid his finger under the envelope flap. He slipped a card out, and together they bent their heads down and read:

To the both of you—

Try, if you might, not to be complete idiots.

The note was unsigned, but there was no doubt who wrote it. The long, graceful handwriting was familiar to them both, but it was the words that definitively declared Lady Danbury the author. No one else could possibly be so delightfully rude.

James cocked his head to the side. "Ah, my loving aunt."

"I cannot believe she tricked me like this," Elizabeth grumbled.

"You can't?" he asked doubtfully.

"Well, yes, of course I can believe *that*. I just can't believe she would use the blackmail plot as bait. I was quite terrified for her."

"Ah, yes, the blackmail." James regarded the unopened envelope, the one marked *Read after you've recon-*

ciled. "I have a sneaking suspicion we'll find something about that in here."

Elizabeth gasped. "Do you think she was making it up?"

"She certainly never seemed overly concerned by my lack of progress in solving the crime."

"Open it," Elizabeth ordered. "Immediately. Sooner than immediately."

James started to, then stopped and shook his head. "No," he said in a lazy voice, "I think I'll wait."

"You want to wait?"

He smiled down at her, slow and sensual. "We're not yet reconciled."

"James . . ." she said, in a voice that was half warning and half longing.

"You know me," he said. "You know more of my soul than any other person alive, maybe even myself. If at first you didn't know my name . . . well, all I can say is that you know why I didn't reveal myself to you right away. I had obligations to my aunt, and I owe her more than I could ever repay."

He waited for her to say something, and when she didn't, his voice grew more impatient. "You know me," he repeated, "and I think you know me well enough to know that I would never do anything to hurt or humiliate you." His hands landed heavily on her shoulders, and he fought the urge to shake her until she agreed. "Because if you don't, then there is no hope for us."

Her lips parted in surprise, and James caught a glimpse of the beguiling tip of her tongue. And somehow, as he stared at the face that had haunted him for weeks, he knew exactly what he needed to do.

Before she had a chance to react, he reached out and took her hand in his. "Do you feel this?" he whispered, placing it against his heart. "It beats for you."

"Do you feel these?" he echoed, raising her hand to his lips. "They breathe for you.

"And my eyes—they see for you. My legs walk for you. My voice speaks for you, and my arms—"

"Stop," she choked out, overcome. "Stop."

"My arms . . ." he said, his voice grown hoarse with emotion. "They ache to hold you."

She took a step forward—just an inch or two—and he could see that she was close, her heart was so close to admitting the inevitable.

"I love you," he whispered. "I love you. I see your face when I wake up in the morning, and you're all I dream about at night. Everything I am, and everything I want to be—"

She rushed into his arms, burying her face in the warm haven of his chest. "You never said it," she said, her voice nearly strangled by the sobs she'd been holding in for days. "You never said it before."

"I don't know why," he said into her hair. "I meant to, but I was waiting for the time to be right, and then it was never right, and—"

She put a finger to his mouth. "Shhhh. Just kiss me."

For a split second he was frozen, his muscles unable to move in the face of such supreme relief. Then, overcome with the irrational fear that she might disappear in his arms, he crushed her to him, his mouth devouring hers with a mix of love and longing.

"Stop," he murmured, pulling slightly away from her. And then, while she looked at him with confusion, he reached for her hair and pulled out a pin. "I've never seen it down," he said. "I've seen it mussed, but never undone, shining over your shoulders."

One by one, he pulled the pins loose, each lost pin freeing a long lock of pale golden hair. Finally, when it cascaded freely down her back, he held her at arm's length and turned her slowly around. "You're the most beautiful thing I've ever seen," he breathed.

She blushed. "Don't be silly," she mumbled. "I—"

"The most beautiful thing," he repeated. Then he drew her back to him, lifting a fragrant lock and running it over his mouth. "Pure silk," he murmured. "I want to feel this when I go to bed at night."

Elizabeth had thought her skin had felt warm before, but that comment sent her right over the edge. Her cheeks burned, and she would have used her hair to shield her blush had not James touched the underside of her chin and tilted her head up so that he could look into her eyes.

He leaned forward and kissed the corner of her mouth. "Soon you won't blush anymore." He kissed the other. "Or maybe, if I'm lucky, I'll keep you blushing every night."

"I love you," she blurted out, not sure why she was saying it now, only sure that she had to say it.

His smile spread and his eyes burned with pride. But instead of saying anything in response, he cupped her face and brought her to him for another kiss, this one deeper and more intimate than any before.

Elizabeth melted into him, and his heat seeped into her body, fueling a fire that already threatened to rage out of control. Her body was tingling with excitement and need, and when he swooped her up into his arms and carried her toward the bedroom, she made no murmur of protest.

Seconds later they tumbled onto the bed. She felt her clothing slipping away, piece by piece, until she was clad only in her thin cotton shift. The only sound was that of their breathing until James rasped, "Elizabeth ... I won't ... I can't ..."

She looked up at him, asking all her questions with her eyes.

"If you want me to stop," he managed, "tell me now."

She reached up and touched his face.

"It has to be now," he said hoarsely, "because in a minute I won't be able to——"

She kissed him.

"Oh, God," he moaned. "Oh, Elizabeth."

She should have made him stop, she knew. She should have raced out of the room and not allowed him within twenty feet of her until she stood next to him in a church as husband and wife. But love, she was discovering, was a powerful emotion, and passion ran a very close second. And nothing, not propriety, not a wedding band, not even eternal damage to her reputation and good name, could stop her from reaching for this man right now and encouraging him to make her his.

With trembling fingers she reached for the buttons of his shirt. She had never before taken such an active role in their lovemaking, but heaven help her, she wanted to touch the hot skin of his chest. She wanted to skim her fingers over his powerful muscles and feel his heart pounding with desire.

Her hands trailed down to his abdomen and lingered there for a moment before gently pulling his linen shirt from the waistband of his breeches. With a shiver of pride, she watched as his muscles bunched and clenched under her gentle touch, and she knew that his desire was something too great for him to contain.

That this man, who had chased criminals across Europe, and, according to Caroline Ravenscroft, *been chased* by countless women, could be so undone by her touch—Elizabeth was thrilled to the core. She felt so . . . so *womanly* as she watched her small hand trace circles and hearts on the smooth planes of his chest and stomach.

And as he sucked in his breath and groaned her name, she felt infinitely powerful.

He allowed her to explore him like this for a full minute before a rough growl came from deep in his throat, and he rolled over onto his side, taking her along with him. "Enough," he gasped. "I can't . . . Not another . . ."

Elizabeth took this as a compliment and curved her lips into a secret, sensual smile. But her thrill at having the upper hand was short-lived. For no sooner had James rolled her onto her side than he'd rolled her onto her back, and before she could draw in even one complete breath, he was straddling her body, staring down at her with raw need and a very male look of anticipation.

His fingers found the tiny buttons that marched between her breasts, and with startling dexterity and speed he undid all five. "Ah," he murmured, sliding the garment over her shoulders, "that was what we needed."

He bared the tops of her breasts, letting his fingers tickle into her cleavage before sliding her shift down lower.

Elizabeth clawed at the bedclothes to keep from covering herself. He was staring at her with such burning intensity that she felt heat and moisture pool between her legs. He remained still for nearly a minute, not even raising a single finger to caress her, just gazing down at her breasts and licking his lips as he watched her nipples peak and harden.

"Do something," she finally gasped.

"This?" he asked softly, grazing one tip with the palm of his hand.

She didn't say a word, just fought for breath.

"This?" He moved his hand to the other side, and gently pinched her between his fore- and middle finger.

"Please," she begged.

"Ah, you must mean this," he said roughly, his words lost as he bent over and drew her into his mouth.

Elizabeth let out a little shriek. One of her hands twisted the bedsheet into a tight spiral while the other sank into James's thick hair.

"Oh, that wasn't what you wanted?" he teased. "Maybe I need to pay more attention to the other side." And then he did it again, and Elizabeth thought she surely would die if he didn't do something to release the incredible tension that was building inside her.

He tore himself from her for just long enough to pull the shift over her head, and then, while he was yanking off his belt, Elizabeth pulled the thin bedsheet over her.

"You won't be able to hide for long," he said, his voice thick with desire.

"I know." She blushed. "But it's different when you're next to me."

He eyed her curiously as he slid back into bed. "What do you mean?"

"I can't explain." She shrugged helplessly. "It's different when you can see *all* of me."

"Ah," he said slowly, "so does that mean I can look at you like *this*?" With a teasing glance, he tugged on the sheet until he bared one silky shoulder, which he proceeded to kiss lovingly.

Elizabeth squirmed and giggled.

"I see," he said, adopting an odd foreign accent just for fun. "And what about this?" He reached down and yanked the sheet off her foot, then tickled her toes.

"Stop!" she shrieked.

He turned back around to give her his most devilish look. "I had no idea you were so ticklish." He tickled her some more. "This is certainly important to know."

"Oh, stop," she gasped, "please stop. I can't bear it."

James smiled down at her with all the love in his heart.

It had been so important to him to make this first time perfect for her. He had been dreaming of it for weeks, of how he was going to show her how exquisite the love between a man and a woman could be. And if he hadn't exactly pictured himself tickling her toes, he *had* pictured her with a smile on her face.

Rather like right now.

"Oh, Elizabeth," he murmured, leaning down to press a gentle kiss on her mouth, "I love you so much. You must believe me."

"I believe you," she said softly, "because in your eyes, I see what I feel in my heart."

James felt his eyes go wet with tears, and he had no words to express the torrent of emotion her simple statement had unleashed. He kissed her again, this time tracing the outline of her lips with his tongue as he slid his hand down the side of her body.

He felt her stiffen with anticipation, her muscles quickening beneath his touch. But when he reached the core of her womanhood, her legs parted slightly to receive him. He toyed with her curls, and then, when he heard her breathing grow shallow and raspy, slipped in farther. She was already ready for him, thank God, because he wasn't certain he could wait another moment.

He nudged her legs farther open and settled between them. "This may hurt," he said, hearing regret in his voice. "There's no other way, but it will get better, I promise."

She nodded, and he noticed that her face had tensed up slightly at his words. Damn. Maybe he shouldn't even have warned her. He had no experience with virgins; he didn't have the slightest idea what to do to lessen her pain. All he could do was be gentle and slow—difficult as that was in the face of the most intense desire he had ever felt—and pray for the best.

"Shhhh," he crooned, smoothing his hand over her forehead. He moved forward an inch or so, until the tip of his manhood was pressed up against her. "See?" he whispered. "I'm nothing out of the ordinary."

"You're huge," she retorted.

To his utter shock, a burst of laughter escaped his lips. "Oh, my love, normally I'd take that as the highest compliment."

"And now . . ." she prodded.

His fingers trailed lovingly over her temple to the line of her jaw. "Now all I want is for you not to worry."

She gave her head a little shake. "I'm not worried. A little nervous, perhaps, but not worried. I know that you will make this wonderful. You make everything wonderful."

"I will," he said, his words fervent against her lips. "I promise I will."

Elizabeth gasped as he nudged forward, entering her. It all felt so strange, and in an odd way, so right, as if she'd been made for this moment, crafted to receive this man in love.

His hands stole around to cup her buttocks, and he tilted her slightly. Elizabeth gasped at the difference that made as he slid easily in until he reached the proof of her innocence.

"After this moment," he said, his voice hot against her ear. "You will be mine." And then, without waiting for a response, he pushed forward, capturing her surprised "Oh!" with a deep kiss.

His hands still wrapped beneath her, he began to move. Elizabeth gasped with each thrust, and then, without consciously realizing it, she began to move as well, joining him in an ancient rhythm.

The tension that had been tickling her insides grew stronger, more urgent, and she felt as if she were straining against her own skin. And then something changed, and she felt as if she were falling off a cliff, and the world exploded around her. A second later, James gave a hoarse shout, and his hands clutched her shoulders with impossible force. For a moment he looked as if he were dying, and then his face was washed with a look of complete bliss, and he collapsed atop her.

Several moments passed, the only sound their breathing as it slowed to an even pace, and then James rolled over onto his side, pulling her against him and nestling against her like two spoons in a drawer. "This is it," he said, his voice drowsy. "This is what I've been searching for my entire life."

Elizabeth nodded against him, and they slept.

Several hours later, Elizabeth woke to the sound of James's feet moving across the wooden floors of the hunting lodge. She hadn't felt him leave the bed, but there he was, slipping back into the bedroom, naked as the day he was born.

She was torn between the urge to avert her eyes and the temptation to stare shamelessly. She ended up doing a little of both.

"Look what we forgot," James said, waving something in the air. "I found it on the floor."

"Lady Danbury's letter!"

He raised his brows and gifted her with his most rakish smile. "I must have dropped it in my haste to have my way with you."

Elizabeth thought that with all that had happened, he wouldn't still be able to make her blush, but apparently she was wrong. "Just open it," she mumbled.

He set a candle on the nightstand and crawled into bed beside her. When he didn't move quickly enough to open the envelope, Elizabeth grabbed it from him and yanked it open. Inside, she found another envelope, with the following words across the front:

You're cheating, aren't you? Do you really want to open this before you've reconciled?

Elizabeth clapped a hand over her mouth, and James didn't even bother to silence the chuckles that welled up in his throat. "Suspicious, isn't she?" he murmured.

"Probably with good reason," Elizabeth admitted. "We did almost open it before we . . ."

"Reconciled?" he supplied with a devilish grin.

"Yes," she mumbled, "exactly."

He motioned to the envelope in her hands. "Are you going to open it?"

"Oh, yes, of course." Proceeding with a bit more decorum this time, she lifted the envelope flap and pulled out a delicately scented sheet of white paper, folded neatly in half. Elizabeth unfolded it, and, heads burrowed together in the candlelight, they read:

My dearest children,

Yes, it's true. My dearest children. That is how I think of you, after all.

James, I shall never forget the day I first brought you to Danbury House. You were so suspicious, so unwilling to believe that I might love you for yourself. Every day I hugged you, trying to show you what it means to be family, and then, one day, you hugged me back, and said, "I love you, Aunt Agatha." And from that moment on, you were as a son to me. I would give my life for you, but I suspect you know that.

Elizabeth, you entered my life when the last of

*my children married and left me. From the first day,
you have taught me what it means to be brave and
loyal and true to one's beliefs. During these past
few years it has been my delight to watch you blos-
som and grow. When you first came to Danbury
House, you were so young and green and easy to
fluster. But somewhere along the way, you developed a quiet poise and wit that any young woman
would envy. You don't fawn over me, and you never
allow me to bully you; that is probably the greatest
gift a woman of my sort can receive. I would give
all that I own to call you my daughter, but I suspect
you, too, know that.*

*So was it so very strange that I should dream of
bringing you—my two favorite people—together? I
knew I could not do it through conventional means.
James would certainly resist any attempts on my
part at matchmaking. He is a man, after all, and
therefore stupidly proud. And I knew that I could
never convince Elizabeth to travel to London for a
season at my expense. She would never participate
in any endeavor that would take so much time away
from her family.*

*And so my little deception was born. It started
with a note to James. You have always wanted to
rescue me as I once rescued you, my boy. It was
easy enough to devise a blackmail plot. (I must di-
gress for a moment to assure you that the plot was
a complete fabrication, and all of my children are
legitimate and were, of course, sired by the late
Lord Danbury. I am not the sort of woman who
strays from her marital vows.)*

*I was fairly certain that if I could arrange for
the both of you to meet, you would fall in love (I
am rarely wrong about these sorts of things), but*

just to plant ideas in Elizabeth's head, I located my old copy of HOW TO MARRY A MARQUIS. A sillier book was never written, but I did not know how else to start her pondering marriage. (In case you are wondering, Lizzie, I forgive you for stealing the book from my library. You were meant to do so, of course, and you may keep it as a memento of your courtship.)

That is my entire confession. I shan't ask your forgiveness since, of course, I have nothing which begs it. I suppose some might take offense with my methods, and normally I would not dream of orchestrating such a compromising situation, but it was clear that the two of you were far too stubborn to see the truth any other way. Love is a precious gift, and you would do well not to toss it away over a bit of foolish pride.

I do hope you enjoy the hunting lodge; you will find that I have anticipated your every need. Please do feel free to spend the night; contrary to popular belief, I do not control the weather, but I am putting in a request with the gentleman upstairs for a violent rainstorm—the sort in which one would never venture outside.

You may thank me at your wedding. I have already procured a special license in your names.

> *Fondly,*
> *Agatha, Lady Danbury*

Elizabeth's mouth fell open. "I can't believe it," she breathed. "She engineered everything."

James rolled his eyes. "I can believe it."

"I can't believe she left that bloody little book out, knowing that I would take it."

He nodded. "I can believe that, as well."

She turned to him, her lips still parted in amazement. "And she even has a special license."

"That," he admitted, "I can't believe. But only because I obtained one as well, and I'm a bit surprised that the archbishop would issue a duplicate."

Lady Danbury's letter slipped from Elizabeth's hand and fluttered down to the bedsheets. "You did?" she whispered.

James took one of her hands and raised it to his lips. "When I was in London, searching for Agatha's bogus blackmailer."

"You want to marry me," she breathed. Her words were a statement, not a question, but she sounded as if she could not quite believe it.

James shot her an amused smile. "I've only asked you a dozen times in the past few days."

Elizabeth jerked her head, as if waking up from a dazed dream. "If you ask me again," she said mischievously, "I might give you a different answer."

"Is that so?"

She nodded. "Most definitely so."

He ran one finger down the side of her neck, his blood running hot when he saw the way his touch made her shiver. "And what changed your mind?" he murmured.

"One might think"—she gasped as his finger moved lower—"that it had something to do with being compromised, but if you really want the truth . . ."

He leaned over her, smiling wolfishly. "Oh, I definitely want the truth."

Elizabeth allowed him to close the distance between them to a mere inch before she said, "It's the book."

He froze. "The book?"

"How to Marry a Marquis." She cocked one of her brows. "I'm thinking of writing a revised edition."

He went white. "You're joking."

She smiled and wiggled beneath him. "Am I?"

"Please say you're joking."

She slipped down farther in the bed.

"I'll make you say you're joking," James growled.

Elizabeth reached up and wrapped her arms around him, not even noticing the loud clap of thunder that shook the walls. "Please do."

And he did.

Epilogue

A uthor's Note: It is universally agreed upon by scholars of nineteenth-century etiquette that the copious scribblings found in the margins of this unique volume are the work of the Marquis of Riverdale.

Excerpts from

HOW TO MARRY A MARQUIS
SECOND EDITION
BY THE MARCHIONESS OF RIVERDALE

Published 1818
Copies Printed: One

Edict Number One

NEVER SET YOUR CAP FOR A GENTLEMAN UNTIL YOU ARE COMPLETELY CERTAIN OF HIS IDENTITY. AS ANY SENSIBLE YOUNG LADY MUST KNOW, MEN ARE EVER DECEPTIVE.

Good God, Lizzie, haven't you forgiven me for that yet?

Edict Number Five

POPULAR CONVENTION DEEMS THAT YOU SPEND NO MORE THAN TEN MINUTES IN CONVERSATION WITH A PARTICULAR GENTLEMAN. THIS AUTHOR DISAGREES. IF YOU FEEL THIS MAN MIGHT BE A CANDIDATE FOR MARRIAGE, IT BEHOOVES YOU TO KNOW HIS MIND BEFORE YOU COMMIT YOURSELF TO SUCH A SACROSANCT VOW. IN OTHER WORDS, HALF AN HOUR OF CONVERSATION MAY SAVE YOU FROM THE MISTAKE OF A LIFETIME.

No arguments from this quarter.

Edict Number Eight

NO MATTER HOW WELL YOU LOVE YOUR RELA-TIONS, COURTSHIPS ARE BEST CONDUCTED WITH-OUT THE PARTICIPATION OF YOUR FAMILY.

Ah, but don't forget the hunting lodge . . .

Edict Number Thirteen

EVERY WOMAN MUST KNOW HOW TO DEFEND HERSELF FROM UNWANTED ATTENTIONS. THIS AU-THOR RECOMMENDS BOXING. SOME MIGHT CON-SIDER SUCH ATHLETIC CONDUCT UNBECOMING TO A GENTLE YOUNG LADY, BUT YOU MUST BE PRE-PARED TO DEFEND YOUR OWN REPUTATION. YOUR MARQUIS WILL NOT ALWAYS BE CLOSE AT HAND. THERE MAY BE TIMES WHEN YOU HAVE TO PRO-TECT YOURSELF.

I will ALWAYS protect you.

Edict Number Fourteen

SHOULD THE AFOREMENTIONED ATTENTIONS NOT BE UNWANTED, THIS AUTHOR CAN OFFER NO ADVICE THAT MAY BE LEGALLY PRINTED IN THIS BOOK.

Meet me in the master suite and I shall advise YOU.

Edict Number Twenty
(The Only One You Truly Need Remember)

ABOVE ALL ELSE, BE TRUE TO YOUR HEART. WHEN YOU MARRY, WHETHER IT BE A MARQUIS OR AN ESTATE MANAGER (or both!), IT WILL BE FOR LIFE. YOU MUST GO WHERE YOUR HEART LEADS AND NEVER FORGET THAT LOVE IS THE MOST PRECIOUS GIFT OF ALL. MONEY AND SOCIAL STATUS ARE POOR SUBSTITUTES FOR A WARM, TENDER EMBRACE, AND THERE IS LITTLE IN LIFE MORE FULFILLING THAN THE JOY OF LOVING AND KNOWLEDGE THAT YOU ARE LOVED IN RETURN.

And you ARE loved, Elizabeth. Until the last breath leaves my body, and for eternity after that. . . .

Dear Reader,

Sexy Scottish heroes, tantalizingly long nights spent mesmerizing a man, love stories that won't be forgotten...all this—and more—awaits you next month from Avon romance!

Linda Needham is fast becoming a rising star of romance, and her latest, *The Wedding Night*, is a wonderful, sensuous love story filled with all the power and passion of her earlier books. When a young woman is forced to marry a dark and dashing nobleman she expects to do her duty...but she never dreams she's also lost her heart to the one man capable of breaking it.

Lois Greiman's *Highland Brides* series is at the top of many readers' list of favorites. Her latest sweeping, sexy love story *Highland Enchantment* is sure to please anyone looking for a thrilling hero...and a powerful love story. If you haven't read the earlier books in the series, don't worry! This title is supremely entertaining romance for you, too.

Susan Sizemore is a name many of you recognize, and her Avon debut, *The Price of Innocence* is filled with the lush sensuality and powerful emotion that her fans have come to expect. When Sherry Hamilton looks across a crowded ballroom, she never expects to meet the eyes of the man who once took away her innocence. Can she now face a man she has never stopped hating—and loving?

Mary Alice Kruesi's *Second Star to the Right* is a must read for lovers of contemporary romance. It's tender, poignant, and one of the most magical love stories I've read in years. A single mother comes to London to escape her past, and finds her heart stolen by a man who makes her once again believe that dreams can come true.

It's all here at Avon romance! Enjoy,

Lucia Macro

Lucia Macro
Senior Editor

Avon Romantic Treasures

*Unforgettable, enthralling love stories,
sparkling with passion and adventure
from Romance's bestselling authors*

❋❋❋❋❋❋❋❋❋❋❋❋❋❋❋❋❋❋❋❋❋❋❋❋❋❋❋❋❋

TO CATCH AN HEIRESS *by Julia Quinn*
78935-3/$5.99 US/$7.99 Can

WHEN DREAMS COME TRUE *by Cathy Maxwell*
79709-7/$5.99 US/$7.99 Can

TO TAME A RENEGADE *by Connie Mason*
79341-5/$5.99 US/$7.99 Can

A RAKE'S VOW *by Stephanie Laurens*
79457-8/$5.99 US/$7.99 Can

SO WILD A KISS *by Nancy Richards-Akers*
78947-7/$5.99 US/$7.99 Can

UPON A WICKED TIME *by Karen Ranney*
79583-3/$5.99 US/$7.99 Can

ON BENDED KNEE *by Tanya Anne Crosby*
78573-0/$5.99 US/$7.99 Can

BECAUSE OF YOU *by Cathy Maxwell*
79710-0/$5.99 US/$7.99 Can